To Elizabeth Rose and all of you "K" Kids · you are loved more than you'll ever know

With admiring affection to Andrew, Ariel Alexis, Chloe, Donques, Emma Kate, Estefany, Hannah, Jade, Jake, Lindsey Marie, Nic Adam, Savanna, Shelby, and Talya · and to Cindy with love and admiration

To the staff, volunteers, and deaf and hard of hearing of Bridges, Nashville, Tennessee · you helped to awaken this novel's creation

To the wonderful management and crew of Brentwood Skate Center, where "It's Fun you can Feel" is more than a slogan · it's unbeatable family good times rolling on wheels!

With affectionate hugs to Rose D for scrutinizing these words long before they appeared in print

Eva Roblins and the Enchanted Gate

Book One
Return of the Princess

By
Eva Roblins

Mention of the U.S. Central Intelligence Agency is in keeping with a long tradition of portraying the Agency in novels of espionage, spying, and intrigue. Mention of the office of the President of the United States also is in keeping with the same literary traditions. We applaud the Agency's employees for their sacrifices to keep our nation free and likewise hold the Presidency in high esteem.

We give credit to Walter Rollin Brooks (1886 - 1958), author of short stories and children's books, for mention of the talking horse, Mister Ed. We likewise give credit to *Grimm's Fairy Tales*, for mention of *The Elves and the Shoemaker* (circa 1806).

Finally, a special thanks to Brentwood Skate Center, Brentwood, Tennessee for allowing us to mention their business name and slogan in this novel.

Cover Design by EbookLaunch

ISBN 978-0-9861861-1-0

www.evaroblins.com

PREFACE

Imagine the thrill of receiving something on the eve of your birthday, only to have it change your life. One minute you're you, the next minute you're something else · well, maybe not something else entirely, but you're definitely no longer you. Imagine going places, doing things, meeting others, and witnessing events that seem too magical, too impossible, too amazing to be real.

This fictional autobiographical novel contains these exciting items and many more incredible events within its pages. This novel is a fantastic tale of paranormal powers, physical limitations, anti-bullying, boundless friendship, and never-ending optimism. It contains a plethora of funny stuff, some hatred, and gobs and gobs of the supernatural. There are bizarre creatures, a large amount of reality and, as expected, a wicked being who wants to take over the world. More often than not, this novel is about special youngsters who possess amazing powers, extraordinary skills, keen intellect, and enduring courage.

This novel's main persona has traveled the world, had exciting adventures, and encountered countless good people along the way. However, nothing can compare to the heartwarming times shared with the true-life young people who embody the primary and secondary characters portrayed in this novel. The main persona met these youngsters while roller skating. A few · they know who they are ·

were befriended as pre-teens. Now some of them are all grown-up, soon to be adults. They are loved and admired very much. This novel is dedicated to all of them and to a special friend, Cindy.

Yes, Cindy - an astute professional, a charming lady, and an enduring friend. Cindy embodies the strength of character, intellect, audacity, and a skilled wisdom rendered in this novel's main persona. The free world is a safer place thanks to Cindy's expert leadership. It is an honor to portray Cindy as a character in this novel along with the others.

There are additional people who have inspired the penning of this novel. As you can well imagine, there only can be so many characters in a story. Otherwise the characters' attributes tend to fade away like clutter in a crowded attic, mislaid forever. But all is not lost. We promise you - other inspiring young people will appear as characters in sequels to this novel.

You will find this novel is not so much about the story's main persona as it is about others. Others who go through life unseen by the masses as they deal with day to day challenges. They are the blind, the deaf, the voiceless, those with disabilities and incurable diseases, heroic veterans suffering from wounds and PTSD, and the poor and impoverished. They are those unfortunates who live alone on the streets, are subject to ridicule, bullying, prejudice, and social stigma. They are those who live dejected and forgotten in homes for the elderly or suffer abuse and neglect and lack companionship.

As you read this novel, and when you have an opportunity, take a few moments to reach out to someone in need. Maybe, just maybe, your single act of love will give someone a ray of hope. Then maybe, just maybe, his or her dreams can come true just like yours.

SPRINGTIME

By Mary (Polly) Hall

Strolling down a Country Lane
Watching nature's glory
Trees all budding once again
Speaking out their story

Violets with their heads of blue
Daffodil bills of yellow
Tulips with their pretty hue
Soft scents sweet and mellow

Birds now are on the wing
Filling the air with song
Heralding a bright new spring
Helping nature's work along

Lambs are playing in the sun
Tis a very pretty sight
They don't stray but romp and run
Their mother watching day and night

The bright blue sky, the birds that sing
The beasts and pretty flowers
The budding trees, the gentle breeze
We thank you, God for everything.

Contents

I DID NOT HEAR A THING

What is this? I cannot hear a word these people are saying! Why do they look worried? I pinch myself to see if I am awake. It hurts. So I know I am not in a dream. Papa rushes into the room. Thank goodness he is here! He looks at me, smiles and then he blows me a kiss. He is talking to a doctor. At least I think the man is a doctor. He has a stethoscope hanging around his neck like an actor in the movies. But what is with these two stern-looking nurses in the room? I do not like them. They scare me.

I must have been asleep for a very long time. My body is hurting badly. My eyes will not focus, and my eyelids feel puffy. I also feel scrawny, like I haven't eaten in weeks. I encircle fingers of my right hand around the wrist of my left. My wrist is boney, and it aches like crazy. I am left-handed. However, I cannot move my left arm. For some strange reason, it is strapped to the bed. I almost scream when I notice creepy tubes and eerie wires protruding from its forearm.

I reach beneath the sheet to touch my breasts, my waist, and my rear end. Each feels so thin like I have no muscle remaining. I also touch my ribs. They stick out through my skin. I know I have lost a lot of weight. But why - what happened to me? Why am I here in this hospital bed? And why do I feel as if a ton of bricks has slammed into me?

Papa approaches my bed. My heart quickens. He attempts a meek smile, but I can see he has been crying. His lips move. However, I cannot hear what he is saying! It looks like he's saying, "Eva, you're awake - thank goodness!" But I cannot be certain. He could have said something else. I do not know - and I never will.

Papa holds a small yellow lined pad in his hand. He scribbles with a pen, "I love you!" I smile and say in return, "I love you too, Papa." But what is this? I cannot hear my voice! Plus, I need to know - why is Papa writing on a pad? Tears begin to race down my cheeks. Something has happened to me! Am I speechless? Then it dawns on me - I am unable to hear Papa's voice as well. My goodness, I cannot hear a thing!

I know something has ruined my life when I read the next note Papa writes. "Honey, you have been sick. You have been in a coma for three weeks. You are now deaf, but thankfully alive! I am very sorry. I truly am. I will be with you as we work this together. I love you!"

He quickly scribbles a subsequent note, then seemingly endless note after note. He rips each one from the pad in desperation as he hands it to me. It is as if he wants me to know in a matter of minutes all that has happened while I was in a three-week coma. Tears cascade down his unshaven ruddy cheeks as he writes. His tender tears plunge as heartbroken droplets, forever staining the yellow pad together with my aching heart.

Because my eyes are bleary from crying, I can barely read what every one of his scribbled words is saying. Papa writes I am lucky to be alive. My deafness is a small price to pay for beating the near-death odds of meningitis. But it is his last hastily scribbled note that conveys the most ominous warning. When I read what he had written, the words promise to destroy nearly everything I have come to cherish.

"Children who survive meningitis sometimes lose their hearing. There is no cure. No reversal. I am sorry, honey. I truly am."

I abruptly sit up in total shock. How I manage to do this, I do not know. I am dreadfully weak. Papa responds to my sudden, shocked reaction. He hugs me close. As we embrace, I can feel his sobbing, broken heart convulse in gasping shudders. I know, if he could, he would willingly trade places with me. I know in my heart that my Papa loves me as much as I love him.

Now the doctor is talking to Papa. But what he says he says to Papa alone. He's talking in what appears to be a guarded whisper. The man won't even look at me. He simply glances my way now and then. When he finally turns to address me his lips move bit by bit, like in slow motion. His lips over-exaggerate what he says which makes him look like a stupid moron. It is as if he thinks I am an imbecile, and he wants me to understand what he is saying.

I do not recognize your words, doctor! I cannot read lips! I - cannot - hear! I am deaf, you idiot! You of all people should know that!

I already know this deafness has ruined my life - my world! My world that heard a sweet voice that belonged to me - it is forever gone! That sang songs of the heart. And said I love you, time and time again with richness and sincerity that matched the love I hold close to my heart. A voice I always thought was wonderful to listen to as it spoke and sang and laughed. And to think I was going to study at university as an operatic singer - what a joke!

Even if I still speak with my same voice, I can no longer hear what my voice is saying. While I can see, feel, taste and love and laugh and even cry, I cannot hear. I am deaf! But why, oh why did this happen to me?

The doctor abruptly grabs the tear-soaked pad from Papa. I watch with horror as the pen scratches words I know I will never hear spoken aloud. A flood of nonstop tears and an anguished anger swell from deep inside me until I feel as if I have to burst with emotion.

Impulsively, I scream as loudly as I know how. But I cannot hear my tormented cries of anguish. My unheard screams make my suffering even worse. As a result, I scream and scream and scream. I can feel my eyes bulging, my neck muscles tightening, my face turning beet red. I try to scream even louder. It is as if I am going crazy in a make-believe world of absolute, horrible silence! If only I could scream loudly enough to hear the pain that I feel in my heart! At least then I would know there is a ray of hope.

Without glancing at what the doctor has written, I tear the sheet of paper he handed me into a dozen pieces of yellow confetti. I hate him for not making me capable of hearing again. I want him to go away, as far away from me as possible. And I wish with all my heart for my life to be ripped to shreds like the yellow paper confetti now littering the floor. I want to be cast away with the wind to the farthest corners of the earth, to exist no more.

I try to get out of bed to escape this nightmare, but I am too fragile. My hands thrash at the air in panic. Tubes and wires rip from my veins. I cry out in pain. Papa and the doctor hurriedly reach to restrain me. A nasty-looking old hag of a gray-haired nurse with nauseating peppermint breath gives me an injection. Almost immediately, my sobbing begins to lessen. My entire world encircles over and over in a whirlwind of absolute quiet as I begin to relax.

I watch in horror through the soundless deepening fog as the doctor, nurses, and Papa mouth unheard words I cannot fathom, words I will never hear. Knowing I will never hear again causes me to cry myself to sleep.

I dream I am soaring in a noiseless sky. Then I am dropping, twisting and turning in an endless spiral until I finally crash to earth in a mangled heap.

As I expected, I did not hear a thing.

CHAPTER TWO

REDHEADED ELFIN

When I awakened on that ill-omened day, I instantly knew something was wrong, terribly wrong. It was three weeks to the day after my fifteenth birthday, a little over fourteen years ago from today. I need to tell you, my life up to that point was not a bed of roses. True, I had my share of fun as most kids do · at least those who are healthy and grow up in a somewhat safe environment. However, my life was plainly miserable, to say the least.

My parents were dreadfully poor. We drifted from town to town in search of work for my father. I guess you could say we were nomadic wanderers, contemporary gypsies. After my mother had passed, things got even worse. After I had become deaf, I had every excuse in the world to quit trying to live a normal life. I could have screamed at the top of my lungs, poor, poor, me. However, I persevered.

I learned to read lips skillfully. Most people, who meet me today, have no suspicion I am deaf. I also learned American Sign Language, abbreviated ASL. I can *hear* by reading lips. I can communicate verbally using the voice I remember hearing as mine. Even so, I'm not certain if eve·

ry word I say sounds correct. I suppose I slur words now and then. It is inevitable when one is deaf.

My deafness was distressing for me when I was a teenager. I more often than not cried myself to sleep, especially right after my hospitalization. Even my nightmarish sobs caused me pain. I knew my cries must forever fall on my deafened ears. There was no outlet, no closure, and no escape.

Weeks turned into months. Demanding months of learning ASL and retraining my voice to speak without hearing its spoken words turned into years. All the while my Papa was my supportive guiding angel. He learned to sign in ASL as his work schedule allowed. The two of us had fun attending classes together. We stopped at the local soda shop after class to spoil ourselves with hot fudge and strawberry ice cream sundaes. We couldn't afford it, yet we did it just the same.

Papa had a funny saying when it came to treating ourselves when money was in short supply. He would say, "Sometimes ya got to do what ya got to do because ya got to do it." So we indulged ourselves, and he worried it about it later. Sweet memories - tasty hot fudge and strawberry sundae goodies are my favorites even today.

As a teenager, I knew my speech was more than slightly impaired, perhaps ridiculous-sounding at times. My acquaintances sometimes smiled when I talked. They often asked me to repeat what I had said. However, they supported me as acquaintances are supposed to. A few of my closest school companions also learned the rudiments of ASL.

Today, I have come to accept the fact that my voice is a bit slurred from time to time. I still cannot form certain complex words easily. I know how they should sound. Sounding them correctly without hearing them is a different story.

As I said, I never gave up. If I stop to think about it, I guess I had no other choice. I recognized a second chance at life was too precious to abandon all hope of normality because of a minor physical impairment. I carried on bravely, and I tried to live as normal as life as possible despite my deafness.

I frown and slowly shake my head back and forth. I should know better. It's not healthy to loiter on the past, especially long-ago nightmares. It was bad enough those nightmares left me sleepless for too many nights when I was a youngster. It does no good reliving them now.

I grab my silver hairbrush to caress my shoulder-length bright red hair. As I brush my hair, I stare without purpose at another dull day beyond the window pane. The scene outside my window pane reflects my frame of mind - uninteresting. It should come as no surprise. The rain has drizzled nonstop for two days now. Quite frankly, it's just a typically blasé mid-winter day - chilly and wet.

Today is my day off from work. So I'm lounging around the house being lazy. I'm wearing my typical lounging around the house being lazy outfit - an extra large shirt and baggy pants. The shirt says *Help Support the Fight*. The familiar breast cancer awareness pink ribbon appears next to the words. I paid ten bucks for the shirt - a bargain at twice the price.

I set my brush on the table to take hold of my coffee mug. I collect mugs. I must have thirty or forty of them. They include Hello Kitty, Popeye, Betty Boop, and Harry Potter, among others. My Harry Potter mug is the coolest. Tiny footprints begin to walk on a map after I pour hot liquid into it. I also have an oversized mug shaped like a chocolate-covered glazed donut. Although the cup is too large to drink out of, it is unique. That's why it's part of my collection.

Of all of my mugs, I do have a favorite. It's the mug I'm cradling in my hands. This mug is the official mug of the Central Intelligence Agency or CIA. My name appears below the CIA logo - Eva Roblins Special Agent.

Certainly, any Tom, Dick, Jane, and Harry can buy a CIA mug for themselves on the internet. They can also get their name embossed on the flip side - Tom What's-his-name, Special Agent; or Jane Schmuck, Special Agent; maybe even Special Agent Tricky Dickey.

But my CIA mug is the real McCoy, no joke - it's the real deal. I earned it a hundred times over. I'm proud to call it mine.

I have filled my CIA mug to the rim with mouth-watering hazelnut-flavored coffee. Hazelnut is my favorite flavor when it comes to coffee. I'm in a sour frame of mind today. So this brew contains an extra heaping teaspoon of sugar. Maybe it'll sweeten my mood. It's my fourth mug, fairly close to a record. At least I think it is. I may consume more coffee in the field on any given day. But here at home three mugs of coffee is my max.

Thus far, four doses of caffeine and a ton of sugar haven't done the trick. My mood hasn't changed a bit. Does more coffee equal a better disposition or vice versa? Hmm, I wonder. I'll have to wait and see and hope for the best.

To get my blood flowing, I consider hopping on the treadmill. Naw, that's not going to happen today. I'm far too lazy. Besides, I ran a 5K for breast cancer awareness last weekend. I'm still sore from that.

I'm also worn out from traveling. I returned last night from an official Agency trip in Nashville, Tennessee. While I was there, I skated at what I believe to be the finest roller rink in the land, Brentwood Skate Center. I skated Friday night and Saturday and Sunday. It was great seeing my young skating friends, as well as a handful of BSC workers. I was particularly pleased to see Lauren and Meredith and their dad, Steve, along with tons of super-talented skaters like Chloe, Olivia, Diana, Billy, and Antonio.

And there was Emma, sitting on Lucky Number Game number three (number four ended up being the lucky number). I was standing. We noticed each other, she stood, and we hugged. Later, we caught each other up on what was happening in our lives. I hadn't seen Emma and her mom in nearly a year. Emma's grown up now, tall, and very pretty, just like her mom.

Someday, when this CIA nonsense is complete, I'd like

to be a roller skating floor guard. I'm certain it's the best job in the world.

My attention straight away wanders to the window-sill's planter. The dismal-looking box once nurtured the brightest crimson petunias imaginable of summer's glory. But today it looks pitifully weather-beaten, nothing more than what it is - an uncared-for, ugly-looking wooden box. The box's paint job has peeled badly. Little flecks of red float in splotchy rain puddles inside its walls. The flecks look like small ruby fishes barely staying afloat in a muddy sea.

I make a mental note to repaint the planter in spring. Then I will stuff it with plastic perennial blooms that should last all four seasons. I mean, think about it. Who honestly cares if spring flowers bloom in winter? Not me, that's for sure. Anything will be better than the ugly box with red paint fishes floppily floating within it.

Everything seems sadly comatose today. The grass recently turned brown seems dead to the world. Just a few weeks ago it was wide awake with a vivacious green. I wish spring were here. Spring's my favorite season. It would have chased away today's dullness.

Of course, winter is not all bad. Winter with glistening snow is wonderful, along with snowmen, sledding and hurling snowballs. Yes, I still hurl snowballs - at trees. However, winter lacking even the slightest wisp of snowy white is mind-numbing. Today fits that wearisome description to a tee.

In spite of everything, I must admit a bit of outside activity is obvious. Playful brownish-gray squirrels undoubtedly scold one another as they play tag in the brown branches. A brown sparrow beneath the squirrels' lofty romper room scrounges for something to eat on the brown infertile ground. But everything is painted a dreary color today, the squirrels, the sparrow, the trees, the grass, the relentless rain - and my mood.

I focus my attention to the heavens beyond the hills. A lightning storm is raging over there. A brilliant flash of pure-white light startles me now and then. Of course, I cannot hear the ensuing thundering sounds. When I look away, the storm's hubbub disappears beyond the hills of my apartment in Washington DC suburbia. Now it is nothing more than a make-believe event of which others speak and hear.

During stormy times like this, I consider my deafness a bit advantageous. Please do not misunderstand me. I don't think being deaf is pleasurable - on the contrary. Deafness dishes me a heaping plate of challenges every day. All the same, when having to face something I would rather tune out my deafness is a way to escape reality.

I glance at my smartphone weather app. I am vigilant when it comes to inclement weather. I cannot hear pelting hail, the rain, or roaring sounds of an imminent tornado. For this reason, I rely on my smartphone as a defense of sorts, from unnatural as well as from natural events.

My phone is my link to the world, at least the hearing world most people take for granted. Probably just like you, I often ponder how I ever managed in the past without my handy-dandy smartphone. I rely on my phone for everything. The marvel's hi-tech memory contains every detail about my life. I never jot down what I should to back up the phone's data. So I dread the thought of losing the device. I would lose a goodly part of my life forever. Then where would I be?

Coworkers - all, of whom I must admit, are males - have told me that I am a stunning redhead. Despite their compliments, as a freethinking, successful woman, I don't like it when guys gawk at me. Maybe it's an anxiety caused by my deafness. I don't know for sure. I only know that, when guys gawk at me, I get this uncomfortable feeling in my gut. Perhaps it's that way with all women when they notice guys staring at them.

On the other hand, I never feel vulnerable. I am never frightened. I am well-trained in martial arts. I have a permit to carry a concealed handgun. And carry it I do. Carrying a firearm on my person is obligatory given my profession. I think all adult women should carry a concealed weapon - with a permit, of course. If they do not like handguns, learning self-protection skills is a must. We live in a dangerous world. The more we can do to defend ourselves the better. Predatory creeps roam the earth. We have a moral obligation to stop them cold.

Allow me to say a bit more about gawkers, mainly as it relates to the human psyche. I consider it comical when guys stumble over their own two feet to catch another glimpse as a gal passes by them. Without a doubt, a lot of guys, but surely not all, are two-legged, chauvinistic klutzes.

I guess it is normal human behavior to look. I notice women stare and stumble just as often as men when they see a good-looking guy. And yes, some men stare at men, and some women stare at women. I'm okay with all of this. The diversity of human behavior is what makes life powerfully interesting. I honestly believe people should live their lives any way they want. As long as they're not hurting others then leave them alone.

As I mentioned a moment ago, my hair is red. It's the natural curls type. I wrap it tightly in a bun to keep it manageable when I am on assignment. Sometimes I weave it into a French braid. A few months ago I considered cutting my hair. It certainly will be easier to control, especially when I am in the field. All the same, the more I think about it, the more I dread cutting my long red locks. So I'll let my hair grow.

My hair is a reminder of carefree days when I was a little girl, before my deafness. I wore my hair much shorter when I was a child. I had to. It was forever and a day dirty, tangled and untidy. I bet I looked like a female version of that filthy little kid in the Sunday morning comic's section. What was his name? Oh yeah, Pig-pen. Like Pig-pen, I seemed to trail a dust cloud that made me awfully filthy as I walked. Pig-pen Eva Roblins - I cringe just thinking it!

Now, I don't want to appear conceited. But ask any natural redheaded guy or gal at school, work or church, and when you meet him or her on the street. Being a red-head carries with it a remarkably cool, unique mystique. There is no getting around the truth. Redheads, natural or dyed, stand out amongst the crowd. I read somewhere that less than two percent of the world's population is naturally redheaded. Marvelously awesome · I like being different, standing out from the crowd.

I look in the mirror and smile at the countless freckles that adorn my pale face. My freckles appear as infinitesi-mal light-colored chocolate stars dotting a moonlit whitish sky. Two dozen or so minuscule freckles surround my nose. They bunch into a brownish mass when I squint or laugh.

A few dozen prominent freckles rest on my upper lip. It makes me cringe that people looking at me from a distance might think I am sporting a slender cookie duster. I have freckles everywhere, on my arms and legs, on my back and my chest and most places in between.

I laugh when I think back to when I was a young teen-ager trying to pop my freckles to nothingness. I teetered on a step stool in front of the mirror squeezing the most prom-inent freckles, clearly to no avail. I am happy my childish attempts to pop freckles like adolescent zits were unsuc-cessful. I have come to love my freckles, almost as much as my bright red hair, pale skin and, of course, my deafness.

There was a time I did not like who I was. I guess most kids go through a similar stage as they grow up. I was the brunt of bullying in high school, and most certainly gram-mar school. The teasing usually concerned my many freck-les and my red hair.

My classmates called me too late for supper, red on the noodle like a (blank) on a poodle. They also called me car-rot top, freckled face, fly dung nose; the list goes on. My eyebrows were light red, so they were just about colorless. Mean bullies would often tease me, shouting during gym, "Hey carrot top! What happened to your eyebrows? Did they fall off your head?"

There were few redheads in the city where I lived as a teenager. In fact, I was the only redhead in my entire school. I was in the minority · at least as it concerned my hair color. Back then, if you were in the minority, you were fair game for teasing, bullying, name-calling and even physical abuse.

Schoolmates also teased me about my ragged clothes. Papa could not afford to buy me new ones. I wore hand-me-downs. After I became deaf spiteful classmates in my sophomore and junior high school years would also tease me about my deafness and, true to form, my slurred speech.

I was only five-foot-five inches in high school, the same height I am today. Because of my petite stature, taunting youngsters never had to fear my revenge. Besides, it was not in my nature to be violent or to strike out against another in anger. I was the kind of girl who lovingly released a wasp through an open window. I could not allow classmates to pulverize it with a rolled up magazine. I abhorred violence back then, and I still do.

The taunting continued mercilessly until one fateful day when the infamous school bully, Francis, went right up in my face and screamed taunts at me. Francis was an enormous six-foot tall brute, an unintelligent, boorish jerk, your typical bullying jock. Everyone was afraid of him. Francis and I were in our junior year. I could read lips fairly well by then. I understood everything he said. His spiteful words haunt me to this day.

> *Eva, Eva, stone-cold deaf*
> *Clothes in tatters, hair's a mess*
> *Freckles like fly-dung on her mug*
> *She's too late for supper, a redhead slug.*
>
> *I'd kill her, but that's not swell,*
> *She slurs too much ever to tell.*
> *So out of my sight you filthy witch,*
> *Or they'll find your body in a ditch!*

POW! One left-handed slug to Francis' nose that

cracked and started bleeding profusely was the result of my comeback. Francis doubled over in pain straight away. What followed was my well-placed kick to an area that causes boys agonizing pain. Years of pent-up anger held within my bosom had exploded like a deluge of water bursting from a dam. I had had enough of the mean-spirited bullying! My left-handed hook and expertly-aimed kick were all it took for the school bullying to stop once and for all.

I received a week's suspension for the excruciating retaliation I inflicted on Francis' nose. He received two week's punishment for his never-ending school torments. But it was only fair and just. From then on everyone referred to me as the redheaded elfin heroine who knocked the notorious school bully on his butt. One and all knew taunting five-foot-five deaf redheaded elfin, Eva Roblins was to be no more.

Unlike today, bullying was a tolerable form of behavior when I was in school. Bullies were a terror in school, on the playground, at the pool, even in church. Then they went on as adults to bully at work, at ballgames, at their local bars, in their neighborhoods - you get the picture.

Luckily for kids nowadays, bullying is recognized as an unnecessary destructive behavior. Bullying is unacceptable. All the same, you and I know it often lurks as a silent marauder beneath the radar, particularly on social sites frequented by young people.

Just the same I would not be surprised if an anti-bullying sign is hanging outside my former high school principal's office right now. If it is, I bet it reads something along the lines, *Attention Bully's. Beware of elves!*

CHAPTER THREE

MUSTACHE BOBBY
AND A WARNING

I've just received an email notification on my phone. A parcel will arrive sometime this afternoon. What is in the parcel, or who sent it for that matter, I do not know. I know I didn't order anything. Wait a minute - maybe it's a surprise birthday present! Then again, it's most likely mis-addressed. In all probability, I'm not the intended recipi-ent. But it sure would be nice to receive something exciting - a surprise of sorts for my birthday. A birthday present would certainly brighten up this dull day, not to mention sweeten my vinegary mood.

I'm in the kitchen pouring myself a record-setting fifth mug of coffee. I glance up and see the tiny red light blink-ing above the sink. This light, I had similar ones installed throughout my apartment, blinks whenever someone rings my doorbell. Without these little LED marvels, there is no way for me to know someone is at the door. I quickly stroll into the living room to see who it is.

As I peer through the door's eyehole, I instinctively make a face. The delivery man is Mustache Bobby. Mustache Bobby is my nickname for Bobby Malone. He's a nice enough fellow, maybe forty, give or take, and more or less good-looking. The trouble is he has a bushy mustache. His mustache makes my reading his lips more difficult than other delivery persons say, Vivian or Pete. And Pete has a serious lisp at that! When Mustache Bobby speaks, I have to watch carefully as he forms his words. My confusion is due to his mustache hairs going up and down, to and fro, and round and round as his lips move. It is pure madness to comprehend what he is saying!

"Hi, Bobby," I call through the door. "Can you leave it on the stoop? I'm not properly dressed to open the door. I'm sort of hanging around today looking a bit ragged if you know what I mean. It's my day off from work."

As I look through the door's eyehole again, I can barely see Mustache Bobby's lips move. The distorted, wide-angle image in the door's eyehole makes it all the more difficult. As expected, his mustache hairs are going up and down, to and fro, and round and round.

I do catch one word near the end of whatever he has been saying, "Sign..." I slap my arms to my sides in frustration and groan. Darn the bad luck. I have to sign for it. Darn! I don't have a clue what it is or if it's even for me!

"Okay, then," I shout through the door. "Just give me a sec to get a bit decent-looking before I open up. Hold on Bobby." I count slowly in my mind, one Mississippi, two Mississippi, and three Mississippi until I tally ten Mississippi's in all. I open the door.

Ta-da! Here stands good ole Mustache Bobby! He looks debonair (not!) in his heavy gray jacket, gray slacks, gray ear muffs, gray gloves, and gray scarf - he fits in perfectly with this dull gray day. He's soaking wet. I take a quick glance at the envelope in his gloved hand. It's not a document. A thin rectangular box stretches from within the rubbery container.

He exclaims, "Dang, Miss Eva! Although you had but a few seconds to get decent-looking, your words, not mine, you look wonderful here! I can't wait to see what you look like when you're dolled up here!" He laughs at his boorish joke.

I force a lighthearted grin. I laugh in return - best not to offend a deliveryman. What's more, Mustache Bobby is a nice guy. "Ha-ha," says my fake laugh, followed by, "Well, I did have to comb my hair a bit. We gals can get ready in a flash when you guys least expect it."

I watch his lips say, "Well, I just need you to sign this here machine here on the line here and then I will be on my way. Good thing you're not out in this rain here. It's miserable here. Why, is that coffee I smell here? I sure could use a cup of hot coffee. I surely could - and maybe enjoy a bit of warmth too, to dry off a bit if I could rest inside here a spell."

That is mightily bold of him. The rain must have saturated his brain cells. Maybe that explains why nearly every one of his sentences has the word *here* in it. I say apologetically, "Sorry, Bobby, I truly am. I have a ton of work to do. I have no time to visit with you. An important project is due tomorrow. I can give you a cup of coffee to go if you would like."

I feel badly about lying, but what Mustache Bobby does not know will not hurt him. He is likable as I said. But I would go totally bonkers if I had to try to read his lips for ten minutes or longer. Standing here as he talks is bad enough!

I sign the formatted screen on the machine he holds in his hand. I look up just in time to catch his reply as he hands me the package. "No ma'am, I guess that's okay..."

Now I'm staring at him in a shadowy fog, not discerning what words follow from his mustached lips. I'm indifferent as his mustache hairs go up and down, to and fro, and round and round for at least a half-minute more. I cannot seem to focus my eyes properly. I feel peculiar. It has to be the envelope. It's much too warm for this cold day. It's giving off some eerie energy - I can feel it!

Poor Mustache Bobby, he must think I'm nuts. Here he is talking away, and I have no clue what he is saying! I'm just staring at him like a dim-witted fool! What in tarnation is happening to me?

Peculiar shivers run up and down my spine. I am wobbly-kneed and lightheaded. Something out of the ordinary is in this envelope. If it's good or bad, I do not know. Nor do I care. One thing is for certain. I have had this feeling a few times before in my life. Once again my life is about to change, I'm sure of it.

I do not know how I know this. I just do. They say the deaf, voiceless, and the blind possess a unique sixth sense, an unusual power of perception. So it is with me. I have a sixth sense, a strong one for sure. I cannot sense every detail - you know, I cannot predict the future or anything like that. All the same, I get just enough info to have a general idea of strange things. Whenever my sixth sense tells me something is wrong or about to happen, I always pay close attention.

Mustache Bobby finally turns away and trudges down the walkway to his delivery truck. He probably thinks me rude. I did not thank him or say goodbye. Oh well, he'll get over it.

I slowly close the door. After it closes, I lean against the door jamb to keep from falling. I feel very lightheaded now. And my ears are twitching and itching like crazy. I have not felt this sort of strangeness since a bullet bore a hole in my stomach. That was over two years ago.

I'm examining the envelope. It has the standard stuff - computer barcodes and the delivery company's logo. It also has my full name, street address, township, and zip code printed on it. Strangely, there is no sender's address.

I stare at the envelope as I patiently wait for this dizzy feeling to subside. All of a sudden I instinctively grab the doorknob with my hand to keep from falling flat on my face. Red words miraculously appear on the envelope below my address.

Eva Roblins - do not open until the stroke of midnight, the exact moment you are twenty-nine years of age.

Now, as incredibly as the words had formed, they vanish! I stumble to lie down on the couch for a spell. I have to try and escape this dizziness · it's like I'm barely motion-less while everything in the room whirls around me.

I lie still for the longest time, my eyes watching the chandelier in the dining room as it seems to spin in place. After what seems like forever, I begin to feel a whole lot better. I'm just nervous as can be. I get up from the couch. Then I walk back and forth between the kitchen and the dining room for the longest time.

I have finally returned to normal. Well, I guess you can say I've returned to normal · I've been walking in wide cir-cles around my living room coffee table for what seems like endless hours. It is highly unusual for me to pace back and forth nervously, particularly when I am in the comfort of my home. Even so, that's what I've been doing since Mus-tache Bobby delivered the envelope at two o'clock. I glance at the wall clock. It is now six o'clock in the evening.

The coffee pot is working overtime. Its payoff is mug af-ter mug of hazelnut flavored coffee. Now I have the jitters. They're not solely due to the extra caffeine soaring through my body · I'll tell you that. My hands are also shaking a lit-tle. I wonder · are they shaking because of the coffee or are they shaking because I am jumpy?

Since my legs ache from walking in circles, I plop on the couch to thumb through magazines. I'm not reading a word, just staring at pictures. Every so often I get up from the couch to use the bathroom. I also stare out the dining room window · anything to pass the time hurriedly. I don't want to check my phone to see what time it is. I'd be afraid only a few minutes will have passed since the last time I looked. I know it's corny, but I'm a firm believer in my screwy version of the Latin phrase "tempus fugit" · *time flies when you stay occupies.*

After a while, I check the time. Yippee! More than three hours have passed since I last checked. It is a few minutes past nine o'clock. I can feel my stomach grumble. No wonder it's complaining · I haven't eaten since break-fast, over twelve hours ago. Standing on my tippy-toes, I rummage through the cupboards for something to eat. I grab a can of tuna and open it. I empty the excess water into the sink. I plop the stringy, gooey goop into a bowl. To make it somewhat palatable, I slap in a tablespoon of mayo and a teaspoon of relish. As I mix the creation together, I scowl. It looks horrible! Too bad · I'm hungry, so it'll have to do.

I spread the slimy, green-speckled brownish concoction on top of two slices of whole wheat bread to make a super fat, sloppy sandwich. Unattractive gooey goop oozes out from all sides. I slice the sandwich in two. Then I stroll into the dining room with the fat, sloppy sandwich and a tall glass of ice water in hand. I peer outside. The rain has moved on. It's about time. Two days of nonstop rain are enough.

While I eat my nasty-tasting sandwich · I'm eating it more for nourishment than enjoyment · I start to relax. I also think about *what is* and *what was* as it relates to my existence. To be sure, I have been in worst situations in my life. There is no reason to get all worked up about an envelope and funny warning words that miraculously appeared then disappeared. As if to pacify my anxiety, I think back to some tough spots I have been in since joining the Agency.

There was the time I awakened to find my hands and wrists bound behind me. I was sitting speechless, my eyes unblinking in a darkly lit storage trailer. I laugh as I recall that the very person I had been trying to capture drugged me. My immediate supervisor, Cindy Wickham, finally captured him. I was a novice agent back then, and it showed.

Then I remember when I was on assignment in the Philippines. I was off-duty, enjoying the sights as a wandering wide-eyed tourist. I had plunged without a second thought into a swiftly flowing river to rescue a little boy who was being swept away. I had managed to get the boy safely onto a sandbar · hooray me! Just to be swept further down the torrent.

Luckily, I managed to grab onto a tree limb jutting

from the river's banks. So here I am today, perhaps no wiser but here. I laugh. That incident certainly wasn't the highlight of my career at the Agency. I was off-duty at the time. So not a soul at work knew what happened. I'll never tell. You shouldn't either, eh?

I cringe when I think back to when a drug dealer shot me on the left side of my stomach. Despite my being shot, my undercover effort had wrecked an immoral international drug dealer's evil trade. It also resulted in his fellow gang members serving lengthy sentences behind bars. I tremble as my fingers unconsciously grope the spot where the bullet entered my body. It entered my body a half-inch below my rib cage. I intend no pun - that event has been the lowest point in my professional career at the Agency, no doubt about it.

Despite my attempt at digression, I'm still thinking about that blasted envelope and what's inside. I try a different approach, contemplating *what ifs*. What if something poisonous is inside the envelope, like a box of powdered anthrax! No, that cannot be. The package delivery company has a sophisticated screening process to detect hazardous materials.

What if it's a severed finger or something equally gross? The Agency has been known to take delivery of similarly disgusting, thought-provoking vulgar parcels. If you think about it, the box appears to be roughly the same size as an index finger. Naw, that's pretty lame.

Oh my goodness, what if it's an itsy-bitsy bomb! No, that's also ridiculous. The object is too small to be an explosive device - then again...

I try dozing. It doesn't work. Whenever I open my eyes, they move straight away to the rosewood coffee table where the envelope sits happy and proud. I try reading. That also doesn't work. My mind wanders until my eyes zero in on the darned envelope just itching to get my attention. I try closing my eyes just for the heck of it. Nope - ain't going to work either. Pallid flashing images of the envelope skate back and forth as eye floaters beneath my shut eyelids. It is utterly nerve-wracking. The envelope is driving me nuts!

Out of the blue, I have this impulse to take hold of the envelope and open it. So I do. As I begin to tear at it, I exclaim aloud, "I will not allow an envelope and silly words to keep me on the edge like this!"

I fight with the elastic rubbery plastic. It is super hard to open. As I struggle, I cannot help but wonder who designed it - probably a brawny architectural genius who holds the only clue for opening modern-day rubbery envelopes. I finally tear the envelope. I tear it just enough to see it contains what I thought was inside - a tiny rectangular box. To my alarm, I am abruptly jolted back onto the couch cushion as if a bolt of electricity slammed me.

I exclaim in a high-pitched, slurred voice, "Gaoush! That hurt like the dickens!" It is obvious the envelope does not like being ripped apart, at least not yet. For whatever reason, it propelled a jolting charge into my fingers. The charge pulsated up my arms like a lightning bolt. I am now feeling mixed emotions - totally ticked-off and slightly terrified.

I turn my palms up. Perhaps the jolt burned them. Okay, okay I confess. The bolt of energy was not intense enough to cause burns. But the bolt of energy hurt, it honestly did!

I glance at the fireplace mantel where Papa's vintage 20th Century German chime clock sits. The time is eleven twenty-six in the evening. I believe it prudent to wait another thirty-four minutes to open the envelope before a charge zaps me again, or worse.

Thirty-three minutes and two mugs of coffee later, I watch as the minute hand on Papa's clock strikes midnight. Of course, I cannot hear its chime. It is fortunate I cannot. The clock is an old wind-up timepiece. So it's not as accurate as the time display on my phone. I would be tempted to tear open the package when Papa's clock struck midnight. The envelope could have zapped me again had I opened it too early.

I stare at the digital readout on my phone as it slowly

ticks off the remaining seconds. Twenty · ten…four · three · two · one. It is now the ninth of January, my twenty-ninth birthday! I shout loudly, "Happy birthday to meeeeee!"

Being zapped again is the last thing I want to happen. I instinctively hold my breath while my fingers warily tear at the remnants of the rubbery envelope. It is hard going. These sturdy envelopes are made to last a lifetime. I'm sure of it. I doubt they're even recyclable. The tiny box seems stuck inside the rubbery mess. Being trapped inside the plastic goo makes matters worse. I need to open this envelope like right now. I've been holding my breath this entire time · I need to breathe!

Okay. It took a bit of effort, but I finally open the envelope. I exhale a long sigh of relief, and then I inhale deeply. I remove the tiny box and set it on the coffee table. I stare at it for a few moments. It is quite old. It appears to be handmade. Its wood surface is marred and cracked. It looks as though flames scorched it at some point.

I pick up the curious-looking box and turn it over and again in my trembling hand as I examine it. Printed in faded red letters on the top is this inscription · *ælf*. I recognize the word as the Old English version of the modern day word *elf*.

Goodness, this box must be a hundred years old or older! It belongs in a museum. Why did I receive it, or better yet, who sent it to me? Is it supposed to be a birthday present? Is that why I could not open it before my twenty-ninth birthday? But why did it zap me? That's no way to treat the birthday girl!

I continue to inspect the box. But I'm hesitant to open it so I can peer inside. I'm afraid I'll get zapped another time. Just now, I am acutely aware my ears are twitching and itching yet again. I have this creepy feeling my ears are growing · and stretching. I hesitantly touch my right ear. My ear is longer than it's supposed to be! I leap to my feet shouting, "Goodness has my ear grown? Does it have a point on it?"

Now I'm more frightened than ever! I toss the box onto

the table and dash into the dining room to get my mirror. I stare at my reflection. I look at my left ear then at my right. I immediately fall on my knees to the carpet in disbelieving, bewildering panic. I can barely breathe. In an anguished tone of voice, I whisper aloud, "Oh my goodness! My ears have grown by at least an inch. They also have tiny points - it's as if..."

There is no way my ears are changing into elf ears! No, no, no, no - no way! What in the world is happening to me? Oh my goodness, for the love of Peter, could I be turning into an elf? What does this have to do with my twenty-ninth birthday? And what does it have to do with whatever is inside that mysterious box? Ah, the box - perhaps it contains the answers to my questions!

Everything around me is spinning once again. I'm afraid I will pass out if I attempt to stand. I crawl back into the living room on my hands and knees. I upset the floor lamp near the couch. As I pull myself onto the couch, I catch the lamp before it crashes to smithereens on the floor. I switch the lamp to full brightness.

My hands are trembling more noticeably than before. I reach for the tiny box. Dreading the thought of being shocked yet again, I hold my breath as I open it. Thankfully, nothing happens.

A round silver medallion rests upon a silvery hue of silvery silk. The medallion is one inch in diameter, perhaps a bit more. It hangs from an intricately woven thin silver chain. There's a small piece of rolled up parchment inside the box. I take the medallion in my hand. It is handmade of what looks to be sterling silver. It is old but in mint condition. I could be wrong, but it looks like no one wore it.

An artistically engraved facial image of a beautiful elf with long flowing curly hair adorns the medallion's front. I am flabbergasted. The image looks exactly like me, diminutive freckles, and all! The image even includes the tiny mole on the lower portion of the left side of my chin. That tiny dot of a mole is barely discernible in real life, but it's there.

24

I turn the medallion over in my hand. An inscription reads, *with love life and glory reign.*

I retrieve my handheld mirror I had tossed to the floor when I reentered the living room. I glance over and over from my reflection in the mirror to the medallion's image and back again. The image looks exactly like me - now that I have elf ears! But how can this be? What does this medallion have to do with me? What am I supposed to do with it? Ah, the rolled up piece of parchment - I bet it holds the answer!

I carefully unroll the parchment. It is old and fragile. I am afraid it will fall to pieces in the palm of my hand before I can read the words inscribed on it. I gently press it smooth on the living room coffee table. The parchment contains five words: *Eva Roblins Princess of Spardom.*

What in the world is Spardom? And me, Eva Roblins, the supposed princess of a place called Spardom? Is this someone's idea of a joke? But no, there was a shock and the warning on the envelope and, of course, my elfish-looking ears! No one could dream up a practical joke like this!

I dash into the dining room to retrieve my phone. As I hurry back into the living room, I search the Internet by typing the word *Spardom* on my smartphone. I'm not surprised with words that appear on my phone's screen: *We found no results for your search terms.*

It is at this precise moment I notice I have an email from my former head supervisor at the Agency. How can this be from him? The darling gentleman died one year ago. Goodness, this is starting out to be one insane birthday! Before I open the email, I carefully type on my phone to Google, *Dr. Raymond D Brown, CIA.* The Internet search results pop up on the display.

Dr. Raymond D Brown, Central Intelligence Agency (CIA) Deputy Director, National Clandestine Service (NCS).

As expected, there is no further mention of his service with the CIA. There is, however, a lengthy list of his many philanthropic contributions to the local community and his scholastic achievements. Luckily, at least for me, and to confirm I am not going insane, there it is · at the very bottom of page two.

Deceased · survived by wife Bette Hall Sinclair-Brown and two children, Raymond D. Brown Jr. and Edgar Brown; fourteen grandchildren, and so on and so forth.

Okay, not only am I supposedly the Princess of Spardom, but I'm also receiving emails from dead people! Should I open the email? Maybe I should ignore it, delete it before reading. Perhaps I should get in touch with my present supervisor or report it to the police! But no, I knew something like this was going to take place. My sixth sense is on red alert. It is telling me I should not allow this mystery to go unchallenged. I open the email and begin to read.

CHAPTER FOUR

WORDS FROM THE GRAVE

"Dearest Eva,
First off, I beg you not to be alarmed you are receiving this note long after my passing. I know I have but one more chance to make things right in my life. Thus, I have chosen one single item of extreme import to reconcile before I pass on. I am preparing this email before I succumb to my illness. I likewise have directed my attorney to send it on your 29th birthday. I also directed she destroy any record of this email upon ensuring my communiqué was received by you with a receipt of delivery confirmed.

You have undoubtedly received the package I instructed my attorney send to you. Otherwise, you would not be reading these words. I directed sending of this email after you received the package.

Eva, I had access to many issues in my line of work for many years as Deputy Director, NCS. Those on the street could not fathom what I knew. Such is the medallion you hold in your hand · or will shortly after you read these lines. The value of the medallion to the average man and woman is beyond his or her understanding. To them, the

medallion would appear to be nothing more than an old rel-
ic. Of course, it would seem priceless for its intrinsic value
and of course for its age. You will soon see its value is unri-
valed. In my view, there is nothing in the world that can
compare.

I imagine you know very little about your family's her-
itage. How could you, given the poverty and detachment
you endured as a child? Yes, I know how your family strug-
gled when you were a youngster. I know your father mi-
grated from one menial job to the next after your family
left Canada. You were a toddler at the time. And I know -
and these facts pain me to mention them - how your mother froze to death in your car as she slept. She had placed
her blanket over you to prevent you from freezing to death.
I believe you were only seven years old at the time.

Yes, I know that you and your parents had to live out
of your dilapidated vehicle. As a nomadic child, it was the
only place you could call home for years on end. Living in
such squalid conditions explains that your health markedly
deteriorated over the ensuing years. An environment like
that weakens one's immune system. I am certain your sad
surroundings ultimately resulted in your meningitis and
deafness.

Yes, Eva, I am aware of all these dreadful things when
you were a youngster. I often wished we could speak of
them. I trust you realize I could never to do such a thing in
respect for your privacy. In this regard, I deeply apologize
you have had to endure those terrible, nightmarish memories on your own.

You had an undeserved childhood, inequitable and
quite sorrowful. However, you never lost sight of your abilities. You never gave up. You always strengthened your
pronounced potential by looking forward to your future.
You always strove to better yourself, to outdistance your
peers, and in the end, you became a model Agency agent.

Your impeccable record speaks for itself. You have
achieved honorable successes. Your exceptional hand-to-
hand combat skills and sharpshooter marksmanship doc-

ument your drive. Your daring courage under fire, when M. Rodriquez shot you, reflects your bravery. These attributes echo your dedication to your country and pay tribute to your uncanny strength. I salute you, Eva Roblins. I truly do.

But enough of these kudos, for I know you are not the sort to put up with excessive praise even if it is well-deserved. Let us now move to the real purpose of this email. Let us address the medallion and the legend. I am not certain if the legend is fact or fiction. I only know what I have read. However, the existence of the land is real.

First, let me say this. Eva, you are the only known lineage descendant of the legendary, ancient Isle of Spardom's monarch. You are the sole, surviving bloodline descendant of the Isle's only known queen. That makes you, Eva Roblins, Princess of Spardom.

The following paragraphs, of which I paraphrase, are from the Isle's Chronicles. The Agency obtained the Isle's Chronicles from an unknown entity shortly after the Second World War.

Spardom was purportedly an out-of-the-way Isle located near the Equatorial line of exotic atolls and coral islands in the western portion of the Pacific basin. It was roughly one thousand kilometers east-northeast of the tropical island of Nauru in Micronesia. Spardom reportedly was a paradise to behold. It had a warm climate and abundant sea and land life. Its beauty was something to behold - rolling hills of vibrant green fields, majestic snow-covered mountains, and lush agricultural fields.

During the rainy season, red blossoms of dainty flora, found only on Spardom, dotted the entire landscape. When the flora was in bloom, it resembled a million tiny candles blinking delicate crimson embers beneath the sunshine's warm glow. At night huge true-life, tropical lightning bugs flickered. The lightening bugs were indigenous to Spardom and found nowhere else in the world.

The combination of the flora and lightning bugs brought a mysterious aura of seemingly starlit panoramas to the rolling hills of Spardom both at daytime and nighttime. To the rare visiting sailor's untrained eye, it was difficult at night to distinguish between stars above and iridescent flickering of surrounding hills below. These beautiful panoramas were said to be a tribute to the monarch of the Isle, the lovely Queen April of Spardom.

According to legend the queen was so enchantingly exquisite, Islanders called her April. The name April refers to the second month of the Greek calendar when attractive buds of spring come into flower and forest creatures raise their young. It is considered an incredible time of rebirth and cheer.

Islanders were fond of narrating stories about their queen to the occasional sailor who was allowed to visit the Isle. Islanders said Queen April had special powers and had outlived many generations of her peoples. In all that time, as she reigned, she had never grown a day older. She supposedly had lived more than a hundred years but looked much younger, perhaps thirty or so years of age.

A few, who have read the Chronicles, have noted her land as one of the first true democracies on Earth. Attesting to the manner in which she held others in great esteem as equals, she married a commoner. She and her husband reportedly had two children. The oldest was a son named Thurman.

They also had a daughter named Eva. Eva was destined to become Princess Eva of Spardom, heir apparent to the queen. The child Eva, so the Chronicles stipulate, had reddish hair and an abundant number of freckles adorning her face, arms, and back. Many said her eyes shone with the light blue hue of the surrounding seas. Her skin was as white and delicate as albino butterflies that dwelled in the Isle's deepest forest.

Then one day the Isle vanished. Able seaman, who had visited the Isle on previous voyages, could never again locate the island or its peoples. Some speculated at the time a huge tsunami had washed over the Isle, submerging it and its inhabitants forever.

Others contend a huge earthquake beset the island. Historical records say an enormous earthquake occurred when the Isle disappeared. Perhaps the Isle had fallen into the abyss.

We find this hypothesis most remarkable, given the Isle was supposedly one-third as large as the continent of Australia. Understandably, many legends have spoken of the Isle's existence. Some fables stipulate Spardom was equal in splendor to Atlantis, perhaps being the legendary lost land of Atlantis itself.

Infra-red satellite and radar imagery taken by (name of the agency redacted) reveal a vast land mass impression on the seabed floor. Its area is approximately one million square miles, again more or less one-third the size of Australia. I could tell you much more. In view of the unclassified nature of this communication, I trust others will provide classified supplementary details at a later date.

Now, please permit me to speak of the medallion. Fourteen years ago, nearly three weeks to the day after you turned fifteen years of age, I came into possession of the medallion. A weather-beaten old man, who sported a long white beard, gave the medallion to me. He hid his identity beneath the covering of his hooded white cloak.

When I inquired as to the man's name, he wished not to be identified. He simply said, "Ensure this gets to its rightful owner, sir. You know the tale, the Chronicles as they are, and you know its importance. Please carry out my wishes." He then scurried away out of my sight.

I immediately opened the box when I returned to my office. I saw your name on the parchment and orchestrated a modest research. I quickly learned all there was to know about you and your family. You were in the hospital in a coma on the very day my inquiry began. The doctor told me you weren't expected to survive our illness. Fortunately, you did survive. I am happy to say the legend of Spardom and its lovely princess, if both facets of this rather bizarre legend are, in fact, true, live.

So, there you have it, my dear Eva. No matter what

you do with this information, or with the medallion that is rightly yours, I want you to know I wish you all the best. If I were a betting man, I would bet you will not hesitate to embark once again on an exciting adventure. Something tells me it may be the most exciting adventure of your life.

Bless you, my dear Eva Roblins · Princess of Spardom. Good luck. I am yours everlastingly, Raymond."

I'm a strong-willed woman. I like to think I'm also pretty darned tough. I confess I haven't had it as bad in my life as some people. Nevertheless, I've had to triumph over my share of life's speed bumps during my twenty-nine years. But this · this email and everything else that has happened since I received the envelope takes the cake. I'm not lying to you when I say this. I am scared out of my wits!

As I sit cross-legged on my living room couch, I'm rocking back and forth and shaking from head to toe. I have not felt this scared since the day I found out I was deaf. A hot, flushed redness covers my face. I have a nagging headache. This evening's events have drained my body of its energy. My sixth sense is going berserk. It's trying to tell me all will be okay, not to be scared.

But c'mon · who wouldn't be scared? Weird feelings, a cautionary note, a sudden electrical shock, mirrored images. Then there is an email from the deceased, tales and legends, strange lands beneath the sea. Along with, of course, supposedly being a human princess with, of all things, elongated elf ears! I mean, you tell me · what could top all of this?

I read the email two more times. I've committed the Chronicles' highlights to memory. A part of me wants to save the email. It might be helpful to have proof of the email's existence in case I'm seen blabbering to myself on the street. It just could keep me from being committed.

Of course, if I save the email, others will know about Spardom's existence. My sixth sense tells me others do not need to know. I delete the email and clear it from my trash bin. As you and I know, things never disappear from the Internet - there is always a trace. Deleting the email from my account is, however, the best I can do.

I check the time. It is twelve-thirty in the morning. I notice another email notification has popped on my phone. I do not know the sender, a Kristopher Bales. Forever and a day curious, I open the email and begin to read.

"My dear, Eva Roblins, Princess of Spardom,

May I have the pleasure of your company for lunch on or about 1:30 this afternoon? I will be resting on a check-ered blanket beneath the leafless shade trees on the left-side area to the rear of the Jefferson Memorial. The day promises to be a bit cool temperature-wise. However, thankfully, the weatherman forecasts a warm sun. I will be serving a delicious light lunch of your favorite German po-tato salad and Tilsit cheese, along with saltine crackers.

May I indulge upon you to bring along a carafe of your delicious non-alcoholic Cabernet Sauvignon if you please? I will have three plastic wine glasses, so you need not bother with those. I regret I cannot bring along the wine. I am un-able to purchase wine of any kind in your land, even if it is non-alcoholic. It seems I do not hold proper identification, a rather out-of-date, ill-mannered rule if I do say so myself. I hope you do not mind my humble request.

And please milady, do try to sleep before our rendez-vous. You have undergone quite a bit of excitement during the past half-hour. I can only imagine you are exhausted. I have many things of significance to convey to you. I trust you will sleep well.

Finally, if I may be so bold as to suggest, I would pro-pose you do not sleep on the couch where you are sitting at this moment. It appears none too comfortable for a good night's rest.

I am reverently yours, Kristopher Bales III of Toriam."

Well, I'll be darned. Now I am getting strange invites from a strange man. I wonder if it has anything to do with the medallion, Spardom, and the last half-hour of absurdity. But no matter, I'll follow-through on the request. Besides, this Kristopher guy somehow knows I was thinking of sleeping on the couch tonight. So I'm certain he has something to do with all of this. Plus, how in the world does he know I have a carafe of Cabernet Sauvignon in my refrigerator?

I am in a disagreeable mood, to say the least. To (nervously) prove I'm still in charge of my human life, I grab two pillows and an afghan blanket from the closet. I deliberately make my bed on the couch. Of course, I know I will not sleep well. I'm over-tired and keyed-up. I'm also a side sleeper. It will not be easy sleeping on my side with larger than normal ears - I'll tell you that!

When I awaken later in the morning, the sun is shining brightly through the living room window. I guess I was more tired than I thought last night. I forgot to close the curtains before I sacked out on the couch. I shower. As I shampoo my hair, I pay particular attention to the locks near my elf ears. It feels weird having to scrub around ears that nearly doubled in size in less than twelve hours.

I blow-dry and brush my hair. Then I eat a toasted onion bagel with cream cheese. I swallow three mugs of hazelnut flavored coffee to perk my senses. I check myself in the mirror (I ensure I cover my elf ears with my white beanie), smile, wink, and then I cringe. My sixth sense tells me today is going to be extraordinarily odd.

I hop in my car and head to the Nation's Capitol. There's not much traffic at this hour, with the exception of those bold enough to drive their cars to lunch. Most DC employees walk to lunch or eat at their desks.

It is now one-thirty in the afternoon. I am happily twenty-nine years of age plus one-half day give or take an hour. And I'm still alive - remarkably! I wasn't spirited away by some paranormal alien life form to the Isle of Spardom or outer space for that matter. Now, as I sit on the blanket, my mind is racing with thoughts at twice the speed of sound.

Well, that explains the three plastic glasses he mentioned in his email. There is one for me, one for this strange-looking character with a long white beard who calls himself Kristopher, and the third one is for my Agency supervisor, Cindy Wickham. But what the heck is going on and why is Cindy here? Better yet, why am I here?

I sip my wine as calmly as I can. I'm trying to act nonchalant. All the same, I cannot take my eyes off of the carafe as it sits on the checkered blanket. I could have sworn Kristopher opened the carafe with a mere wave of his hand. Then again, I probably imagined it. I didn't get much sleep last night. I should not have slept on the couch.

I notice Cindy is speaking. Her lips are saying "...so I thought I would come unannounced, so there is no credible, documented trace I was here. Others will believe I am enjoying a pleasant, unseasonably warm picnic lunch with two charming people."

After reading Cindy's lips, I frown. My frown causes my eyes to squint and the sides of my nose to squash together. I recognize this causes freckles on both sides of my nose to bunch together into brownish, freckled creases. I may look silly. But I do not care. I am angry, and I want it to show. My angry-looking frown will do nicely and go along with what I am about to say.

"Okay, Cindy, could you please tell me what's going on? And what you and the Agency have to do with the rather amazing things that have happened to me in the past twenty-four hours, eh? Why I knew nothing about this beforehand - why I had no clue, no inkling to keep me from almost going bonkers since that darned envelope arrived? Then I get an email from a man who is dead. Then there's this medallion with an image on it that looks like me. Finally, there's this princess stuff - plus the fact I've grown preposterous elf ears, it's enough..."

Cindy waves her hand to interrupt my tirade. She laughs and says, "You are too cute when you are upset,

Eva, do you know that? In addition, you ramble on and on uncontrollably as well." She smiles the sweetest, most in-nocent smile imaginable. I'm usually a sucker for her en-dearing smile. However, her smile is a waste of time today. And one thing's for certain. I'm in no mood to smile in re-turn.

Cindy's lips continue to speak. "I apologize I could not tell you beforehand what this is about or what Raymond had to do with it. You see, Eva, as Raymond said in the email... Now, please do not give me that angry scowl again Eva. You must understand we sometimes look at agents' email. Believe me when I say this is the first time in your case. Okay? Give me some breathing room here, will you? Please? Okay then..."

I quickly wave my hand back and forth to bring Cindy's words to a halt. I know for certain my face shows the anger boiling from within me. I only hope my voice will mirror that anger.

I hiss softly, "You did what? You read my email from Raymond? Why does the Agency do that Cindy, eh? What happened to the mutual trust factor? For crying out loud that email was private. Raymond had written that email before he died a year ago. His attorney sent it to my per-sonal email account this morning. How am I supposed to trust you or the Agency or this guy Kristopher?" I give a purposeful side-glance of annoyance at Kristopher. He just stares at me.

My tirade continues. "You've been privy to my personal email all along and then you keep me totally in the dark? You may be my supervisor, Cindy · but you're also my friend. For crying out loud, you raised me for a year after Papa died. You're like my surrogate mother. How could you, Cindy, how could you, eh?"

"Eva," Cindy replies, "Calm down and take it easy. First off, I just told you we never have, not once, read your emails since I have been Director for the past eleven months · not until now, of course. Second, that email was official. Our Agency attorney sent it as directed by Raymond. It was not, by any stretch of the imagination, sent by a personal civilian attorney. Do you think Raymond could entrust a non-cleared lawyer with the information contained in his email? It would be scandalous if the media ever learned of its contents!"

I say skeptically, "Cindy, I want to believe what I see you are saying. But put yourself in my shoes. Also, let me be candid here. If you weren't beside me right now, I would have already beaten the dickens out of this man Kristopher. I would have stuffed his potato salad and Tilsit cheese in my bag for good measure. Then I would have been on my merry way. At least I would feel some comfort for the anxiety I have suffered since yesterday afternoon. Thank you both very much...and Raymond too for that matter!"

Just to prove my point, I take another side-glance of irritation at Kristopher. As if to show my unsociable remarks do not bother him, Kristopher smiles. He also continues to stare at me. His staring is annoying the crap out of me. I defiantly return his stare.

With his maddening blank eyes staring into mine, he gestures toward the carafe with his hand. I watch in disbelief as the carafe miraculously rises above the blanket! It floats in midair until it is above the wine glass Kristopher holds in his hand. The carafe tilts slowly on its end and pours wine into Kristopher's glass!

Now the carafe floats to hover above Cindy and my glasses sitting on the blanket. It refills our glasses in turn to within an inch of the rim. It unhurriedly descends until it rests upright on the blanket once more. It hadn't spilled a single drop of wine the entire time!

I look at Kristopher with disbelief. "Well, I'll be darned!" I say with a chuckle. "I am still angry at the two of you. Nevertheless, I take back everything I said about kicking your butt, sir, every last bit of it. That was incredible. How in the world did you do that, eh?"

I look over at Cindy. She is smiling. I then glance back to Kristopher and stare. He has just finished a sentence. I was barely able to grasp the very last word his lips spoke.

I am shocked. I can feel my redheaded fury beginning to boil within me. "I beg your pardon, sir," I challenge. "Did you just call me what I think you called me?" I momentarily pause to mull over what I will say next. The only words that escape my mouth are seething accusations that threaten, "How dare you..."

"No, no, no my fair lady," I watch Kristopher's lips reply. "I would never call you anything but my fair lady. I said you were a *wizardess*, not that other word you thought I said." He laughs.

Realizing my mistake, I laugh awkwardly in return. I inwardly cringe as well. I can feel my freckled face turning as crimson as a sugar beet. That's the way it is with us redheads. When we blush, we blush until our faces just about match the color of our hair. There is no getting around it.

I apologize saying, "It's your mustache sir. I have trouble reading your lips. The mustache masks your lips' pattern as you speak. It causes me to fail to notice or misunderstand a word here and there. You see, I am deaf."

Now a word Kristopher just said pops in my brain like a firecracker. I guardedly whisper, "Wait a minute. What did you just say? Did you say I was a *wizardess*? Yes, you darned well did! I watched your lips say I was a wizardess!" I look from Kristopher to Cindy then back again. I say, "Goodness you two, what's going on here, eh? I'm no wizardess. I seriously doubt I'm the Princess of Spardom either. Tell me all of this is a birthday joke - an insanely in-poor-taste birthday joke."

I look intently at Kristopher as I wait for him to explain. He waves his hand in front of his face three times. His mustache vanishes! No way - he made his mustache disappear with three waves of his hand! He may look utterly absurd with a long white beard that lacks a mustache. However, his mustache is no longer on his face!

He begins to reply to my question. But I need to interrupt him. Yes, yes I know - I know! I have a bad habit of interrupting people when something bothers me. But it's my way, okay? I can't help it. Besides, I'm going bonkers with at least a hundred questions running through my mind right now. I need answers. I need them right away. I'm certain you can't blame me! You'd probably do the same.

I say, "You are something, Kristopher. How did you make your mustache disappear, eh? And how did you do those amazing things with the carafe? Are you a wizard?" I look at Cindy and inquire, "Or is this a clever physics-defying supernatural phenomenon developed by the Agency?" I look back at Kristopher and add, "And what in the world does this have to do with me?" Kristopher does not answer. He simply stares as before.

I look back at Cindy. The expression on her face is serious. Even so, it is apparent to me that she is not going to offer anything, at least not at this point. I look away from her to address Kristopher. "Certainly, I am no wizardess, sir. You are the one with magical powers. I saw them myself. What you did is out of this world!

"First you open the carafe without using your hands. Then you have it magically refill our glasses all by itself. Then, with three waves of your hand - poof! Your mustache disappears. Please explain yourself. What does this have to do with me and all the craziness that has happened over the past twenty-four hours?"

Kristopher turns his head toward Cindy. He appears to be staring at her. He shrugs his shoulders as if he's saying, "It's up to you, Cindy."

Cindy gently touches my shoulder. I turn my head to watch her lips. I also focus on her facial expression. The expression on her face is one I have come to know over the years as tender honesty. I love that look. It's because I know Cindy is going to be straight with me - no lies, no deception, no beating around the bush, and no bull.

Her lips say, "Kristopher is not supernatural when it comes to moving things with his mind, honey. His power is temporary. To be frank with you, he derives his telekinesis power from you. He will be unable to move things in such a fashion when you are once again some distance from him."

She takes my hand in hers and says, "Eva, there is only one entity on this blanket that possesses incredible magical powers. That entity is you, my dear. It is you and you alone. You are now an elf wizardess. I know this comes as a shock to you. However, please believe me. What I am saying is true. You know I would never lie to you, hon."

I stare at her. I do not want to believe what she just said. Tears of compassion are welling in her eyes. She understands I am both shocked and scared. I start to tremble, a little at first, and then I am shaking all over. As tears start to flow down my cheek, she squeezes my hand. Her lips silently say, "I love you, honey. I always will. Be brave, Eva, be brave. Be brave for your Papa. Be brave for me."

It is all that I can do to keep from running back to my purple Volkswagen Beetle to escape Cindy's mind-boggling pronouncements. I am frightened. I am panicky. I am confused. Most of all, I am bone-tired, bordering on physical and mental exhaustion. I did not sleep well. I should have slept in bed like Kristopher recommended! To make matters worse, it feels as if gallons of caffeine are soaring through my body. That is making me jittery as ever.

All the same, I am no defeatist. My sixth sense was one-hundred percent correct. My life is going to change. In fact, my life has already changed. If you need proof, just take a look at my elf ears!

In spite of everything, a nagging question cries from somewhere deep within my mind, *how much more is my life going to change?*

CHAPTER FIVE

THE MAKINGS
OF A WIZARDESS

I sit on the checkered blanket staring for the longest time at delicate clouds floating in the afternoon's deep blue sky. All that has happened has emotionally drained me. I cannot stop shaking. Nonetheless, I am determined to see this, whatever this is, through to the end.

Mercifully, my ears have stopped growing. It is a good thing, too. They grew another half-inch overnight. The delicate points at their uppermost parts are also more pronounced than they were last night. They no longer itch like crazy. I hope with all my heart that this is a good sign. I can deal with ears this size. I shudder to think what I would look like if my ears grew any longer.

I know for certain that my ears are now elf ears. Could it have been, when high school classmates started calling me their elfin heroine, they somehow made their endearing words come true? I mean am I no longer human like Cindy said? Am I really an elf wizardess?

Always one to look on the bright side of otherwise gloomy, mystifying circumstances, I poke fun at myself in secret.

Hey, Santa baby, ya got yourself a new elf here - make room for Eva, the benevolent wizardess elf! Let me tell 'ya, she's got it all, magical powers, a cool-looking medallion, and amazingly cute elf ears!

Yeah, yeah, I know. It's not particularly funny, but it is the best I can do in consideration of the current state of affairs. Please do not judge me - I need to find some joviality in this sobriety. Otherwise, I will go bonkers!

I now bring my wandering mind back into focus. I sigh. I look at Cindy and smile. Then I quietly say, "Okay, give it to me straight if you please. I want to know it all, from top to bottom, beginning to end, the whole caboodle."

After I say this, I cannot help but stare at Kristopher as he stares back at me intently. His eyes never waver, his eyelids never blink. But enough of this - everything that has happened is as crazy as it can get. Why should I get worked up about a strange, magical man staring at me? I need answers. I need them now. I look at Cindy and shrug. She smiles at me. Finally, her lips say, "Kristopher, tell her the whole story if you please."

It is obvious that Kristopher is primed and ready to go. He does not hesitate a bit. I watch intently as his lips begin to move.

"My fair lady, as Raymond wrote, you are the Princess of Spardom. You are the only known living descendant of Queen April. As you read in Raymond's email, Queen April married a commoner who was not of Spardom. His name was Percival Winchester Roblins. Percival was intelligent, poised, and well-educated. Some aspects of Chronicles regarding his origins and background are a bit hazy. We are fairly certain he was a British sailor, undoubtedly an officer and a lieutenant perhaps.

"When he was in his late teens his parents emigrated from Great Britain to Canada. We believe Percival wished to learn the ways of a seafarer, so he remained behind in Great Britain. According to what we know, his performance as a mariner was admirable. We think he received his commission when he was in his late thirties.

"During the final voyage of his career Roblins' merchant ship smashed upon the Isle's shoals during a severe typhoon. To our knowledge, he was the only known survivor. Queen April and Percival fell in love, and they married. The couple's wedding was the most celebrated event on the Isle.

"Queen April and Percival had two children of that we are certain. There was mention of a third child, a younger girl. We believe the existence of a third child is a myth. Islanders almost certainly fabricated it. However, there is no way of knowing for certain.

"The eldest child was a blond-haired boy with coal-black eyes named Thurman. Prince Thurman was an ill-tempered child. He had behavioral problems, often quarreling with other children his age. He was notorious for pilfering goods from island merchants, usually jewels and silver trinkets. Chronicles do not give a complete account.

"Thurman was presumed to have drowned in the deep lagoon on the northeastern part of the Isle. His companions told of his swimming out to deep water, going under, and never surfacing. He was reportedly twelve years of age when he drowned. They never found his body.

"The queen and her husband's other child was a fair-skinned, red-headed daughter with light blue eyes named Eva - your namesake. Princess Eva was younger than her brother Thurman by five years. She was well-mannered but feisty, shy but adventurous, modest but daring.

"When she was fifteen years of age plus three weeks, Eva disappeared from the Isles, eight years to the day after her brother drowned. We do not know the year. Chronicles say she was spirited away from the family dwelling on a moonless night. No one is certain how or why she disappeared.

"There are two theories regarding her disappearance. One, she was abducted for the slave trade by islanders of a more primitive island across the sea. Two, she was spirited away by sorcerers who lived in a remote part of the Isle.

"Queen April and Percival were understandably brokenhearted by the disappearance of their beloved daughter, heir to the throne. They directed extensive searches afloat and lengthy expeditions ashore to look for her, to no gain of her whereabouts. Chronicles claim the royal couple never gave up on their quest to find their daughter.

"Now you are thinking milady, how do I know you are the descendant of Queen April of Spardom? The answer lies within Chronicles for they portend your destiny. The section of Chronicles is the Prophesy. The Prophesy is from many centuries ago. It has numerous entries. Of course, one pertains to you. I will now render the ancient text of the Prophesy that addresses the Isle's Princess. I have committed it to memory."

Princess Eva Roblins of Spardom shall reign o'er the Isle upon reaching the age of twenty-nine years. Ye shall know thy beloved Princess by her scarlet-swept hair brilliant as hues of flames; eyes blushed as sapphire pearls; inherent magical powers to move about unhindered; her mind's skill to speak with and rule men and beasts; and ye shall pay due loyalty to thy Princess' eminence - for Princess Eva rules supreme.

"The proof of who you are is already with you, milady - as evidenced by your elf ears and the medallion with your exact likeness. Plus there is all you have learned and what you have seen here today. Despite what you know up till now, I recognize you need more credible proof. Hence, I shall give it to you.

"Please watch my lips carefully so you can understand everything I am about to say. When I finish speaking, I want you to close your eyes. Then think silently to yourself, *Carafe, gradually rise from the blanket.* After that, count to three slowly before opening your eyes."

Although it feels weird doing what Kristopher asked, I close my eyes as instructed. I then think to myself, *Carafe - gradually rise from the blanket.* I silently count to three unhurriedly and then I open my eyes.

The carafe vanished! But where did it go? Did I really

make it rise? I notice Kristopher's finger is pointing above our heads. The carafe is six feet above our blanket! It is slowly but surely floating higher in the air by the second! Kristopher's face is beaming. I notice his lips are moving again.

He says, "Now as you look at the carafe with your eyes open command it to descend. Then tell it to do something else, perhaps to set itself on the blanket or pour us more wine. This time, I would like you to tell the carafe out loud what you want it to do. Don't forget to keep your eyes open."

I follow Kristopher's instructions. The carafe slowly descends toward the blanket. You can imagine how fast my heart is beating as I watch the carafe as it moves! I cannot believe this is happening! After a few moments, I say, "Pour more wine into my glass."

Obedient to my command, the carafe stops descending. It steadily tilts on end and pours wine into my glass. However, from a height of about three feet above the blanket, the carafe overfills my glass. That causes wine to splatter everywhere. The now empty, tilted on end carafe continues to float in the air as it awaits further orders. The wine splattered little droplets of dark purple on my white winter jacket and ruined Kristopher's checkered blanket. Even so, I could care less. I did it!

The three of us laugh uncontrollably. I look from Kristopher to Cindy then back again to Kristopher. I am sporting a huge grin on my face. I feel like singing and dancing and telling the world. I have magical powers, and I can move things with telekinesis! You have to admit · this is too cool!

Over the course of the next hour or so, Kristopher shows me the basics of using my magical powers. He does so with a handful of marbles, a pencil, and origami shaped like a bird. I cause marbles to roll across the blanket simply by using my mind. I can (more or less) get the pencil to scribble on a pad of paper in the same fashion. And I can make the origami fly, just by telling it to do so. Except I can't get it to flap its wings · darn!

Kristopher says I will need more practice before I can move objects with ease. He also says I will learn new spells that will enhance my powers.

Words cannot describe my excitement. Yes, I am exhausted. Plus, I am not used to having elf ears, at least not yet. But who cares? I am a wizardess. And I know magic. Talk about being one completely amazing redheaded deaf lady! It is like all of my most precious childhood dreams have come true. Now I'm totally, awesomely, fantastically special, let there be no doubt about it!

CHAPTER SIX

SPECIAL YOUNGSTERS IN MY LIFE

We snack on a bit of Kristopher's potato salad, Tilsit cheese, and crackers. I'm just glad Cindy had the foresight to bring along a few bottles of mineral water. Otherwise, since I spilled all the wine, we would have nothing to wash down the cheese and crackers. Now it's time for business once again.

Kristopher gestures for me to look at four youngsters to my left. They are perhaps eleven or twelve to around sixteen years of age. They have been frolicking and picnicking a half-dozen yards from where we sit. I had noticed the four youngsters when I first arrived. Since I could not hear their shenanigans, I focused my attention on things happening on the blanket. To be completely honest with you, I've been having too much fun. I forgot the youngsters were there. They are playing a game of some sort, maybe a quieter, less robust form of tag. I am aware Kristopher is talking to me.

I catch his lips mid-sentence saying, "...are here to assist you. Like you, they are elves. They too possess varying magical powers but to a lesser degree than your own. I implore you to allow me to explain." He gestures toward the elves and begins to speak of each elf one by one.

"The tallest female elf is Ariel·e. She is the oldest of the four elves. Ariel·e is from the sea. She is an elf mermaid. As you can see, she can sprout legs and walk on land but only for a few days. She must replenish her core with salt or fresh water at least once every four days. If she does not, she will weaken rapidly and ultimately perish. Even pouring a minuscule amount of water over her body replenishes her core, but only somewhat. Ariel·e will accompany you to your home along with the others. Since she has been away from water for two days now, she will top off her energy level in your bathtub.

I watch as Ariel·e interacts with the other elves. She is strikingly good·looking. She has lightly tanned skin. Her eyes are dark brown. Her long brunette hair cascades in delicate curls down her back to fall well below her waist. Her smile is wholly captivating, extraordinarily charismatic.

Ariel·e is tall and willowy with long legs. She is muscular, and she looks quite strong. I guess Ariel·e is around sixteen years of age. She is putting on a show like she's an actress on a stage. She also appears to be singing.

Kristopher continues to describe Ariel·e's powers, which he sums up as having everything to do with water and water vapor. She can physically change water molecules into ice. She can form forceful waterspouts, small but vigorous waves, and frozen spears. She can also cause water to boil without the benefit of heat or flames. "However," Kristopher says, "Her powers are on a much lesser scale in comparison to nature's passion." He then gestures to the elves once again.

Kristopher's lips say, "The dark·skinned male elf is Donas. Donas is the second to oldest of the four. He is highly intelligent, quick·witted, and cunning. He is also nimble and extremely fast. He can run faster than anything on earth, faster than a cheetah. No creature on earth is capable of seeing him as he moves, he is that speedy. Donas can also skip amongst tree limbs more rapidly than a peregrine falcon can fly. However, he is not capable of actual flight.

"As I said, he is as cunning and bright as he is quick. By some fashion, he will overcome nearly every complex obstacle that comes his way. His only weakness is the night. He must find his way as slowly as the slowest living being. If there is no moon, or if a thick cloud cover is present, he walks even slower. Luckily, his hands remain lightning fast in darkness as well as in light."

It is at this very moment I espy Donas' amazing quickness. One moment he is high in a tree. Then in less than a blink of an eye he is standing behind Ariel-e. Even as I watch intently, I cannot see Donas move. He is astonishingly fast, in one place one second, in another the next.

Donas is slightly shorter than Ariel-e. He looks quite powerful and unquestionably sly. He is particularly handsome with dark hair and bushy eyebrows. He has a strong jaw line. I guess Donas is fifteen years of age, perhaps a few months younger than Ariel-e.

Kristopher is talking once more. I watch his lips carefully. "The light-skinned male elf is Andrial. He has the seeing ability of an eagle. He can see over vast distances that are nearly incalculable. His nighttime eyesight is that of a jaguar or lion. His perception is that advanced. He also has an exceptional sense of hearing. His hearing is that of an owl. He can locate vertical positions of sound.

"He can see and hear perhaps upwards of twenty-five miles or more. However, Andrial cannot speak. He has no vocal chords. He must converse with hand signals. Fortunately, for you, milady, he has mastered ASL. Andrial is the second to youngest of the four."

As I once more glance in the direction of the four elves, it is obvious Andrial has been eavesdropping. He signs, "Hello." I grin and sign hello in response adding, "I am excited to meet you!"

Andrial is much taller in comparison to the other elves. His hair is light brown as are his eyes. He is wiry and very thin, but muscular. He is good-looking. I guess his age as thirteen or fourteen, maybe fifteen. Like the others, he looks strong.

Looking back at Kristopher, I watch as he describes the younger of the two female elves. He says, "The younger female elf is Lindsial. She is the youngest of the four elves. She is strong-willed, very intelligent and the others' leader. She will direct their actions according to your bidding. She is also the most extraordinary of the four elves. She can become invisible. Like you, she possesses remarkable telepathy skills. However, her powers cannot compare to your thought transference and extrasensory perception powers."

I look at Lindsial and guess she is probably eleven or twelve years of age. Similar to Ariel·e, Lindsial is gorgeously attractive. I believe she is the most beautiful youngster I have ever seen. Her chocolate-colored hair falls well below her shoulders. Her hair appears wondrously alive. Its silky strands seem to float in the breeze as she moves.

When Lindsial laughs, her light blue eyes are barely noticeable. Just like me her eyes tend to squint when she expresses amusement. Her figure is slender but with muscular arms and powerful legs. She is assuredly athletic.

For some odd reason, Lindsial reminds me of a young person I see now and again at the skate center I mentioned earlier. That youngster is very supportive to a particular floor guard, marking hands of winners and rolling the lucky number game die. The floor guard treats her as if she is special. Perhaps she is. She is a terrific skater. She always wins the skate races, even beating the boys, many of whom are older than her.

Lindsial's likeness to the pretty girl at the skate center is amazing! But this cannot be · Lindsial is an elf, and the girl at the skate center is a human. Hmm, I wonder. Is it possible Lindsial merely hides her elf ears beneath her long hair when she's out in public?

Lindsial turns her head in my direction. She vigorously waves her hand back and forth. She smiles a big grin as her lips say, "Hello, hello, hello!"

I cannot help but laugh when I read her lips. She is energetic and cheerful. I'll for sure give her that much credit! Then something pops into my mind. What in the world - how did she know I was looking at her? Did she somehow read my thoughts? Just as I think this, something Kristopher said a moment ago also comes to mind. What was that he said?

I turn to look at Kristopher and ask, "What was that you were saying, Kristopher? I thought you said I had telepathy skills, just like Lindsial. If I read your lips correctly, you also said I have extrasensory perception powers. Was I correct in what I saw?"

"Yes, milady, you are correct," Kristopher replies with an earnest smile. "While you are wearing the Princess of Spardom medallion, your extrasensory perception powers, to include your telepathy powers will strengthen. Eventually, your telepathy powers will become more powerful than Lindsial's, and hers are quite strong.

"Over time your extrasensory perception powers will increase dramatically. Then you will no longer need the medallion's influence. Before long you will find yourself possessing psychic abilities more powerful than anything you can imagine.

"You will gain what is called *clairaudience* powers. Clairaudience is the ability to hear in a paranormal manner. Since you are deaf, you will not hear in the physical sense of the word. Quite the opposite - what you think you hear you will sense in your mind.

"You will also acquire *claircognizance* powers. Claircognizance is the talent of knowing something without a physical explanation of why you know it. I would equate this to your sixth sense, only much more powerful. Your claircognizance skills will grow so potent you will eventually see into the future.

"Just as notably you will develop increasingly strong *clairsentience* powers. Clairsentience is the capacity to obtain psychic knowledge simply by touching a living organism or inanimate object. When you touch a living organism or object, you will have the power to look into its past and to read its memory.

"Truthfully, my fair lady, you will possess the greatest paranormal skills imaginable, more powerful than anything in the history of the magical world. It will take a bit of time for these skills to mature. You already possess limited use of these skills as you have seen here today. Trust me when I say they will grow stronger minute by minute, hour by hour, day by day."

I cannot believe everything Kristopher has been saying. It is like I am in a dream. I have never heard of some of the psychic powers he has been describing - clairsentience and clairaudience. Yes, as I mentioned earlier, I have always known I possess a special intuitive power, my sixth sense. But I never dreamed of one day having the ability to hear without hearing. I cannot imagine seeing the past simply by touching something. And to look into the future - it is all too incredible! Despite the thrilling thoughts racing through my mind, I try to focus intently as Kristopher's lips continue.

His lips say, "Now, milady as you can see each of the four elves has certain powers to compliment your own. Ariel·e has the gift to make water do fantastic things. Donas moves more swiftly than the eye can see, either on land or in trees. He is as cunning as he is quick.

"Andrial can see over vast distances. He also has indescribable hearing. Lindsial can turn invisible and converse with you telepathically. Like you and your deafness, each of the four elves has weaknesses. Their weaknesses will present challenges to them as well as to you."

"I saw you say all four have weaknesses," I whisper softly. "But you spoke of only three having weaknesses. You mentioned Ariel·e must replenish her core with water. You said Donas must walk slowly at night. You said Andrial is voiceless. You have not spoken of Lindsial's weakness. What is her major weakness?"

Kristopher closes his eyes for ten seconds or more. Then, as a tiny teardrop caresses his cheek, I watch his lips say, "Lindsial is like me. She is blind."

Kristopher's blindness explains why he seemed to be staring at me intently! Now it is also apparent to me why Lindsial did not run and play as the other three. She simply twirled in circles. When she did walk about, she walked slowly and deliberately.

"I am so very sorry, Kristopher," I say. "It must be horrible for the two of you to go through life without seeing. I am sad, Kristopher. I am truly sad for you and Lindsial."

"Oh, my lady Eva, please do not fret," Kristopher replies. "We have adapted to our blindness as you have come to accept your deafness. In Lindsial and my minds, we can glimpse life's wonders for we have limited clairvoyance powers. That is how I knew last night you were thinking of sleeping on your couch. I simply read your mind."

He laughs and says, "Lindsial also has a gift commonly referred to as *echolocation*. The power of her echolocation is similar to the physical qualities of a flying bat. Since she is blind, she can make out things in her mind. She senses simple shapes and outlines. She locates objects by emitting soft calls. By employing her echolocation, she also navigates as easily as one who can see.

"You probably know blind humans do the same thing by using clicks produced by a device or their mouth. Blind humans use echolocation by tapping their canes, snapping their fingers, or stomping their feet. Sounds Lindsial whispers when she uses her echolocation are beyond the hearing of human and elvish ears. So you see, milady, Lindsial's sightlessness is not as awful as it could be otherwise. She can perceive objects in her mind by echolocation.

"In addition to their astonishing gifts and powers, the elves are skilled in weaponry. These include archery, sword, and throwing of the spear. You will learn how to use these weapons expertly in due course.

"Before I forget, please allow me to add one more thing about Lindsial's invisibility power. All things she touches, when she becomes invisible, turn invisible as well. These things might include a weapon, a living being, or even a glass of water · practically anything. This fact is important for you to know just in case you ever need to vanish. When she becomes invisible, Lindsial will hold your hand to turn you invisible as well. Having her turn you invisible could someday save your life."

"Goodness, Kristopher," I stammer. "All of you are in-credible! You have telepathic powers as does Lindsial. Al-though she is blind, she can also turn invisible and navi-gate with echolocation. Ariel·e can summon waterspouts and other water·related phenomena with her hands. Donas is intelligent, cunning and quick. Andrial, while voiceless, can see and hear over long distances. These gifts are truly amazing, sir!

"About all those startling things you mentioned about me. How do you know I possess extrasensory perception powers, such as clairsentience? How do you know for cer-tain I have clairaudience and claircognizance abilities? How can you be certain when I do not understand these powers, eh?"

Kristopher smiles and says, "Milady, your powers are spelled out in the Isle's Chronicles. Think about all have seen and learned in the brief span of one day. When the courier handed you the envelope, you felt the medallion's power. You also have what you refer to as your sixth sense. I dare say your sixth sense has saved your life on more than one occasion.

"Your magical powers have been with you over the course of your entire life. You did not know their existence or their potential. No one ever told you. No one taught you. There was no way for you to have known about your extra-sensory perception powers. Going forward you will learn everything you need to know. You will learn many things due to the efforts of your loyal elves and your medallion's magic. While the elves cannot invoke the spells themselves, they know of them. They will describe a spell, charm, or enchantment, and tell you how to say it. You will do the rest."

CHAPTER SEVEN

SPELLS AND STORYTELLING

Exhaustive, mind-boggling, perplexing, frustrating, often confusing - yet totally exhilarating. These handful of words describe our three months of in-house training. I am learning how to cast spells. Let me tell you, it is loads of fun.

I swiftly become skilled with the basics of moving and controlling inanimate objects with a wave of my left hand. To do this, I cast what is called a *labor lapsus* spell. My labor lapsus spell compels things to glide across the floor.

I manage to move the couch and office bookshelf on my very first day of training. As the bookshelf moves, it topples and deposits everything onto the floor. The other elves and I laugh as we collect fifty or more books scattered across the carpet.

On the second day, I command my queen-sized pedestal bed to slide across the floor. This feat takes loads of concentration since the bed is heavy. With each practice session, I learn to master the technique of controlling the speed and direction in which objects move. A lot of things strike the walls and bang into furniture as I move them. As time goes on my control over my spells dramatically improves.

The elves also tell me of a spell to make objects fly across the room. It is the *moveo* spell. I have no idea what to expect as I get ready to utter the spell for the first time. However, I cannot wait to give it a go.

I point to the end table lamp and shout *moveo!* The lamp flies through the air at high speed. It slams against the wall with such force it shatters into a few dozen pieces. I also move smaller objects using my moveo spell. Broken remains of knickknacks soon lay in pieces in the waste can along with the destroyed lamp.

What's more, I learn to disarm an opponent with a simple hand gesture using an elvish spell called *exarmo*. Lindsial instructs me how to use my mind as the controlling force. Pointing with my hand as if it were a wand, objects readily respond to my command. Donas is my primary target given his quickness and continual darting about when I try to neutralize him.

He usually holds a broom to simulate a sword, club, or spear. I am seldom able to disarm him given his speed. Now and then I send his broom flying across the room. I doubt I will ever encounter someone as fast as Donas. Disarming him from time to time is a big deal to me.

Lindsial helps me refine my telepathy skill, which I will often refer to as thought transference in this story. Thought transference is the easiest of all my powers. Lindsial and I have hours-long conversations without speaking aloud or making eye contact. We sometimes sit in separate rooms as we convey our thoughts via telepathic conversations. Our thought transference sessions frequently continue well into the early hours of the morning. Lindsial and I are now the best of friends. I firmly believe our thought transference powers helped to make it so.

The five of us seldom venture outdoors. When we do, we stroll in the fenced-in backyard for fresh air. We eat catered meals. As a result, I do not have to go shopping to buy groceries. The Agency or I should say you, the taxpayer, foot our entire food bill. I microwave the day's catered fare or pop it in the oven.

To tell you the truth, I enjoy this part of our training the most. I love to eat. However, I hate to cook. The thought, of cooking three meals a day for five over a three-month period, is utterly frightening, to say the least! So yeah, the catered food is a stroke of good fortune indeed especially for me. Most meals taste fairly decent. It's not gourmet food, but it keeps our tummies happy.

Dinnertime is the most fun. The others tell stories about their adventures when they lived on a remote, uninhabited island in the Pacific Ocean. Ariel-e lived near a shoal off the island's southern coast. When the elves ask me to tell stories, I simply wave off their requests good-naturedly. My adventures pale in comparison to their exhilarating journeys. One story told by Ariel-e is as moving as it is entertaining. It is worth retelling.

One sunny day Ariel-e was enjoying a playful time in the ocean close by her shoal. She was frolicking with a pod of dolphins, jumping somersaults, racing through the waves, catching fish - merely doing her usual thing.

Now, you may not know this, but dolphins are a competitive lot. They like to race beneath the waves and dance competitively on their flippers. Above all, they enjoy seeing how many times they can somersault through the air. Ariel-e said sea legends tell of one dolphin named Desultor somersaulting three times in the air!

Ariel-e invented a spirited game the dolphins could not play without her help. It was called *Catch and See*. The object of Catch and See was for a dolphin to catch a fish in its jaws Ariel-e had tossed in the air. Then the dolphin would have to complete as many somersaults as it could before it hit the water.

Most dolphins cannot somersault. They simply jump from the ocean into the air and flop back down on their bellies. Only the most gifted dolphin's play Catch and See. The dolphin that jumps the highest, while catching the fish and does the most somersaults, is declared champion for the day. As a reward, a trophy of sorts, the champion does not have to catch its fish for the rest of the day. Others have to bring its dinner.

All of a sudden, Ariel·e heard the telltale thumping of a ship's propeller as it drew near. It was a luxury cruise ship making about ten knots through a sea state four with moderate swells. Since the dolphins are intelligent, curious, and playful, they right away sped off to jump alongside the ship and in its wake. They liked showing off for the ship's passengers. The more the passengers oohed and aahed as they watched the dolphins' antics, the better. Ariel·e was more cautious, so she kept her distance.

Usually, when ships or boats drew close to her, Ariel·e would vanish beneath the waves. Then again, sometimes she would peek at passing vessels, more often than not at night. She did not want seamen or ship passengers to spot an elf mermaid in the water. Humans would try to capture her, not for hateful purposes she guessed, but for curiosity's sake.

She had to relocate one time before in her life because she was careless during daylight. Divers searched for her throughout the day and the night for weeks on end. Besides, she liked her shoal off the southern coast of the island. It was close to where her elf friends lived on land. More importantly, elves have to keep their existence secret. Few humans today know that a handful of elves is alive and well on the planet.

For some reason, even though it was daylight, Ariel·e decided to take a peek at the passing cruise ship. It was a massive twelve-deck beauty, its upper decks full of cheerful passengers basking in the tropical sun. At that moment, something odd caught Ariel·e's attention. A young man, perhaps sixteen or seventeen, was sitting on top of the railing as he stared out to the sea. Ariel·e thought how dangerous it was for the young man to be sitting precariously on the railing. He could fall.

Suddenly, the young man and Ariel·e's eyes met. Seeing Ariel·e in the water shocked him. He loosened his grip on the railing to point Ariel·e out to his friends. In a flash, he was catapulting head over heels into the ocean!

It only took a few seconds for the ship's bells to clang and the loudspeaker to cry, "Man overboard!" Someone threw a life preserver into the water. Unluckily, the ship was moving too quickly through the waves. The flotation device fell short. The young man was unable to reach it as it drifted further away from him in the swells.

Through the waves, Ariel·e could see the ship's decks come alive with scurrying deckhands. The ship was struggling to turn one-hundred eighty degrees. Ariel·e was just about to dive under the ocean's waves when she heard the young man's cries, "Somebody, come save me! I can't swim! I can't swim!" Help me, please!"

Judging by the ship's slow turn · ships take grueling minutes to come about, particularly when the sea state is moderate · Ariel·e knew the young man would drown before the ship could come to his aid. She had to rescue him, despite the fact that doing so could put her life in danger.

She dove beneath the surface and headed straight for the red and white life preserver bobbing in the ship's wake. Remaining hidden just below the surface, she grabbed the preserver in her hands to haul it across the surface of the water. She maneuvered the device until it was directly in front of the young man's face. However, he would not grab onto it. He had already gone down once and was now struggling to breathe. He was thrashing at the water with his hands as he sputtered wordlessly and coughed up sea water.

Risking all, Ariel·e surfaced just enough so her head was barely out of the water. She tried her best to stay hidden behind the young man's head. If she were lucky, the ship's crew and passengers would not see her. She looked straight into the young man's hazel eyes and whispered.

"Sweetheart, you have to take hold of the flotation device. I know you're scared, but it'll keep you from drowning. The ship is making a one-hundred-eighty degree turn. It'll lower a lifeboat. You'll be safe soon enough. I promise you.

Now pass your arms through the ring all the way to your elbows and hold on, okay?"

The young man complied with Ariel·e's request, all the while staring into Ariel·e's stunning dark brown eyes. Then he said, "Who are you? Are you a mermaid? You just saved my life. How can I ever thank you?"

Ariel·e kissed him on his cheek. She said, "You can thank me by promising you will not tell the others I was here. Perhaps they can see me through their spy glasses, perhaps not. Please deny I was ever here if they question you. If you do not, they will try to capture me. Promise me, okay?"

He said, "I promise. You're too pretty to be captured by anyone! Can I ask your name?"

Ariel·e whispered, "I am Ariel·e. I am an elf mermaid. I live in the sea next to a shoal. What is your name, sir?"

The young man replied excitedly, "I am James, James Allen Williams. Gosh, you're an elf mermaid. You're so pretty too. It's incredible!"

Ariel·e noticed the ship had completed its turn. A lifeboat was being lowered. Good · the young man would be rescued in no time.

Ariel·e said, "Well, James, I must away. It was nice meeting you. Take care of yourself, don't ever sit on railings, and try to keep your promise. I will remain close by you beneath the surface until the lifeboat crew rescues you. Goodbye handsome man. Maybe we'll see each other in our dreams."

Ariel·e kissed him on his cheek once again. Then she slipped beneath the waves. As far as Ariel·e knew, no one sought to discover her in the ensuing weeks and months. James had kept his promise.

Now, please allow me to say a bit more about these four adorable youngster elves sharing my apartment. When I first saw them, I had guessed their ages as between eleven to sixteen years of age. I figured Lindsial was the youngest at eleven or twelve and Ariel·e the oldest at sixteen.

I don't think I was anywhere close. My miscalculation of their ages has to do with their storytelling yarns. They sometimes tell of a time when gas lanterns lighted the shoreline. They also describe ships of sail roaming the sea ⁃ of muskets, cannons, horse-driven carriages and genteel ladies and gentlemen attending lavish balls and concerts.

I do not want to risk embarrassing them by asking their actual ages. It is apparent to me, however, that they are considerably older than they look. Perhaps they are over a hundred years old or older. While they have the vitality and look of youngsters, their minds and experiences are highly advanced. Then again, maybe they are reincarnated. As you and I know, stranger things have happened.

When we are not eating, sleeping, or training, we stay busy with assorted tasks to ward off boredom. With the exception of Lindsial, the others eagerly read from my voluminous book collection. They particularly enjoy reading history. Donas tries surfing the Internet on a few occasions, but he says it is too boring. Like the others, he has acquired a taste for adventure and is used to exploring the world.

Ariel-e enjoys watching downloaded movies on my computer, mainly those in black and white. She also busies herself with basket weaving or other handicraft projects, such as crocheting and sewing. What's more, she practices with her sword and spear in front of the mirror. She is lightning fast and highly skilled.

Lindsial tells me Donas and Andrial are expert archers. They are also skillful fletchers. So it comes as no surprise to me when they wile away their time making arrows. Their leather quivers are overflowing. They also fuss with their bows, waxing strings and polishing the wooden parts, called limbs. Donas' bow is an English longbow, popular during medieval times. It is almost as long as he is tall. Andrial prefers to use a recurve bow. Since we are inside and they cannot shoot arrows outside, I have not seen them shoot. I look forward to the day I can see their expert archery skills for myself.

Like Ariel·e, Lindsial is also skilled with a sword. Taking into consideration her blindness, I find her swordsmanship to be unbelievable. Despite her weaponry skills, she prefers to pass her free time playing a golden hand·held harp. Ariel·e, Donas, and Andrial play a small flute. Each of their flutes is a single piece of wood with six open finger holes. The flutes are replicas of medieval recorders.

I watch attentively as the four of them play together. When they sing, I can only imagine the beauty of elf ballads sung since the beginning of time. I wish with all my heart I could hear. Fortunately, not all is lost because of my deafness. When Lindsial sings ballads, I can sense her words in my mind.

I am still working for the Agency and on the payroll. So my status is listed as *on assignment during training*. I do not have to report to work in the flesh. It is a good thing, too. My coworkers would certainly notice my elf ears. I can just imagine their comments if I reported to work.

"Oh, Eva, what happened to your ears · they're so, uh, how do I (tactfully) put this, *different?*' What in the world could I say to that?

The others and I discuss the likelihood our in·house training must be nearing an end. There is insufficient room to train properly as a team. The five of us are starting to get antsy since we're cooped up within the four walls of my dinky apartment. We eat well, get plenty of exercise on my treadmill, and keep ourselves busy. We also enjoy each other's company. That's probably the paramount thing. However, we long for change. Change it does via an email from Cindy.

"Agent Roblins,

Mr. Bales has been monitoring your training progress via his typical means. We have decided it is time to deploy you and your team to the next phase of our operation. An Agency van will arrive at your apartment Monday at 0400. Each of you is advised to bring along one day's change of clothes and any toiletry necessities. Instruct your team members to carry their weapons as well. Well done on your progress to date. I hope you're well. I wish you all the best, Cindy Wickham."

CHAPTER EIGHT

POWER IS KNOWLEDGE

The van arrives at my apartment precisely at four o'clock in the morning. The self-important-looking shiny black behemoth on four wheels is your standard eight-passenger U.S. Government van. Much to my surprise its windows are blackened out. Before we hit the road, our uniformed driver raises a partition that separates him from us, his passengers. The partition is also blackened out.

I think that this is one heck of a way to treat one's passengers. Not a single courtesy escapes our driver's lips, such as, "How are you this morning, or can I help you with that? Wow, it's a bit nippy today, don't you agree?" Or maybe, "We'll be on the road for such and such amount of time. If you need anything or have to go pee, just holler, okay?" He says nothing as we struggle with our weapons and bags. We get in, and then he slides a partition between us. Pooh!

I have ridden in my share of Agency vans. Nevertheless, this one takes the cake. Given the blackened windows and partition, it is apparent we are en route to a highly classified covert location. It irks me some bureaucratic idiot thinks we do not need to know where we are going. My sixth sense is screaming. I don't like what it's telling me. Let me tell you, something is wrong with all of this!

Lindsial and I attempt to read the driver's mind. We are unsuccessful. I'm not surprised when it comes to my mind reading ability. Except for reading Lindsial's thoughts, I haven't been able to read another's thoughts these past three months. I wonder if our driver is trained to block others' intrusions into his mind. That is one theory.

Here's the second theory. Most likely the glass partition produces electronic magnetic interference or EMI, which makes it impenetrable to eavesdropping both aural and visual. But how it can block telepathy stumps me unless, of course, telepathy is also blocked by EMI.

"Well, this stinks," I convey to Lindsial via telepathy. "It is obvious they do not want us to know where the driver is taking us."

"I think I know where we are going," Lindsial conveys in her mind. "I eavesdropped on a conversation Cindy and Kristopher had before I met you. They spoke of a special facility in Virginia where we will go sooner or later. Cindy described the facility as a transporter center of sorts. Given the way she described it, I doubt it's a training facility. We need a large area in which to train to improve our team's performance before we do anything else. That's my opinion, for what it's worth."

"What in the world is a transporter center," I convey. "Do you know? Did she describe it further?"

"I don't know what it is. Given Cindy's description, I think it's a place where they move stuff. They move people and things from one place to another using unconventional means."

"Goodness," I exclaim. "Are we going to a place that will somehow move us through space or something equally bizarre? I hope not. Plus it doesn't make sense. Wherever we need to go for training, outdoors or indoors, they can transport us in a van like now. Or they can move us by train, bus or plane. No doubt we would need to be disguised or move undercover. It's no big deal. I do it all the time."

After what seems like forever, the van slows. It makes a few roundabout turns. As it stops, our driver finally low-ers the partition. He exclaims, "Everyone out, please. Stay close." Now that the driver has lowered the partition, I can read his thoughts. Weird and wonderful - that's the only way to describe how I feel. I gather my belongings and exit the van along with the others.

The driver parked the van inside a tunnel. I convey to Lindsial, "By the way I read our driver's thoughts."

She replies via thought transference, "Way to go, Eva! Now that we're out of your apartment I expect your telepa-thy skills will improve dramatically. You were somewhat stifled in there, too cooped up to expand your mind. At least I guess that was the reason you could not read the other elves' minds."

We walk a hundred yards or more through the tunnel until we arrive at a large steel door. The door is bright green. A sign on the door, printed in bold red letters reads, *Property of the United States Government. Do not enter. Violators will be prosecuted - Title 18, US Code.*

I read our driver's thoughts. "You are to remain here." He gestures with his hand to a row of chairs lined up along the left side of the tunnel. "Please take a seat along the wall. I will return in a few moments." We move to take our seats.

I perceive a barely discernible silhouette speedily dart across the floor toward the door. After our driver closes the door, I notice Lindsial and Donas' chairs are empty. They must have followed the driver into the room when the door swung open. The momentary, fleeting shadow I saw must have belonged to Donas. Lindsial probably turned invisible as soon as the driver stepped into the doorway.

"Yes, we are inside, Eva," Lindsial's thoughts convey. "Donas and I are seldom content when someone implies we cannot go where he or she goes. I suspect Donas is scurrying about as he checks out this place. I was walking right next to the driver. Then our driver went into a room. Donas said a sign on the door reads *men's clean room.* It may be a men's bathroom. I didn't accompany the driver into the room for obvious reasons. Men's clean room · you have to admit it is a strange name for a bathroom. Then again, Eva, your Agency friends tend to be a bit weird at times."

I laugh. She is right · about the weird part on behalf of Agency employees. I guess they, similar to me, need to be a bit peculiar to do what we do day in and day out. If only our countrymen knew what we had to put up with to protect our nation from those who would try to harm our nation and its peoples.

After a few moments, Lindsial conveys, "I was correct. Donas said this isn't an indoor stadium. It isn't a training facility either. It is probably the transporter place Cindy and Kristopher discussed. Donas said there is a rather large odd-looking contraption, like a flying saucer or something, in the center of a spacious room. He also said there are offices and an enormous control room with rows of monitors in it. Donas says every room has a sign that reads, *Restricted Access.*" She suddenly adds to her thought transference, "Uh-oh, I detect Cindy's presence. I also sense trouble."

"Lindsial and Donas," Cindy exclaims loudly. "Show yourselves straight away!"

Lindsial becomes visible. She is blushing. Donas rapidly runs to stand beside Lindsial. He has a satisfied look on his face. He is also grinning.

With a glare on her face that could toast a marshmallow, Cindy barks, "While you may think it is endearing to come into this chamber unescorted, I do not. This entire building is a clean environment. You need to put on protective clothing that will not foul the equipment. Now please turn around and go into the clean room so you can suit up. Thank you."

Lindsial's mind conveys via thought transference, "Well, Eva, we got caught. Our driver went into the clean room so he could change into some ridiculous protective garb. I'm putting mine on right now. It smells like petroleum-based plastic. Ugh! Donas said the driver is returning to you three. We were supposed to wait outside so the driver could escort us to the clean rooms to put on outer clothing. As I said, I am in here now. Donas is in the men's portion of the room. What a way to start our journey. I am sorry."

I cannot help but laugh. I convey, "Sorry? I think it's hilarious. I salute you and Donas for being bold. You did what I would have expected you to do. You demonstrated resourcefulness and originality. Well done, Lindsial, well done! But you have to admit, Cindy can be mightily imposing when she's annoyed, don't you agree? I couldn't read her mind of course, but knowing Cindy the way I know Cindy..."

"Yes, she certainly can," Lindsial conveys. "However, at least she was courteous. I probably wouldn't have been as nice if I were in her shoes. To be truthful with you, Eva, we would have gotten away with our little scheme if it weren't for Kristopher. He said he was standing in the back of the room where the big contraption sits. He must have tapped into our telepathic conversation. He probably felt obliged to tell Cindy we were inside. It makes sense. Although he squealed on us, he seemed pleased with Donas and my audacity. Kristopher has always said, *to win one must be audacious - when audacious one must never waiver.*"

Ten minutes later the five of us are sitting at a long table in a large briefing room. We're wearing transparent, stupid-looking, stinky plastic clothing. It is suggestive of the see-through plastic garb I've seen workers wear in Third World open air meat markets. We're also wearing see-through booties over our shoes. We can see our street clothes through the attire, which makes us look outright dim-witted. Oh well, at least all of us in the room look the same - laughingly ridiculous!

Darn! - And I forgot my camera so I could take a pic for posterity. It doesn't matter. Signs everywhere protest *no cell phones - no cameras!*

The room's metal shelves and cabinets are as sterile-looking as the brightly polished steel floor. A large projection screen is on the wall at the far end of the room. I'm happy to see a coffee mess on the counter. Various condiments, flavored coffee creamers, and an assortment of munchies sit on the counter as well.

Hooyah - I can't help but smile! I see a container of liquid hazelnut coffee creamer. It must be Cindy's doing. She knows how much I love the stuff. Things are looking better by the minute!

And here comes Cindy, Kristopher, and the bigwigs. The bigwig entourage accompanying Cindy and Kristopher consists of a four-star Admiral, and two four-star generals, one Marine one Army. I recognize the Marine general. But I cannot place him or recall his name. There is also a civilian doctor and a civilian ASL interpreter. As the bigwigs stride in, we stand. I notice Cindy is wearing the pleated skirt and long-sleeve cotton blouse I bought her for Christmas. That brings a happy smile to my face.

Now we're going through the customary *meet and greet* routine, with intros, handshakes, and fake "It is a pleasure to meet you," smiles. Meet and greet is always a precursor to what follows at Agency briefings, *mandatory fun* - at least that's what I call it. I don't like these meet and greet evolutions. So many lips moving in one fell swoop drives me bonkers. I barely catch a word!

The seating arrangement allows the briefers to remain in their seats as they speak. I am directly opposite the sign language interpreter. She has a flag officer on either side. The Navy admiral is to her right, the Army general to her left. I assume the Navy and Army officers will brief since they are sitting on either side of the interpreter.

The Marine general is sitting to the Admiral's right. Cindy is sitting to the Army general's left. Kristopher and the doctor sit at either end of the table. That leaves the other members of my team and me on the opposite side of the table. The elves are sitting two by two's on both sides of me, lady elves to my right, gentlemen elves to my left.

Two handsome-looking uniformed soldiers are serving breakfast. It's a good thing too. I am starving! We had spaghetti for dinner last night, so I didn't eat much. Spaghetti sauce sometimes gives me heartburn, and I can never eat it late at night. It just seems to come back up in noxious waves as I sleep. To be honest with you, dinner was horrible-tasting, to say the least, especially the soggy, stringy asparagus spears smothered in slimy cheese. Suffice it to say, the last catered meal of our three-month training period sucked big time! I felt sick to my stomach after eating a small portion. I've been somewhat nauseous ever since.

I served both ashore and afloat with a multi-national force during a recent three-month Agency assignment. As a result, I recognize military members' nationalities, service corps, and pay grades. The two American soldiers serving us are sergeants. They are wearing golden amulets on their shoulders. The golden amulets mean they belong to a flag officer's staff.

Their dress uniforms display row after row of ribbons that would humble even the most heroic of military heroes. They've earned the Global War on Terrorism Service Medal. One soldier is wearing the Purple Heart ribbon, signifying wounds in action. The other soldier is wearing the Bronze Star.

Lindsial and I exchange good-natured questioning thoughts about the two servicemen until Kristopher chides us. He says via telepathy, "Please stop fooling around ladies. Concentrate. There is much you will need to learn today. I encourage you to pay attention. You and your fellow elves' lives may depend on how well you pay attention to what is being said."

I manage to smile despite Kristopher's mild admonishment. My telepathic skills are becoming stronger. I read the driver's thoughts, and now I can read Kristopher's thoughts. I wonder if Kristopher knows. Then again, maybe he can force me to read his thoughts. I will have to ask Lindsial about this later.

After an appetizing breakfast of ham, eggs, toast, two mugs of coffee with hazelnut creamer for me, and pastries, we're ready to start. Admiral Shelly Jones, United States Navy is the first briefer. I divide my attention from the interpreter to the Admiral and back again. As I focus on the Admiral's lips, I sense her thoughts entering my mind. Now thoughts of others around the table are crossing the threshold of my mind as well. I am thoroughly confused, to say the least.

To be honest with you, my mind is a mumble jumble mess of too many thoughts entering it simultaneously. I try to center my attention exclusively on the Admiral's lips and thoughts. My mind dismisses the others' thoughts little by little. I purposely glance at the interpreter now and then as she signs. I want it to appear as though I am relying on her to some extent for the information being presented.

I do not want to give anything away when it comes to my telepathic skills. *Knowledge is power,* as they say. When you think about it, in my case, given my telepathic power, *power is knowledge.* No matter - I loathe giving any more knowledge of the elves and my abilities than is necessary.

I can only hope I will soon learn to filter thoughts that enter my brain from all directions. If I do not, I will surely go bonkers! I can picture myself now - wandering around town muttering aimlessly to no one, in particular, *Uh, duh, yeah, I am her, Eva Caroline Roblins, uh-huh the nonsensical extrasensory perception idiot who can read minds - duh. It's a pleasure to meet you - how do you do?*

Admiral Jones begins her brief. She says, "Let me begin by welcoming you, Eva Roblins and your group of elves to the Universal Transporter Program. This program is a cooperative project jointly run by governments of the major Western powers.

"The information, which I am about to deliver, is classified Top Secret. It is Special Compartmented Intelligence, Codeword *Sea Blue.* You have before you folders containing information from this particular program and other classified programs as well. We ask you to study these programs carefully over the next several days. After today's briefs, we will ask the five of you to sign indoctrination forms to document your access to the classified information.

"I will now provide you with an overview of the ancient Isle of Spardom. Please direct your attention to the screen. The ancient Isle of Spardom is a vast landmass one-third the size of Australia. It was a thriving, beautiful, and prosperous land before it sank beneath the ocean around 1760 AD. As you can see on the chart, the Isle is located in precisely the same place stipulated in the Chronicles. Chronicles are the official laws and historical documents of the Land of Spardom.

"We confirmed the Isle's existence on the seabed floor via satellite infra-red and radar mapping. The Chronicles are fairly accurate in describing the Isle's size, shape, and landmass. Twenty years ago, during the Cold War, we covertly mapped its topographical characteristics. It has high mountains and deep valleys as well as plateaus.

"These topographical facts are fascinating in and of themselves. The land of Spardom is still with us, resting on the ocean floor. It has all the uniqueness one would expect of a continent, perhaps the eighth continent of the world. These facts are indisputable. They are also intriguing, to say the least. One could even argue the Isle is the fabled land of Atlantis. Its location, however, is nowhere near where the legendary site is thought to be.

"What is equally intriguing - and I am certain this will astound you - the island is alive. By alive, I imply the grass is green. Dense, thriving forests cover the plains and mountains. There is evidence of snow at the uppermost peaks of mountains. There are verdant valleys, flourishing fields and flowing waterways, lagoons, rivers, a lake, a desert, and streams. All of this exists in the sea covered by over one thousand fathoms of water.

"To put it in other measurements - the Isle lies nearly two thousand meters, six thousand feet, or nearly one and one-tenth miles beneath the ocean's surface. That, Miss

Roblins, is astounding given the enormous water pressure exerted on the Isle, not to mention there is life on its surface!

"We discovered these astonishing truths purely by accident a few years ago. One of our nuclear-powered submarines was conducting a routine deep-sea nighttime training operation in the vicinity of the island. It had deployed a Special Forces team via a submersible vessel. We use the vessel for intelligence-gathering and pre-staging U.S. Navy Seals in support of stealthy missions ashore.

"Shortly after the vessel deployed from its mother submarine, one of our Navy Seals spotted dimly-lit lights on the Isle's landmass. The sailors exited their vessel to investigate the sources of lights. They snapped numerous photographs. We analyzed the photographs at our Joint Intelligence Center in Hawaii. Although the Navy Seals took the photographs from a great distance, we were able to discern the source of the lights. The lights were campfires.

"Five subsequent visits confirmed that which the sailors captured on their cameras. Deeper depth dives by scientific research submersibles determined the Isle is certainly alive. As I said, it has breathable air, thriving vegetation, streams, and a lake, and living creatures with sufficient intelligence to create campfires."

Admiral Jones pauses to gauge our reaction. During this pause, I convey to Lindsial, "I cannot believe this! Have you ever seen, heard, or experienced anything of this sort?"

"No," Lindsial replies via telepathy. "Even for us elves, used to extraordinary events not known to humans, such a place is unimaginable. It is wholly beyond even our understanding. It is indeed incredible."

Admiral Jones continues briefing. "From the looks on your faces, you undoubtedly do not accept as true what we discovered. At first we did not believe it either. Please trust me when I say the Isle, as told by the Chronicles exists. It is alive, probably with life of various forms, including intelligent beings.

"There is one more incredible detail that is completely beyond our comprehension. A translucent bubble of unexplained energy encloses the Isle. This unknown energy source protects the Isle from the ocean's enormous pressure. Equally exciting is the Isle somehow harvests oxygen molecules from the sea. The Isle has atmosphere of its own. The Isle also has periods of sunlight and darkness similar to that on surface earth." Admiral Jones pauses to gauge our reaction.

"That is correct. The Isle has periods of sunlight and darkness that coincide with those on the surface. The sun rises as usual, and then the sun sets. There are stars and even a moon that completes its monthly lunar cycle. It is as if the Isle's celestial structure is a carbon copy of the astronomical view we have here on surface earth. Remarkably, the Isle is one thousand fathoms below the ocean's surface!

"On numerous occasions, our research ships tried to communicate with whoever is on the Isle, to no avail. Either our communications cannot penetrate the Isle's protective barrier or those who dwell there opt to remain silent. Perhaps they are incapable of communication. We simply do not know."

"Or," I convey to Lindsial, "Whoever lives on the Isle is deaf just like the supposed Princess of Spardom."

"Perhaps," Lindsial conveys, "They are deaf and voiceless, maybe even blind. It would not seem odd for those on the Isle to have similar physical characteristics as us elves. You know, Eva, I think I am beginning to understand what may be happening here."

Before Lindsial can finish conveying her thoughts, Admiral Jones says, "I now conclude my presentation. Are there any questions?"

I slowly rise from my chair. I walk unsteadily to the counter to refill my coffee mug. The room has been spinning round and round for several minutes now. I do not feel well, and I am nauseous again. I've been burping up breakfast. It sure does taste nasty! I wonder if I feel ill because of last night's dinner. I try to ignore my nausea.

Having refilled my coffee mug and added my dearly cherished hazelnut creamer, I turn to face the Admiral. Despite my queasiness, I gather all my strength to project my voice in a strong manner. I ask, "Admiral Jones, why did you people summon us today? What do we have to do with any of this, even if I am as everyone says, the Princess of Spardom? I saw you say no one has been able to contact the Isle's inhabitants. In addition, I seriously doubt you know how to enter its protective bubble, correct? So Admiral Jones, why are we here?"

I lean my hip against the counter to keep my balance as I await Admiral Jones' reply. Nevertheless, I am dangerously off balance. I feel weightless and I cannot right myself. Why in the world am I so wobbly? My goodness, I feel as if I am going to faint!

CHAPTER NINE

REVELATIONS

Admiral Jones says, "The reason we asked you here to-day is simple enough, Miss Roblins. You are indisputably the princess of the ancient Isle of Spardom. Each of the four elves, in all likelihood, is also a descendant of the Isle. Each of the elves, including you, has similar DNA characteristics. That means the five of you are relatives - generations removed perhaps, yet related just the same.

"There is one more piece of information we feel you have the right to know Miss Roblins. Each of the elves in this room, including you, is most certainly more than one hundred fifty years old. You may be two hundred years old, perhaps even older, say three hundred years old. There is no way of knowing for certain. For some strange reason, the other elves stopped growing at some point in their childhood. They appear today as youthful as when their growth stopped.

"Additionally, and I do not know how to say this but to give it to you straight. Eva Roblins, you are the missing daughter of Queen April of Spardom and her husband, Roblins. You are heir and princess of the ancient Isle. You merely think you lived your childhood the way you remember it. In actuality, you were reborn in another's body. You assumed that child's memories when she was in a coma so many years ago. To put it candidly, you are reincarnated. I know this comes as a shock to you. Trust me, it is the truth. And yes, Miss Roblins, as I said, you are probably as old as the other elves.

"We have no idea how this happened. All the same, we do know this. A teenager, who suffered meningitis, is not the same teenager who lived from that day. She became you, and you became her. You absorbed the memories of the body and mind you inherited - hers. Then the two of you switched places. But all along you remained and were to this day, Eva Caroline Roblins, princess of the ancient Land of Spardom.

"So to answer your question frankly Miss Roblins, you are the reason we are here today. We are here to capitalize on your powers and those of your distant relatives, the other elves in this room. We do not know all of the powers you possess. However, please trust me when I say, we will learn about all of your paranormal skills. We have our ways." She laughs as she glances around the room. The others in the room snicker and nod their heads.

Admiral Jones continues, saying, "You must also agree with this, Miss Roblins. We need to know the Isle's technology, how the creatures living on the Isle can thrive beneath the sea. We need to know how it is they can harvest sunlight, darkness, and breathable air. We need to understand how they have managed to stay alive after sinking below the surface. We need to know how their protective bubble can withstand inestimable pounds of pressure.

"Cannot you see, Miss Roblins, we desperately need to know the Isle's technology. Our knowledge of that technology will advance our space programs. It will better lives for humans on surface earth. Knowing how the Isle survives may also help us rein in global warming. For sure we yearn to live an amazing life as those on the Isle. These reasons and many more are why you and the elves are here today,

Miss Roblins. We need you to do what we cannot."

Oh my goodness, if what you say is true, I am ancient -
I am perhaps one hundred fifty years old, maybe as old as
three centuries! No - no - no! There is no way. What you
are saying is not remotely possible! I remember growing
up. I remember my mother and my dear Papa, my childhood, my sickness, my friends, my entire life damn you! I
sang, and I danced, and I skipped and jumped and I enjoyed Christmas and my favorite foods. I have lived twenty-
nine years, and I remember all of it. I remember every bit
of it I tell you. You are wrong! You are completely wrong!

And no, I will not help you! I will not allow you to destroy the Isle's beauty to satisfy your self-serving greed.
The history of the world is fraught with conquerors' deceitful lies that eventually became a reality of horrible abuses.
There were killings and the slaughter of whole populations
and the ruin of entire cultures. All was accomplished to
better the stronger one at the expense of the weaker one. I
will not be a part of your devious plan - ever!

And dear Papa, I loved you. But wait! You were not my
real father. It would appear I loved a stranger - a person
fabricated by the Agency so they could use me as a pawn in
their grand scheme. It was all a lie, an Agency conspiracy
from the start, over fourteen years now. My Papa, oh my
Papa - you are not real, at least not since my illness! Everything - you, my childhood, my dreams and my nightmares - everything was a lie, a horrible, fraudulent,
heartless lie!

And you, Dr. Raymond Brown, I hate you with all my
heart and soul. You and the Central Intelligence Agency
took me away from myself. May you never rest in peace
and may your soul be cursed!

Stop it I tell you. Leave me alone! I need to sort out
this nightmare. I dislike these people. The people in this
place are evil. How can I escape this loathsomeness? Go
away, I tell you.

Familiar clairvoyant thoughts unexpectedly invade my
mind just as someone continues to shake me gently. "Eva,

Eva! Wake up, Eva. It is me, Lindsial. Eva, please wake up - wake up now!"

I awaken with a start. I sit up in bed. My first thought is that this is not my bed. I am in a comfortable enough bed for sure though freshly-laundered U.S. Government-issued starched and stenciled sheets cover it. I mean, come on - who stencils their sheets?

There is also the typical gray wool blanket folded at the foot of the bed. I stare at the blanket with anger. I disliked my wool blanket while I was on assignment with the U.S. Navy on board the frigate *USS Vandegrift*. The blanket was one hundred percent wool. It made me itch like crazy. Thank goodness a crypto tech crewmember loaned me his fleece blanket.

I slowly search the room. For what, I do not know. I eventually look to my left to see Lindsial sitting on a chair close beside my bed. I stare at her and pleadingly ask via thought transference, "What happened, Lindsial? Where am I? How long have I been asleep? What did I miss? Are you and the others okay?"

Lindsial conveys, "Thank goodness you're awake! You fainted Eva. You have been asleep for a very long time now. I believe it is mid morning, the day after we arrived. The doctor said you would be okay after a day's rest. You have endured so much the past three months. The doctor said it was amazing you did not give way much sooner. He also said you had been in overdrive, going full steam ahead for a very long time.

"Yesterday's revelations about the Isle only added to the strain. The doctor said you have had a touch of food poisoning - probably from the asparagus with cheese we ate the other night. To be honest with you, it tasted funny to the rest of us. Spoiled food doesn't bother us like it does humans, so we didn't give its sour taste a second thought."

"But Lindsial, they want us to go to Spardom," I convey via telepathy. "They want to steal the Isle's technology. They want to ruin Spardom like humans ruined the Maya and Aztec's cultures. They want to obliterate the Isle's culture just like Americans subjugated the American Indian's traditions. They also want to learn more about our elvish powers, to probe our bodies and minds with experiments or something. I will not let them, Lindsial. I will not be a part of anything like that."

"No, Eva. They do not want us to do anything of the sort," Lindsial's mind conveys. She is smiling, her lovely face full of love and understanding. I notice her beautiful light blue eyes sparkle with a dazzling intensity in the dimly-lit room. I wonder how such dazzling eyes could be blind. Lindsial's calm composure makes me feel a bit more at ease.

She continues conveying her thoughts via telepathy. "None of that is true. No one is going to try and make us steal anything from anybody. No one is going to conduct experiments on us. At least no one has told us that up to now. I certainly hope they do not intend to. Besides, I have the feeling Cindy and Admiral Jones are on our side. They won't let anything nasty happen to us."

"But I saw Admiral's Jones lips say those things, Lindsial," my thoughts contradict. "She also said I am as old · please do not be offended. She said I was reborn, reincarnated · that I am as old as you or older. Oh my goodness, Lindsial! She said Papa was never real! She also said I possessed a dying child's body and assumed her memories. From what she said, everything was of that poor girl's life and not of my own!

"She went on to say, and of this I have no problem. In fact, if it's true, I'm blessed. She went on to say you and me, Ariel·e and Donas, and Andrial · we are relatives! I saw her say these things with my own two eyes, Lindsial. You must have heard the Admiral's words."

"Eva, I am so sorry you had to endure those thoughts," Lindsial conveys. "I was going to wake you earlier. The doctor told me to wake you hours ago. But I resisted. I wanted to absorb everything going on in your mind. What you thought your eyes saw Admiral Jones say was someone entering false information into your psyche.

"In fact, you fainted before Admiral Jones answered your questions. You were leaning against the counter. I sensed your body was swaying to and fro. I rose to rush toward you, to keep you from falling. Just as I did, I think your coffee mug slipped from your hand. I heard it crash to the floor. Then blam! You followed in a heap a fraction of a second later. I dare say, Eva, I believe you may have ruined Cindy's precious uncontaminated outer clothes. The others told me you spilled coffee everywhere." She laughs.

I give her hand a firm squeeze. As I do my thoughts pleadingly inquire, "Please tell me everything I thought I saw Admiral Jones said was false · my Papa not being my true father · that I was reborn. Please tell me those horrible bits and pieces about me being reincarnated · that I'm one hundred fifty years old or older are false. Please tell me what I saw in my mind is untrue, Lindsial. Please tell me I am who I think I am. Because if I am not who I think I am, I will surely want to die."

"Everything you thought you saw the Admiral say after you fainted is a lie," Lindsial's thoughts convey. "Honestly, the other elves and I have no idea why we are here. The humans have not answered your question. From reading the humans' thoughts, I do not think the humans know why we are here. Even Kristopher does not know the reason we are here.

"But I do know one thing for a fact, Eva. Someone or something is trying to destroy your mind. Whatever it is, it is trying to change your thought processes. It wants you to see and hear in your mind things that are false. It probably wants you to do things you otherwise would not do. Whatever this thing is, it is pure evil."

My thoughts question, "What can we do to keep whatever it is from entering my mind? How can I block it from trying to control my actions, from reading my thoughts?"

Lindsial conveys, "While I may be wrong, I do not think it can read your thoughts, Eva. It certainly cannot read my thoughts, or I would know. So I doubt it can read yours. I think it was reading the humans' thoughts. Then it twisted

their thoughts into something bizarre as it entered false-
hoods into your mind. At present, however, whatever it is,
it can make your mind think what is false is real and what
is real is false. Even so, there is good news on the horizon.
Your powers will continue to get stronger. Then this thing
will be unable to penetrate your mind no matter how hard
it tries.

"My mind captured its power, Eva. All the same, as
hard as I tried I could not break through the sender's
thoughts. I could not enter its mind. Nor could I receive its
thoughts directly in my mind. I had to read its thoughts as
you interpreted them in your mind. Whatever it is that is
doing this to your mind, it is much more powerful than me.
This is most disturbing. Whatever it is, it is far away from
where we are."

Lindsial sits on my bed. She gives me a reassuring hug.
Her thoughts say, "I know a few very old magical enchantments we can try, Eva. They should aid you in blocking this thing's thoughts from entering your mind. So try
not to worry about it for now. We will figure out a way to
block its intrusions.

"However, please allow me to explain a few things as it
pertains to the mind, or brain, whatever you want to call it.
As you know, our brains are controlling life forms. While
our brains are alive and functioning normally, they can
compel us to do whatever they want us to do. It does not
matter whether acts or thoughts are good or evil. Our
brains are in total control whether we like it or not.

"So if our brains want us to walk, we walk. If our
brains want us to talk, we talk. If they want us to do something stupid, we do stupid things. If our brains have a dark
side, they may want us to hurt, steal, lie, cheat, and yes,
even kill. There is no getting around it. We have to do what
our brains tell us to do.

"So, Eva, please think about this. When the mind, the
brain, possesses extrasensory perception powers, then
things can get mightily scary. A mind with extrasensory
perception powers is virtually unstoppable. I assume what-

ever or whoever it is that is trying to influence your mind is wicked. In contrast, thank goodness you and your brain are compassionate. If not, we could be in a world of hurt."

CHAPTER TEN

THESE ELVES ARE CUTE

"Well, here we are once more," I watch the Army general's lips say. "Ah, give me a sec. I seem to have my notes out of kilter."

There is something about this character I do not like. He gives off a tone of superiority. As he fidgets with his notes, I read his mind. Yup, I knew it. He does not take pleasure in briefing inferiors, especially females. And he's ticked off about having to brief as he puts it, *these so-called weird-looking elves.*

But look here · he does think Lindsial, Ariel·e, and I are cute, darling, in fact. He likes the way our butts wiggle when we walk. But wow! If he had to tell the truth, he has the hots for Cindy. He might even ask her out for dinner tonight.

C'mon General, you're at least ten years her senior! Plus, you have a wedding ring on your finger! Besides, Cindy is also married, and she has a lovely teenage daughter. You better retire soon, buster, before your chauvinism gets the best of you!

Lindsial squeezes my arm. From the corner of my eye, I

see she agrees with me. She is smiling. I convey, "Yeah, but he thinks we are cute, darling, in fact. Imagine that." The two of us stifle a giggle.

I refocus my attention to the General. He is finally prepared to brief us. I cannot help but inject one last thought of my own. *It's about time you opinionated, self-centered, sexist moron.*

The General says, "Okay, here we go. I was on the wrong page. I am General Bobby Powers of the Joint Intelligence Center that Admiral Jones mentioned yesterday, abbreviated title J-I-C. First off, let me say we are relieved you are feeling better, Miss Roblins. You gave us quite a scare. But enough of that · let's move on to business.

"My portion of today's presentation will be brief. At approximately thirteen hundred, we will receive an EO, an Execute Order. The EO will come from the Office of the Secretary of Defense. The President of the United States will have authorized the EO. None of us in this room are privy to the exact details of the EO. As such, Miss Roblins, to answer the question you posed to Admiral Jones yesterday morning we do not know. None of us knows for certain why we are here. So, I ask you to be patient.

"Suffice it to say, if the EO directs we deploy I will brief you on what the transport entails. If the EO tells us to stand down, I will debrief you on everything classified. That would include, Miss Roblins, your viewing of Dr. Brown's email three months ago.

"If we are ordered to stand down, all five of you will then be asked to sign an NDA, non-disclosure agreement. The NDA will bind you to your obligation to keep silent about each and every aspect of these proceedings. If you do not adhere to its restrictions, there will be stiff penalties involved, including imprisonment and fines. We take this stuff seriously. We expect you to do the same. Are there any questions?"

"Well, that was brief and to the point," I convey to Lindsial. "This guy is beside himself. Plus, I think he's full of garbage. I'm going to find out for certain. As they say, it's time to test the waters."

I stare at the General for a few moments. I smile prettily, and then I say, "Yes, General, I have a question. What do you mean when you say the word *deploy?* What exactly does that imply, sir? Could you please further define the word deploy?

The General says, "That is an excellent question, Miss Roblins. When I say the word deploy, I suggest transfer or convey you from one place or another with our transport machine. It is the bulky machine in the center of this building. I am sure you have seen it by now. It's pretty noticeable."

"I see," I say tentatively. "And have you used the machine on previous occasions? Is it safe? Does it actually take a person to the exact place a person is intended to go?"

"Oh, yes, Miss Roblins, the machine works satisfactorily. We have transported entire squads of Special Forces to specific geographical locations around the world. We have experienced no problems at all. However, I must insist · what the machine does and how it works has a strict need to know caveat."

"And do we have a need to know, sir?" I ask. "Do we have the need to know what the machine does?"

The General shakes his head in a rude way as he laughs. "Unfortunately, you do not have a need to know, Miss Roblins. As I mentioned earlier, the EO will determine when and where and if we are to deploy."

He now crosses his arms in front of his six rows of service ribbons. Without thinking, he has assumed a controlling pose with his non-verbal expression. He tilts his head and stares. His lips seem to sneer. I am subordinate to him by a wide margin, and he's making certain I don't forget it.

I surprise myself with the arrogant laugh that somehow escapes my mouth. I do not intend it. I cannot hear it, but I know it happens just the same. I sit back in my chair. I want to match the General's controlling demeanor no matter what. I cross my arms across my chest with similar mocking disdain. We stare at each other for a few moments, our eyes never wavering. The General tilts his head to the other side and sneers once again. It's as if he's saying by means of his non-verbal expression, "Your move sweetheart."

I love a challenge. I say, "Do you honestly think we are going to set foot in some machine without a briefing on its function? To put it another way, General - do you honestly believe the five of us do not have a need to know? I dare say we do, sir. Because, if we do not have a need to know, there is no way in the world we're going to step one foot into that stupid machine - period!"

"Hmm," General Power's lips mouth as he laughs. "I was told you were going to be difficult to work with, Miss Roblins. I see that's one hundred percent true. My orders are quite clear. I am not authorized to brief you on the machine's capabilities until we receive the EO at thirteen hundred. I wish I could, but I cannot. You'll just have to wait, like it or not. Sorry."

After the General finishes talking, I read afterthoughts in his mind. He's calling me, and I quote - A brainless, arrogant civilian sand crab, low-life, and redheaded, freckle-faced stupid idiot! I decide to let the General's afterthoughts pass - for now. I cannot let anyone in this room know I am able to read his mind. However, I avow - someday I will get my revenge for his narrow-minded remarks. I promise you.

I rise from my chair. I shove my chair back with so much force it tips over to crash (I can only hope) deafeningly loud onto the floor. I address the other elves, "Well my fellow, merry band of elves. We are on our way. Please wave goodbye to the nice General."

The elves' contempt for the General's discourteous manner toward me is apparent. To my delight, after they push themselves away from their chairs they smirk and, at the same time, wave goodbye to the General. Their actions are almost too comical to believe. Gosh, I love these four youngsters!

I turn to exit the briefing room. The four elves follow

closely behind. Out of the corner of my eye, I notice Cindy is frantically waving her hands in the air. She is trying to get my attention. I stop to face her. I stare as if I am waiting for her lips to move. Lip reading at this point is a ruse. I can read her thoughts easily enough, just like I can read the thoughts of every other human in this room. And let me tell you - some thoughts concerning how some of the humans feel about me right now I cannot repeat. They are too offensive and crude. They make what General Powers just said about me in his mind seem like childlike baby talk gibberish.

Cindy says, "Crying out loud, Eva! Why in the world are you so difficult? Can't you just wait until we receive the EO? We won't know what our orders are going to be for another two hours. As the General said, it could be a go. Then again, it could be a stand down order, a no go. We just do not know, Eva. Give us a break, will you?"

Turning to General Powers she appears to shout, "I really cannot blame Eva for getting angry! Everything about you today is sarcasm and unfriendliness. What is your problem, Bobby? Is it because you do not like them because they're different? Well, too bad. They probably possess more powers and intellect than all of us in this room combined. Now..."

"Hold on a minute, Cindy," I interrupt with a shout. I'm waving my finger in the air. "No need to know no can do. You know how I operate, Cindy. Unless I know every aspect of this process, I am not putting these elves in harm's way. That is my final word. So, all of you can just kiss our butts goodbye. We're out of here." I once again turn on my heels and head toward the exit. The elves dutifully follow.

I had to interrupt Cindy. She was about to dig herself a deep hole from which she might not be able to escape. She has to work with these clowns. Plus, she is a political appointee. I do not want her to hitch a one-way ride on Washington's political scapegoat slippery slope because of me. I love and respect her too much.

As everyone in the room stands stock-still, except for us elves - we're marching toward the doorway - the Marine general is addressing General Powers. I read his thoughts. I feel a sense of relief. I'm relieved at least one of these male bureaucrats has the guts to give it to my team of elves and me straight. I look over my shoulder. As I stop walking, I turn to face the Marine general as if I'm reading his lips.

"Give them the damned access, Bobby," the Marine general barks to General Powers. "We can worry about the authorization and stupid paperwork later. There is no sense us sitting around here for another two hours while these five go to heaven knows where. Miss Roblins is too valuable, we all know that. The other elves are as well."

The Marine general turns his head a little so I cannot read his lips. He probably wants to lessen the shock of the butt chewing he is about to unleash on General Powers. I read his mind. "Bobby, watch your step. Cindy is right. Your brief came across as both haughty and sarcastic. You humiliated Miss Roblins with your challenging, disrespect-ful demeanor, and you embarrassed her in front of her en-tourage. That was uncalled for and unprofessional. Please express regret for your flippant answers, sir. Then tell Miss Roblins and the others what they need to know. I encour-age you to make it snappy!"

The Marine general turns to look at me. He says, "Miss Roblins, I do believe everything is now under control. You will have access to the information. I apologize if we have upset you."

I turn around to face the elves and say, "My fellow elves - it would appear we do, in fact, have a need to know. So, if you please, let us take our seats like the good sports that we are."

"Wow!" Lindsial conveys to me as she slides into her seat. "You have some backbone there, missy! You are start-ing to act more like a princess with each passing moment. Good for you! And Cindy - holy cow! Now I know where you get your spunk. Cindy is incredible!"

General Powers' face is now a shade deeper than bright red. It is obvious he's taken aback by my insolence and the Marine general's butt-chewing. I watch with satisfaction as his pen taps nervously on the table as he speaks. He says, "Miss Roblins, please accept my regrets for being overly cautious. As a soldier, I readily abide by orders of my seniors. Since the Chairman JCS has issued the latest order that countermanded the previous order I had received, directing that I brief you, brief you I shall." He sorts through his notes once more.

"But oh, this General certainly is one ticked off hothead," I convey to Lindsial's mind. "And he knows how to mince his words and how to cover his butt. He is trying to make it look like what he said wasn't his fault. But wait, the Marine general - now I know why I recognize him. He is the Chairman of the Joint Chiefs of Staff, head honcho of all U.S. military services. His name is Fuller, General Michael J. Fuller, of the United States Marine Corps. He is the President's recent pick as Chairman, JCS. He has had the job less than a month. I like this guy. I like this guy a lot."

General Powers' tedious thoughts once again hammer in my mind like a troublesome headache. "Miss Roblins, the transporter machine I referred to earlier is called the Universal Transporter Device or UTD. It is but one component of the Universal Transporter Program Admiral Jones mentioned yesterday. It does not take a person or object from one place to the next by means of time warp. That's nonsense for sci-fi novels.

"The capsule inside the transporter moves at one-tenth the speed of sound. It transports whatever, or whoever is inside across the planet in a matter of minutes. It is primarily used to transport US Army Special Forces and US Navy Seals to terrorist hotbeds as quickly as possible.

"There are two exact replicas of the UTD in this facility, one each in Great Britain and Japan. We use them predominately as a counter-terrorism transport mechanism. The UTD located in this building has deployed on twenty-seven occasions. The ones in Great Britain and Japan deployed thirteen times and four times, respectively. Each operation has been flawless.

"There is only one limitation to the UTD. We can transport troops to exact locations anywhere on earth. Retrieving the troops is an entirely different matter. It is then when we employ more conventional means. These include airborne recovery platforms, submarines, or staging our troops to safe houses and clandestine pick-up points. That pretty much sums it up, Miss Roblins." Turning to General Fuller, he adds, "Did I miss anything, sir?"

Before the Chairman, JCS can reply I have something to add. I say in a barely audible, challenging whisper, "You overlooked a few things, General - if you do not mind me saying. This machine of yours is pretty amazing if it does everything you say it does. Getting troops to a hot spot rapidly is darned right smart. There may be one tiny problem in our case."

General Powers' face is once more displaying its customary look of annoyance. For some reason, this makes me glad. His lips move to say, "Not again. And what problem would that be, ma'am, huh?" He crosses his arms and scowls.

"Well, sir," I say, "Admiral Jones stated the bubble surrounding the Isle of Spardom is impenetrable. Even our attempts at communication have been fruitless. If that is the case, sir, how in the world do you expect us to get there? How do you expect our fragile flesh and bone bodies to penetrate the bubble when radio waves cannot, eh? Plus, how in the world do we return? You said so yourself - you cannot return people from whence they came by using the device."

The General responds, "Nobody said anything about going to Spardom, Miss Roblins. As you are well aware, we have not received the EO." He looks at his watch and then he says, "We will not have it in our possession for another one and three-quarter hours. So I ask you to remain patient." He pauses, and then he adds, "...if that's at all possible."

Not only is the General being annoyingly discourteous, he never answered my third question. *How in the world do we return?* I say in a tone of obvious exasperation, "Oh, come off it, General. Do you think for one moment, if the EO says execute, you will stage us to an island paradise close to Spardom?"

I have a sudden urge to be equally discourteous as he was to me. Yes, I know, I shouldn't do it, but I do it anyway. As a come back to the General's uncivil behavior, I offer, "So if the EO says we execute, my goodness! We'll have to ensure we do not forget to pack our fancy umbrella drink concoctions, sunscreen, and flip-flops. That is because we're not going to Spardom, eh?"

I haven't finished with my diatribe. I state, "Let's be honest with each other here, sir. If the EO says execute, you will attempt to transport us precisely to where the Isle is. You will transport us dab smack in the middle of the ocean, to the middle of nowhere. Now, that is how I define the word *executing* my dear sir. The five of us will drown. That's if we do not implode with the sea's pressure! And if that's not enough to ask of us, there's no way for us to return if we somehow manage to survive." I smile, and then I lightheartedly say as I wave my arms in the air, "Wow! Talk about one super-cool, once in a lifetime opportunity! It's much better than winning the lottery. Sign us up!"

Just as I finish talking, I glance over at Cindy. She is shaking her head and laughing as she stares at the folder in front of her. She's accustomed to my spirited, redheaded challenging ways, so her amused reaction to my conduct doesn't surprise me in the least. But let's be honest here, the General is narrow-minded, chauvinistic, impolite, and shrewd. He deserved everything he received and more! Plus, he called me a redheaded, freckle-faced stupid idiot! You remember what happened when I was in high school. I won't put up with anyone calling me names!

I look at the General. He is about to lose his cool. His hands are trembling. His face is bright red once again.

Good! Desperately trying to maintain his composure he finally stammers, "We have the capability to transport to - to a certain depth as well - as well as to a precise geographical location. Perhaps you're not as trusting of our machine's abilities as I am. However, you'll have to believe - you'll have to believe what I am saying, because I know what I'm saying. I've seen - I've seen the machine in action. You haven't."

Of course, I'm reading Powers' mind. Now he's calling me everything under the sun, to include an *obnoxious idiot. He's* calling *me* an obnoxious idiot? I'll buy off on the obnoxious part. However, I am no idiot. He is!

I have had enough of this - I'm going to give him everything I have, guns blazing! I say in a gentle tone, "Have you ever tried it to a specific depth, say one thousand fathoms below the surface of the ocean, General? Better yet, have you ever tried it on a *person* to a depth of one thousand fathoms? How about a measly two hundred fathoms, have you?"

General Powers stammers, "Well no - I mean yes, an object to a specific depth - two hundred feet - at least I think so. It was quite successful if I recall correctly."

"If you recall correctly," I say sarcastically. "Come off it, General - how many times, how many times have you tried it on a living person? Be honest with us."

"Never," the General replies in an apparent whisper. He is overwhelmed by my relentless questioning. I honestly can't blame him. I bet he never had a lowly CIA special agent like me speak to him in such a way. However, good manners go both ways. Besides, I didn't start this. He did.

The General adds, "Honestly, Miss Roblins, we have never tried it on a living organism - a person if you will. I am more than confident it will succeed. You'll have to trust me if that's even possible in your case."

I notice the Chairman JCS has thrown his hands up in the air with obvious frustration. His thoughts say, "This tit-for-tat is getting us nowhere. What do you say we take a break? Try to relax, sneak in a nap, have a snack or use the treadmill, study our briefing material. Do anything to take our minds off as to why we are here. To be perfectly honest with you, I do not know why we are here. Not knowing is about to drive all of us, including me, insane. Now let's adjourn for a brief spell. Also, please remember we are in this together - whatever the heck this is."

CHAPTER ELEVEN

SPARDOM SPONSO DIRECTO

The four elves and I are in the common room. The others of our group are just as concerned and worked up as I am. Even so, they are pretending to be completely bored to tears. Andrial is doodling on a writing pad. Donas and Ariel·e are playing a hotly contested game of chess.

Lindsial is resting her head against the wall as she sits. She has closed her eyes. Maybe she is taking a nap. Then again, she may be in deep thought. I attempt to begin a thought transference conversation. She waves her hand a few times. She is telling me she doesn't want a telepathic conversation right now. I respect her wishes.

General Powers' inane stupidity and obvious contempt riled me. I am exhausted from our verbal attacks and counterattacks. I'm also fairly weak from the suspected case of food poisoning. My head continues to swim occasionally with wooziness. I cradle my head in my arms on the table. Before I know it, I am sound asleep. Another's thoughts now enter my mind.

"Let it go, Eva Roblins that is what you should do. Let it go. Simply walk out with the elves and forget you were ever here. Lindsial will know how to hide you. The others will use their powers to keep you safe. The Washington bureaucrats do not care about you, Eva Roblins. They only want to know the Isle's secrets. Once they have used your power to their gain, they will abandon you. That machine they're speaking about, it'll kill you, Eva Roblins. It will kill you and the others.

"Leave with the elves now, before it is too late. Or perhaps you should leave them behind. If you think about it, they are of no value without you. Maybe they scheme behind your back. You suspect Lindsial has been against you since you two have met. You are being deceived by her Eva Roblins. Leave now, before it is too late. Leave without Lindsial and the other elves immediately. Do it now!"

I open my eyes. What is this? No! There is no way Lindsial would betray me. I will not allow you lie to me anymore. I want you to leave me alone. Leave me now I say, leave now.

"Eva? Eva?" Lindsial's thoughts question in my mind. "Are you okay? I could tell you were angry. You were telling someone to leave you alone. Is that evil thing back in your mind, Eva, is it?"

"Yes it is, Lindsial, at least it was. It told me to leave, to not trust you or the others. Its thoughts were compelling. When it mentioned you betraying me, I instinctively fought back. I knew the thoughts were not my own. I fought it, and now it's gone."

"Well, I am glad you were able to stop it," Lindsial's thoughts reply. "I'm also relieved the others are not talking about what is happening here. Donas has been spying on the humans while he has been playing chess. The humans are worked up about something · they seem anxious and worried.

"Donas says some of the humans are carefully watching us. Uniformed men in the control room monitor and record our every move. Donas says there are hidden cameras and microphones in every room, including this one. He has probably told the others by now. They will not speak of what is going on in this awful place."

I convey, "What in the world is happening here? It's almost as if they are our enemy, the Admiral, the two generals, perhaps even Cindy. Or, maybe they're frightened. I know firsthand how improper orders from oblivious, noncaring bureaucrats in Washington can upset underlings. Maybe Cindy and the others know the EO will direct us to enter the UTD with no guarantee it will work?"

"I believe you are correct, Eva. They're worked up about something for sure. Andrial was almost certain he overheard the doctor saying they'll use tranquilizers if need be."

My mind conveys, "I have this nagging feeling, my sixth sense kicking in I guess. I feel as if we're not supposed to leave this place unless it's in that idiotic transporter. It hasn't been used to transport a living soul to a deep depth at sea. There is also the issue of the Isle's bubble being impenetrable. We will drown, or worse. Our bodies will implode with the pressure. If we do manage to survive, there is no way for us to return."

Lindsial conveys, "Eva, Kristopher is listening in via telepathy. He and I were exchanging thoughts when I waved away your attempted thought transference. He shares our concern. He has an idea that concerns a very risky plan. It involves a spell you can make possible with the help of your medallions magic. I will let him explain. Kristopher, if you please."

I am surprised I did not read Kristopher's thoughts as he and Lindsial had a telepathic exchange. I read his thoughts earlier, but not this time. I wonder if Kristopher can select who can and who cannot read what he is thinking. It wouldn't surprise me in the least.

Lindsial departs the common room as Kristopher outlines his plan to me in my mind. She strolls to the women's restroom. There are no cameras in the restrooms, as far as we can tell. She enters a stall, latches the door, turns invisible, and then she crawls beneath the stall door. With Donas serving as her guide in the corridor, she tiptoes to the office where Cindy and the flag officers are meeting. The door is wide open. For some strange reason, Lindsial cannot enter the room. An invisible energy force keeps her from proceeding any further. Donas tries to enter the office as well, also without success.

Donas is rapidly moving back and forth from the common room to Lindsial. He wants the monitors to see him playing chess. Despite his swiftness, he finally has to give up. He whispers into Lindsial's ear. "I cannot continue. It is far too difficult to keep the cameras recording my presence in the common room while I am here. I am sorry." He departs to resume his chess match with Ariel-e. Lindsial snoops around a while longer, and then she returns to the women's restroom. She slips under the stall door and turns visible once more.

Now that Lindsial has returned to the common room, Ariel-e asks, "Where were you, my dear Lindsial? You missed it. Master Donas had me in check two times, but I ended up beating him. You should have seen the look on his face when I said *checkmate!*"

"I was in the lady's room," Lindsial replies. With her back to the camera, she whispers to Ariel-e and Donas, "Ahsom forton li bie vay socolom."

Ariel-e asks, "Forsom na vay taolm Eva?"

"Solonk mo routel vy mastonat," Lindsial replies.

Donas whispers, "Forsom na vay taolm Andrial?" Lindsial nods her head in reply.

Unbeknownst to me, Lindsial has just told Ariel-e and Donas they are to follow my lead after receipt of the EO. Now Lindsial is speaking to Andrial in the same elvish language in which she spoke to Ariel-e and Donas.

"Andrial, you must think the words in your mind when the time comes. But I caution you - do not practice it now. If you do, I dread what might happen. Since you have never spoken Fortunomy, Eva will explain how to sign it in ASL as well. One of the two methods should work. At least I hope so."

"Okay, Lindsial," I convey via thought transference.

"Kristopher told me his plan. He said he told you as well. I only hope with all my heart it will work when the time comes. We cannot speak of it out loud. So how will the others know what we plan to do? And what was that strange language you were speaking? I sensed it in my mind, but I could not understand it."

Lindsial conveys, "I already told Ariel·e, Donas, and Andrial our plan by using our ancient elvish language. At the right time, they will know what to do. They will follow your lead. Then our fate will be in your hands."

All of a sudden Lindsial deliberately turns to look in the direction of the camera high on the wall. Of course, since she is blind, she cannot see the camera. Just the same, she pretends to stare at it. Then, of all things, she closes her eyes, sticks out her tongue and shakes her head back and forth! Next, with her eyes open and her tongue hanging out of her mouth, she puts her thumbs to her elf ears and waves her fingers! She is mocking those who are watching us! Good for her!

Despite my best efforts, I am unable to control myself. I laugh along with the others in the room at her sudden, silly outburst. Lindsial has managed to lighten the moment to put us a bit more at ease and to cheer us up.

With her face still facing in the direction of the camera, Lindsial says via thought transference, "The language you sensed is the ancient elvish language called Fortunomy. Elves have spoken Fortunomy since the beginning of time. Fortunomy helped us to survive mankind's cruelty many times over. You will learn Fortunomy soon enough, Eva. Trust me when I say this."

She continues conveying, all the while pretending to stare at the camera, "I will pass on in my mind the words to make our plan work. The only difficult part is getting Andrial to understand. He has heard the words spoken in Fortunomy. Of course, he has never spoken the words. I told him, when the time comes, he is to think the words in his mind. I also told him you will tell him how to say it in ASL."

"Kristopher already told me the words," I convey. "Let me see if I understood them correctly. I'll communicate them in my mind · *Spardom sponso directo!* Is that correct?"

"That is correct, Eva. However, do not say the words aloud until it is time. Whatever you do, ensure you pronounce them as accurately as possible. Otherwise, the spell may not work, and we could found ourselves in China, on top of Mount Everest, or worse. Now, all we have to do is show Andrial how to say the words in ASL."

I glance at the wall clock. I convey, "There isn't enough time. Besides, it will not translate in ASL. Only three minutes remain before we have to report back to the briefing room. I am going to risk everything right now. I will write the words for Andrial and pray for the best."

On a post-it slip of paper, I pen the words, *Spardom sponso directo!* I discretely show the post-it to Andrial by cupping it in my hand. With my back to the camera, I sign, "Read carefully. It will not translate in ASL. Look at me when we are holding hands. When you see my lips move, I want you to think these words in your mind. Try your best and pray it works." I tear the post-it into a dozen pieces and stuff it in my bra.

CHAPTER TWELVE

EXECUTE!

The bureaucrats, Cindy, and the five of us are sitting at the table right on schedule. I notice Kristopher is not present. The doctor is also missing. As a rule, I would not give a doctor's absence from a presentation a second thought. In view of what Andrial thought he overheard about the doctor tranquilizing us, I consider it likely the crazed maniac is just outside the door. I imagine him excit-edly rubbing his hands together as he foams at the mouth like a madman. I also picture in my mind an equally eager battalion of white-cloaked insane nurses ready to shoot sedatives into the five of us.

"Two minutes to go," General Powers earnestly ex-claims as he points to the screen. "The EO should appear on the screen exactly at thirteen hundred. We will then know our orders. I trust you are as excited as me. We final-ly get to see what is going to happen!"

I'm disgusted with this empty-headed excuse for a flag officer. The General's latest burst of emotion reminds me of a small child standing on a neighborhood street corner on a hot summer day. With wild anticipation, he waits for the ice cream man to arrive. After the ice cream man pulls up to the curb, the little boy, a.k.a. General Powers exclaims, "Oh, yes please mister. I'll take one of those and two of those and oh! Mister, this day is exciting! I can't wait to tell all of my friends. I trust you are as excited as me!" Bleah!

I convey, "I don't know about you, Lindsial, but I'm as excited as a dog in a pound."

"I do not know anything about a canine in a monetary amount," Lindsial replies jokingly via thought transference. "However, I am very worried our plan will not work, especially when it comes to Andrial." She adds with a chuckle, "By the way, I do like your analogy of General Powers and the little boy's reaction to the ice cream man. Plus, I double the bleah!"

I'm staring transfixed at the red folder sitting on the table in front of me. It reads Top Secret SCI, Codeword Sea Blue. I never did open the folder to look inside. Perhaps I should. Just as I flip the cover, I feel the mood in the room change. I look up. The dreaded EO is on the screen.

By the Order of the
President of the United States
Execute Order 17864

Top Secret Special Intelligence
Codeword - Sea Depth

Chairman, Armed Forces Joint Chiefs of Staff, is directed to employ the five mission volunteers to the undersea Land of Spardom via the Universal Transporter Device (UTD). Employment will be within five hours after receipt of this Execute Order or as soon as practicable after that. In the event of a significant delay, the Chairman is directed to advise the Secretary of Defense immediately.

The volunteers' mission is to locate the human or artificial power source that sustains life on the Isle of Spardom beneath the Pacific Ocean. Once mission volunteers locate the power source, they shall deploy a transceiver device to communicate with naval forces. Naval forces will provide further instructions to the mission volunteers at that time.

Additionally, intelligence relating to sustenance of life on the Isle shall be collected and documented for further analysis. As a precaution, mission volunteers will carry with them a crystallized chemical agent specifically designed to neutralize any opposing forces. This agent is lethal. Administer an antidote to the volunteers prior to dispersal of the team in the UTD.

Mission volunteers should make all efforts to avoid detection and capture. In the event of capture, mission volunteers will attempt to utilize all possible means to escape. If their capture is unavoidable, they shall consider consuming a vial of cyanide. A word of caution: Mission volunteers should make no mention of the UTD. To do so will jeopardize national security. Attempts to retrieve mission volunteers at some time in the future will be made using submersibles.

//s// George W. Fulbright

I jump up from my chair, yelling "What un tarnation is this supposed to be? We're not volunteers! We didn't volunteer for a darned thing!"

As I shout, the room fills with ten to twelve uniformed soldiers. Each soldier has an M-4 rifle slung over his or her shoulder. I imagine the doc and his fanatical cohorts are outside the door - licking their chops, just itching to stick us with their delirium-inducing garbage. I try my best to ignore the soldiers assembled at parade rest. But it's not easy, I'll tell you that.

I continue to bellow. "The EO's intention is to execute the five of us! How are we supposed to find this power of life source, let alone figure out a way to get us off of the Isle! The EO is a one-way ticket to our death. Plus, it's apparent to me we are one hundred percent expendable! Additionally, how are we supposed to communicate with you when you cannot communicate with what's down there? If that's not enough garbage to fathom · how are we supposed to gather food and find shelter? And cyanide · what is that, your bright idea version of a mission impossible James Bond spy flick? You folks are insane, totally gone bonkers insane!"

"Now Miss Roblins," General Powers' lips say, "We know how this looks to you. Trust me when I say I have thought this through carefully. I firmly believe you will be able to find the power source. Once you locate it, communicate with us using the transceiver device we will give you.

"The device you will have in your possession is compatible with a similar device on the guided missile destroyer, USS Spruance. The ship is sailing in the area. You will receive further instructions once the device is operating. Suffice it to say your mission will change at that time.

"Yes, you may have to deploy the chemical agent if threatened. Each of you will be given an antidote before you depart to negate its poison. Let's be reasonable here, okay? If you somehow became neutralized, you are of no benefit to us in future assignments, correct? So, calm down, all right?

"Bear in mind, Miss Roblins, you are an agent of the United States Government. You took an oath to serve and protect. You know as well as I this is a matter of world security. It is imperative we learn the Isle's technology.

"In addition, there are other reasons you are to deploy · reasons we cannot go into at this time. As I said, you will receive further instructions once you are on the Isle and the transponder is operable. Now follow your orders like the obedient public servant that you are."

As if his last sarcastic remark wasn't insulting enough he's smiling his customary arrogant sneer. I think to myself, someday buster, someday I'll get even. I promise you!

I breathe in deeply. My mind is racing. I need a few moments to collect my thoughts. I have to come up with a ploy of some sort, something · anything to put Kristopher's plan into action. But one thing is for sure. There is no way the elves and I are going to set foot into that idiotic, untested UTD! They'll have to drag me screaming and kicking before that happens.

As I stand, I slowly flip through the pages of the briefing folder on the table before me. I pretend to study each of the pictures and bulletined notes. I nod my head a few times, trying to appear as if I agree with what I see. After a few moments, I look General Powers squarely in the eye. I let out a long submissive sigh.

I act as if I concede defeat by saying, "Okay General, I guess there is no sense fighting the inevitable. After all, this is the reason I signed up with the Agency. I fully accept the risks. I guess I have to trust you when you say you honestly believe we will be okay. After all, we are on the same side. General Fuller said that himself."

I turn to look at General Fuller. He is the ranking officer. Only he can approve what I am about to request. I say, "General, I do have a request if you please?" I read General Fuller's thoughts. He says, "If we can grant it we shall. What is it, Miss Roblins?"

With an innocent expression, I say, "I thank you, sir. May we assemble in that corner over there for a moment of reflection?" I point to the corner wall near the snack bar counter where I fainted yesterday. "It is an elvish ritual. We have been doing it the past three months. It helps to soothe our nerves. It also strengthens our bond." I nod my head in the direction of the guards, smile and add, "In any case, it's obvious we're not going anywhere. We will be well covered by your soldiers as you can see."

General Fuller glances around the room. The army captain in charge of the soldiers says, "I don't have a problem, sir. There's no getting past us. I can assure you."

Cindy and Admiral Jones nod their heads in approval. Cindy winks at me. I bet she somehow knows of our plan! I wouldn't be surprised if Kristopher told her. I hope her wink suggests she concurs with what I am about to do.

General Powers and the ASL interpreter stare at me

solemnly. They do not say or do anything. By their disgusted-looking scowls, it is obvious they do not concur with my request. If it were up to them, they would already have had us tranquilized and well on our way to our doom. I would read their thoughts, but I'm too nervous to do so.

"Okay, Miss Roblins," General Fuller says, "I'll give you a few minutes. Then I must insist the five of you accompany us to the UTD for further instruction. I must caution you. Do not try anything rash. We are under orders to subdue you. That includes tranquilizing you if necessary. I am sorry, but our orders are quite clear. Please proceed to that corner over there and do what you must. But please do it quickly. We have much to discuss, and there's no time to waste."

The elves and I assemble in a semi-circle facing Cindy and the others. The now wary guards inch closer until they are fifteen to twenty feet away on the opposite side of the table. Three guards block the doorway. I position myself in the middle of our group. Lindsial and Donas are to my left, Andrial and Ariel-e are to my right. I ask the elves to hold hands. I momentarily let go of Lindsial's hand and sign to Andrial, "When my lips move I want you to think the written words."

Before I can utter the spell Kristopher gave me, I watch in horror as the interpreter's eyes meet mine. She has interpreted what I signed to Andrial. I sense her words shrieking, "General, they are not meditating or whatever they call it! They are trying to escape!"

It is déjà vu time in my mind once again as a couple dozen thoughts from the others inundate my sanity. I frown as I see General Fuller's lips form a single frightening word, "Guards!" In response, soldiers hasten to us from both sides of the table. It will be a matter of seconds before they are on us.

A split second before the guards reach us, I look at Andrial. I slowly exclaim in a loud voice, enunciating as carefully as I can, "Spardom sponso directo!"

Nothing happened! Something is wrong! I am still here

standing in the same spot. The other elves are here as well. We did not disappear! What in tarnation did I do incorrectly? I cry out, "Lindsial! It did not work! I must have mispronounced the spell when I spoke the words out loud. I tend to slur my words when I am excited. My goodness, what have I done? I am sorry. I am so very sorry."

The entire room is now in an agitated state of total mayhem. I begin to shiver uncontrollably as the guards rush toward us. I notice Cindy is looking straight at me and - what's this? She is smiling! She is also signaling thumbs up. That makes me happy. She is pleased with my escape attempt. But Cindy, it did not work - we're still here!

General Fuller points at us as hurrying soldier's yell unheard commands. The sign language interpreter is sneering. She is mocking me, undoubtedly pleased with herself for discovering my plan to escape. General Powers' arms are forming a huge letter Y as he holds them high in the air. He looks totally ticked off! I see Admiral Jones is smiling at me and nodding. Like Cindy, she almost certainly approves of our attempted escape.

To my horror, I watch as the devilish doctor dashes into the room. Five male nurses bedecked in long white Frankenstein smocks accompany him. Each nurse has a syringe in his hand. Andrial was right - they are going to tranquilize us! Now there is no escape!

I suddenly become aware of something extraordinarily odd. Everyone in the room is moving and gesturing in slow motion. Despite the scene's disordered sluggishness, the guards are nearing. However, they progress at a snail's pace. I see they are yelling unheard whatnots, but their lips move sluggishly. Perhaps the doctor drugged them as well!

What is more, I feel the room spinning, slowly at first, then more quickly as it rotates round and round on its axis. I am mesmerized, unable to move or react as the terrifying chaos unfolds before me.

The soldiers are now upon us. The five nurses are a

step or two behind. I involuntarily jump back as a stout guard with arms outstretched before him passes all the way through my body. Even as I sense his bulk, I feel nothing. There is no pain, no physical connection.

My goodness, what is happening? I can see them, and they obviously can see us. But they cannot touch us. They pass right through us! It is as though we are transparent! Does this mean we are safe? Or is this just a brief sensation? Will they soon take hold of us and knock us unconscious? Perhaps they have already tranquilized us! Maybe what I am seeing is a surreal Agency-conspired hallucination!

Then as incredibly as the confused slow-motion scene unfolds, I am now witness to a spray of brilliant colors. The colors are twisting in a circle, their kaleidoscopic panorama overpowering my sense of sight. I feel my body uplifted as it makes countless loops in step with the vibrancy, yet in the opposite direction. It is as if I am spinning like a misguided top inside a gyroscope. My body gradually increases speed. I watch in awe as dazzling colors twist here and there. Now I am consumed by a whirlpool of vibrancy. It is so intense I have to close my eyes against its clarity. Its strength is that overpowering! Suddenly, there is total blackness.

Oh no, they tranquilized me! Everything is slipping into total darkness as before. I am starting to black out. I failed! Does this mean all of us are going to die?

CHAPTER THIRTEEN

ANCIENT ISLE OF SPARDOM

Amazingly, I have returned to the past - two years ago. I am standing in a courtyard surrounded by shouting CIA and FBI Agents. Hysterical women clutching bewildered youngsters bawl panicky tears. As they watch the handcuffing of wicked souls, the women frantically tug at their hair. These devilish men being handcuffed are husbands, boyfriends, brothers, and sons.

I notice Miguel is staring at me. His look is one of hate. He knows. Someone deceived him, and he knows it was I. His lips read ugly curses. Although I am shivering with fear, I somehow manage to smile meekly. His hand reaches into his pants pocket. I am stock-still as he slowly retrieves the weapon. For some strange reason, I cannot move. It is as if paralysis has enveloped my body. I am unarmed, and he knows it. I am powerless to do anything.

I know what he is thinking. He despises me - probably as much as I despise him. Now he is smiling an evil grin. I am certain the devil possesses his soul.

I submissively watch as he unhurriedly brings the weapon to the level of my forehead until it is mere inches from my skull. I stare seemingly apathetic as his forefinger deliberately depresses the trigger ever so slowly. He wants to torment me to the unavoidable end. His lips continue to scowl a hideous grin.

Just before his finger completes its forbidding task I grimace at the sight of a tiny red hole that unexpectedly appears on his forehead. I react in horror as the air behind his head fills with fine reddish mist. Now everything starts to fade unhurriedly into nothingness. I am in shock from intense pain. I am bleeding profusely from a bullet wound on the left side my abdomen.

Miguel's aim was off as the marksman's bullet hit his head. Miguel had his revenge just the same. He managed to squeeze off two rounds before his cursed brain stopped thinking forever · one in the air as the bullet hit him, the other at me as he fell.

I somehow know I am dying. However, I manage a meek smile. That is because I know the raid was a complete success! All the same I should have been more attentive. I should have trusted my instinct. Everyone in the Cartel had his hands in the air. Miguel did not. Policemen were handcuffing men and women. For some reason, Miguel stood alone. He stood unmolested in the center of the courtyard, his hateful eyes staring into mine. Why?

Why did I not recognize what Miguel was going to do? Why did I not anticipate he would know it was I who had tricked him · his wide-eyed, innocent, naïve pretend girlfriend? His cute little Americano redhead, as he called me. He wanted to introduce me to everyone in the village. He could hardly wait to show everyone how proud he was of the one he was going to take as his bride.

He had invited me to his village to meet his parents and all of his drug-dealing friends · his village, its courtyard adorned with streamers and *Welcome Gloria to our Village* signs, and brightly-colored balloons. After all, an event involving the all-powerful international drug czar called for a celebratory village fiesta · with lots of cheer, booze, drugs, and sex.

A week ago everyone in my task force was euphoric. We finally had the means to capture Miguel and his henchmen on their turf. We had the element of surprise. And, it had only taken me four months to complete my mission, not too shabby for a rookie. I had tricked Miguel with my Agency-construed ruse and my fake name.

I pretended to enjoy the extravagant dinners and cruises in the bay and romantic sunset vistas and boxes of candy and flowers and jewelry bought with his evil drug cartel money. Despite his gifts, I silently loathed him and his wicked ways. I never allowed him to kiss me, although he tried on many occasions. If he had kissed me, I would have vomited right then and there. I hated him that much. I had repeatedly said, "I want to save myself for that special day."

As I lay on my side in the dirt bleeding to death Federal agents continue to swarm the town square. I watch through the expanding haze as little girls and boys stare wide-eyed. Their bittersweet tears stream from unblinking, tearful eyes. They do not know why their mamas and papas and older brothers and sisters are being handcuffed and led away by strangers.

Of course, they are too young to know how lucky they are. Someday they will be thankful for their deliverance from a life of drugs and crime. I suddenly feel content, at ease. Knowing children and other innocents in the village are now out of harm's way gives me a sense of joy.

Ghostly shadows reach out to envelop my being until I am floating. I can no longer feel the pain that wracked my body just moments before. I can feel that my heart has stopped its beating. I am at peace. I am ready to go.

What's this? My head is throbbing. Now the pain in my side is intense yet again. Am I alive, or is this how it feels to die? Wait! Someone is speaking to me. That cannot be - I am deaf! Yes, someone is speaking to me - speaking to me in my mind! I recognize these thoughts. They belong to...

Lindsial!

"Eva? Eva, please come back to me! Do not allow it to

take you away again. Eva, please listen to me, I beg you!"

I say in my mind, "I am dying Lindsial. I failed all of you. As punishment, this thing in my mind has recreated my past. It is delivering Miguel's finishing vengeance. He shot me, Lindsial. It hurts dreadfully bad. I thought I was to live, but I am being punished for failing you. It is the only way, Lindsial. I shall miss you. I love you so much!"

Lindsial conveys, "Eva, do not allow this thing, or whatever it is, to deceive you! You did not fail us, Eva. We are here on your Isle, your Isle of Spardom. It is beautiful, Eva, wondrously, gloriously beautiful! You delivered us, Eva. Dispel that thing's thoughts from your mind."

My mind pleads, "What is this you are telling me? Am I not dying? Are we truly on the Isle? Please tell me more, Lindsial · my mind is full of contradictory thoughts. I can feel the pain, Lindsial. It hurts from my head to my upper thigh. The thing said it was going to punish me for my failure. It wants to take me away, Lindsial. Please don't let it take me away, Lindsial, please..."

"You are fine, Eva, well somewhat fine I guess. We just entered Spardom on a barren field covered with huge boulders and rocks. You apparently hit hard and fell a ways to the ground. You've bruised your side terribly. I looked · the bruise is on the same side as the bullet wound, Eva. That is why this thing is trying to trick you to remember the shooting because you are in pain. Otherwise, you are okay. So concentrate, Eva, concentrate! Open your eyes!"

I open my eyes wide and stare into Lindsial's beautiful, light blue sightless eyes. With my fingertip, I reach to catch a teardrop as it slips from her eye. I bring my fingertip along with her teardrop to my lips with a kiss. I smile and say aloud, "Thank you, Lindsial. Please do not cry."

"You are welcome, Eva," Lindsial replies out loud. "You gave me such a fright. It pains me to know you undergo that evil thing's torment. I love you too much to know you are hurting the way you do."

I reply, "I am sorry to have frightened you, Lindsial. I guessed I blacked out after seeing all those brilliant lights.

Then my thoughts retreated back to the day Miguel shot me."

"Please do not apologize, Eva," Lindsial's lips plead. "The others and I blacked out as well. However, we didn't land as hard as you, and we didn't fall ten feet like you did." She laughs. "So, we're in better shape than you by a wide margin."

She continues speaking. "I was able to read your thoughts, your memories. I could sense you standing in the courtyard with that evil man pointing his gun at your head. You were brave, Eva, so wonderfully brave. When that thing possessed your mind once more, telling you to stop living, I had to intervene. I am afraid that whatever it is, its power is much stronger than my own. I could barely enter your thoughts while it had you under its spell."

"Thanks," I say. "I do not know how I could survive these intrusive thought episodes without you. Now, please tell me about the others. Are they here? Are they safe? Is Andrial here? Is he okay? And you, Lindsial, are you okay? Were you hurt?"

Lindsial laughs, and then she says, "Why can't you just ask one question in a sentence rather than three or four questioning sentences? I can't keep track." She laughs again. "Everyone is here and everyone is safe. Donas skedaddled to explore." Lindsial points to my right. "The ocean is over there. Ariel-e is replenishing her core and gathering seafood for our dinner. Andrial is off in the distance exploring the shoreline. I'm fine too."

My left side aches. I lift my blouse a bit as I sit up. I also pull my skirt down slightly. I look at the bruise. The contusion is gigantic. The bruise's disgusting-looking blackish-blue discoloration runs from my shoulder blade to my upper thigh. The scar, where Miguel's bullet entered my body, is bright red and hot to the touch.

I say, "What in the world happened to me? Do we know where we are? Do we know what part of the Isle we have come to?"

Lindsial replies, "Well, as best as I can figure, you

came to rest on that boulder there." She points to a massive boulder ten feet high that's three or four feet from where I'm sitting. "Then I guess you rolled off of it and fell onto the rocks. I have no clue on what part of the Isle we landed."

I say, "My goodness, no wonder I'm aching all over. Was anyone else injured badly?"

Lindsial replies, "Not really. We have a few minor bruises, cuts and the like, but nothing serious, nothing as terrible as your injuries. I just wish we could have picked a better spot to land. These plentiful little lookalike rocks are unmerciful. Be careful where you step. They seem to be everywhere. It would appear you also hit your head. You were unconscious for a long time. You bloodied the side of your head when you fell. You may have a concussion. Let me feel it. I want to sense in my mind how deep it is."

As Lindsial examines me, I gingerly touch the left side of my head with my fingers. I can feel the dried, caked blood in my hair. That explains the severe headache. "This is a glorious way to begin my reign," I say with a laugh. "It will take a week or so before this bruise fades. I am relieved the others are okay. So, what's our plan?"

"Eva, it's all up to you," Lindsial's lips say with earnest. "Andrial has a topographical map of the Isle with him as he explores. Donas had stolen it from that nasty General Powers a split-second before you uttered the spell. He gave the map to Andrial. He figured Andrial might as well have it since Andrial will consult it often as he walks. Donas also repossessed our weapons before the spell took effect. Unfortunately, he did not have enough time to retrieve our extra sets of clothing and toiletries. You have to admit, Donas is one cunning elf."

"Yes, he is, and quick-thinking on his behalf," I say. "Well, I guess we should find ourselves a safe and comfortable campsite near the trees. Then await word from Donas and Andrial and see what Ariel·e will bring us for supper. I don't know about you, but I'm hungry. We didn't have lunch at that rotten place." I laugh. "It's probably a good thing · they would have laced our food with knockout drugs."

"I'm hungry as well," Lindsial's lips reply. "Eva, I feel it necessary to discuss a few things with you while the others are away. Do you mind?"

"Sure, go ahead," I say with a smile. "What is on your mind? Oh, don't bother. I can tell, and the answer is I agree, but with one condition."

"And what is that one condition?" Lindsial's lips say. She tilts her head and shrugs her shoulders mischievously.

For sure she has already read my mind and knows what I am about to say. I have done the same. Even so, we continue to voice our thoughts out loud. It is good practice to say our thoughts out loud. That way, when the others are around, they will feel as if they are part of every conversation. Even so, Lindsial and I will continue to use our thought transference powers often.

I say, "I agree the others should address me by my rightful title or milady as you suggest, as should you. Nevertheless, I am positive it will take a while for me to get used to all this nonsensical pageantry. I do insist, when you and I are alone, or when we are exchanging telepathic thoughts, you call me Eva. Is that agreeable with you?"

"Yes," Lindsial answers with a cheerful laugh. "Anything you say your Excellency, Milady Eva Roblins, Princess of Spardom."

I laugh in response and say, "Oh stop. Now, let's see if we can find a suitable site to spend the night. Perhaps that area over there will do." I point to an area near the forest. It's circular-shaped, about twenty or twenty-five feet in diameter. Tall boulders six or seven feet tall practically enclose it on three sides. The enclosure's only opening faces the stream. That is convenient. Low hanging branches shade it from the sun. There is no protection from the rain. If and when it rains, we will get drenched.

I say, "Judging by the temperature in the shade right now, I expect it will be somewhat chilly after it gets dark. Since we do not have anything with us but the clothes on our backs, we should try and build a fire. Do you know how to start a fire, Lindsial? I tried it once as a teenager during a camping trip with my Papa. I failed miserably."

"No, Eva, I do not know how to make fire," Lindsial's lips say. "However, you do. I can tell you the spell now if you'd like. I have heard the spell spoken many times. As you know, I have no powers to summon magic. I will convey the spell to your mind so you can pronounce it properly."

Lindsial shows me the proper hand movements and, through thought transference, the spell to create fire. As she runs off to gather firewood, I decide to give the spell a go. I stare at a stack of twigs on the ground. With my arm and fingers stretched before me, I silently think *credo auduro!*

I jump up and down like a child and laugh at the top of my lungs. The spell ignited the twigs! I point to a large tree limb lying on the ground and once again think in my mind, *credo auduro!* Bright orange flames completely cover the log.

"This is breathtaking!" I exclaim aloud. "Is there any way I can control this spell - you know, can I make a huge bolt of fire, stuff like that?"

"Yes, there are variations of the spell we can teach you," Lindsial conveys in her mind. "All the same, I suggest we slowly proceed before you perform an enchantment you cannot control. We don't want you burning down the forest." She laughs and then conveys, "You can always say the words out loud as you think them with your mind. In fact, I suggest you practice saying them aloud for now. Otherwise, one slip of the words in your mind and we could have a disaster on our hands."

"Okay," I say with an add-on moan of disappointment. I truthfully want to create and control a huge fire bolt, similar to what I saw in comic books as a child. However, I know Lindsial is one hundred percent correct. I must be patient, or something disastrous could happen.

"All right, Lindsial. I will try to be patient and take it

one spell at a time." Then I whisper, "I have the strangest feeling Donas is trying to connect with me, at least I think it's him. Are you also able to read his thoughts?"

Lindsial says, "No, I cannot read his thoughts. He must be too far away for my powers to work. My powers only work over a certain distance. But goodness, it appears your telepathic power is getting stronger if you can sense his thoughts, especially from a distance. The increased power of your telepathy is great news, great news indeed! Try to concentrate, Eva. Erase everything else from your mind, to include my thoughts. Attempt to connect with his mind and his mind only."

I do as Lindsial says. I close my eyes and concentrate. After a few moments, I begin to receive Donas' thoughts clearly in my mind. His thoughts say, "…up a tree outside creatures' cave, many miles from where we entered Spar-dom. I heard voices. I peeked into the cave. It was nearly pitch-black inside except for a large fire at the distant end of the cave. My presence inside the cave was concealed by a large kettle…" Donas continues relating in his mind what he saw inside the cave.

After a few moments, I convey to Lindsial, "Donas says there are hideous beasts inside a cave. He says there are many of them. He is safe, up a tree. He will pass along more info if he sees anything of importance."

She conveys, "Did he describe the beasts?"

"Yes, as a matter of fact he did. Let's see if I can recall everything he said. He said the creatures have three eyes in the middle of their foreheads. Their skin is like leather. They have disgusting-looking bumps over their bodies comparable to knots on a buckled tree. The beasts are brown in color and powerful-looking. Donas said he did not recognize the exact dialect they were speaking. He said it is similar to the elvish language Fortunomy. He could under-stand most of the words although some were difficult to discern."

"Those must be *spargnarls*," Lindsial conveys. I am glad she is using telepathy. Otherwise, I would be unable to comprehend the word on her lips had she spoken it out loud. It is a strange word, to say the least. Both syllables give me the impression that they sound the same. I some-times have difficulty pronouncing words that have rhyming syllables. I continue to read Lindsial's thoughts.

"Spargnarls are revolting creatures. They live in caves. They are mostly carnivores. They have formidable strength and are very tall. If I remember correctly, they are thirteen feet or so when fully mature. They're nearly doubled in two when they stand and walk. That's probably from the heavy knots or gnarls on their bodies. They hunt in packs by trapping their prey with snares made of rope. As Donas said, their language is similar to that of elves. Fortunately, many, but not all, are dim-witted. Some are extremely in-telligent. Surprisingly, they can move fairly quickly through the woods. Given their size they make a colossal hullabaloo when they walk. We will surely know if they come this way."

Lindsial is gathering firewood a few dozen paces from where I stand. I want to say the word aloud since it is for-eign to me. I stroll over and tap her on her shoulder. When she looks up, I carefully say the word aloud. "*Spargnarls* is that correct?" She nods.

I say, "I can imagine they are disgusting by how you and Donas described them. But tell me, Lindsial, how do you know what they are? You have never been to Spardom. You said that yourself."

"No, Eva, I have not been here before now." With a lighthearted laugh, she adds, "I am a castaway on this Isle as much as you and the other elves. You see, in the elf kingdom we elves grow up as children hearing stories about ancient lands. Some tales are true, and some tales are nothing but make-believe myths. I assume I heard a tale of spargnarls once or twice, probably from my parents. When you described the creatures to me, I somehow knew what they were."

"Ah, I see," I say. "Since they are no threat to us right now, perhaps we should carry this firewood to our little campsite and get a fire going. What do you say I use some more of my magic, eh?"

My heart is fluttering as I say this. It was thrilling when I tossed and slid things in my apartment by using my spells. But making fire, now this is what I call a real spell! Seeing I have more room to maneuver, I can't wait to learn even more clever spells.

As the sun begins to settle near the horizon, the temperature drops noticeably. Despite the sudden chill in the air, we should have no problem keeping warm. Lindsial and I gathered an ample amount of tree limbs and brush to keep the fire blazing throughout the night. I only wish the others would hurry back to our camp, especially Ariel·e. I'm hungry as a bear, and oh · do I ever craze a mug of coffee with hazelnut cream!

CHAPTER FOURTEEN

BIRDSEYE VIEW OF SPARDOM

I watch as Ariel·e walks to our do-it-yourself campsite. She is toting a large basket woven from strands of kelp. The basket is expertly designed and completely waterproof. It even includes a handle on either side for ease in carrying a heavy load. The basket reminds me of old fashioned chubby wicker tubs I used to see at roadside fruit stands when I was a child. I now know why Ariel·e spent a great deal of time in my apartment weaving baskets of all shapes and sizes.

I peer inside the basket. It is filled halfway to the lip with a mixed bag of freshly caught fish. "Wow, this is like super remarkable," I say aloud. "You are something, Ariel·e! Thank you for catching so many different kinds of fish. They look splendid. Allow me to compliment you on your basket weaving. The basket doesn't leak, and it is quite sturdy."

Ariel·e smiles brightly. "I thank you, milady. Please tell me, how would you desire tonight's evening meal? Would you prefer your fish steamed, served sashimi style, or as kebabs? If you prefer steamed or sashimi, seaweed lining the inside of the basket can serve as a moist, but delicately salted, mouth-watering delight." She laughs adding, "If you desire kebabs, we can gather twigs of the suitable thickness to serve as skewers to roast our fish over the fire."

"Goodness," I reply. "Our first dinner on Spardom and we have three delicious entrees from which to choose. I think steamed will do quite well if you do not mind."

"As you wish, milady," Ariel-e replies. She is beaming from ear to ear. "I shall return to the ocean to gather oysters and clams to go with the fish. It will be an honor to prepare milady's first meal on Spardom. I trust she will enjoy it."

Ariel-e curtsies. She curtsies to be cute rather than to be formal. She exclaims, "But first, we need to keep these little darlings of the sea fresh." I watch in amazement as Ariel-e performs a water spell. She is encasing each fish in a cube of ice.

"Your personalities are amazing," I convey to Lindsial. "And Ariel-e's manner is wonderfully proper and charmingly poignant. She is too sweet! I am both happy and relieved. Each of you has the temperament of a saint. With your combined powers and given what I have learned and hopefully will gain knowledge of, we should be fine. Goodness, if only I knew why we were here."

"Thank you for the compliments," Lindsial conveys. "As to why we are here, that is, without a doubt, the million dollar question of the day. Perhaps we shall know the answer soon enough."

My body is still aching. I sit down and lean my back against an ebony-colored boulder. I ponder the scenery within my view. The sky is a deep blue just like on surface earth. Delicate clouds of white are drifting in the sky. Now and then a solitary pure white bird gracefully arches in the wind just above the horizon.

There is something unusual about the bird. Whenever I look at it straight on, it abruptly dives to disappear from view. It is when I watch the bird in my peripheral vision that it begins soaring through the air once more. I have this uncanny feeling the bird is spying on me. Why else would it dive to the horizon when I look at it directly? Then again, I am quite tired. Maybe I imagine things.

The sun is setting in front of me. So, I guess I'm facing west. Then again, we are one thousand fathoms beneath the sea. I can't be certain in which direction the sun sets. Here on Spardom the sun could set anywhere, in the east, in the north. Or else it could set in the south, any number of ways. Perhaps it doesn't set at all. I will have to wait and see.

The view is spectacular from where I sit. The exceptions being the ebony-colored boulders and countless grayish-black small, mirror image rocks that dot the area. A few of the boulders loom as large as a storage shed. The majority are the size of a medium-sized dog house on surface earth.

The rocks scattered on the ground are as small as my hand. There must be thousands of them. Every rock is the same size and shape as the one next to it. How strange - something has cloned the rocks. Remarkably, they are exactly alike.

I pick one up to weigh it in my hand. I guess it weighs about six ounces, give or take. It's about three inches in diameter. It is as smooth as polished glass. I can see my reflection in its looking-glass sheen. Its edges are quite sharp. I would not want to stub my toe on it or any of its lookalike cousins.

I toss the rock to the ground. It lands precisely in the spot from where I retrieved it. That is odd. I could have sworn I tossed it farther than it landed. I must be more tired than I thought.

As I continue looking around, I am pleased with what I see. Majestic tall trees line the banks of the gently flowing stream to my left. Lovely green fields with clumps of brownish grass that resemble wheat are to my right. I can also see rolling hills of red flowers beyond the fields. Just as Raymond described them in his email, the flowers flicker like delicate crimson embers beneath the sun.

In front of me, beyond the boulders and rocks, I can just about make out windswept sandy peaks of copper-colored sand dunes. Ariel-e said the ocean was toward the low sun, just beyond our encampment's line of sight. I plan to explore the water's edge at daybreak.

A dense forest of massive trees is behind me. The forest looks shadowy and unfriendly. If the huge girths of trees on its periphery are any indication, it is no small wonder the wooded area looks menacing. Lindsial and I could not reach half-way around a few of the smaller tree trunks with our arms outstretched and fingertips touching.

I close my eyes and sigh dreamily. Ah, but Spardom feels so much more blissful than surface earth. I cannot think of a more beautiful and serene place on earth - well, below surface earth. The landscape is spectacular. The company is enjoyable, and the air clean and fresh. The temperature is still cozily warm, at least here in the sun where I sit. One could effortlessly fall fast asleep merely by imagining all the beauty that surrounds.

As you would expect, I am fast asleep in nothing flat. As I fall deeper into sleep, the strangest dream enters my mind. I am flying parallel to the ground. I have not flown in my dreams since I was a little girl. I am soaring high in the sky like a graceful bird. Perhaps I am the very bird I thought was spying on me. Then again, maybe I see what the bird sees as it soars through the air.

But wait - this cannot be. The bird I saw off in the distance was flying above the ocean. I am flying over a forest. I wonder if it is the same forest that abuts our campsite. On the other hand, maybe this is nothing more than a vivid figment of my imagination. After all, that's what makes dreams so exciting. They appear to be real.

Before long I can make out a desolate wasteland as it comes into view. It is a desert. Now it makes perfect sense to me. The bird must have met me on the outer edge of the forest where I sat. Then it scooped me up to carry me above the forest. Now, with me on its back, it is flying over the desert. That is the only logical explanation. But a bird carrying me aloft · I must be crazy!

I soar effortlessly in the air currents above the expansive, featureless wilderness of the desert for what seems like an eternity. The barren region's vastness appears to stretch forever. It is beautiful in a wild and rugged, serene kind of way. Of course, given my deafness, everything is serene to me. Perhaps I should have said tranquil or restful? In either case, I trust you know what I mean. It looks delightfully peaceful and heart-stopping beautiful.

Everything below me, as far as the eye can see, is brown, except for a splotch of green here and there. And look! There is a lake far off to my left. And I can see a stream and hills and valleys and what looks like crisscrossing trails that go on forever. Or are they dirt roads?

At this moment in time, an interesting thought enters my mind. I have this uncanny feeling as if I am flying. However, I experience no movement. Nor do I feel the wind in my face. Perhaps I am not flying at all. Maybe I'm still at the campsite. Then again, maybe it's a figment of my imagination, a dream that seems too real to be true!

Suddenly, out of nowhere, I sense unexplainable foreboding. The bland desert scene is changing into a cluster of mountains. In an instant, I am approaching the border of the land I somehow know I am not welcome. I am not certain how I know this. I just do. Sinister evil penetrates my heart with sharp pains. Ripples of stinging shivers crawl up and down my spine. In this instant, I know. This land is where the Evil One dwells on the Isle of Spardom.

I soar safe and sound in seemingly endless circles beyond the fortress' periphery. As I do, the finer points of what I see enter my mind. From my safe vantage point high in the sky, I can see that the fortress is massive and impenetrable. Something begins to speak to my mind. Are these thoughts of the bird? Then again, am I the one who somehow knows firsthand all the details of what I see and what I sense in my mind?

Surprisingly, I seem to know quite a bit of the landscape below. Magigro sits on the northeastern end of the Isle to the east of Lake Namoni and the Hidden Valley. The kingdom of Banned Borders lies to its south. The desert, over which I just flew, lies to the west. The desert region is called the Land of Abeti.

Magigro is an agriculturally rich land inhabited by two-headed, four-armed trolls. The laboring creatures work the fields by day and well into the night. They inhabit caves located within the fortress walls. The numerous gaping caves are natural rock formations. The impenetrable fortification that surrounds the caves is unnatural, forged by hand. The fortification's walls consist of solid granite blocks. The walls are seven feet thick and fifty feet high. The fortification is in the center of Magigro.

Soldier trolls stand guard as lookouts on the fortress walls. About a third of the soldier trolls carry sword and shield. The remaining soldier trolls are archers. Each of the archer's quivers holds twenty iron-tipped arrows.

Trolls also man four gigantic, impenetrable gates, the only entrance points into the extensive fortress. These trolls bear shield, sword, *and* spear. All of the trolls wear identical armored headdress on both of their heads. They wear an iron breastplate to protect their upper body.

Since trolls have four arms, they can shoot with bow and arrow and fight with spear or sword while holding a shield. With two heads, they can look in two directions at once. They are formidable warriors. Their uncanny strength and bizarre two-headed, four-armed capabilities are frightening.

Inside the wall's perimeter, a dozen or so catapults are ready to unleash their doom. Huge slabs of granite piled next to the catapults serve as deadly ammunition.

The ruler of Magigro and the fortress is King Parston. He is not a troll. He is a human, a wicked man who destroys his enemies without hesitation and with no remorse. He takes no prisoners. The sea bore him on a raft many generations ago. Legends say he has not aged one day since being cast ashore on the Isle.

My mind unexpectedly begins to capture an ongoing conversation of significance. I somehow single it out amongst all others. King Parston is shouting at the troll sorcerer he calls Felcio.

At eight feet, Felcio is much taller than other trolls. Most trolls are six foot in height. He is wearing a green robe with satin cuffs and ruffled collars that adorn his two necks. I focus all of my attention on the conversation between him and King Parston.

"You insolent fool. How many times must I tell you?" The king demands.

"But your highness," Felcio cries. "The elf is helpless without the medallion. Likewise, the medallion is powerless without the elf. I know this to be true as the Chronicles portrayed it. Hence, I implore you to tell me what it is you wish me to do."

King Parston shouts, "You are wrong, Felcio! The Chronicles are wrong! Yes, the medallion increases the elf's power the longer she bears it upon her breasts. However, her magic is already potent I tell you - perhaps more potent than your own! She is merely unaware of its power.

"So let me say again, Felcio - it is not the medallion I want, it is the elf. The medallion is nothing more than an ornament to me. Go back to your chamber, search your crystal glass and locate her. Then bring me the elf I tell you, bring me the one they call Eva Roblins. She is the one who dares to call herself Princess of Spardom!"

"As you wish master, I will have the elf brought to you as soon as we capture her," Felcio replies. "I must ask, however - will she know the spell to open the Enchanted Gate? For it is what is behind the Enchanted Gate I do believe you honestly seek."

King Parston says, "You ask too many questions you wretched sorcerer. I should strike you down at this moment and end your miserable ways. But I am in your father's debt. On his deathbed, I swore I would let no harm come to you. Now go away and use your magic that is, if you still possess any. Consult your crystal glass and find me that elf!"

I watch as Felcio bows deeply. He slowly backs away, for one never turns his back to the king. After he departs the king's chamber, Felcio does not proceed directly to his chamber as King Parston directed. Instead, he visits the chamber of Zarof, the Great Wizard of the Land of Abeti. Zarof is visiting Magigro. My mind now focuses on the sorcerer and wizard's conversation.

"Let the greedy king have his elf," Felcio stammers to Zarof as he uncorks a bottle of wine. "We must have the elf's medallion. It will give us unimaginable power."

As Zarof takes a cup of wine offered by Felcio, he says, "Ah, Felcio, you too have become greedy in your old age. You have become less wizened as well. You said yourself to the king a mere moment ago - the medallion is powerless without the elf and vice versa."

"Yes, I said that to the king," Felcio responds. "You and I both know that if the elf is to die, the medallion's allegiance will be to the one who carries out the task."

"You?" grunts Zarof. "You wish to become ruler of the Isle - ridiculous. You are rude and vile, a nasty-smelling, brainless troll who learned his trade from books. No man, elf, dwarf, or phantom on this vast Isle will follow you!"

Although he does not like the insults, Felcio nevertheless forces a smile. As he cowers in front of all powerful wizard Zarof, he whispers meekly "I am not referring to me, Zarof. It is you who should become the leader of the Isle."

"Hmm, that does sound enticing, Felcio," Zarof says. "Perhaps I was a bit too unkind a moment ago when I insulted you. I take back what I said about you being brainless. On the other hand, I meant everything else I said, every last bit of it."

Felcio asks, "But the key question is when we find the elf will she have the wherewithal to open the Enchanted Gate? It is what lies behind the Enchanted Gate that shall reward us with undreamed supremacy and riches. If anyone can open the Enchanted Gate, it is Eva Roblins, the one they call Princess of Spardom."

My mind watches as Zarof walks toward a tall object that stands in a shadowy corner of his chamber. He casts aside the dusty cloth that conceals the object. It is a looking glass, a vague mirror as black and opaque as the darkest depths of death. Zarof turns to face the mirror. I can hardly stifle a cry of torment as his reflection slowly appears.

A large gray reptile, with four expansive wings and a tail with spiked barbs, is reflected in the mirror. Crusty scales cover the creature's body. Spiked barbs protrude from each of its four wingtips. The creature's two heads are those of a hideous-looking human being. The ghastly image in the mirror looks like the devil himself!

Now I sense scornful words that pierce my mind like taunts of chilling omens. The frightening creature in the mirror seems to stare straight into my eyes as its words taunt, "Ah, Eva Roblins, I am coming for you. It is only a matter of time. So prepare yourself. In the meantime, do enjoy the company of your fellow elves. For they shall soon die one by one. You shall watch as they suffer unspeakable torment.

"Afterward you shall give me everlasting life. For it is I - it is I who shall reign as King Immortal on surface earth and the Isle of Spardom. Along with you, my dear elf, Eva Roblins - for you shall be granted your wish. I shall place you on your throne, but not as Princess of Spardom. I shall seat you as Queen of Spardom beside your everlasting husband, the immortal King Zarof of Spardom."

CHAPTER FIFTEEN

KINDLY CAMPSITE ROCKS

I am now wide awake. I vigorously shake my head. I want to rid my mind of the frightening scenes and conversations I have just witnessed. In my peripheral vision, I notice the bird continues to soar above the ocean as before. Just to confirm my suspicions I look directly at it. It descends straight away to the horizon out of view.

I know for certain the bird does not want me to look directly at it. But why would it not want me to look at it that way? It must recognize I know it is the same bird that somehow carried my mind to Magigro. Then again, just maybe, the bird and I are one and the same. No, that is impossible and unmistakably crazy. I am a former human turned elf. Now I'm talking about being a bird? Nope · I am not going to fly down that path!

I glance over my shoulder at the campsite. Lindsial is sitting on a log as she plays her harp. Seeing that she has her harp on the Isle surprises me. Perhaps Donas grabbed it for her before we left surface earth. I hope he brought their flutes as well. Lindsial looks so peaceful and happy. I smile as her soft brown hair seems to float delicately in the unseen breeze.

Ariel·e is cooking dinner. Let me correct myself. Dinner is cooking all by itself. It has to be. The woven basket is a good distance away from the campfire. Bubbly steam flees from its inside like clouds of boiling mist. Well, I will be darned · Ariel·e's water magic strikes again! Ariel·e ap-pears to be singing as she dances in place. I cannot help but smile · she's always singing as she acts out a story of some sort in her mind.

I notice Andrial has returned. He is sitting close to the fire, undoubtedly warming himself since it is a bit chilly. He is peeling tubers with a broken seashell. The tubers, when cooked, are a dull purple in color. They remind me of the delicious purple tubers I ate while I was on assignment in the Philippines. Filipinos call those tubers *ubi*. Ubi is a primary ingredient in jams and candies. I wonder how An-drial is handling the tubers without gloves. Raw ubi tubers have a sap that stings the hands. Then again, this is Spar-dom, so maybe these tubers are different. Or, more likely, the stinging sap doesn't bother elves.

Andrial notices I am looking at him. He signs, "Have a good nap, milady?" I smile and nod my head in response. Then I sign, "I am afraid I napped far too long. How was your walk?"

He signs in response, "It was good, milady. I did not see much, but I heard quite a bit." I reply in ASL saying, "Okay, if it's all right with you, let's discuss it during din-ner."

I convey to Lindsial, "Can you tell me where Donas is? Has he returned?"

Lindsial does not answer me via thought transference. Instead, she walks over to me and replies aloud, "We do not know, milady. We thought maybe you could tell us, that he may have tried to connect with you while you were nap-ping."

Lindsial is speaking vocally for the benefit of the oth-ers. I appreciate her doing so. I need to get in the habit of speaking aloud when I am with the others.

"No, unfortunately, I have not," I reply out load. "I can only hope he is okay. It is nearly dark, and he cannot move quickly after nightfall." I then say via thought transference, "Were you able to read the thoughts in my mind just before I awakened?"

Lindsial conveys, "Yes, sort of, at least I think so. In any event, I am frightened for you, Eva. The message from that thing sounds evil and dreadfully immoral. Whatever it is, its telepathic powers are so strong I was able to read its thoughts. It was - it was as if it was standing beside me. But no, that cannot be."

She tilts her head in thought for a few moments. With a puzzled look on her face, she adds, "Now that I think of it, I was not reading its thoughts - it was certainly too far away for that. I was reading your thoughts, Eva. It was like you were there, witnessing firsthand what was being said. The thoughts did not come from the other's mind - they came from yours! But how could that be? I sensed you were napping right here." She points to where I am sitting.

"And, unless I'm mistaken, you haven't moved an inch. So, how in the world did I discern its thoughts, unless - no, that's not possible, right? There's no way you could be in two places at once, Eva! You were here all along! Besides, you couldn't possibly travel a great distance in such a short period, right?"

"I do not know, Lindsial. There is one thing I do know for certain. I somehow understood everything that was happening at a location far from here, perhaps on the far side of the Isle. It was like I was dreaming. I was accompanying a bird. My soaring through the air felt real, except I felt no movement, no wind rushing around me. It was a weird sensation, to say the least.

"Maybe, just maybe, and I know this sounds crazy - maybe *I was the bird flying through the air*. I don't know. I honestly don't know. It is somewhat confusing. In any event, I was circling in the air, and I saw everything below. Plus I understood in my mind everything being said. I had flown over the forest, then over a desert on my way...

"Lindsial, I know this is hard to believe, but I saw a fortress! I saw trolls! They are two-headed beasts with four arms! I also know what he wants. I know what the Evil One wants, Lindsial. He has accomplices, too - a mortal who calls himself king and a troll sorcerer. The Evil One, who has been conveying thoughts in my mind, is called Zarof. The king is Parston, and the king's sorcerer is Felcio.

"But that is enough for now. Although I dozed, I am more tired than ever. I feel as if I have returned from a long journey. Who knows, eh? Perhaps I have. I will narrate everything I have learned during dinner."

Lindsial's thoughts say, "Eva, I know you want to take a break before we discuss it further. Even so, I need to ask you something very important. Are you saying you know who this thing is? If so, your powers have gotten much stronger! It is remarkable you were able to penetrate his mind."

I stare at Lindsial quizzically for a few moments. I convey, "No - I do not believe I penetrated his mind. It was amazing, Lindsial. It was as if I was there! I was in the chamber! I was listening in on conversations, reading lips, or sensing things in my mind! But, of course, that is impossible. At least I think it is. Please give me a bit more time to unravel the confusing parts before I tell you and the others everything I learned."

"I understand, Eva," Lindsial conveys. "But whatever you do, you must try to block him from reading your thoughts. You do not want him to know what you have discovered. And oh, before I forget, please let me try to sense what's happening with that cut on your head."

I lower my head for her to feel my scalp. She says aloud, "It doesn't appear to be oozing gooey stuff anymore. I can feel scabs are forming over the wound, so it's not as deep as I feared. It should heal nicely. Keep it clean, okay?"

As Lindsial scurries away to resume her harp playing, I cannot help but wonder if my - what had Kristopher called it? Yeah, clairaudience - I cannot help but wonder if my clairaudience power is beginning to kick in. Maybe it came into play while I slept. It is the only logical explanation of how I knew what was being said. But how does that explain the things I saw? I saw the fortress, two-headed, four-armed trolls, Zarofs chambers and · I shiver when I recall its reflection. Perhaps I saw the devil himself!

Then again, perchance all of it was due to my claircognizance powers, my ability to foresee the future. Perhaps those powers caused me to see what being said in the future rather than what was being said at the moment? But that doesn't explain how I got from here to there and back again in an hour or so, or however long I napped. Nor does it explain how I sensed flying like a bird. It is all too confusing to think about right now. So I close my eyes and nap some more. This time nothing unusual invades my dreams.

Shortly after I awaken, the sun sets. As we warm ourselves by the fire, we recount the day's adventures. I provide details of what I saw and heard in my mind as I flew like a bird. I purposely leave out parts. I have to sort out some of what I experienced before I can discuss it further.

We also talk about our miraculous escape from surface earth. It appears the others saw what I saw, sluggish movements of the guards, General Fuller barking orders, Cindy smiling, the interpreter sneering. They also witnessed brightly spinning kaleidoscopic colors as we slowly faded from surface earth. Our bodies uplifted just prior to losing consciousness.

We were not supposed to have lost consciousness when we left surface earth. Lindsial says I must have mispronounced the words. We all laugh at this disclosure, quite happy and relieved we made it to Spardom. We could have ended up somewhere else entirely, Antarctica, the Sahara Desert, or on the moon. It doesn't make a bit of a difference. We're here, and we didn't have to use General Powers' brainless machine to do it.

While we enjoy a mouth-watering dinner of steamed fish, clams, and oysters, we tease each other and tell jokes. Despite our somewhat jovial mood, Donas' absence troubles us. For me, it feels like I have somehow failed the others. I'm supposedly their leader, the Princess of Spardom. We've been on the island less than one full day, and already one of us is missing.

"I wonder where he could be," Ariel·e suggests. "It is not like him to miss a delicious meal of steamed clams. It is his favorite seafood."

"Perhaps he ventured so far into the forest he could not make it back before nightfall," Andrial signs to me. "You know how sluggish he gets when nightfall hits."

After Lindsial reads Andrial's thoughts, she automatically repeats his comments out loud for Ariel·e's benefit. She and the other elves have been around each other for many years now. It is a force of habit for Lindsial to repeat Andrial's thoughts straight away.

"I have not received any more of Donas' thoughts," I say aloud. "I must admit I am worried. Even if he is slow in returning, he should be able to contact me. Then again, if he is a good distance away he may not think I can read his thoughts."

"Or," Ariel·e lips say, "He may be asleep high up in a tree where it is safe. He tends to be sound asleep and snoring away when dusk approaches." She laughs. "Perhaps he will try to return to us at daybreak. I will keep a pot of clams warm for him."

"Well, Andrial," I inquire, "When you heard that sound you spoke of, from what manner of beast did it come? Do you know?"

Andrial signs in response, "I have no idea what it was, but it was horrible, milady. Like a howl, or maybe an anguished cry, way off in the distance, well beyond a distant mountain range. It gave me the creeps, let me tell you. I wanted to climb to the summit of a hill so I could listen better, but I ran out of time. I thought it best to return here before dark.

"From my vantage point a ways up the hill, I did get a good look on this side of the Isle. I could not see anything moving except for high flying birds. I did not see any beasts or other land creatures. But that cry was terrifying, to say the least, and it continues up to now."

Having read Andrial's mind as he signed to me, Lindsial once again repeats for Ariel·e everything Andrial said. Let me tell you, Lindsial's one gifted elf. I think she repeated everything Andrial said word for word!

The sky is now jet·black. It appears storm clouds are moving in from the ocean. It is rather chilly. I'm shivering, despite the blazing fire I started with my credo auduro spell. I look at the others. Ariel·e and Andrial seem to be okay. Like me, Lindsial is also shivering. Even so, I know she is a resilient elf. I am certain she will not allow the night's chill to bother her.

Perhaps she has read my mind. She says, "Well, milady, Ariel·e, and you too, Andrial, we should get some sleep. We have had a trying day. I suggest three separate watches tonight. I will take the first watch. Ariel·e, please take the second. Andrial, you take the third if you please. You are undoubtedly very tired since you trekked quite a distance today."

I truly hoped Lindsial would include me in the watch rotation. However, I know it is imprudent for me to stand watch since I am now the Princess of Spardom. I smile and say, "That sounds good to me. I just napped, so I am not sleepy. I shall stay awake and keep you company as you take your watch, Lindsial."

Lindsial and I sit side by side just outside of our camp's enclosure. Our backs are warmed somewhat by the heat of the fire, yet we continue to shiver. We sit as close together as we can to share our body heat. We are discussing the day's happenings in our minds.

I convey everything I learned about King Parston, the Kingdom of Magigro and the seemingly impenetrable fortress. I describe in detail the sinful·looking two·headed, four·armed trolls guarding the fortress. I also relate the conversation between the king and Felcio, and the one between Felcio and Zarof. Lastly, I make mention of the Enchanted Gate.

By the light of the flickering flames, I notice Lindsial is nodding her head in recognition of something I have just said. "What is it?" I convey. "Did I say something that has sparked your memory?"

Lindsial conveys, "I have heard tales about the Enchanted Gate. The Elixir of Immortality is rumored to lie hidden someplace beyond the Enchanted Gate. There are other magical objects behind the gate as well · books of charms and spells and enchantment treasures. What's more, there are instruments of amazingly wonderful magic and indescribable powers. I have heard mention of the Land of Magigro as well. The kingdom came about after Princess Eva disappeared. If I recall correctly, Kristopher may have mentioned the Land of Magigro to me."

Once again, Lindsial has surprised me with her knowledge of Spardom. I convey, "Lindsial, if you knew of such things, why have you not mentioned them before now? Perhaps there is more that you know that could help us."

Lindsial's mind conveys, "My dear Eva, as I said previously · an elf hears many stories during her lifetime. I am certain most stories were nothing more than fables. Storytellers try to keep the hours of darkness exciting on otherwise dreary, starless nights. Unless I hear the name or a place, or a beast's portrayal, it is impossible for me to know what may spark my memory. Besides, and it breaks my heart to say this, I believe I have lost some of my memory. I don't know why. It only comes back to me whenever something sparks my attention. As hard as I try, I cannot seem to remember things from long ago.

"It's uncanny, Eva. I'm certain I heard the word Spardom before the briefing on surface earth. I somehow knew what spargnarls were when you mentioned them to me. And now, I recall hearing about the Enchanted Gate and Land of Magigro. Try as I do, I cannot remember anything else about them. It is like something erased my mind and my ability to recollect.

"To be honest with you, the Enchanted Gate and the

Kingdom of Magigro may be nothing more than make-believe myths. We have not seen them, so we cannot be certain they exist. Could it be this thing, this wizard Zarof you speak of, is trying to mislead you? It is quite possible you know."

"I appreciate what you are telling me, Lindsial, and I agree with your reservations. But the visions I saw in my mind, Lindsial - the visions seemed real. What my mind sensed being discussed within the fortress' walls seemed vividly authentic as well."

"Yes, I'm sure they did," Lindsial conveys. "Just the same I beg of you to consider this. Whatever powerful thing is entering thoughts into your mind, it may also be trying to control your mind. It may want you to sense what it intends for you to know, not what is, in fact, true."

As I wrap-up telling Lindsial about my mind's journey, I describe to her just about everything I sensed at Magigro. I purposely omit the part about Zarof's hideous evil-looking reflection in the mirror. I do not want to shock her needlessly. I am certain I saw the devil. At least he looked every bit the devil to me. I will not be surprised if I have terror-stricken nightmares tonight.

I kiss Lindsial on her forehead and say goodnight. As I enter our campsite enclosure, I see Andrial is lying close to the fire. Surely he is in deep sleep. His eyes move rapidly beneath his lids, and his arms twitch wildly. I can only imagine he is exhausted from today's hike. I bend to kiss his forehead. Although he is not shivering, I place more leaves on his shoulder to keep him warm.

Ariel-e has just about finished tidying up after dinner. She and I chitchat for a few moments. I give her a hug and kiss her on the forehead. She leaves to replenish her core in the ocean. She will return to assume the watch in an hour or two.

Lindsial continues her guard duty. She is invisible as she sits on a shoulder-high boulder. As the air pressure changes, she senses an imminent cloud burst is about to drench us. Understandably, she is getting more anxious with each passing minute. She says aloud to no one, in particular, "We are going to get sopping wet tonight. Tonight would be a great night to be an elf mermaid. At least Ariel-e will be comfortable standing watch when she returns."

All of a sudden her amazing power of echolocation detects the movement of many objects beneath her. The small rocks are beginning to move a bit on the sandy ground! At first their movements are random. Some move to the left, some slide gently to the right. Others move forward or backward.

Before Lindsial can react, she senses the rocks are speedily merging into three distinct groups. The three groups of rocks noiselessly slide up the boulders enclosing our campsite. They quietly fasten together to form an intertwined rainproof cover. As if on cue, the rain begins to fall. It rains a little at first, and then it rains more steadily.

Of course, Lindsial could not see what the rocks accomplished. She sensed their progress as they slid to and fro. By tracking the mass with echolocation, she realized the rocks had covered our encampment with a protective canopy.

With a wide grin on her face, she slides from her exposed perch to move beneath the shelter. Once inside, she touches the ceiling of rocks here and there with her fingers. She sighs deeply and whispers, "I do not know how you did what you did, but thank you for keeping us dry. You are by far the sweetest rocks I have ever met. I can't wait to tell our lady Eva in the morning!"

A bit later, Ariel-e arrives to stand guard. She and Lindsial giggle when Lindsial tells how bewildered she was when she sensed the rocks' movement · then how happy she was to be out of the rain. After a bit of small talk between the two of them, Ariel-e says, "Good night my dear Lindsial. Sleep tight and don't let the grayish-black rocks bite." Lindsial lies down next to me. I am sound asleep, but I unconsciously know I am now more than toasty warm sandwiched in between my two elf friends.

Ariel-e takes up her spear and reenters the downpour.

Water is her best friend. Her core will benefit from standing guard tonight in the pouring rain. As usual, she softly hums to herself.

When I wake up in the morning, the sun is shining brightly overhead, and the temperature is warm. Unbeknownst to me, the rocks had disassembled themselves as a canopy a few hours before. Then they scattered hither and dither amongst the large boulders. Lindsial will tell me about the rocks via thought transference a while later as I explore the coastline. Of course, I will not think much of it. To be honest with you, I will suspect she is pulling my leg. As events will soon show, I should have paid more attention to what Lindsial said.

I notice Lindsial and Andrial are sound asleep. Ariel-e is nowhere in sight. I presume the lovely elf mermaid has returned to the sea. I bet she is having fun. I imagine her now, flipping upside-down as she performs ocean-deep cartwheels. She is probably swimming here and there as she plays tag with other sea creatures. Then again, she may be exploring unfathomable crevices along with octopuses and other bulgy-eyed creatures.

I have never known a more free-spirited and happy-go-lucky creature than Ariel-e. I expect whatever she is doing she is having the time of her life. Then something comes to mind. I wonder if she sings beneath the waves. I'll have to ask her next time I see her.

I am raring to go. And I am greedily hungry as well. I plunge my fingers into the basket of fish and scoop out three huge handfuls of steamed goodies. I wrap each handful in a sheet of moist seaweed. The seafood is warm, and it smells delicious. It may not be bacon, eggs, and toast, but it hits the spot. But once again I think to myself - if only I could have a cup of hazelnut-flavored coffee to go with breakfast. Coffee is the only thing I truly miss about surface earth, along with Cindy, of course.

I'm ready to venture off to see the ocean and walk the shoreline. Maybe I will come across Ariel·e as she swims in the ocean. Come to think of it, I have never seen Ariel·e without her legs. I wonder what she looks like with a mermaid fin · or is it a tail? Whatever Ariel·e has in place of legs I just know it is just as beautiful as the rest of her.

CHAPTER SIXTEEN

ERANBA LIKES SECRETS

Donas has been in an enormous steel kettle since the early hours of darkness the night before. He is frantically trying to untie ropes that bind his hands behind him. Ropes also bind his legs at the ankles. Despite his struggles, he is not having much success.

He had intended to return to our campsite before sunset. He had slid off his perch high in a tree where he had been spying on the spargnarls. Then he ran at top speed in the direction of our campsite. In his haste to return, he sprung a rope trap set by the spargnarls. He found himself hanging upside-down from a tree limb. The last thing he remembered was a conversation between two spargnarls.

"Well, look what we have here, Bratle," the smaller of the two spargnarls said, "It is an itsy-bitsy, tiny elf!" The spargnarl was Eranba, one of the two spargnarls who had set the trap that ensnared Donas.

"Aw, quit your shouting Eranba, you will scare the game!" Bratle whispered as he glanced about the immediate vicinity. Bratle is Eranba's cousin. "Cut him down from the tree and make sure you bind him tightly. We do not want him to escape. We have not seen an elf in these parts for ages. Gonialit will want to question him. And make sure you don't injure him!"

After being cut down from the tree, Donas had fallen hard to the ground and landed on his back. He was knocked unconscious. When he awoke this morning, he found himself inside the large steel kettle where he sits bound by hand and foot. His back is aching, and his head hurts. Fortunately, no bones are broken - just a few bumps and bruises here and there.

Cautiously peering with his head just above the lip of the kettle, he sees countless spargnarls in the yawning, dimly lit cave. A number of spargnarls are sleeping. Others are fumbling with ropes, presumably making snares. A few others are roasting game over a roaring fire. Still others are chatting away in whispers. All of a sudden a loud ear splitting yell breaks the cave's stillness. Donas recognizes it is Eranba that is yelling. He is the spargnarl who cut Donas loose from the tree.

"He is my elf!" Eranba screams. "I found him. I cut him down from the tree. I dragged him here, and I want to keep him as a pet! Maybe I can train him to fight the trolls. He could be my bodyguard. He could! He is mine, and I want him!"

A booming voice answers, "Elves are not pets!" The voice belongs to Gonialit, chief of the spargnarl district in this part of the forest. Gonialit is a huge spargnarl, much taller and full-bodied than the others.

Gonialit continues bellowing. "Elves are wise and devi-ous. This one will trick you. I can feel it. I want you to leave him alone for now. When he awakens, I do not want you to draw nearer. Just come and tell me. I will question him to see why he is here. Do you understand, Eranba the Freak?"

"Yes, I understand," Eranba answers with a whimper. He does not like being called Eranba the Freak. Just be-cause he has no gnarls on his body, other spargnarls in the district say he looks freakish. So they bully him, calling him Eranba the Freak. However, he knows they are wrong. When he looks at his reflection in the pond, he thinks he looks better than the other spargnarls, much more handsome. He does not have hideous gnarls all over his body. They do.

He sneaks on all fours to the kettle that holds Donas. He peeks inside and sees Donas is wide awake. He also notices Donas is trying to untie his leg ropes with his teeth. Donas and Eranba's eyes meet.

Eranba shakes his head several times and whispers, "No, no, I would not do that if I were you. If you try to escape, they will bind you to the tell-the-truth board. If you do manage to escape, it will be of no use. There are traps everywhere outside the cave and all the way to the end of our district. Besides, Gonialit wants to talk with you. If you are untruthful, he will slay you for your misdeeds sooner than later. Why are you here, little elf? I like you, but I already have too many pets. Gonialit says elves do not make good pets."

"I intend you no harm, Eranba," Donas says softly. "I am here with my friends and the proud lady, Princess Eva of Spardom. I simply got lost wandering in the forest."

"Oh, you lie!" Eranba scolds. "You are trying to trick me just like Gonialit said you would. Spardom is dead. You are in the Land of Fogreia, my home and district of us proud spargnarls. The Princess of Spardom, this Princess Eva you speak of, she is nothing but a fairy tale. I like fairy tales, but only when I want to be scared or lied to for a laugh."

"She is real, I tell you, and that is the truth," Donas stammers softly. "And what is this land of Fogreia of which you speak? What happened to Spardom?"

"You ask too many questions elf," Eranba replies. He peeks around the kettle at the other spargnarls to ensure they are not listening. "But for now you are my elf. So I will provide you with answers, but only as few as I see fit.

"As I said, Fogreia is the forest of spargnarls as well as other creatures. Far to the northeast is the Kingdom of

Magigro where the ugly trolls live under the protection of King Parston. The trolls are our mortal enemy. They have been our enemy for as long as I can remember.

"The Banned Borders are far to the east of our land way beyond the desert, the Land of Abeti. It is in the Banned Borders where ghosts, goblins, and other phantoms dwell. They are unspeakably powerful beings. At least that is what I know of the Banned Borders' creatures.

"The Land of Abeti is in the Middle World as we call it. A mean and powerful wizard lives there. And to the north, well, I do not know. None has been able to pass over the tall mountains that are hidden by white clouds. But that is enough. You ask far too many questions for one who shall soon wish he had not."

"I thank you for explaining the various kingdoms," Donas whispers. "But what of Spardom, what happened to the Kingdom of Spardom?"

"We do not speak anymore of Spardom, my dear elf," Eranba boasts. "Spardom is gone. That is all I know. In addition, the Princess of Spardom is nothing more than a fairy tale like I said. I dare say you are quite small. What do you eat that makes you so tiny? Are you hungry? I could slip over to the fire and get you some food if you are hungry."

Donas realizes it is useless to ask further questions regarding the Isle of Spardom. He thinks it best to try and bargain with Eranba so the creature will release him. He tries a different tactic. He asks, "What are they going to do with me? If I tell Gonialit the truth, will he let me go free?"

"No, my little elf, Gonialit will not let you go free, whether you tell the truth or if you lie. He will use a powerful tonic so you will tell the truth. It is senseless to lie. So you will tell the truth, I promise you. When Gonialit is finished learning the truth, he will cook you in this kettle and then carve you up as bait. It is a rather nice kettle, do you not agree?"

"No, it is not a nice kettle. It is not nice at all," Donas squeaks. He adds gently, "Well, I hope you realize it would be unfortunate for him to cook me. I know far too much, things only I know and others should not. Things perhaps you should like to know as well · but no, you just want to cook me."

"What do you know, little elf? What is it an elf as small as you could know?" Eranba asks.

Donas peers above the lid at the other spargnarls. He whispers, "I cannot tell you. If I told you, then the other spargnarls would want to know how you came to know my secret. It could be far too dangerous for you to handle. We should not talk about my secret anymore. The others might hear us."

With a doubtful laugh, Eranba asks, "And what secret is that? I like secrets, as long as they are mine. In addition, you need not worry yourself about my safety." He clenches his fists, and then he slams them together. With a tenacious look on his face, he hisses, "Nothing is too dangerous for Eranba!"

"Hand me that small cup that is hanging on the hook over there," Donas says. "You can watch it disappear before your very eyes as it moves faster than a bird's flight. Before you do, you must undo my hands. I must use my hands to perform my secret magic."

"I think your secret is not possible, little elf," Eranba scolds. "Invisible disappearing is not possible. However, I am curious. I shall get you the cup so you can show me the secret. I shall be happy to watch your secret's disappearing act, as long as you do not disappear as well. I think I will keep your legs bound so you cannot escape."

Eranba unties Donas' hands. He hands Donas the cup. In an instant, the cup is in Donas' right hand, then in his left hand, then teetering on the lip of the kettle. Each movement is in a blink of an eye. Making sure Eranba's sees the cup teetering on the kettle's lip, Donas moves it again and again even faster than before. In a flash, the cup is between his legs, then resting on Eranba's hand, and then perched on top of Donas' head. The quick movements of the cup continue for another minute.

Almost immediately, Eranba is lightheaded. His three eyes are swimming, seemingly uncaring if they will ever focus once more. His dizziness is causing him to teeter. He is barely able to remain on all fours without falling. He stammers, "This is entertaining my little elf pet!"

Donas can barely stifle a laugh. Eranba looks absurdly funny with his two outer eyes crossed toward his now drooping middle eye. His eyes appear to be spinning without purpose inside his massive head.

Eranba says, "The cup moves too quickly. It makes my head spin and my eyes cross-eyed. I can hardly see straight ahead. Is this your secret? Can you show me how to do it? Then I will have a secret, and I shall keep my secret from the others. I like secrets as long as they are mine."

"Yes, I can," Donas answers. "You must allow me to go outside the cave. This kettle is too cramped, and I can barely move. I need more space to teach you the secret proper-like. Plus, my legs are aching terribly."

As you know, Donas is telling a lie. And he is getting desperate. The last thing he wants is for Gonialit to question him. He is confident he can eventually trick Eranba. Then, hopefully, he can escape.

"Aw, you are trying to trick me," Eranba whispers. "I was told you would try to make me look foolish. I may not be all that clever, but I am very smart. I am no fool."

Donas pleads, "But I am your pet elf, Eranba. I want to be your friend, too. With my secret, you will learn how to move amongst trolls undetected. And you will be a hero among all spargnarls. Just this very moment I showed you the quickness of how I make things disappear. You can learn to do it as well. Afterward, just dare them to call you Eranba the Freak when you slaughter more trolls than all other spargnarls combined!"

Donas shows his amazingly fast, secret hand tricks with the cup one more time. As Donas had hoped, Eranba eagerly frees his legs from the knotted rope. With barely a grunt or groan, Eranba lifts Donas onto his shoulder with ease. If you recall, Donas is as tall as a youngster of medium height. Eranba, while also a youngster, is over eight feet tall. Although Eranba may be much shorter than full grown spargnarls · they are nearly thirteen feet tall · compared to Donas, Eranba is a giant.

"Now you be very quiet, my pet elf," Eranba whispers. "You make one sound and I will put you back in the kettle."

With Donas riding on the back of his huge, muscular frame, Eranba slowly backs out of the cave on all fours. In short time, the two are safely outside. Hanging vines covering the cave's entrance hide them from the other spargnarls' view.

Donas recalls Eranba mentioned rope traps concealed in the vicinity. Being trapped again is the last thing he wants to happen. He persuades Eranba to walk with him along the trail. All the while he focuses Eranba's attention on his practically undetectable swift movements. Eranba shrieks with joy as Donas thrills him with indescribably fascinating bursts of high-speed delights.

Donas crawls up trees in a flash. Then more quickly than the eye can follow he hops from limb to limb. He juggles sticks and stones found along the trail in a blink of an eye. He throws sticks high in the trees and retrieves them before they can even begin to fall to the ground. He plays tag with Eranba, streaking here and there and everywhere, moving faster than Eranba's eyes can follow.

Donas keeps Eranba off-balance and spinning in place as he appears standing before the creature in one instant. In the next instant, he is to the spargnarl's left. Then he is behind Eranba, to his right, after that high above him in a tree. All the while Donas and Eranba continue down the trail gradually moving further and further from the cave.

After a few hundred yards of trail, dodging visible rope snares as they go, Eranba suddenly yells, "We should not go any further little elf. I cannot allow you to step one foot beyond this point. The traps end here. This place is also the end of my district. Now, please let me see that trick..."

Before Eranba can finish his sentence, Donas vanishes. He hurdles through the forest as quickly as he can. As he increases his distance between the spargnarl and himself, he hears Eranba's rapidly fading, threatening shouts.

"You tricked me my pet! I do not like you anymore. You took away my secret. You have shamed me. But I will find you yet again. When I do, I will make you teach me more magic secrets! If you do not, I will cook you myself!"

Donas is thankful he managed to trick the young spargnarl to escape the unthinkable, terrible fate of that horrid kettle. Nevertheless, he has not seen the last of the spargnarls. Spargnarls almost never mislead each other. To them, trickery or lying or being deceitful are as inexcusable as treachery, which they scorn. And Donas tricked them. More importantly, Gonialit will want to know more about Donas' swiftness powers. He will also want to know why an elf suddenly appears in his district after all these years.

CHAPTER SEVENTEEN

SPARGNARLS!

I am walking the shoreline as Donas is speeding through the forest toward our camp. I have been away from the campsite for the better part of two hours. The sparkling blue water and amazing white sands of the beach are incredible. Despite the beauty that surrounds, the late morning's hot sun is making me thirsty.

Darn, how could I have forgotten to bring along water? What wouldn't I do for a quenching sip of Ariel-e's deliciously cold, magically-made fresh water?

I sense Lindsial's thoughts in my mind. "I can bring you a seaweed container of cool water from the stream if you would like. Perhaps we can meet halfway. You'll get it much faster that way."

"Oh, I do not want you to make a special trip just for me," I convey. "Thank you just the same. I will head back to camp in a bit and get some water from the stream. I think I am only an hour's walk away; that is if I walk in a straight line back to the camp and don't meander too much. Besides, I might run into Ariel-e. She can fix me up with fresh water with ice to boot."

Just as I say this, I am abruptly aware of Donas' thoughts entering my mind. "Milady, milady Eva, I am returning to camp! The spargnarls held me captive last night. There is a loud commotion behind me in the distance. I believe the spargnarls are heading toward our camp! I will try to lead them to the left, away from the camp. Please tell the others and leave the camp as quickly as you can!"

Before I have time to react, Lindsial's thoughts are in my mind. "Donas cannot be too far away. I was able to read his thoughts. I am the only one here at our campsite. I imagine Ariel·e is in the ocean. I do not know where Andrial is. He will hear the spargnarls soon enough if they are making as much noise as Donas said they were. Andrial will know better than to approach the camp. Eva, you stay where you are. I will vanish from sight and let you know what is happening. With any luck, the spargnarls will see no one is here, and they will return to their cave."

I convey, "You cannot see the spargnarls, Lindsial. They may be able to detect your presence somehow! You need to get out of the camp as quickly as you can!"

"I will be okay," Lindsial's thoughts reply. "Remember, I can *see* things with my acuity power. You just find someplace safe to hide. Whatever you do, do not go into the forest. The forest is not safe. I will hide our weapons in a cluster of rocks near the stream. Be careful!"

Gonialit, ruler of the spargnarl district holds his hand high in the air. "Stop!" he commands. He is out of breath and panting. The enormous giant has been dashing through the forest with his soldiers at top speed. In their haste to catch up to Donas, the spargnarls trampled everything in their path, including luckless small saplings and thickets.

Gonialit addresses two of his most senior subordinates. They are Stanquerl and Pagriol. "Stanquerl, take your group and head to the north. Remain parallel to the shore. Before you go, have two dozen of your members join Pagriol's group." Gonialit takes a few moments to count the spargnarl's in each group.

He turns to Pagriol. "I am sending you south. There are more places along the shoreline for the elf to hide down south than up north. For this reason, I'm giving you the bulk of our strength. Like Stanquerl, make certain you stay parallel to the shore."

Addressing both subordinates, he adds, "Both of you stay on the Old Path within the confines of the forest. I will proceed directly from here westward toward the ocean with my group. Emerge from the forest when you think it is appropriate. In that way, we will put this elf in a squeeze. And this time I will not hesitate to ask questions of him.

"Sound off four times with your sea horn if you capture the elf. As usual, three blasts means stay put. Two means unite with me or with whoever made the call. One, you have found something of interest. It goes without saying five blasts means retreat. However, I do not think that will be required here given he is but one elf." He laughs loudly and says with contempt in his voice, "He may be quick, but he is alone. We are a good deal more than a hundred."

"But Gonialit," Eranba stammers, "The elf is too quick. We shall never catch him. I saw his magical secret with my own eyes. He moves faster than a lightning flash."

"Shut up, you freak fool," Gonialit shouts. "We will catch him. Then I will interrogate him. After that, I will throw his boiled entrails to the rodents. I may cook you as well, you clumsy slipshod idiot!"

Turning his attention away from Eranba, Gonialit yells, "Okay everyone, let us proceed with haste!" Then with a disapproving glare at Eranba he says, "Eranba the Freak, you go with Pagriol. After we catch the elf, you will carry him back to the cave as punishment for allowing him to escape!"

Now that they have received their orders, the spargnarls separate into three groups. They clumsily crash through the tightly packed forest as they scurry in three separate directions.

After a half-hour or so, Pagriol's clamoring group abruptly quickens its pace. Pagriol sees Donas standing motionless on the Old Path. Pagriol is a disrespectful spargnarl who flaunts authority. He is in line to assume the tribe's leadership if something happens to Gonialit. To further his standing in the tribe, he wants the glory for recapturing the elf to go to him and his group. He doesn't sound his sea horn one time as he is supposed to.

As soon as he is certain the spargnarls have seen him, Donas turns and jogs along the path. He is leading the spargnarls away from our camp. He is unaware the spargnarls have split into three groups. He also doesn't know Pagriol's group consists of fifty spargnarls. Lastly, Donas is unmindful he is leading Pagriol's group directly toward me.

I am standing behind a large boulder in the ankle-deep surf. My back is to the ocean. Every once in a while I peek from behind the boulder. All seems well. There is no sign of spargnarls. Of course, I am oblivious to the racket heading in my direction through the forest. As usual, my sixth sense is telling me something is wrong.

I lift my head to sniff the air. I get a whiff of a faint, sickening stench carried aloft by the prevailing wind. Whatever it is I smell it stinks like months old rotten eggs. I ponder my predicament. I have no weapons. They wouldn't do me much good. I'm still fairly awkward when I use them. I'm thirsty. I'm standing in ankle-deep water to the rear of a boulder. It's going to be high tide in a half a dozen hours. I am baking beneath the sun. If I don't get out of this direct sunlight, I will look like burnt toast before long. I do know a handful of spells to protect myself. Maybe I can use my moveo, credo auduro, or labor lapsus spells against the spargnarls. Well, enough about me. I wonder how the others are doing.

"Lindsial," I convey. "I have a couple questions. Have you heard anything yet of the spargnarls? Do you know if any are coming toward you? Do you know how many there are? Are the others safe? Are you safe, eh?"

Lindsial replies via telepathy, "You and your couple

questions - that was like four of five."

I cannot hear it, but I bet she's chuckling to herself right now. Once again, she is correct. I am inclined to ask a string of questions in one or more sentences from time to time. It has been that way ever since I became deaf.

She conveys, "Yes, Eva, I can hear the spargnarls now. They are noisy as they proceed. It appears they are heading in my direction. I'm still at the camp. But don't worry, I'm invisible. I will be okay. Are you safe?"

I convey, "Yes, I'm safe. Plus I'm glad you're confident all will be okay at your end. I worry about you, you know that."

I sniff the air again - whatever it is that stinks to high heaven is getting closer. "Lindsial, can you tell me if you smell a horrible stench, a nasty smell that stinks like sulfur or rotten eggs?"

"Yes, I'm getting a trace here and there," Lindsial's mind replies. "I bet it's coming from the spargnarl's offensive body odor, although I'm not certain. Why do you ask?"

"I can also smell it," my mind responds. "I think it is getting stronger by the second. Now, I could be wrong, but I believe some of the spargnarls may be heading in my direction."

"Eva, milady," Lindsial's thoughts pervade strongly, "Please tell me you're not to the left of the camp."

I ponder her question for a moment, and then I convey, "Well, I do believe I am to the left. I waded across the stream when I strolled toward the ocean earlier this morning. So let me see - yup, I'm to the left. Why?"

Lindsial's thoughts seem to shout. "Goodness, Eva, Donas said he was going to lead the spargnarls to the left of the camp! He is leading them directly to you! But that doesn't explain the smell I... Wait! I detect their presence in my mind now."

Lindsial begins to count the images forming in her mind. It is not easy since she is blind. However, she has had years of practice. More often than not she's practically one hundred percent accurate when it comes to detecting shapes and sizes.

Her mind conveys, "There seems to be a group of twenty-five to thirty spargnarls emerging from the forest in front of me. Of course, I cannot be sure since I am blind. But, it's a bunch, of that I'm certain. One massive spargnarl is in the front of the others. I bet he's their leader. He seems to be much taller and heavier than the rest. He's also the one barking orders, at least I think it is him. As I said, there could be more than twenty-five or thirty creatures. I just do not know for certain."

"Well, Lindsial, I do not want to be the one to tell you this, but..." I momentarily pause to take a peek from behind the boulder to confirm what I thought I just saw. "A group of spargnarls just emerged from the forest in front of me. Hold on a sec..."

I peer once again around the boulder to do a quick headcount. "Lindsial, I guess my group consists of forty, maybe forty-five to fifty spargnarls. Since you have a group near you, I wager there are three groups at least, possibly more. I bet they had separated before they emerged from the forest. I would have done it. It's a sensible encircling tactic, especially with the ocean providing no means of escape.

"So let me see. Given what you told me, and what I see before me, we can assume..." I do a quick calculation in my head as I count on my fingers. "Lindsial, in the worst case scenario, we can assume there are least one hundred thirty to one hundred fifty spargnarls. That is if there are three groups. If we add a fourth group, we're looking at a considerably larger number of spargnarls.

"So, if I am even close to my calculations, we are talking about some awful odds - at least as it concerns us. We're outnumbered by at least twenty-five to one. As they say on surface earth, Lindsial - It doesn't look good for the home team! I guess we'll just to have to wait them out. We don't stand a chance otherwise. I just hope they don't see me. And wow! These critters sure do stink!"

"Goodness, Eva! Where are you now? Are you well-hidden, somewhere safe where the creatures cannot see you?"

I convey, "I'm standing on the other side of a large boulder. It protrudes a half dozen feet into the ocean. I'm in six inches of water. I'm safe for now. The spargnarls are resting on a grouping of rocks just outside the forest. But, Lindsial, we need to come up with a plan. We need to do it quickly."

I jump as someone touches my shoulder. I let out a long sigh of relief. It is Donas. I grab him by the shoulders to pull him close to me in a tight embrace. As I hug him, I whisper near his ear, "I am relieved you are okay. We're in a pretty dire situation here."

I read his mind as he says, "Milady, I am so sorry to have put you in danger. If I had known you were here, I would not have led the spargnarls in this direction. Please forgive me. Where are the others? Are they safe?"

I tell Donas in a whisper all that I know up to this point. I say I am mainly worried about Lindsial. She is at the campsite and has twenty-five to thirty spargnarls nearby. I also tell Donas I would not put it past the spargnarls to have a third group to the right of our campsite. I tell him I suppose Ariel·e is safe in the ocean. I add Andrial is surely able to hear what is happening. So he is safe as well, at least I hope he is.

I ask Donas to address his thoughts to me in his mind. I want to keep our aural exchanges to a minimum. I, of course, will have to whisper to him. He cannot read minds like Lindsial and me, and he is unable to sign.

I am suddenly aware of Ariel·e's thoughts entering my mind. "Milady, please do not be alarmed. I am behind you and Master Donas, just below the water's surface. It will be dark in at least half a day. Although it's a bit of a delay, I think it best we wait until dark before we try to escape. If you need anything, please gesture with your hands. I can see you and Master Donas clearly from where I am at."

What I need more than anything is fresh water and shade from the sun. I have been without water for well over two hours now. I bet Donas could use a quenching drink as well. I'm also getting sunburned. My fair, whitish skin cannot take the sun's burning rays for much longer. With my thumb and pinky finger extended I move my hand to my lips as if I am sipping a drink. I point to Donas. He probably needs water more than I do. I wipe my sweaty brow with the back of my hand and point to my sunburned arms. I need something to cover my shoulders, neck, and arms.

In a few moments, two small containers made of sea-weed gently float toward Donas and me. Ariel-e filled the containers to the brim with cool, fresh water. Donas greedi-ly scoops up the containers. He hands one to me as he hast-ily drinks from the other. I read his mind. He has not had a drink of water since yesterday afternoon.

Moments later a large, crude-looking, sombrero-shaped hat, also made of seaweed, emerges from the ocean's depths. It is followed by a seaweed shawl. The shawl is supple and large enough to cover my shoulders. From my side of the boulder, I look to ensure the spargnarls cannot see me as I get into my marine outfit. I place the sopping wet hat on my head and drape the salty wet shawl over my shoulders. I feel instant relief from the burning sun. Donas and I sip the cool water from the woven seaweed contain-ers. I turn my head to mouth silently to the ocean, "Thank you."

Ariel-e's thoughts reply, "Milady is most welcome. I am honored to help. I shall away for now to venture in the vi-cinity of the campsite. I will return shortly with more fresh water."

Donas tells me in his mind that a horn abruptly trum-peted three times off in the distance. Peeking from behind the boulder, I watch as the spargnarls suddenly become restless. Donas also tells me that one of them, probably their leader, barked, "Be patient you fools! You know what we must do. Relax. Take a nap if you must. No matter what you idiots do, do it quietly! Besides, we saw the elf exit over there."

I watch as the spargnarl points to his left, to the south. He is pointing in the general direction where Donas and I are hiding. Donas' thoughts tell me the spargnarl yelled, "We surely cut him off. So he's probably lurking behind one of those boulders. We'll eventually find him. It is too hot now. We will look for him as soon as the sun sets."

Back in camp, Lindsial is invisible. She is creeping closer to the spargnarls. She wants to eavesdrop on their conversations. She listens as Gonialit says angrily, "I do not care if you are hot. Quit your complaining. Are you so stupid to not see what remains of that campsite over there? That is where the elf hides at night. It makes sense, too. It's close to the stream, up the hill from the ocean, and there's plenty of firewood."

Gonialit points, "And by the looks of the half-dozen seaweed cups and plates lying about, we may be seeking more than one elf. See those? There are far too many footprints for one solitary elf as well. Also, I suspect an elf that moves as quickly as the one Eranba the Freak speaks of cannot move nearly as speedily at night. He may rule the day, but we command the night. So we stay put. We wait him out. Nighttime is our friend. Darkness is his enemy."

I sense Lindsial's incoming thought transference. She conveys, "I have been reading thoughts from Donas and you. I'm relieved Ariel-e has provided you with some shade, as well as fresh water. Eva, you're right. We're in a serious state of affairs. The spargnarls know there is more than one of us. Their leader also knows of Donas' abilities as well as his nighttime weakness. I have a plan. But, we must act quickly before the sun sets and Donas is defenseless. Please convey my plan to Donas if you concur with it. I'll outline it now."

Once I receive Lindsial's plan, I tell it to Donas. In a flash, he is gone. He has plenty of time before the sun sets to put the plan into effect. I'm gritting my teeth in frustration. I bounce up and down in place to stretch my aching legs and to pump some life into my cold feet. As I do, I ponder that this is a great second day as so-called Princess of

Spardom. Yes, I have telepathic skills. I can do a few supernatural tricks. But I assuredly have more magical powers than I know of at this point. All the same, it is
aggravating standing here in ankle deep water and doing
nothing. I have to do something! Then it dawns on me ·
oops, I forgot Lindsial can read my thoughts.

As I anticipated, she comments. "Eva, please be patient
and wait until nightfall before you try anything rash. Yes,
you do have more powers. We haven't had time to explain
them to you that's all. However, you can move objects with
ease. Remember the incidents in your apartment? You tore
holes in the wall moving your couch and knickknacks. Your
spells are strong. When the time comes, use everything
that you've learned up to this point. In the meantime,
please remain patient."

"You are correct as usual," I convey. "But you know me.
I am a person..." I pause, and then I convey, "Or more correctly I should say I am an elf of action. I've been cowering
behind this blasted rock for over an hour now. Although I
have this hat and shawl over my shoulders, I'm being
roasted alive from the inside-out. Nevertheless, I shall try
and remain patient." I change the subject. "Have you seen
Ariel-e?"

"No, Eva, I have not. And I honestly don't expect to.
The spargnarls have posted guards on all sides of our
campsite. It's too dangerous for her to show right now. She
will undoubtedly wait for nightfall before she makes a
move outside of the ocean. The leader also mentioned he's
confident the others will eventually see something of interest. The big bloke boss who calls himself Gonialit says everyone is to stay put for now."

"Have you seen anything of Andrial?" I ask. "And how
about Donas, have you seen him?"

Lindsial conveys, "I'm fairly certain Donas was just
here. I thought I detected him with my echolocation. Hold
on a sec while I try to sense if he was here." She silently
walks to where she hid our weapons. After a few moments
she says, "Yes, I think he retrieved Ariel-e's weapons. I

sense your sword is not here as well. How Donas was able to retrieve the weapons under the watchful eyes of the spargnarls is truly amazing. Andrial has his bow, arrows, and his sword with him, so we need not worry about him being without weapons."

"Oh, here is Donas now," I convey. "He has my sword, what good it'll do me. You know I'm not skilled enough to use it properly. Donas also told me he placed Ariel·e's spear and sword behind a boulder near the shoreline. Hopefully, she'll see them before the spargnarls do."

Now Andrial's thoughts enter my mind. "Milady and Lindsial, Andrial here. I am to the right of our encamp·ment along the tree line. If the sun sets here on the Isle like on surface earth, I am to the north. I have been listen·ing to three distinct groups of spargnarl conversations.

"There is a group near me. There is a group surround·ing the encampment. A third, much larger group is located some distance away, perhaps to the south of the encamp·ment. I am not positive. The creatures know about Donas' nighttime weakness. They also suspect there is more than one of us.

"The leader of the spargnarls is Gonialit. His group is the one nearest our encampment. The leader of the group nearest to me is Stanquerl. To my knowledge, Stanquerl has not seen anything of interest in this vicinity. I am well hidden and will remain so until dark. The leader of the group farthest from me to the south is called Pagriol. He also has not seen anything of interest as far as I can tell. I hope you can read my thoughts. I will relay more infor·mation later if it is of any value."

Lindsial and I now know what we are facing. I tell Do·nas all that Andrial has conveyed.

Remaining invisible, Lindsial carefully walks toward the shoreline. When she reaches the ocean, she intends to become visible once more. She is hoping Ariel·e will see her so she can tell Ariel·e what she knows. Lindsial's plan, to contact Ariel·e, is risky.

She is acutely aware of one fact. As soon as she turns

visible she is a target. Given she is blind, even her power of echolocation will be insufficient to assist her if a spargnarl spots her from a distance. She purposely did not tell me of her plan so I wouldn't worry.

"Lindsial," I convey, "Have you tried reading the spargnarls' thoughts? I have tried again and again, but I cannot detect a thing."

"Yes," Lindsial conveys via thought transference. "I have tried as well. I cannot read their minds. They are primitive beings. I doubt their minds are advanced sufficiently to have their thoughts read, at least by me. It is the only reason I can render. If you recall, Donas said they speak a dialect similar to the elvish language. Like Andrial, I can pretty much understand what they are saying aloud. By the way, I am visible here at the ocean. Hopefully, Ariel-e will see me. I need to tell her what we know."

"Oh, no, Lindsial," I convey. "That is far too dangerous. You are standing in the open. They may see you. Please take cover. I can tell Ariel-e everything she needs to know when she returns. She should be here soon enough. Please turn invisible."

"Oh, do not worry yourself," Lindsial's thoughts say. "I am safe enough. I don't think any of the spargnarls has left the campsite area. Besides, I will instantly know if someone approaches me."

Lindsial suddenly hears a brusque shout a short distance away. A spargnarl is yelling, "Over there! Look over there! An elf is standing right there! But wait, it is now gone. It disappeared like the wind in the trees. But I saw something!" He points excitedly adding, "I saw a young female elf standing over there."

"Where did you see it?" another voice scolds with annoyance. "I do not see anything. You have been in the sun far too long you dolt. Perhaps you need to go back to the forest and rest in the shade. There is nothing out here but boulders, sand, and water."

The spargnarl growls, "I saw a young female elf I tell you. Right there standing near the water, just to the right of that boulder. I am going to tell Gonialit. I must tell Gonialit an elf is invisible here!"

I am oblivious to what has just happened. All the same, I am immediately aware of three minds conveying thoughts at the same time. "They saw me, darn it!" Lindsial's mind conveys.

"Lindsial, they saw you!" Ariel-e's thoughts seem to scream. "You have to get away from here straight away. Run to the left along the shoreline as quickly as you can. That is where our lady Eva and Master Donas are. I will guide you along the way if you turn visible now and then but for a brief second."

Andrial's anxious thoughts also enter my mind. "Lindsial, Andrial here. I just heard a spargnarl tell another he saw an elf disappear. You are in danger, Lindsial. Please leave immediately. The spargnarl has already told Gonialit. They are developing a plan to find you. Do not walk on the shoreline. Walk in the water. They said they would track your footprints in the sand. Move, Lindsial, move now before it's too late!"

Just as I finally interpret the three separate thoughts entering my mind at the same time, Lindsial conveys, "My goodness, Eva, now I've done it. I'm moving to the right - to the north I expect, in the opposite direction of you. I will speak aloud to Andrial in a moment, so he knows my intent. I refuse to allow the spargnarls to unite where you and Donas are hiding. You have enough trouble with all those beasts near you. You do not need thirty additional spargnarls in your vicinity. That would be nearly a hundred! I will walk in the sand for a bit. They can track me when I do. Then I'll confuse them by walking in the weeds. Tell Ariel-e and Donas of my plans if you please."

"Okay, Lindsial," my mind says, "Perhaps you are correct. It is better that we split into two groups. We will have a better chance of outwitting these beasts or beating them if need be. We just need to figure out how to do it. They do not know of Andrial up north or Donas and me down south here. I'm almost certain they certainly do not know about

Ariel-e. Please stay in contact with me. I will do the same. Don't do anything foolish. And be careful, my dear friend, be extra careful."

Lindsial purposely walks in the sand, so her footsteps are visible. Then she walks in the surf for a distance, re-emerges onto the shore and walks straight into the forest. Further along the tree line, she walks toward the seashore, making sure her footprints are visible in the sand once more. She turns her invisibility on and off. She hopes to confuse the spargnarls.

"That ought to keep them guessing," she says aloud adding, "Andrial, I am walking toward your location. I think it best I move away from our lady Eva. We can split our forces while forcing the spargnarls to do the same. I would expect you will soon see more of these dreaded crea-tures as they head in your direction. I will speak to you aloud when I detect your presence. If I cannot detect your presence, I will tell you where I am so you can guide me. I'm turning invisible now."

"I understand, Lindsial," Andrial's mind says, "Please be careful."

CHAPTER EIGHTEEN

COME AND GET ME!

The hours tick by slowly, more slowly than usual since I'm standing stock-still. The sun's relentless heat is seeping beneath the now dried out marine outfits covering my torso. My stomach is cramping. My legs are aching and nearly unbendable. They're also badly sunburned. They could be burnt to a crisp if it weren't for Ariel-e making me full-length seaweed leggings a couple of hours ago. To make matters worse, my feet feel waterlogged. I'm being honest with you when I say this - I feel miserable.

I can only imagine how absurd I look. I'm standing motionless, covered from head to ankles in dark green strands of woven seaweed. Oh, but only if Cindy and my fellow CIA agents could see me now! I bet they would double over in laughter.

Maybe I should come out from behind the boulder, spread my arms out wide, snarl ferociously, and pretend I'm a sea monster. Maybe, just maybe, with any luck, the spargnarls would head for the trees. Then again, they might butcher me, thinking I was something delicious to eat!

As I rest my head against the boulder, I feel drowsy. I know I cannot nap; that's for certain. I'm so tired I'd probably fall smack on my butt while asleep and make the loudest splash ever. That could spell disaster!

Ariel·e has given me four containers of fresh water. Yet I am showing the first signs of dehydration. I have a splitting headache. I can barely produce a stream of pee, my mouth is dry, and I am starting to get lightheaded. The sun has been baking me from the inside·out the past several hours. Just as I think this, Ariel·e produces another container of water. I gulp it greedily and silently mouth my thanks to the sea. As I do, Donas reappears next to me.

His thoughts say, "I've been spying on the spargnarls, milady. As Andrial said, there is a group to the north, one near our campsite and, of course, the one here. More must have arrived in the past hour or so. I count nearly one hundred fifty spargnarls. I am going to remain here with you. The sun will set soon. I cannot move rapidly after dark as you know. All the same, I swear I will do everything I can to protect you." He unsheathes his sword and stands behind me to block the sun's rays.

As Donas and I stand motionless behind the boulder, we play whispered riddle games to pass the time. I have my eyes closed. Even so, I can tell that the sun is starting to set beyond the horizon. I'm in such a foul mood; I don't bother to turn around to look. All of a sudden, the glow of the setting sun hurriedly turns into a virtually pitch·black moonless sky. I open my eyes and see iridescent stars as they awaken to blink naively in the heavens. Their innocence appears indifferent to what is happening far beneath their gaze.

The forest likewise seems to come alive as it winks with limitless tiny lamps of flickering lightning bugs. I stare fascinated from behind my shielding boulder as the captivating panorama unfolds all around. The vista is breathtaking! I am positive the nighttime's tranquility and beauty emerging before me are befitting of the Isle's splendor. My sour mood turns a bit agreeable.

Then as stylishly as tranquility came into view the peaceful moment is crushed. I grimace as dozens of shining torches begin to illuminate our surroundings. As the flickering lights begin to move about in all directions, their gloomy shadows they cast seem to match my frame of mind. Donas touches me on the shoulder and points. A handful of spargnarls holding torches high above their heads is getting dangerously close to our hiding place.

"They are searching for food," his mind says. "One of them said he spotted huge sand crabs crawling all along the shoreline. We must be on our guard. They could spot us." He sheaths his sword, and then he takes an arrow out of his quiver and places it on his bowstring. I think to myself, huge sand crabs - great! I hope they don't like waterlogged female elf ankles!

Just as I think this, a meandering torch light starts to move dangerously nearer. Then it abruptly veers in our direction. A spargnarl is walking in a straight line toward us. In a matter of seconds, the creature is on the opposite side of the boulder a few feet from where we stand!

Out of the blue, a towering wall of water in the shape of an angry rogue wave emerges from our left. The huge wave completely engulfs the spargnarl knocking him off his feet. It snuffs out his torch as well. The aim of the expertly timed, expertly-formed elf mermaid wave was perfect. Donas and I did not feel even the tiniest bit of salt spray.

"What in the devil was that?" The spargnarl stammers. "That darn wave just ruined my torch. Look at how ferocious the waves have become! I bet there is a dreadful storm out to sea." He shrugs his wide gnarled shoulders, turns and walks toward the tree line.

I ponder Ariel-e's huge wave. It gives me an idea. We have to do something - anything to confront the spargnarls head-on. What's more, I have had enough of this hide-and-seek waiting game. If we do not do something soon, Donas and I will be standing in knee-high water in a matter of hours. The tide is gathering that quickly. Besides, I am sore, hot, unhappy, sunburned, and totally ticked-off.

What's more, I haven't eaten a thing since early this morning. I'm starving!

I whisper in Donas' ear. "Okay, I have a plan. But first let me ask Lindsial a question." I convey via telepathy, "Lindsial, can you tell if Gonialit and his group have moved far enough away to be momentarily out of action at our campsite?"

Lindsial conveys, "Yes, Gonialit's group is pursuing me to the north. Their loud noise, as they stumble through the weeds, is unmistakable. They are a good distance from the campsite, maybe twenty to twenty-five minutes, perhaps more. The going is rough for them. They're complaining about everything being pitch-black. I presume the sun has set."

I convey, "Thanks, sweetie. And yes, the sun has set. It is pitch-black tonight with no moon."

I tell Donas to tell Ariel-e to come closer. I say, "Okay, Lindsial and Andrial, please listen as I whisper my plan to Donas and Ariel-e." I pass on my plan via a barely audible whisper and, of course, in my mind so all will know what I am thinking.

My plan is simple enough. Lindsial and Andrial are to join forces to the north. Once they do, they are to turn around to work their way to the campsite. I will run to the campsite along the shoreline under cover of Ariel-e's huge waves. She will also produce a drenching downpour up and down the coast. It should extinguish the spargnarls' torches. Tonight is a moonless night. The spargnarls' visibility will be close to zero. So will ours, but there is not much we can do about it. All of us, except for Donas, who needs to remain hidden, will converge at the campsite. It goes without saying - we will battle on the go.

While the spargnarls have many more soldiers, outnumbering us significantly, we have an element of surprise. We also have a powerful elf that can battle undetected from the sea, Ariel-e. She can unleash powerful water spells. When it comes time to fighting on land, she is an expert with her sword and spear.

Even if she is blind, Lindsial can fight like the finest of warriors when she is invisible. Andrial has sword and archery skillfulness as able as a knight. I, of course, have my powerful magical spells. Then there is Donas. Even though he cannot pursue the spargnarls, he has his bow and arrows.

In a few moments, Ariel·e produces a drenching downpour that extinguishes the spargnarls' torches. Her cloudburst forces the spargnarls to regroup grudgingly near the forest. She then forms waves ten feet high that wash well inland. The waves are from the shoreline. That allows me to dash behind the waves in ankle deep water. The towering waves also shield me a bit from the spargnarls' view.

As I run along the beach, I get a sudden urge to taunt the spargnarls. Yes, I admit it. Sometimes I can be pigheaded and do foolish things. What do you say we blame it on my feistiness due to my red hair? I yell at the top of my lungs, "Come and get me you stinky things! You cannot catch me. I'm a lot faster than you! Gosh, you ugly things need a bath! You stink!"

The spargnarls are confused. They did not expect to hear a female voice from behind the unexpected wall of waves. They also did not anticipate a voice shouting absurdities in both English and Fortunomy. It appears, unbeknownst to me; I have already learned some words from the elvish language. What I am yelling in two languages must sound like bizarre nonsense spoken by a creature from outer space.

Pagriol orders his group to follow the sounds of my shouts. I glance through breaks in the waves. I make out a few hapless spargnarls being swallowed up inside whirling waterspouts produced by Ariel·e. The creatures are powerless in the water's spinning furor. As I glance to the sky, they appear to plead feebly for pity. I know their screams go unheeded, for there is nothing anyone can do to help them. Ariel·e's waterspouts quickly take them far above the ocean where they fall into the deep water.

Donas remains hidden behind a boulder. As you know,

he is powerless to engage the spargnarls on foot after dark. Even so, he unleashes volley after volley of stinging arrows that fell many spargnarls. He's shooting them in the legs so they can no longer pursue me. He's paying particular attention to those that try and cut me off as I dash through the water. In a few moments, however, the spargnarls are out of Donas' view. He throws his bow and arrows to the ground in disgust, and then he collapses to the ground dejected. His short-lived, but vital part of the battle has ended.

Meanwhile, as I run, I cast spells at spargnarls that come dangerously close. I point with my left hand yelling *moveo!* I toss some of the creatures far away into the water. I imagine their bodies are too heavy to float. I hope they can swim. I do not want them killed. I simply want them out of action for a bit. I propel others head-on onto boulders. Some spargnarls hurled onto boulders quickly recover to resume their chase. Fortunately, for me, the spargnarls are slow-moving beasts. None comes close to catching me. I take a split second to thank myself for staying in shape and running 5K and half marathons from time to time.

Up to the north, Lindsial and Andrial are stealthily moving through the grassy fields as they proceed toward our encampment. Since Andrial is holding Lindsial's hand, he is invisible. Suddenly, Lindsial, Andrial, and Donas' thoughts exclaim that they hear two blasts of a horn. The sound originates from somewhere down south in the vicinity of where Ariel-e and I are battling the beasts as we rush to the camp.

"Pagriol is calling the others as he pursues our lady!" Andrial's mind seems to scream to Lindsial. "We must hurry or our lady Eva and elfin Ariel-e will be overwhelmed. There are far too many spargnarls for the two of them!"

I consider our dilemma. Darn! That's the last thing Ariel-e, and I need right now given our situation, spargnarl reinforcements! I didn't count on that. Hopefully, Lindsial and Andrial can head-off the beasts from the north that are surely heading toward the campsite.

While I know the fall of some spargnarls is inevitable, I convey to Lindsial, "Please tell Andrial to try and wound the beasts. I want you to try and keep them out of action, nothing more. For sure, do what you must to ensure your survival. Thank you."

After a period of fifteen to twenty minutes, Ariel·e and I arrive at the campsite. I am reinvigorated and raring to go. It is much too dark to see what is happening around us. I set a stack of logs on fire using my credo auduro spell.

The spargnarls converging from two directions are soon upon us. A raucous battle ensues. I hold my sword in my right hand, but it is useless. I have no clue how to use it against a real foe. I can only hope its presence serves to intimidate the spargnarls to some extent.

In contrast to my difficulty using my sword, the spargnarls have no problem wielding theirs. They immediately begin slashing away. Fortunately for Ariel·e and me, they are slashing away at thin air, at least for now.

We need to keep the spargnarls from getting too close to use their expert slice and dice skills deftly. With my sword clutched uselessly in my right hand, I'm casting spells dutifully with my left. I toss spargnarls head over heels one after another with a simple flick of my hand using my moveo spell. Some land with a hard thud on the ground, while others fall helplessly against boulders. A few remain in place after they smash headlong into boulders. I believe they loudly moan in pain where they fell. Most that I hurl through the air are only temporarily stunned. They quickly recover to rejoin the fight.

I employ my labor lapsus spell to cause a few spargnarls to slide back and forth brutally. They eventually slam sideways into boulders and tree trunks. My spell causes them to be knocked unconscious. A few slide completely out of view toward the ocean. I suspect they will continue sliding until they hit sea bottom. I also disarm many spargnarls with my exarmo spell. Even after I disarm them, they come charging at us with brute force. They look like huge three-eyed battering rams on two gigantic, powerful legs.

Ariel-e is unable to summon up the ocean's naturally occurring, devastating fury this far inland. Nevertheless, she can use her powers to create other vicious water-borne weapons. She produces solid icicles with pointy tips that pierce the toughened hide of a few spargnarls. She hits others on the head with huge blocks of ice thrown through the air. She douses other spargnarls with steaming hot water. When she gets close enough to one of the beasts, she jabs her metal spear into its leg. Again, like me, Ariel-e does not want to cause any to die if possible.

She holds a sword in her other hand. She uses it expertly, slashing the bellies and arms of wretched spargnarls that come too close. The butchery of Spargnarls is mounting. Yet I know more are on their way. Despite our best defensive efforts, Ariel-e and I are steadily besieged on all sides.

Amidst the bedlam, I receive Lindsial's thought transference in my mind, "Eva, we cannot get any closer for now. Spargnarls have blocked our path both in the forest and along the shoreline. We are engaging them. I will tell you when we can come to your aid. There must be a dozen or more of the beasts from the north that turned around. They advance your way. Please be careful, milady, and good luck!"

The sheer number of spargnarls is slowly overwhelming Ariel-e and me. We are gradually forced to retreat with our backs to the campsite's narrow opening. We do not want the spargnarls to trap us within the three-walled enclosure. We will have no means to escape. So we do our best to confine the battle to the front of the enclosure's opening.

Despite the ever-growing number of spargnarls and our increasing exhaustion, I have to say we put up a darned good fight. I hurl spargnarls left and right. Some slam forcefully into branches high in the trees. Some spargnarls fall with a heavy thud upon boulders.

Now I consider putting boulders to work. I pick up boulders with my moveo spell to hurl them at the spargnarls. Using boulders to my advantage seems to help our cause quite well. The boulders knock out some of the spargnarls as they slam into the creatures. My spells manage to squash other spargnarls beneath the boulders' substantial weight.

Ariel·e and I gallantly fight side by side, not once being touched by the spargnarls. However, how much longer can we endure this onslaught against lopsided odds?

CHAPTER NINETEEN

DONAS AND ERANBA

Further south, away from where the fight is raging, a miserable Donas is resting his still aching back against a boulder as he sits on the sand. His incredible quickness skills are useless at night.

Without doubt, he accurately shot arrows at the spargnarls as they chased me, and he felled many. He can hear their moans and groans as they crawl on all fours into the forest. For certain, he contributed to the battle at first. All the same, he now feels disappointed. As he broods over his predicament, he detects a presence nearby. He cringes when he hears a familiar voice. The voice belongs to Eranba.

The young spargnarl whispers, "I know you are here, little elf. I cannot see you. However, I know your smell. You are my pet, remember? You still have to teach me your secret magic. Perhaps you should do so before the others return. I won't let them imprison you as long as you show me the secret you possess. This time you better teach me proper like."

Donas thinks there is no way he is going to get out of

this predicament. Even relatively, slow-moving Eranba can move faster than he can at night. Donas decides to appear blameless and defenseless. He managed to trick the young spargnarl once. Perhaps he can do it again.

He whispers, "I am right here, Eranba, behind a boulder. I am sorry I tricked you earlier today. Please picture yourself in my place as I sat in the kettle. How would you like to be boiled into mush as bait?"

"I do not think I would like that at all," Eranba replies. "You tricked me just the same, just like Gonialit said you would. Then you ran away. Now everyone thinks I am a fool. I simply wanted to learn your secret. As I told you before, I like secrets, as long as they are mine. Besides, I like you little elf. I honestly do."

Donas says, "Well, it is no use right now. I cannot perform my secret magic after the sun sets. You are faster than me tonight, of that I assure you."

"Me faster than the little elf," Eranba scoffs, "Surely you make fun of me once more. Are you trying to trick me by telling lies as before?"

"No, Eranba, I am not," Donas replies. "You see, my secret is only doable in daytime. At night, I am weak and nearly defenseless. True, my hands are fast. Yet when darkness comes, I move slower than the slowest creature. Tomorrow, after the sun rises, I can again show you my magic. I promise I will."

Eranba moves from the other side of the boulder where Donas sits. He towers over Donas. Donas is incapable of escape. He can only prepare himself for Eranba to strike him with his huge sword. For sure he can strike out with his blade, perhaps slicing at Eranba's massive knees. That would incapacitate the huge brute. However, something tells him Eranba is not going to harm him. He senses Eranba is different than the other spargnarls.

"Please do secret magic," Eranba cries. "I like it when you do secret magic. I like secrets, as long as they are mine. I want to have fun. Please my elfin friend, please."

"Eranba, I am completely honest with you. I cannot do

any secret magic right now. If you must strike, strike me now. All I ask, however, is you strike me quickly." As he says this, Donas readies himself to ward off any incoming blows. He may slowly ramble when he walks at night, but his hand is still quicker than the eye. His blade is just as swift.

Eranba sighs, "Strike you? Oh, I could never hurt you little elf. I do not like hurting things. I know how it feels to hurt. Others are always calling me Eranba the Freak. It upsets me so. It hurts me so much my heart cries."

"You are not a freak," Donas whispers. "You are more handsome than every other spargnarl I have seen. You are just different. That is all. Being different does not make you less of a being than others. It makes you special. In fact, why not leave the others behind and come on a journey with me and my fellow elves. We would treat you nicely. What's more, we could use a guide who knows the area."

"Oh, I could never do that," Eranba replies. "I am ugly, and I am a freak · everyone says so. The other elves will not like me. I am repulsive to look at."

Donas says, "You are not hideous or vile, Eranba. As I said, you are more fine-looking than the others of your kind, at least to me. Please listen attentively, for I am going to tell you a secret very few know." Eranba crouches to listen to what Donas has to say. After all, he likes secrets as long as they are his.

"Eranba, every elf in my group of five is different from others of our kind · just like you. One elf, Eva, the Princess of Spardom, is deaf. One elf is blind. Another elf is voiceless. One elf has flippers like a fish, although she can sprout legs to walk on land. She must immerse herself in the water every three or four days, or she will perish. Then there is me. While I am swift during daylight as you know, I walk as slowly as a crawl after dark.

"Each of us has amazing powers that, even though we are different from others, make us very special. So you see, Eranba, being different is okay. It helps you to stand out amongst the crowd, to be something special. I am certain all of the elves will like you as much as I like you."

"Do you really think so?" Eranba cries. "If the other elves will like me, then I shall accompany you on your journey. I do not like being called Eranba the Freak - it hurts me right here." Eranba points to where Donas supposes the young spargnarl's heart beats. "Oh, I am thrilled to accompany you, little elf. I will finally have friends."

"Well, okay then, it is settled," Donas says with a smile. "Let us wait here a spell. There's a battle going on, and I am powerless to help. I walk quite slowly at night. Now, would you mind taking a plunge in the ocean? I do not intend any offense. You smell a bit stinky if you don't mind me saying."

CHAPTER TWENTY

HOW CAN THIS BE -
YOU LIVE!

Here at the campsite, in the thick of battle, Ariel·e and I are close to being overwhelmed by the enemy. The spargnarls almost have us where they want us · dab smack within the enclosing walls of our campsite. Despite our slaying of immeasurable spargnarls, there are too many of the creatures for the two of us to engage at once.

Just when all seems lost, suddenly, from nowhere, countless grayish-black look-alike rocks in the sand unexpectedly hurl through the air. Nothing is propelling the rocks. They are launching themselves like magical disks destined to avenge wrongdoing!

Most of the rocks seem to seek out the spargnarls' massive heads. Others go for the spargnarls' abdomens. As I mentioned earlier, the rocks are razor-sharp. They're doing a number on the beasts. Ariel·e and I speechlessly stare as the astonishing scene of rocks flying through the air unfolds before us.

Without a doubt, the spargnarls are now the ones being overwhelmed. Countless rocks are being flung from many directions. The spargnarls have no other choice but to retreat. Since the rocks are now on the offense, the hour-long battle begins to end in less than a few minutes.

I read Ariel-e's mind as she tells me Gonialit is ordering a retreat. The spargnarl leader screams, "Retreat - back to the cave! You there, trumpeter - blow your sea horn five times. I want all to know they should fall back, to retreat! Blow it over and again five times. Do it now!" Then, pulling one of his fallen comrades to his feet, Gonialit scampers into the forest. Others that are able follow Gonialit without delay.

From somewhere up north, Lindsial conveys in her mind that spargnarls in her vicinity are retreating. With my sword hanging lifelessly by my side, I watch as spargnarls rush toward the darkened forest. Some of the creatures help wounded comrades from the scene. Others remain behind moaning in pain. Many more are lifeless. I'm certain they are dead. I also notice the rocks have returned to their nests on the ground.

The scene before us is total mayhem. True, I am thankful the battle is over. All the same, I feel miserable. There was no cause for this horrific bloodshed. There was no reason at all.

I am deep in thought, so I do not sense Ariel-e is addressing me. She taps me on the shoulder. I squint in the darkness as her lips say, "Now if milady would be so kind, perhaps she could build a larger fire. The other fire is nearly extinguished. We also need to light torches. I want to see if any battle-ready spargnarls remain behind."

After we pile more firewood onto the fire pit, I shout *credo auduro!* My spell returns this morning's smoldering ashes to a blazing fire. Ariel-e lights two torches.

The two of us somberly stroll among the dead and dying spargnarls. We check the fate of each spargnarl. Ariel-e quickly puts each dying creature out of its misery. In a few moments, our gruesome task is finished. It is obvious to me that the rocks felled most of the spargnarls that have met their maker. It doesn't matter. I still feel miserable.

"I count thirty-four dead, milady," Ariel-e's thoughts say. "Counting the twenty or so my waterspouts were able to eliminate along the way that makes for a total of at least fifty or more spargnarls."

"I more or less agree with your tally," I reply aloud. "Add to that a few dozen seriously injured spargnarls that escaped into the forest." As I look at the dead and dying Spargnarls, I say, "Ariel-e, it is such a disgrace, so many of the creatures had to die. We did not provoke them. We simply had to defend ourselves. I feel miserable seeing the creatures scattered across the ground."

Just as I say this, I stare spellbound as Ariel-e produces dozens of tiny waterspouts with a circular motion of her hands. The twirling waterspouts gently lift each dead and dying spargnarl into the air. The waterspouts will carry the hapless creatures to their final resting place far off to the sea.

I read Ariel-e's mind as it says, "Better to bury the dead at sea then leave them here to decompose in the open. I do believe it's much more dignified and civilized." She adds, "I agree, milady. The death of any creature, no matter how unkind or wicked the creature, is horrible. Now, please excuse me, milady. I shall fetch a late night snack."

I nod my head, saying, "Thank you, Ariel-e, for everything." Now Lindsial's thoughts are in my mind. She says, "Is everyone there okay, Eva?"

"Yes, we're all right. Ariel-e and I are at camp. She's leaving to fetch us a late night snack. I told Donas to stay in place to the south. I am certain he's okay. Are you and Andrial okay?" Lindsial conveys that she and Andrial are unharmed.

Andrial's thoughts now enter my mind. "I am sorry I could not tell you earlier, milady. Lindsial and I were frightfully busy up north here as you know. I overheard Donas speaking a while ago with the young spargnarl he encountered earlier today. It seems they are now friends. Donas asked the beast to accompany us on our journey. The spargnarl, Eranba is his name, agreed."

"Lindsial," I convey, "Please thank Andrial for the information. Tell him I think it's a grand idea to have Eranba join us. I am certain the spargnarl will be useful as a guide. I am also relieved the two of you are safe and uninjured. Where are you now?"

"We are a ten-minute hike from the encampment if we move quickly. I am bone-tired and hungry as ever. Also, Andrial and I are quite thirsty. But tell me, Eva, how did you two manage to slay so many spargnarls? That is incredible!"

I convey, "I am glad you are almost here. About the spargnarls, well, we did have a bit of help at the end of the battle. In fact, those that helped us ended the skirmish in less than a few minutes. It appears these little grayish-black rocks you mentioned earlier today have a mind of their own. There is no doubt they are our friends."

As I say this, the rocks begin to move to and fro just as they did last night. They quickly merge into three separate groups. Then they scurry up the boulders surrounding the campsite to provide a protective covering. As if on cue, the sky opens up, and it begins to sprinkle.

"Well, that is something else indeed," I exclaim out loud. "Good rocks you are, good rocks to be sure. We are blessed to have you as our friends. I think I shall take one of you along with me as we journey, perhaps as a good luck charm. I thank you."

Meanwhile, Donas is hitching a ride on Eranba's back. It is nearly midnight when the pair arrives at the encampment. Lindsial is standing guard. Upon sensing the pair's approach, she turns visible to greet them. She says, "Well, I am very relieved you are okay, Donas." Then turning in the spargnarl's direction she adds, "You must be Eranba."

Eranba replies, "Yes my pretty elf, I am Eranba. Who may I ask are you?"

"I am Lindsial. Would you mind stooping low so I can touch your face? That way I can picture in my mind what you look like."

"Well, I do not know," Eranba stammers. "I think you shall not like the way I feel to your touch. I am not as beautiful and fair-skinned as you my dear elf friend Lindsial. My skin is tough like the leather of a very old used up animal."

"It is okay, Eranba," Lindsial says. "I am the blind elf Donas mentioned. I can sense your presence by your large form. It would be better if I could touch your face. In that way, I can know your features. If you do not want me to, I understand."

"Go ahead, Eranba," Donas offers. "It is all right. Touching another's face is what the blind do. It is their way of *seeing* in their mind how another looks."

Eranba crouches down. Lindsial's fingers gently caress the outlines of Eranba's face. She touches his forehead, nose, lips, ears, three eyes, and then his neck and shoulders.

She says, "Goodness, you do not have gnarls on your body. Is that why the other spargnarls call you that dreadful name?"

"Yes, it is my elf friend Lindsial," Eranba cries. "They call me Eranba the Freak."

"Well, you should no longer trouble yourself about that," Lindsial suggests with a smile. "You appear to be quite handsome to me. Please allow me to show you inside. I want you to see two of the other elves Donas mentioned. Do not make noise when you enter. They are sleeping." Eranba is too tall to stand upright in the enclosure. He drops down on all fours and crawls inside.

Lindsial says, "The male elf closest to you is Andrial. He is the voiceless elf Donas mentioned. He has amazing powers of sight and hearing. The beautiful female elf with long red hair is Princess Eva. She is the deaf elf. Her powers are..."

Before Lindsial can continue, Eranba lets out a barely audible gasp. More quickly than the two elves can react, he reaches out and takes my medallion in his massive hand. I feel Eranba's touch against my skin. I open my eyes straight away. The light is dim, so I can barely make out the face of the creature before me. However, I am not worried. Nor am I alarmed. Something tells me he is not dangerous.

Donas immediately draws his sword and commands in a whispered hiss, "Let go of Princess Eva's medallion and move away from her now!"

Upon hearing Donas' command, Lindsial steps between Eranba and me. She also draws her sword. Her absolute anger is evident. Her physical form rapidly moves in and out of visibility like an iridescent specter.

Eranba kindly releases my medallion. He backs away slowly on all fours. As he does, he never takes his eyes off of me. As our five eyes meet in the dim light Eranba whispers in earnest, "Oh, I am sorry. I meant no harm. But how can this be - you live!"

"Of course she lives," Donas says. He still has his sword drawn although he has lowered it slightly. Lindsial does the same. Donas says, "What did you expect?"

"Oh, my elf friend, Donas," Eranba gasps. "I mean the fair lady of Spardom of which legends speak - she lives! It is the royal one, the elf you call Princess Eva!" Eranba lowers his head in reverence and abruptly looks away from me.

By now Andrial is wide awake. He smiles at Eranba and nods. I sit up, yawn, and say with a sleepy sigh, "Well, you must be Eranba." I offer him my hand. I intend for him to shake it. Instead, he affectionately takes my hand in his and touches it briefly to his forehead. It is a spargnarl custom, a sign of absolute deference and deep respect. Then he quickly looks away.

With his head bowed, Eranba mutters softly, "I am at your service, my dear Princess Eva of Spardom." I cannot hear his words, nor can I correctly see them as they form on his lips in the dim light. Lindsial immediately repeats Eranba's words for me in her mind just as she did a few seconds ago.

I am still groggy from sleep and bone-weary from the

battle. I simply manage to say, "It is my pleasure indeed to meet you, Eranba."

After a bit of talk, as we get to know our new friend a bit more, Ariel·e arrives at the encampment. I introduce Ariel·e to Eranba. She prepares us a quick snack of raw oysters and slices of raw fish delicately seasoned with salt-ed seaweed.

After we eat our snack, I stretch my arms out wide with an accompanying, gaping yawn that is equally wide. I loudly proclaim, "Well, we should all get some sleep. It has been a long, tiring day. We are in good hands with Ariel·e on guard. And you, Andrial, you are on watch in three hours, so you should try to get at least forty winks as well." Then addressing Lindsial, I say, "Would you mind sleeping here next to me. It's cold!"

Before I lie back down on my soft bed of dried leaves next to Lindsial, I call Ariel·e over to me. As she kneels be-side me, I pull her close to hug her. I whisper softly near her ear and say, "Ariel·e, I thank you for your kindness to-day. I also thank you for your courage and resolve. You saved my life on more than one occasion tonight. I want you to know · you are one of the most beautiful creatures on earth. You have a heart of gold, an unequaled charis-matic smile, and a mind of wonders. Plus, you are a coura-geous soldier. I love you, Ariel·e, I truly do."

As I look into her eyes, I see she is crying tears of joyful love, just like me. I kiss her on her forehead and read her thoughts as she says, "Thank you, milady Eva. Thank you very much. I love you too."

I flop down on my makeshift bed and cover myself with the seaweed coverlet Ariel·e crocheted for me early this morning. Lindsial is next to me our backs barely touching. By the feel of her rhythmic breathing against my back, I know she is already sleeping like a baby. I pull a bit of the coverlet over her shoulders.

I stare sleepy-eyed at Ariel-e's silhouette in the campfire's soft glow. I say a silent prayer of thanks. Being with the elves makes me feel more love in my heart than I have ever felt in my entire life. In a few moments, my eyes become unfocused. They finally succumb to sleep. There will be no dreams tonight. My mind's too exhausted to bring them to life.

CHAPTER TWENTY-ONE

HE BEHEADED THE QUEEN

Gray clouds shroud the morning's rising sun. As a result, it is quite chilly. The five of us are wearing the
same springtime clothes we wore when we escaped surface
earth. As one would expect, I am shivering in my knee-high
skirt and skimpy polyester blouse.

Lindsial is a bit more comfortable. She is wearing a
long sleeve shirt and slacks. All the same, she and I snug-
gle close together as we sit. We are sharing the seaweed
coverlet Ariel-e crocheted. It is draped over our shoulders
and down our backs. Thank goodness for the blazing hot
campfire I started. At least the fronts of our bodies are
warm.

Donas and Andrial do not seem to be shivering as
much as Lindsial and me. They are wearing long sleeve
shirts and trousers. They are also gathering firewood.
Staying busy helps them to keep warm. I should be a bit
warmer as well if I started moving. Yet I am too cold to lift
my shivering body from the log on which I am sitting.

Ariel-e does not seem to mind the morning chill as the
rest of us. She has acclimated to the ocean's cool tempera-

ture. When the temperature on land is nippy, Ariel·e goes about her business in her typical merry way. She sings and dances all the while.

She just returned with fresh fish for our morning meal. Thanks to her magic, the sweet·smelling gumbo cooks itself in the pot without using external heat. My mouth is water·ing as I smell the rich aroma of what is certainly going to be delicious·tasting broth. The broth will also be hot, which is what I need more than anything to warm up my shiver·ing body.

As we wait for breakfast, Lindsial, Ariel·e, and I are paying close attention to what Eranba is saying. He is nar·rating legends about the young Princess Eva, Queen April, and the ancient Isle of Spardom.

As I look away from Ariel·e's bubbling gumbo, I catch Eranba mid·sentence. "...the Chronicles' decree, Queen April ensured no evil set foot on the Isle. Only decent and honest sailors were allowed to visit the Isle. Dishonorable and scandalous seafarers such as pirates were unable even to see the isle. The Isle was nothing to them but additional never·ending sea.

"The Chronicles avowed any shipwrecked sailor, re·gardless of his sort, should be granted a place of protection on the Isle. This kindly clause was in keeping with the Is·landers' benevolent spirit and their reliance on the sea. They also believed any sailor granted refuge on the Isle must be beholden to the islanders' kindness. He should not desire to bring injury to the Isle or its inhabitants. This ar·rangement, as far as it concerned the Islanders' expecta·tion, was the same as an honest trade·off.

"This is how King Parston, Monarch of Magigro ulti·mately came to be. Parston, formerly known as Captain Whittaker, was a notorious pirate whose shameful pirate fleet roamed the Seven Seas. Legends state he had con·quered a vessel, a French man of war. After killing its cap·tain, he claimed the ship as a prize. Whittaker never took prisoners. Surviving French sailors were forced to walk the gangplank. They had their end in Davy Jones' locker.

"A few years later Captain Whittaker's pirate fleet was caught in a typhoon. His ship capsized and sank. As fate would have it, Captain Whittaker and four of his fellow pirates were cast upon Spardom's northeastern shore.

"Chests of gold, silver, precious jewels, and firearms also cast upon the shore. Those ill-gotten gains made Captain Whittaker the richest and most dangerous being on the Isle. Over time, he bought friendship and loyalty amongst diverse creatures of the Isle. If he could not bribe creatures, he intimidated them. He slaughtered family members of those who would not follow his devious ways. Word quickly spread on the Isle · Whitaker was a wicked man, a man others needed to fear and obey.

"Whittaker ultimately befriended the trolls and formed an alliance. With the trolls' assistance, he began to claim territory as his own. The alliance was eventually the troll's undoing. It seems Whittaker had befriended an aged, but a powerful troll sorcerer who was as crooked and wicked as Whittaker. The two eventually conspired to enslave the trolls with their combined powers. Then they trained the trolls to fight. They formed a strong army.

"The Grand War followed. Creatures of all kinds fought to the death. A few species died out completely. Countless others had to leave their dwellings, destined to roam the Isle evermore as Wanderers.

"A few years later, thousands of trolls led by Whittaker marched west through the desert, the Land of Abeti. Their conquest was distant Fogreia on the far side of Spardom. They wanted to subjugate the forest's creatures on behalf of Whittaker and the evil troll sorcerer. By doing so, they would vastly increase their sphere of influence."

Donas and Andrial have completed their firewood gathering. They sit next to us. Ariel·e says breakfast is ready whenever we want to eat. We are too intrigued with what Eranba is telling us. Breakfast will have to wait.

Eranba continues with his story. "You probably do not know this. Fogreia is a vast forest. It is inhabited by many diverse creatures. Chief among the forest's creatures is us spargnarls. We number in the tens of thousands. We have eleven districts with two to four thousand spargnarls in each district. Happily, because of our great numbers and superb fighting skills, we were able to prevent Whittaker and the trolls from conquering Fogreia. Not surprisingly, spargnarls and trolls remain mortal enemies to this day.

"Captain Whittaker eventually declared himself monarch of the Isle's northeast region. Then for some odd reason he changed his last name to Parston. He has been known ever since as King Parston, ruler of Magigro.

"After the Grand War the expansive, lovely land of a united Spardom was no more. The Isle now consists of six distinct regions. They are the Kingdom of Magigro, the Hidden Valley, Land of Abeti, Banned Borders, Fogreia, and an unexplored region to the extreme northwest.

"As I said, Magigro lies in the extreme northeast portion of the Isle. The region of Banned Borders is to its south. The Hidden Valley is to its northwest while the Land of Abeti is to its southwest. Abeti is in the center of the Isle. Of course, Fogreia is far-off from Magigro, in the extreme southwestern portion of the Isle. Our encampment is located just outside of Fogreia on the most southwestern tip of the Isle.

"Regarding the unexplored region to the extreme northwest of the Isle, no creature has ventured into it, at least not to my knowledge. Tall, treacherous mountains surround it on two sides. Myths tell of two more regions. Supposedly, one is out of sight somewhere in the Land of Abeti. The other region is thought to be near the Hidden Valley, near Lake Namoni. The reality of these two additional regions is in doubt since no one has seen them."

I am fascinated with Eranba's story. For some strange reason, I am acutely interested in the northwest region Eranba mentioned. I ask, "Eranba, why has no one journeyed to the region to the northwest, the unexplored area?"

I watch Eranba's lips say, "I do not know, milady. Myths say it is inaccessible due to tall mountains. The remaining three sides border the ocean with dangerous reefs.

By all accounts, the region is a peaceful, lovely land. However, none has seen it, at least not to my knowledge. According to myths, the Hidden Valley to the east is linked to this unexplored land. The truth of these myths is uncertain."

I thank Eranba and ask him to continue. He resumes his storytelling saying, "Someone abducted the child princess from her bed in the middle of the night shortly after King Parston declared his monarchy. Queen April suspected Parston was responsible. She thought it was revenge for her refusal to abandon her sovereignty as the rightful ruler of Spardom.

"Queen April readily recognized the evil Parston brought to the peaceful Isle of Spardom. She tried to a great extent to change the Chronicles, to annul the law concerning seafarer castaways. Islanders would not allow it. Despite the disagreement, opposing views speak well of both the Islanders and Queen April. The Islanders wanted to save lives. The queen wanted to save the Isle.

"Queen April was not dissuaded by the impasse with the Islanders. She was determined to save her beloved Isle from further human wickedness. As we know, she prevailed in the end. She made the most of her supernatural magical powers. She cast a potent spell to enclose the Isle and its surrounding ocean in a protective covering.

"She also cast spells for the sun to continue to rise and set as usual. She ensured our moon had its lunar cycle. The rain fell, and the wind blew, and storms pummeled the shores. Before Queen April completed her spells, the Isle had two suns, two moons, and twice as many stars in the heavens. Satisfied the air was fresh and clean, the water crystal pure, and the soil fertile, she submerged the Isle beneath the sea. What you see around you and what you see in the sky are the results of Queen April's miraculous powers.

"At first Islanders did not know what had happened. They were also unaware that the queen's husband, Percival Winchester Roblins, had set sail on the open sea before the Isle sank below the surface. As time went by, Islanders learned of Queen April's magic spells and Roblins' quest. They ultimately accepted the queen's actions. The Islanders knew she wanted to protect the Isle from further harm by wicked humans.

"As I said earlier, the queen suspected Parston kidnaped Princess Eva. She was not certain. Islanders from other isles had showed an interest in the child princess, undoubtedly due to the princess' uncommon red hair. For this reason, before the queen sank the Isle, Percival set out to sail the Seven Seas in search of the child princess. Queen April continued her quest on the Isle of Spardom to find her daughter."

I am intrigued with Eranba's story. I have to wonder if the legends are even close to accurate. Even so, I say, "That certainly clears up a few things. It makes sense why Queen April sank the Isle beneath the sea. She did not want to tarnish the Isle's decency further. It is equally logical her husband should remain on the surface to search for his missing daughter, just as the queen should search the Isle. But I do not understand something, Eranba."

"What is that my dear Princess?" Eranba asks.

"We have no idea why humans on surface earth wanted us five elves on the Isle." Shrugging my shoulders, I add, "Why do you think we elves are here, Eranba? Do you have any idea?"

Instead of waiting for Eranba's answer, Lindsial looks at me and says, "Well, milady, you had mentioned the Enchanted Gate. Maybe that is the reason we are here..."

"The Enchanted Gate," Eranba interrupts as he shyly smiles at Lindsial. "According to myths, the Isle's original magical powers lie behind the Enchanted Gate. When Queen April ruled the whole Isle of Spardom, her citadel was supposedly within the walls of the Enchanted Gate. As far as I know, no creature has ever found the Enchanted Gate. Perhaps it lies to the northwest, in the unexplored, unknown lands."

"Eranba, I have another question," I ask. "Some powerful force, perhaps a being called Zarof, has visited my mind. He's supposedly a great wizard. Does he have anything to do with Parston?"

"I only know what legends say, milady," Eranba responds cautiously. "Zarof, the Great Wizard of the Land of Abeti, was not born on the Isle. All the same he allegedly was involved in helping Parston capture the queen's crown. Legends state Parston derives his powers from the crown he wears on his head."

"How did Parston come about this crown," I ask. "What do the legends say, Eranba?"

"My dear, Lady Princess," Eranba replies hesitantly, "Legends say a finishing battle followed after the Grand War, a few years after the princess disappeared. It involved many of the Isle's creatures. Some fought on the queen's side. Others fought on the side of Parston, Zarof, and the trolls. The battle was Queen April's attempt to defeat King Parston and reclaim her beloved Isle of Spardom.

"In the end, the queen and her devoted aides were captured and imprisoned. A mysterious force had overwhelmed the queen and somehow held her prisoner. The queen's crown was presented to King Parston by Zarof during a ceremony honoring Parston and his conquering army."

I notice the expression on Eranba's face is troubled. I know he has more to tell me, yet he is hesitant. I nod my head and say, "Continue if you please, Eranba. How was it Zarof was in possession of Queen April's crown?"

Eranba says, "I am very sorry to say this, my dear Princess Eva. The Great Wizard of the Land of Abeti, Zarof, presented the crown to King Parston after he beheaded the queen."

My hand involuntarily moves to cover my mouth. I am too stunned to speak. I feel as though my blood is beginning to boil from deep within me. What's more, I am brokenhearted.

If the legends are true, Queen April of Spardom, my ancestor, was murdered by Zarof. The same repulsive wickedness that beheaded the queen has been nauseatingly forcing itself into my mind. This murderous wickedness also vowed to take me as *his prize, betrothed as his bride!* I recoil with revulsion at the thought.

I am upset; so I am unable to speak. Lindsial can read my thoughts. Fortunately, she speaks for me. She softly asks, "So, Eranba, the crown is what gives King Parston his power over others?"

Avoiding my fixed stare, Eranba sighs, "I do not know for sure, elfin Lindsial. Legends say the crown gave the queen her magical powers just as the medallion our princess is wearing gives magical powers to her. So yes, I believe Parston gets his powers from the crown."

I have regained my composure to some extent. I ask, "If what the legends say is true, the Monarch of Magigro can use the crown for both good and evil. Am I correct, Eranba?"

"Yes, my dear Princess Eva of Spardom, I believe you are correct · that is if the legends are true to their spiritual word."

I suddenly stand. The others begin to stand as well. I gesture for them to remain seated. I boldly state, "I now know why we are here. If there is any truth to the legends, we will avenge the queen's death. We will take the crown from Parston. From what I can comprehend from thoughts entering my mind, the man is unspeakably evil. On the other hand, Zarof is undeniably eviler than Parston. Zarof executed the Queen of Spardom by beheading her.

"From this point going forward, we shall no longer refer to Parston as a king of anything. We shall simply refer to him as Parston. And Zarof shall be referred to as the Evil One. For reasons known only to me, I suspect he is the essence of everything evil. While retaking the queen's crown from Parson is our aim, Zarof's demise is our quest."

What I don't tell the others is I know Zarof's stated objective · to rule both Spardom and surface earth. I also do not mention to the others that he wants me as his wife · ugh! As a final point, I'm surely not going to tell the others

I saw his hideous reflection in the mirror. He is evil and depraved!

I sit back down to eat. As we enjoy Ariel-e's delicious, piping hot gumbo, no one speaks. After a while, Lindsial asks me via telepathy, "Milady, Eva, how do you suppose we go about doing the things you said?"

As I look at Lindsial, I give her an affectionate smile. She never ceases to amaze me. Although she is blind, she smiles in return! I respond aloud, "I have no earthly idea."

Donas looks at me and says, "I'm sorry, milady. You have no earthly idea about what?"

"I was just saying I have no idea how we go about taking the crown from Parston. For this reason, Donas, after breakfast I would like you, Ariel-e, Andrial, and Eranba to put your heads together to work on a plan. Lindsial and I will thrash out a counter plan. We will then put the two plans side by side to decide on the best course of action. We could stay here forever with these marvelous caring rocks and the ocean's delicious delicacies. However, we must move on."

Over the next several days, we brainstorm ideas to re-take the crown. Donas and his group study the topographical map Donas brought from surface earth. Eranba provides valuable input. He points on the map where regions lie.

Ariel-e annotates the map using a feather quill. The ink inside her quill is sepia, the brownish ink of a common cuddle fish. She will transfer the paper map's features onto a piece of parchment. All she needs to do is find suitable animal skin for curing in the sun.

Lindsial and I are taking a different approach. Away from the others, we thrash out our ideas via telepathy. Ariel-e joins us from time to time to point out important updates on the map. Ariel-e is highly skilled when it comes to deciphering maps. Her intricate details and map legends are extraordinary. As time will tell, her understanding of maps will lend itself greatly to our expedition.

Lindsial and I are deep in thought, exchanging ideas

via telepathy. "Yes, Lindsial, that is a huge problem. If what I envisioned in my mind is even remotely true about the fortress. We will need much more than five elves and a young spargnarl to face a stronghold defended by thousands of trolls armed to the teeth. The creatures have two heads and four arms. They have doubled the capacity to fight."

Lindsial conveys with a smile, "Yes, milady, they have doubled the capability to fight. Similar to us they also have one exposed heart. We can slay them like any other beast. Besides, there must be creatures or even kind humans we may recruit to help us. We simply don't know who they are or where they reside. Perhaps Eranba knows."

"He may, Lindsial. There may be other elves on the Isle or ghouls, or dwarfs, even giants perhaps. We should also assume if there is one human on the Isle, Parston · there may be other human beings. As you said, we do not know at this point. We're in a rather difficult predicament."

"Eva," Lindsial conveys, "I do not mean to change the topic, but I have a question. Why do you think Eranba suddenly became humble when he saw you? Was it you physically or was it the medallion?"

"That's a good question, Lindsial," I respond. "I think it was a little bit of both. He saw me, long hair and all, and then he saw the medallion, which is the replica of me. Or maybe I'm a replica of the medallion, whatever." I laugh. "Either way, I imagine the legends are the basis of his reaction. However, I am baffled how he equated me to the legends that quickly. Donas may have told him. I have no idea."

"I have no idea either." Lindsial's mind conveys. "All the same, I am glad he is on our side. He's a nice creature, and I'm confident he will help us as a guide. I have one more question. Why do you think Cindy and those bigwig clowns on surface earth wanted us here?"

"You know, Lindsial, I have been thinking about that for some time now. I have two theories. Humans want to gain the technology, the magic if you will, of an Isle thriving on the ocean floor. Think how that technology could change things for the better on surface earth. Perhaps do away with pollution, curb global warming, and protect nations from war, all sorts of things. It might even help to feed the poor. Think what it can do for the space program.

"Then again, knowing the history of mankind, I sort of doubt the world's bureaucrats give a damn about the Isle. Just as they subjugated other cultures throughout history, they may want the Isle for their greedy purpose. Perhaps a lot of natural gas is here. There might be gold or things more precious, such as rare earth elements. I am afraid, however · after they have emptied the Isle of its goodness, they will leave it in ruins.

"As it concerns Cindy, I honestly believe she was compelled to support the bureaucratic scheme. Then again, she may not have had a clue what we were getting into before we left surface earth. Perhaps, near the end, she and Kristopher worked together to ensure our safety. She may have been privy to Kristopher's plan to have us leave surface earth unharmed. It makes sense. From what you told me in the van, she and Kristopher have been involved in this entire plan from the get·go.

"My sixth sense says both Cindy and Shelly were on our side and wished us well. I hope I am correct. Both were smiling when we escaped. Cindy also gave me thumbs up. I hate to think Cindy knowingly betrayed us."

"I agree with your logic as it pertains to Cindy and Shelly Jones," Lindsial's thoughts say. "Regarding the rationale of why they wanted us here, perhaps there is a third reason. Please allow me to explain.

"Imagine for a moment those on surface earth know something incredibly evil is here on the Isle. And they know they are incapable of confronting it without your help. Let's say, just for argument's sake, they are worried the evil will ultimately spread to surface earth. Since the evil is supernatural, they have no means to counter it, except by using your powers.

"Think about it, Eva. Imagine someone or something

with powers similar to yours using magic on surface earth for other than good. Imagine the Evil One or Parston, untouchable on surface earth, using magic for immoral pursuits. It would be a terrible, nightmarish situation for the human population, to say the least."

Lindsial's theory is an eye-opener for me. It makes perfect sense too, especially considering what I know about Zarof. Then again, maybe she read some of my thoughts as it pertained to Zarof's aims. It doesn't matter; she has hit on something and once more demonstrated her remarkable intelligence.

"That never occurred to me." I convey. "Yes, mankind could surely use the Isle's know-how to advance its technology. As you say, imagine something with awesome magical powers running amuck on surface earth. That would be very bad. You may have something here, Lindsial. Maybe those on surface earth know something is amiss on the Isle. They suspect something evil is about to happen. That should explain their urgency in getting us here."

Lindsial manages a timid smile and shrugs. "Well, we screwed that up, Eva. We left before they could tell us what it was they wanted us to do. All the same, I am glad we left the way we did. I didn't trust that UTD one bit."

With a wry smile, I convey, "I didn't trust it either as you and General Powers could tell. Yes, we left without knowing why they want us here. Now that we're here, I certainly know what we are going to do. We are going to destroy Parston, the Evil One, and their cohorts. Then I am going to take back the crown that rightfully belongs to me. If your assumption is correct, that should make everyone happy - here on Spardom and surface earth."

CHAPTER TWENTY-TWO

ARIEL-E PROPOSES A PLAN

Nearly three weeks have passed since I proclaimed my intent to journey to the Kingdom of Magigro. Our deciding on the journey plan has taken much longer than any of us had anticipated. Despite our well-intentioned efforts, the six of us cannot agree on a feasible course of action. We always seem to come across too many sticking points and at least three times the number of unknowns.

We spend a few hours each day brainstorming ideas within our two teams. Now and then we thrash out our thoughts as an all-inclusive group for an additional hour or two. However, we do not reach agreement. After our group sessions, we kick back to enjoy ourselves for the rest of the day. I admit I am just as guilty as the others. The locale, where we are camping, is a miraculous paradise. All the same, I recognize we are wasting too much valuable time.

That is not to say everything is fun and games. Quite the opposite - a few important things are getting accomplished. There are plenty of weapons training events every day. Ariel-e practices with both sword and spear two to three times a day. She also has skill-enhancing swordfights with Lindsial. Donas and Andrial hone their archery skills. I am happy to say they are expert archers. They hit the heart of a bull's eye carved into a dead tree trunk without fail.

I am now an expert at handling my sword. I have almost perfected my spells and enchantments. I no longer have to point with my hand or speak aloud when I cast a spell. I simply think of the spell, what I want it to bring about, and it comes to pass. I do use my hands on occasion, circling them in the air or pointing. But this is more for show than a necessity. After all, an elf wizardess with magical powers has to show off now and then, right?

As I said, we are industrious to some extent. Yet playing trifling games and enjoying hours-long swims in the ocean every day along with valueless frivolity · we are going way overboard. We need to get our act together and come up with a practical plan.

Our plan will need to include winning over the loyalty of others we meet along the way. They could be unknown beasts of Fogreia and the Land of Abeti. They could be phantoms of the Banned Borders and perhaps even humans. We could meet other elves and perhaps even dwarfs if they still exist on the Isle.

Then again, we may not meet any creatures we can befriend as allies. Outside of what we learned when were on surface earth and what Eranba has told us, we will be journeying into the unknown.

Speaking of Eranba, he is confident Gonialit will not hesitate to join us as we journey toward Magigro. After all, as he said, spargnarls and trolls are mortal enemies. The two species of creatures have been enemies since Parston tried to conquer Fogreia after the Grand War.

Eranba does not convince me. I argue Gonialit will not be readily forgiving to join forces with the same group that slaughtered about fifty of his kind with the help of kindly rocks. I promise Eranba I will keep my options open. If I have to appeal in the future to the spargnarls' strength and numbers for aid, I will not hesitate to do so.

"Besides," I say to Eranba, "Let's face reality. What do we have to offer them? We are but five elves and a young spargnarl. Each of us has weapons with which to fight, either ordinary or magical or both, yet we are six companionless fighters. What may we realistically offer to a battle against thousands that are better armed and protected with massive walls?

"We will have to trek thousands of miles through unchartered territory. We will need food provisions to last us many weeks, many months, or even a year or more. We will need to consider shelter, clothing, and water, especially for Ariel·e. Most notably, we will need plenty of good luck."

Now, as we sit around chitchatting after breakfast, I clap my hands together three times. I say, "Okay, the party is over. It is time to put our heads together as one. We must come up with a plan all of us can agree to." I look at the others one by one. Shrugging my shoulders, I add, "Does anyone have a suggestion?"

Ariel·e raises her hand. Raising hands during important discussions such as this is now a necessity. When we are in a group, we tend to chatter away. Normally I do not mind. What we need to discuss this morning is too important for idle babbling. I do not want any of us to miss something important.

Let's be honest here. I cannot hear. Lindsial cannot see. Lindsial and I cannot read Eranba's mind. Andrial cannot speak. He uses sign language only I understand. Lindsial or I have to repeat everything he says in his mind. As you can see, we have a few challenges when it comes to group discussions. For this reason, as childish as it appears, discipline in the form of raising one's hand before speaking is vital.

I nod with a smile for Ariel·e to speak. I watch as Ariel·e traces the topographical map with her slender forefinger. There is no need for me to watch her lips as she speaks. I read her thoughts as her finger moves across the map.

As Ariel·e talks, I take a moment to consider my thought transference skill. Telepathy is wonderful. I no longer have to look to see if others are speaking to me. I simply sense their words through their thoughts. Of course, in the interest of good manners, I nearly always make eye contact with those who speak to me. Since it was a necessity in the past, I also find I still read lips on occasion. However, I no longer have a problem discerning difficult words others form on their lips. I smile. I will no longer have problems with mustaches either.

Ariel·e says, "Milady, we all see eye to eye regarding movement by the sea. None of us has the talent to build a raft. We also do not have the necessary tools. While I can use the ocean's energy to my gain, I cannot direct its fury. Any sudden storm at sea could spell disaster for everyone but me. Begging milady's pardon, I think we should scrap all strategies to travel around the Isle by raft or other sailing vessels."

I nod with a smile and say, "I wholeheartedly concur, Ariel·e. Continue if you please."

"Well milady, as you can see, the Land of Abeti is in the central portion of Spardom. Abeti consists of two distinct deserts. A mountain range is in the middle of Abeti. It divides the land into two separate deserts, one to the north, and one to the south.

"If we assume the map is fairly accurate, a trail begins at the easternmost edge of the Forest of Fogreia and continues straight across the southern desert of Abeti. As you can see, it breaks into three separate trails near the center of Abeti. One trail leads to the Kingdom of Magigro far to the northeast. Another leads to the Banned Borders to the east. The third leads to the northernmost, unexplored territory Eranba mentioned three weeks ago."

Turning to Eranba, Ariel·e inquires, "Eranba, you said you ventured along the southern trail of Abeti's desert with your cousin Bratle a few years ago. Is that correct?"

Eranba looks at me. He forcefully thrusts his hand high in the air. He is asking permission to speak. Everyone laughs at Eranba's eager gesture.

He looks at us one by one with a puzzled look on his

face and then he asks me, "Did I do something wrong?"

"You do not have to raise your hand when someone asks you a question, Eranba," I offer with a smile. "When we ask someone a question, we will assume that elf or spargnarl will respond. So, Eranba, please feel free to speak."

Eranba smiles sheepishly. "I understand milady. Thank you." Turning his head slightly to look at Ariel·e, he says, "Yes, elfin Ariel·e, we traveled all the way to the border of the Kingdom of Magigro. We were told to spy on the trolls and then report to Gonialit what we saw. There were ten of us in our group. Gonialit seemed quite pleased with our report."

"What kinds of provisions did you carry?" Ariel·e asks.

Eranba says, "Well, we had food and water and…"

Ariel·e waves her hand to interrupt him. "I am sorry to interrupt you, Eranba. How much food and water did you have in your possession when you left the border of Fogreia and Abeti before you entered the desert?"

"I guess it was a week's worth. I am not certain," Eranba replies. "When our provisions became in short supply, we slaughtered wild sheep, boar, and other beasts native to the Isle. They are plentiful in the hills along the trail. There is fresh water in the form of springs and a few streams here and there where we refilled our leather hide flagons."

"Thank you, Eranba," Ariel·e says. Turning her head once more in my direction, she states, "Now, milady, it would make perfect sense for a well·traveled trail through the desert to have sources of food and water. If one knows how to look for food and water, one can always find them. Believe me when I say this.

"Continuing if I may, I think it is best that we do not head directly north toward the unexplored region, for two reasons. One, we have no clue what we will find when we get there, and two; as you stated, our quest is to the northeast. After we overthrow the Monarch of Magigro, we can always explore the northern, unexplored area at our leisure. I know the region to the Isle's northwest interests you, milady. However, I see no point in exploring it at this time."

Ariel·e's logic makes perfect sense to me. I nod for her to continue.

"As I see it, milady, we have two options. The first is to take the trail that runs through the Forest of Fogreia into the desert Land of Abeti and beyond." Ariel·e points to the map, tracing her finger from the x, which denotes where we are at present, to the border of Abeti.

Continuing she says, "The journey through Fogreia will be dangerous, especially after our recent battle with the spargnarls. All the same, I suspect our entire journey will be fraught with danger. Why not gain knowledge as we travel, by facing dangers head on, both known and the unknown?

"After we complete our journey through Fogreia, I suggest we follow Abeti's southernmost trail to the Banned Borders. Magigro and Banned Borders share the same border. I have a hunch that the inhabitants of the two domains are enemies. I also suspect Abeti's inhabitants are likewise on unfriendly terms with inhabitants of Banned Borders.

"If you think about it, the name by itself, Banned Borders, has its inferences. One could define Banned Borders as borders that are forbidden, disbarred, excluded, and prohibited. Added to this are milady and Eranba's comments that the wizard of Abeti and the king of Magigro seem to be on friendly terms. It makes perfect sense to me Banned Borders is not on friendly terms with Magigro and Abeti. Given this hypothesis, we may find creatures of Banned Borders willing to ally with us against Abeti and Magigro.

"Once we are inside the land of Banned Borders, we can take the trail or follow the river northward to Magigro. By then we may have, as I said, allies from residents of Banned Borders as well as from other regions through which we have traveled."

It is obvious to me that Ariel·e has carefully thought out her proposals. Each aspect of her proposals makes perfect sense. I nod my head in agreement. I ask, "And what is your second option, Ariel·e?"

Ariel·e once again traces the map with her finger. "Well, milady, the second option is to follow the southern coast to the east until we reach the southernmost border of Fogreia and Abeti. From there, we head upstream along the easternmost river that parallels the border. We will eventually arrive at the trail that leads to Abeti. I spoke of it earlier.

"There is one major difficulty with this second option. We will encounter the high mountain range that juts into the ocean at this peninsula." She points to the mountain range on the map. "This is the same range Andrial spoke of a while ago. If we take this route along the coast, we add weeks, if not a month, to our journey. Perhaps we may even add two months or more to our journey. This second option is also more circuitous than the first option. On the other hand, it could be safer seeing as we may not run into spargnarls along the way."

Lindsial raises her hand. I convey in my mind for her to speak. She says, "Obviously, milady, I cannot see the map. I can sort of visualize it in my mind. Given the thorough manner in which Ariel·e has laid out both options, I think the first option is the best.

"I do not like the second option at all. Proceeding along the southern coast will expose us to danger. Our only means of escape would be venturing into the forest to the north. If spargnarls attacked with any logic, we would be trapped. With the exception of Ariel·e, the entire southern shoreline shall provide us with no means of escape. At least with the first option, we have an entire forest in all directions to escape if need be.

"Heading toward the Banned Borders instead of directly to Magigro makes perfect sense to me as well. What Ariel·e said about the meaning of the Banned Borders' name also seems highly logical. From what I can visualize of the map in my mind, Banned Borders has, as Ariel·e said, a likely enemy on two sides, Magigro, and Abeti. The ocean is on the other two sides. It appears Banned Borders is the most vulnerable region of the Isle, with enemies on two sides and an inhospitable ocean on the other two sides.

"In consideration of this, I agree with Ariel·e once again. We may elicit support from Banned Border creatures to aid us in our quest. It seems promising, particularly if they are an adversary of both Abeti and Magigro. They may not like us in the least. As the saying goes, *the enemy of my enemy is my friend."*

Donas' hand is now in the air. I nod for him to speak. "Well, milady, I also agree with Ariel·e and Lindsial's suggestions. I should offer · there are numerous spargnarl traps in Fogreia. I can personally attest to their effectiveness." He smiles in spite of himself. We laugh. Understandably, Eranba laughs the loudest.

Donas continues, "May I suggest Eranba serve as our scout while we are in spargnarl country? He knows the lay of the land. If we encounter unruly spargnarls along the way, he can alert us, perhaps even negotiate with them. I may be quick. However, I am no match for the hidden spargnarl trap. For this reason, Eranba is my choice for point spargnarl ahead of the group." I smile as Donas and Eranba exchange a spirited high five. Compared to Eranba's hand · it is as large as a New York Yankees catcher's glove · Donas' hand seems tiny.

With a proud look on his face, Eranba raises his hand. I smile and nod my head for him to speak. He says with a smile, "Milady, I also like the plan elfin Ariel·e has proposed. May I offer something?" I smile once again and nod for him to continue.

He says, "I know where there are horses. Either humans or elves first owned them. I do not know which. A few spargnarl tribes use them for carrying provisions. Perhaps I can ask to borrow some. Then at least a few of you can ride a horse, instead of walking. The journey through Fogreia and the Land of Abeti is quite long. It is tiring as well. Horses will do you much service."

"You know where there are horses?" I say excitedly. "Where are they, Eranba? Do you think others will lend them to us?"

Eranba thrusts his hand in the air once again. His three eyes see that we elves are grinning. He withdraws his hand slowly and says with a timid smile, "Sorry, I forgot." He continues to address me saying, "They are in the forest, milady. Spargnarl youngsters ride them until the youngsters grow too large. Others use the horses to carry packs when journeying through the Land of Abeti to the Hidden Valley. There is good hunting in the Hidden Valley. When the horses grow too old or are unable to carry loads, they are slaughtered for meat. I rode a horse when I was very young, milady. They are quite fun. I think you will like them."

I say, "If you think the spargnarls who own the horses will let us borrow them that would be wonderful!"

"Yes, milady, I am sure they would let us borrow them!" Eranba exclaims eagerly. "I have a number of acquaintances who would gladly allow the Princess of Spardom to borrow anything she desires, anything at all!"

"Well, that solves one very important issue, transportation," Andrial's thoughts say as he raises his hand. As he looks at me, I smile. I nod for him to think his thoughts so I can read them in my mind. After he finishes, I will repeat his thoughts to the others.

"Milady, I also agree with Ariel-e's first proposal. I should like to accompany Eranba and Donas as scout through Fogreia. Eranba's knowledge of the area and the location of spargnarl traps shall be crucial. Donas' ability to sprint ahead of us will be equally crucial. Combined with my hearing and eyesight, I do believe the three of us would make a splendid team. The only drawback is I will be unable to talk to Donas and Eranba. Since you, milady, and Lindsial can read my thoughts that should work to our benefit, in the long run."

I signal with my hand for Andrial to pause for a moment. I need to relay the high points of his comments to the others. I recount his comments as best as I can, and then I nod for him to continue.

"I also suggest, milady, once we are in the Land of Abeti desert · I should journey at least one day in advance of the rest of the group. By the looks of the topographical nature of the map, there are plenty of moderately high hills along our path. If I stay in the hills, I will see and hear across great distances free of natural obstructions. I can update you via my mind's thoughts if I see or hear any· thing troubling along our path."

I take a few moments to paraphrase Andrial's com· ments to the others once again. After I have finished, I an· nounce cheerfully, "Well, we have a plan! I wholeheartedly agree with Ariel·e's plan and the comments offered by the rest of you. I thank you."

Addressing Ariel·e, I say, "It is a grand plan indeed! That was also a good call asking Eranba about water sources. How in the world did you assume there was water along the trail in Abeti?"

Smiling her naturally pleasant charismatic smile, Ari· el·e replies, "I thank you, milady. I believe my mind works in an atypical way when it comes to the important mole· cule of water. Agreed, water is vital to all living things. Those of you who walk on land need only to carry water in containers as you journey. When a creature's existence de· pends on being submerged or doused in water quite often, that creature's mind thinks differently. To be frank with you, milady, I had a hunch. Happily, thanks to Eranba's corroboration, my hunch was right."

"Well, congratulations everyone," I say cheerfully. "All that remains in the coming weeks is to prepare for our journey. But first, what is on my mind right now is food." I turn to look at Ariel·e. With a pleading grin on my face, I ask with all seriousness, "Ariel·e my dear, what is for lunch? I don't know about the others, but I'm hungry again!"

CHAPTER TWENTY-THREE

PREPARING FOR
THE JOURNEY

We are full of activity during the next month as we prepare to journey east. Everyone is excited · you can feel the anticipation as we go about our arrangements. While there is much enthusiasm, we are incredibly apprehensive.

Many unanswered questions dominate our discussions. Will we be fully prepared? Will we have enough provisions? Will we have ample supplies of water for Ariel·e, just in case? Who or what will we meet along the way? Will they be friendly, or will they be foes? What if we're wrong about the path that we've chosen to journey, and we get hopelessly lost?

Eranba ventures into the Forest of Fogreia to visit his close acquaintances. He seeks to borrow five horses, one horse each for Lindsial, Ariel·e, Andrial, and me. A fifth horse will carry provisions. Donas does not need a horse. He can run as speedily as a horse can gallop. He also doesn't need to take lengthy breaks throughout the day like the rest of us. On the other hand, as soon as dusk arrives, Donas is typically sound asleep, safely tucked away high in the crook of a tree limb. He never moves from his perch until sunrise.

On the way to his acquaintances' district Eranba drops by to visit his cousin Bratle. If you will recall, Bratle was the spargnarl that helped Eranba release Donas from his trap. Eranba asks Bratle if he would like to go on an adventure. After a bit of discussion about our planned endeavor, Bratle eagerly agrees. He gives his word to Eranba to keep silent about our destination and the route we will travel. When Bratle agrees to join us, we become the *Group of Seven.*

Eranba tells his acquaintances who own the horses the Princess of Spardom is on the Isle. He also boasts he and Bratle are going to accompany us on a journey. Eranba also says we are going to battle the trolls in Magigro. Not surprisingly, Eranba's acquaintances do not believe him. They think Eranba is trying to trick them. They think Eranba is making up wild stories of adventure, perhaps to acquire their horses so he can sell them. They refuse Eranba's pleas to loan him their horses. They also think the unthinkable. They think Eranba is lying to them.

In the kingdom of spargnarls, a spargnarl's word is as important as his reputation. As a general rule spargnarls do not lie. Spargnarls consider lying as shameful as thieving. There is not much a spargnarl friend or relative can do to get in trouble with his fellow tribe members. However, lying is as unthinkable as injuring or killing a fellow spargnarl. Spargnarls loathe lying very much.

As you and I know, Eranba is telling the truth. Not to be dissuaded, Eranba offers his acquaintances a deal. If they swear not to tell others where our campsite is, he will take them to see us. They readily agree. Although they still do not trust Eranba's honesty.

After the spargnarls arrive at our campsite, they apologize to Eranba profusely for not believing his story. More importantly, at least for us elves, Eranba's acquaintances say they will gladly lend us their horses. As you can imagine, this makes me extremely happy. Horses will benefit us greatly as we journey.

After the formality of introductions between Eranba's acquaintances and us elves, what follows is a great quantity of boisterous hubbub, deafening singing, and side-splitting storytelling around the campfire. This merriment will continue well into the early hours of the morning.

I am quite pleased, to say the least. I recognize it is valuable to display friendship to the spargnarls. I do not want to go to the top of the spargnarl hierarchy, at least not yet. All the same, earning the trust of Eranba's acquaintances is a low-keyed, excellent first start. What's more, Eranba's acquaintances are loads of fun. They know how to party. I also notice that Eranba's acquaintances are giving Eranba well-deserved respect. Even though he is different, because of his gnarl-less body, I believe Eranba now has fellow spargnarl's that think of him as a friend.

Ariel-e treats us to a grand feast of assorted seafood delicacies. She serves up roasted crabs, toasted mussels, and clams, and salt flavored fish kebabs. She also prepares raw fish filets tucked inside mouth-watering seaweed. Our favorite fare is milky black cuttlefish morsels pierced with small tree branch skewers that resemble toothpicks. The cuttlefish morsels are delectable. Ariel-e's face beams with evident joy when we compliment her on the many scrumptious entrees she has prepared.

Andrial's purple-colored roasted tubers are an added delight. The tubers have a crunchy exterior and a delectably soft and flavorful meaty interior. They go well with the seafood. We compliment Andrial on his expert cooking. You know how much I like to eat tubers. As a result of Andrial's efforts, I give him a smooch on his cheek to express my thanks. My fleeting kiss causes him to blush for the longest time.

Bratle suddenly produces a large ceramic jug of home-made spargnarl ale. Everyone laughs when he says it is strictly for medicinal purposes. In a teasing voice, he says, "Before anyone samples a mouthful of ale, he, or she must declare sickness - no excuses!"

I am displeased at first because I think the beverage is intoxicating. I loathe alcoholic beverages. I watched the abuse of alcohol sour too many close relationships amongst my coworkers. It also caused havoc within their families. One of my coworkers lived with a physically abusive alcoholic. It was a nightmare until he severed the bond between them. She finally got treatment, and the two of them date from time to time. I can only hope it works out for them. They're nice people.

Happily, Bratle's drink is non-alcoholic ale called *crasthka*. Crasthka's main ingredient comes from a Fogreia berry bush with a similar name, *crasth*. The spargnarls mash the orange-coloured berries then mix the juices with water and shredded needles of a tree that resemble pine. After straining it, they add loads of sugar from root plants that resemble surface earth sugar beets.

There is a fermented, alcoholic version of the ale, robust and less sweet. It is called *crasthkataka*. Our non-alcoholic beverage, crasthka, is mouth-watering and syrupy and pleasingly delicious. It has a fruity taste but easily goes down my throat like tangy Kool-Aid.

A few of our sickness declarations are, "I feel nauseous. My tummy is aching. I've got a throbbing headache. I need a swig before I pass out!" Ensuing edits surpass the absurdness of the last. As we continue to sample the delicious, sweet-tasting non-alcoholic ale, each new edict is met with good-natured laughter. After a short time, follow-on edicts make no sense at all. While I know the beverage is non-alcoholic, I also know I am now on a crystal-clear sugar high. Along with the others, I am having the time of my life.

During the feast, Lindsial brings up the subjects of loyalty and honesty. She has read my mind once more. I was thinking to introduce the same two themes discretely. I now have my opening, thanks to my mind-reading best companion. I ask Eranba's friends and his cousin Bratle if they will help battle the Monarch of Magigro if the need arises. They enthusiastically say yes.

One of Eranba's friends named Jalosht goes a bit further with his eagerness. He says, "If Gonialit had known
you were the Princess of Spardom, there would never have
been a battle. He and his district's spargnarls and every
other spargnarl district in Fogreia would have been at your
service." The other spargnarls nod their heads in agreement.

I caution Eranba's friends they must give their word,
not to mention our presence or intentions to others. If I
deem it necessary to elicit their aid in the future, I will let
them know by the fastest means possible. Only then should
they tell others about my presence on the Isle and our
quest to retake the crown.

Lindsial makes the secrecy process a trifle more formal. She asks the spargnarls, to include Eranba and his
cousin, to swear an oath of allegiance to the Princess of
Spardom. To enact the fairness amongst all, she also asks
the elves to participate. She asks the group to swear to
keep the Group of Seven's intentions secret. With his or her
hand held high in the air, everyone in the group eagerly
responds, "I swear."

I am not too worried about Eranba's friends divulging
our presence or intentions. I know our secret is safe with
them. After all, a spargnarl's word is his bond. All the
same, Lindsial's oath of allegiance adds a bit of ceremony
to the entire secret-keeping process.

A few days after our feast, Eranba and Bratle return
with five horses. There are four young horses, one each for
Lindsial, Ariel-e, Andrial, and me. An older horse will carry our provisions. For now, Ariel-e and Andrial's horses are
nameless. Knowing how much the two elves love animals,
I'm confident the horses will have names before our journey begins. Lindsial's Arabia horse is called Ceria. Ceria is
a younger sister of my horse. Ceria is as beautiful as they
come.

My horse is a gorgeous dark brown Arabia beauty
named Pranzen. Eranba says Pranzen is a gift of love and

respect on behalf of his friend Wordatha. Lindsial's horse is also a gift. Termazle gave it to her. He is another of Eranba's friends. The other three horses are on loan. In due course, the horses' owners will give the three horses to us as gifts.

According to Bratle, Lindsial's horse, Ceria, and my horse Pranzen are descendants of the very horses Queen April rode. Considering these accounts concern the legend of Queen April, I cannot prove their accuracy. Neverthe-less, it feels mightily awesome for Lindsial and me to ride horses that may be descendants of Queen April's steeds.

As the days pass us by, we stay industrious with our preparations. We now have a meaningful mission. Each of us has specific assignments to take the mission to fruition. Ariel·e is in charge of food preparation. She spreads out various species of sliced fish on top of boulders to dry in the sun.

Ariel·e also prepares flasks, bowls, baskets and jugs of varying shapes and sizes. Some will hold food provisions. Others will serve as utensils for eating and drinking. She also salts fresh game caught by Donas and Andrial. She packs the meat in tightly woven seaweed jugs. In addition to her many chores, she shows me how to throw a spear properly. I am nowhere as accurate as her. Yet I can hit a target from fifteen paces.

In addition to hunting for game, Donas and Andrial manufacture knives and spoons from seashells Ariel·e col-lects from the ocean's floor. They also practice their sword and archery techniques and make many arrows.

Lindsial spends the bulk of her free time showing me how to enhance my defensive spells. My credo auduro spell is now all-powerful. I feel as if my childhood dreams to pos-sess supernatural powers have come true. I can create and hurl large fireballs at great speed over any distance with pinpoint accuracy. I also perfect my moveo spell. I can now pick up multiple objects at the same time. In the past, I could not pick up or move more than one object at once.

I also learn new spells. Eranba is fond of one spell,

above all. He is readily willing to have it practiced on him. By using the prefix *praetendō,* with the following word or phrase in Fortunomy, I can compel Eranba to do things of which he has no control. As an example, I look at Eranba and say either silently or audibly in Fortunomy, *praetendō dance!* Eranba pretends to dance. By pretending to dance, Eranba does what I command. He dances! I say in Fortunomy *praetendō run in circles!* Eranba obligingly runs in circles in response to my command, until I tell him to stop. While the praetendō spell is entertaining fun for Eranba and the others, it will be very useful in the coming months.

There is one spell that I learned quite by accident. Even Lindsial was not aware of the spell. I will explain how my knowledge of the spell came to be.

Lindsial had turned invisible for a few minutes to listen to the soft squeaking noise made by a small rodent that sat on a limb. I recognized early in my training that a few of the words I use for my spells come from Latin. I asked her via thought transference, "Lindsial, do you know the Latin word for invisible?"

"Yes, it is *invisibilis.*" Lindsial conveyed.

I mulled the word over in my mind for a bit. In a whisper, I said aloud, "Invisibilis. Now that is a fine word." I happened to be staring indifferently at a blackbird perched on a boulder when I said the word. To my surprise the bird disappeared. I had turned it invisible! "Oh my goodness, will you look at that!" I said aloud.

"What is it?" Lindsial conveyed via thought transference. She was still listening to the rodent's squeaking while she was invisible. She did not want to scare the rodent away by speaking aloud.

"I think I just made a bird disappear," I cried out loud. "Do you know the Latin word for visible?"

"Please, not too loud, I'm working here," Lindsial jokingly said in her mind. "Yes, I do. It is *promptus.*"

Staring at the location where the bird had been a few seconds before, I whispered, "Promptus!" The bird was visible yet again, perched exactly where it had been just moments before!

My invisibilis spell had one limitation at first. I had to look at an object straight on before I could make it disappear. The same was true when turning it visible yet again. It will be many months before I am able to turn something to its visible form without looking directly at where I suppose it is.

I regularly practiced the invisibilis spell on non-living objects. I dared not use it on the others or any creature that was able to move. I was afraid I would be unable to make whatever I had turned invisible reappear. Could you imagine if I turned a bird invisible - just to have it fly away and never again be seen by its mate? Then again, the more I think about it - perhaps that's not a bad thing...

In any case, I did enjoy tricking Eranba and his cousin on occasion with my invisibilis spell. I would cause a tankard to disappear during dinner, innocent disappearances similar to that. I was particularly fond of causing the spargnarls' tankards to disappear just as the cousins were reaching for them. The others and I would act indifferent, pretending nothing strange had occurred.

I would say innocently, "Say what? Your tankard disappeared? C'mon, Bratle (or Eranba) have you been sipping crasthkataka when we're not looking?"

One day Eranba came to me obviously upset and incredibly worried. He said he and Bratle thought dark things were haunting them. Of course, I had to tell the spargnarls of my newfound magic. Laid-back and easygoing as usual, they just chuckled and asked me to demonstrate my brand new spell. They insisted I turn them invisible as well, so they could feel the sensation. I was hesitant at first because, you know, I was afraid they'd move about, and I couldn't find them again. Happily, all went well.

Over time, I will become skilled at routinely casting my invisibilis spell on living creatures as well as on inanimate objects. Just like my praetendō spell and other powers, I will put my invisibilis spell to good use on our journey.

Eranba and Bratle are extremely busy during the

preparation phase of our journey. Fortunately, for us elves, the spargnarl cousins have a flair for sewing. Eranba sews me numerous lovely outfits, as he puts it, "befitting your status as Princess of Spardom." My favorite outfit is a long sleeve white elfin robe. It fits me perfectly. Eranba says I look like an elf princess from the white hood of the robe to the billowing skirts at its foot. I will wear this very robe during an episode of some significance later in the story.

Eranba also makes me two short-sleeved dresses for strolling in the sun, complete with matching hats to protect my fair skin. Riding outfits, sleepwear, and a warm white cloak add to my Spardom wardrobe. Eranba's spargnarl friend, Termazle, donated the fabric for my outfits. Termazle is the spargnarl district tailor. If you'll recall, Termazle gave Lindsial's horse, Ceria, to her.

Bratle makes dresses for Lindsial and Ariel-e. Lindsial's dresses are a soft brown, and Ariel-e's are an emerald green. He also makes the female elves four short-sleeved blouses with matching pants, sleepwear, and cloaks. Like Eranba, Bratle's sewing expertise is apparent. Lindsial and Ariel-e's garments fit perfectly.

Bratle and Eranba's friends assist in the preparation of our group's journey as well. They sew rugged hunting clothes for Donas and Andrial. What is more, they sew waterproof animal skin cloaks to protect all of us, to include Eranba and Bratle, from the elements.

We are over a month into our journey's preparation phase. I am happy to say we are finally prepared to begin our journey. After eating our last delicious meal at our campsite where we arrived on Spardom, I draw one and all together, including Eranba's friends. I want to thank them for their loyalty and hard work.

I say, "I know the road will be hard from time to time. The elements will try our patience. We do not know who or what will come to our aid. However, we know why we journey. We must meet our main enemy face-to-face, and we must defeat him. We must reclaim the crown for all of Spardom.

"We must defeat our enemy for the benefit of all creatures on our beloved Isle. We must also defeat our enemy for all creatures on surface earth. How we shall do this, we do not know. I am confident we will find a way. With that said, I say to each and every one of you, thank you! I love you. I am very proud to call you my friends."

I walk along the elves and spargnarls in front of me. I stop to kiss each one on his or her cheek. Tears of affectionate love and joy fall freely from the eyes of us elves. Spargnarls do not shed tears from any of their three eyes. Judging by the looks on their faces, I know they are just as moved as us elves.

As the sun sets with its dazzling display of reddish orange against a dark blue cloudless sky, I address the others once more. I say, "Group of Seven - at first light let our journey begin!"

CHAPTER TWENTY-FOUR

ARIEL-E IS MISSING!

At last · it is time to journey east! The first thing I do this morning is pick up one of the rocks that came to our aid months ago. I intend to carry one rock along with me as we journey. Who knows, it just may come in handy in case we need to battle. If nothing else, it'll be a good luck charm.

Oddly, the rock weighs next to nothing. Thinking I must have picked up a defective rock, if there is such a thing, I toss it to the ground. As I expected, it lands exactly in the spot from where I retrieved it. I pick up a second rock, then a third. Just like the first rock, these two are practically weightless.

All of a sudden it dawns on me. The rocks changed their physical structure. It is as if they have a mind of their own · but of course they do! They know how to battle, provide shelter, and return to their precise nesting places. They are now as light as a feather and intend to accompany us. We can carry a bunch of them in our satchels!

Holding the two rocks high in the air I shout, "Hey everyone, squeeze as many of these rocks into your satchels as you can. They weigh nothing practically. They want to come along on our journey. I'm sure of it. Besides, they may come in handy."

The others look at me as if I have finally lost my mind. Lindsial's thoughts seem to confirm teasingly what the others may be thinking. Maybe I have lost my mind. Even so, I am thankful they do as I ask.

As we stuff the rocks in our satchels, their mass changes into spongy stuff. Incredibly, they take up little room. They're no longer about three inches in diameter. Now, when we squeeze them, they are the size of large glass marbles. We pack dozens of rocks into our satchels.

We are now entering the forest of Fogreia. It is a less than a half-hour after daybreak. Eranba says spargnarls seldom wake up earlier than mid-morning, especially on rainy days. To our benefit, this path is seldom used by spargnarls. By taking this path, along with our early start, we will travel well beyond Gonialit's domain before the spargnarls stir. As if fate has smiled on us, it is raining. We want to avoid Gonialit and his district's spargnarls at all costs, so the rain is welcome.

Except for Donas, Eranba, and Bratle, this is the first time Lindsial, Ariel-e, Andrial, and I have ventured into the forest. The four of us are a bit anxious. As we take our first hesitant steps into the forest we glance at one another with an uneasy look that seems to say, "I'm not so sure I want to do this!"

As I said, this path is hardly ever used. The going is slow, to say the least. The forest closes in on all sides with thick underbrush beneath our feet. There barely is enough clearance below the tree limbs for us to walk upright. The two spargnarls need to stoop low as they move through the forest. Despite being doubled-over, they are at ease walking along the path, more so than us elves. Due to the path's low ceiling, we cannot mount our horses. They follow along behind us.

Massive spider webs hang low from bushes and tree limbs. The webs are at least three feet across, a width equal to that of the narrow trail. Enormous insects and unattractive vermin are sheathed inside silky cocoons. The unlucky creatures hang helplessly from the spiders' gummy traps as they await their doom. When one of us elves walks into a web by accident, we tug at the sticky gunk with understandable disgust. We wipe our hands on tree limbs and grass to rid ourselves of the gooey mess, grumbling all the while.

The spargnarls and horses do not seem to mind the webs as much as the others and me. After seeing how rattled we three elves get with the spiders' silky mess, Bratle takes the lead of my small group. Before long his entire body is covered in strands of grayish gluey goo. His appearance resembles a huge tousled ball of discolored thread as he walks. His look would be comical to us if it were not for our extreme dislike of the spider webs.

Donas, Andrial, and Eranba are ahead of my group. They are a good distance in front of us, perhaps a half-hour's walk. The two male elves will advise Lindsial and me using their thoughts if they detect danger. My group consists of Bratle, Lindsial, Ariel·e, and, of course, me. We three female elves follow behind Bratle. I trail Bratle with my horse, Pranzen. Lindsial and her horse Ceria follow closely behind me. Ariel·e and her horse bring up the rear of our group.

I had mentioned it shouldn't be long before Ariel·e and Andrial named their horses. Ariel·e calls her horse Dixie Ranger. Ariel·e explains her horse's first name, Dixie, signifies the southern area of America like the state of Tennessee. The horse's middle name Ranger signifies a soldier (in this case a horse) trained for speedy, sudden attacks against the enemy. So, there you have it, her southern brave horse soldier, Dixie Ranger.

Andrial's horse is Mister Ed. His horse's name is in honor of the talking horse in short stories written by Walter R. Brooks. It should come as no surprise · *non-talking* Andrial naming his mount after a *talking* horse. Now, if only Mister Ed could do Andrial's talking for him · that would be magically wonderful! Who knows? Maybe in the future it's possible.

I am happy to note everyone seems to be in relatively good spirits. The happiness of our group is rather surprising. The sweltering mist and nearness of the thick forest make our progress uncomfortable, to say the least. There are the low-lying tree limbs, difficult underbrush, and sticky spider webs that I mentioned.

Ariel·e seems the most content. I presume drops of water raining down on us tirelessly from the waterlogged branches cause her happiness. Unlike Lindsial and me, and our obvious displeasure with the soggy conditions along the path, Ariel·e is in her happy place. For the charming, happy-go-lucky elf mermaid, the more water, the better.

I glance over my shoulder from time to time. I cannot help but smile at Ariel·e's overjoyed dancing as she cheerfully strolls along the path. As I've said before, our lovely elf mermaid Ariel·e loves to sing. She tends to sing a song repeatedly until its words are part of my long-term memory.

At present, she is singing a song composed by Bratle. I cannot hear the words. As Ariel·e forms the words in her mind, I am able to follow along with the lyrics. This song will become our favorite of the many songs we will sing as we journey.

Oh, the elves and me we journey far
To fight a distant war,
Where things unknown and creatures bold
May even up the score;

The march quite long the nights too short
Yet we shall persevere,
To claim what's ours - and rightly so
The unknown we shall not fear;

Yea our foes have upon their walls
The muscle of the troll,
Yet with us journeys a striking elf
Whose reign we shall uphold;

We journey alone with fortitude
During days of toil and sweat,
Yet in our hearts live true desire,
Each struggle we shall not fret,

So delay you not my beloved friends,
For soon we conquer all,
When journey ends in a dreaded land
Where the trolls man the wall;

Yes the day will come when the Isle sings
With awakened songs of dreams,
For Spardom shall smile yet again
When our Princess reigns supreme.

It is late morning when Eranba and the two male elves arrive at a small clearing. Eranba figures it will be a suitable place to stop for the midday meal. It is a rock-strewn area. Some of the rocks are quite large with jagged edges. We have to step carefully around them to avoid tripping or worse. A large slab of granite hangs over a portion of the clearing. It provides ample protection from the drizzling rain.

Ariel-e unpacks her cooking gadgets. Donas and Andri-al collect as much dry kindling wood as they can find. It is slim pickings since it has been raining all morning. Eranba and Bratle haul large flat rocks on which we can rest. They also collect smaller rocks to make a campfire ring.

Once I have the fire ablaze, we plop down on our make-shift stone chairs beneath the natural canopy to relax. It has been a difficult trek along the path. Everyone is eager to rest a spell. As usual, Ariel·e prepares a yummy lunch.

Eranba raises his hand to speak. "Milady, we are not yet past Gonialit's district. However, I doubt my fellow spargnarls will come this way. Gonialit seldom has us set snares in this area. Other groups of spargnarls claim this area as their own. As a result, we must be careful. I propose we continue on for a few more hours then set up camp well before nightfall. The forest is not safe after dark." He looks at the sky and adds, "It looks like the rain will cease soon. We should be rather comfortable tonight, at least I hope so."

I look at the others one by one. Each nods his head in agreement. I say, "Eranba, you and your cousin are the ones with knowledge of the forest. We will set up camp wherever and whenever you suggest."

Bratle raises his hand. I nod for him to speak. He looks at Eranba and says, "Tell our lady about the *morgalps.*"

With a look of dismay, Eranba shakes his head and stammers, "No · I do not want to · you tell her. You have · yes it is you who has seen them. I have not. I do not want · I do not want to think about them. They · they are the one thing that scares me the most!"

"Milady," Bratle begins, "I hesitated to tell you earlier. I did not want to alarm you and the others before we set out on our journey. We will soon spend our first night in Fogreia. For this reason, I must tell you this. Creatures called morgalps rule the forest at night. They also roam the deserts of Abeti and perhaps beyond. They are ferocious, two·legged beasts. Legends say they are a crossbred mutant of elves and wolves.

They walk upright like an elf. Their muscular hind quarters are like those of a wolf. They have a tail. From the waist up they look somewhat like an elf. On the other hand, their head is much larger than that of an elf. Two, three·inch long fangs protrude from their upper lip. Their ear-splitting cry is that of a wolf. They speak the Elvish tongue.

"Their eyes see all when it is dark. Morgalp eyes are as red as fire hidden behind eye slits that resemble eyes of a snake. Their ears are like those of an elf, but much longer and much wider. They have unmatched hearing. Morgalps are intelligent, quick, and powerful."

Bratle's face becomes even more serious as he adds somberly, "That is not all, milady. Instead of arms, morgalps have rubbery, muscular appendages, tentacles if you will. Their appendages resemble leathery coils of rope. The coils spring forth from their bodies at lightning speed. That is how they ensnare their prey. They can capture prey at a distance that is at least the length of two adult spargnarls' height.

"Morgalps hunt in packs but only at night. They sleep in hollows of trees or bed in thick undergrowth during the day. Every so often we catch a morgalp in our traps. They are quite tasty in a stew, once we skin them and remove their rubbery coils."

"Well, that has to the most disgusting thing I have ever heard," Lindsial suddenly conveys via telepathy. "Bratle's description is scary enough, but to cook and eat the revolting things - yuck!"

I can barely suppress a laugh after reading Lindsial's thoughts. Luckily, I manage to keep a serious look on my face as I address Bratle. "Bratle, these creatures sound horrible. Eranba mentioned you had seen them. Please tell us how that came to be."

Bratle tells of when he and his brother, Spormna, were hunting for pachals at night. Pachals are medium-sized hairy rodents prized by spargnarls for their furry pelts. Sometime during the night Bratle and Spormna became separated. At first Bratle thought his brother was playing a trick on him. Spormna was the joking kind, ever ready to tell a tall story or pull a prank on others.

After some time, Bratle started to worry. He began to search for his brother. He knew better than to call out to his brother. Shouting in the forest of Fogreia at night invites trouble. That is when he heard the undeniable howl of the morgalp. Bratle slowly crawled on all fours in his effort to find his brother. When he finally found him, his brother was lying stock-still on the forest floor surrounded by three morgalps. There was nothing Bratle could do. He was unarmed. He slowly backed away. When he was a safe distance from the scene, he ran for help.

It was not until the next morning when Bratle and his family members returned to the scene. Except for a shoulder bag where his brother had lain, there was no noticeable trace of Spormna. He had vanished. Gonialit suspected the morgalps had taken Spormna to their lair. After the incident with Bratle's brother, spargnarls ventured into the forest at night in groups of four or more. They also brought along their swords.

After Bratle finishes giving his account, I say, "My goodness, that is so sad. I am very sorry for you and your family. Are there many morgalps in the forest?"

"I do not know, Milady," Bratle replies. "We see their tracks and droppings now and then, but we have not had any repeat incidents. I believe hunting for pachals in larger groups has kept the morgalps at bay. That is in our district. We will soon leave our district as Eranba said. What we will face tonight and beyond I do not know. There may be a few dozen morgalps out there. There may be thousands. I am sorry, milady. I have no way of knowing their numbers."

Lindsial raises her hand. She says, "Well, we should be on our guard at night. Everyone should stay close to the camp after dark as well." She turns in the direction of Bratle and says, "If you see any telltale signs of morgalps, such as their droppings, please show the others. That way they can better understand what we face. Knowledge makes strength, as they say."

We have packed our gear and stomped out the fire. We continue along the path. The rain has stopped although the air is heavy with dew. The forest seems quite close, more so

than this morning. Ever since Bratle's story about morgalps all of us are keen to new sights and sounds.

I am suddenly aware of distant thoughts entering my
mind. I suppose they come from the Evil One, Zarof. His
thoughts are typically very strong, nearly overpowering.
Unlike when I first received Zarof's thoughts months ago,
his thoughts no longer invade my mind at will. My ability
to throw out his sinister thoughts has strengthened greatly.

I concentrate attentively for a few moments. I realize
the thought transference is coming from someone or something new. These thoughts are far too tender and kind to
originate with the Evil One or one of his cohorts. As hard
as I try, however, I cannot receive the thought transference
with precision. Suddenly, the thought transference becomes strikingly lucid but only for a few brief seconds.

The thoughts entering my mind say, "I am Hannahlo of
the Land of the Unseen. I must connect with you. However,
something is wrong. I cannot open up our communication.
It is as if you cannot heed my words. For us to unite, you
must heed my words. You must..."

Now, as abruptly as the thoughts had entered my
mind, they cease. I attempt to answer via thought transference with no success. Lindsial is the only one to whom I
can transfer my thoughts and have a two-way telepathic
conversation.

Lindsial's thoughts are now in my mind. "Are you trying to convey to me, Eva?" she asks.

"No, I am not, Lindsial. I was trying to send my
thoughts to another. I received words from a so-called
Hannahlo of the Land of the Unseen. Her mind said she
could not connect with me since I could not heed her
thoughts. She said to unite with her I must heed her
words. It is almost as if I must physically hear her words
for successful thought transference. What do you think?"

"For starters," Lindsial conveys, "What is this Land of
the Unseen? It's not on our map. If it was supposed to be on
our map, I am certain Ariel-e would have put it there. We

need to ask Eranba if he knows of this. Next, there is this Hannahlo saying for you two to connect you must heed her words. It appears she must know you can hear what she is saying before the two of you can have a thought transference. Does that make sense?"

"Well, sort of," I reply via thought transference. After a few moments, I add, "It is almost like something said long ago in the military. *A message never received is a message never sent.* What that implies is, even though one party sends a message, a link is not established if it is not received by the other party. The transference never happened. Hence, the supposed message disappears into thin air. It vanishes forever."

Lindsial conveys, "Makes sense to me. When we stop for the night, we need to ask Eranba about this Hannahlo and the Land of the Unseen. Perhaps he knows something. My mind is racing with the inference of a land that is unseen. For some reason, it sounds exhilarating to me. Maybe it's a land of unseen beings. That would be remarkable. I wonder if I could picture them in my mind when I am invisible."

My mind conveys, "You know Lindsial, speaking of unseen beings, I have meant to ask you a few questions, but they keep slipping my mind. Here goes. How do you turn invisible, and how does it feel when you are invisible? And when you are invisible how do you know for certain, you are, you know, invisible?"

"Those are excellent questions, Eva. When I want to turn invisible, my mind takes control. Let me put it this way. Turning invisible is like walking. You do not explicitly or purposely tell yourself to move your legs back and forth to walk. You don't say, *hey legs, start walking.* It's nothing like that. You walk because your mind's power makes it come about. It is automatic I guess. Does that make sense?"

"Uh-huh," my mind answers.

"Okay then, how does it feel when I am invisible? It feels widely different than when I am visible. When I am invisible, I am more aware of my surroundings, and my brain sharpens my senses. Let me explain. Imagine, when I am visible, I am sitting in a crowded room full of boisterous laughter and noisy chatter. Even if I try, I cannot absorb everything at once. My sense of hearing is overwhelmed.

"Remove the noisy crowd as I sit in the same room that is now empty, I am acutely more aware of my surroundings. The floor creaks noisily. Whispers travel effortlessly from afar. Noises barely noticeable in the formerly crowded room suddenly come to the forefront of my senses. Since I am blind, my senses are more and more heightened. I hear things I could not hear previously. Employing my echolocation, I can navigate with no trouble, even though I am blind. In your case, you would see things after you were invisible you normally would not see when you were visible. These are the heightened sensations I have when I am invisible. Do you follow me?"

I say in my mind, "Yes, I do. So how do you know you have turned invisible?"

Lindsial conveys, "Once again, I will use the walking analogy. For whatever reason, your mind decides to walk your legs move. As long as the nerve connection is intact between your mind and muscles, tendons, and whatnots in your legs, it happens. It is the same when I am invisible. I know I am invisible because my mind says I am. Plus, as I just mentioned, my senses become more aware of my invisibility."

"I wish I could become invisible," I say. "Granted, I have out of the ordinary, magical powers. To turn invisible - that would be something else entirely. I tried turning my arm invisible once, using my invisibilis spell. Obviously, it didn't work. It's strange when you think about it. I can turn things invisible with my invisibilis spell, but I cannot turn myself invisible."

"You can become invisible with me, Eva. It would be good for you to experience it. Being invisible as an experiment will prepare you mentally and physically in case you need to become unseen in an emergency. Simply hold my hand when I turn invisible and presto. You are likewise in-visible. I bet it would be weird at first since you can see and all. However, I'm fairly certain you would get used to it quite easily."

"Perhaps we should try it someday." I convey. I think I would like to be invisible if only for a short time."

As we stumble on through the thick forest, I think about the failed thought transference from Hannahlo. I once knew a Hannah when I was a little girl, when I was nine years old, two years after my mother died. At least I pretended I knew her. She wasn't real, just someone I would talk to - a make-believe friend. I'm sure all kids have an imaginary friend at some point in their lives.

Hannah was like my best friend when I was in gram-mar and middle schools - in particular, sixth grade. That was one of the worse grades before my high school days. Hannah was always there when I needed her the most. All I had to do was call her name.

Hannah was my seraph. She kept me safe and helped soothe my pain when I was sad. During the pre-teen years of my life, I was sad quite often. I didn't have a single soli-tary real life friend at all. Hannah was my one and only companion.

I imagined Hannah was about my height. She was slender just like me. Hannah had red hair, not a surprise since I was picked on at school about my red hair. Natural-ly, she had to be a bit like me - only more resilient to teas-ing and much more valiant. Unlike my scarlet red hair, Hannah's hair color was less flushed. She had the most gorgeous reddish-bronze hair imaginable. She wore it mid back length. Her eyes were light brown. When she smiled, my heart glowed. She was that pretty!

Hannah and I would play games together, more often than not way past our bedtime. We would sing and whisper things and tell funny stories. I would read her stories from my fairytale book. Her favorite story was *The Elves and the Shoemaker* from *Grimm's Fairy Tales.* When I played outside Hannah was with me at all times, enjoying hopscotch, jumping rope and playing Hide n go Seek games. We even climbed trees together. We would sit high up on the boughs and survey the land below us.

In high school, when bullying got rough, I would sometimes call out to Hannah wordlessly. We wouldn't play games or tell stories, nothing like that. I was too old for imaginary friends. At least I thought so at the time. All the same, just thinking about Hannah would somehow make things a wee bit better. She was tough, redheaded like me, and she gave me unbelievable inner strength. I even thought of Hannah the day I found out I was deaf. Ah, Hannah, I sure do miss you. Thanks for being there when I needed you the most.

Now a thought occurs to me - what if, say for the sake of argument, Hannahlo is, in fact, my imaginary childhood friend Hannah? It makes sense when you think about it.

My imaginary childhood friend Hannah was make-believe - *she was unseen*. Just a few moments ago I sensed thoughts from Hannahlo from the *Land of the Unseen*. What a twist of fate - Hannah and Hannahlo one and the same. Talk about totally remarkable! Hey, and why not? Weirder things have happened to me in the past. Weirder things are happening to me right now.

The afternoon drags on and on as we plod on and on with it. The dampness and heat are at their azimuth. Nevertheless, we elves do not perspire. When you figure in my magic powers and strong clairvoyance, yes - unquestionably, I am an elf. I notice I do not tire as easily as before. I have quickness of hands and feet and in my mind, more than I could ever imagine. My skin is more silky-smooth fair as well, except for my freckles. My freckles remain as before, prominent and wholly unblemished.

Even if I'm not sweating, I still feel rather ill at ease as we walk. This uneasy feeling is not physical. It is something I sense. It has everything to do with the forest. The forest seems to be closing in on all sides. The path is also noticeably narrower. Spider webs appear more frequently and with increased density. Their sticky mess tangles in our clothing and hair more than ever. To be honest with you, the forest seems alive!

Lindsial becomes entangled in a web. To free her, Ariel·e and I have to hack at the sticky mess with our swords. Thankfully, Bratle is in front of us elves. He does not seem to mind the menacing character of the forest. He easily dispenses with low·lying limbs and spider webs that seem to reach out to take hold of us. It is as if they are alive.

I say out loud, "Is it me, or is this path becoming more and more treacherous and sinister as we progress along its corridor?"

"I do not like it one bit," Lindsial conveys. "I have a weird notion this forest is breathing. It is almost like it's slowly consuming us. It is as if it doesn't want us to continue on." She says aloud, "Ariel·e, what do you think?"

Lindsial waits a few seconds for Ariel·e to respond. When Ariel·e does not respond, Lindsial turns around. She stands unmoving for a few moments. She cannot discern Ariel·e's presence with her echolocation, nor can she read her mind. She is always able to read the elf mermaid's mind, particularly since Ariel·e is all the time singing. It dawns on her · Ariel·e has gone missing!

"Eva, Eva," Lindsial exclaims via telepathy, "I do not think Ariel·e is behind me!" Then she shouts, "Bratle, stop! I think we are missing our dear elf mermaid Ariel·e!" Knowing Andrial will have most certainly heard her shouts she adds, "Andrial, you three must turn around. Come to us at once!"

I look behind Lindsial to confirm that Ariel·e is indeed missing. As I do, I am surprised to see Lindsial has drawn her sword. I admire Lindsial in situations such as this. Her keen intellect and fighting skills are incredible. She is the seasoned sword fighter. I am not. I draw my sword from its scabbard.

Now I'm trying to interpret the overlapping thoughts entering my mind. As you know, I am not skilled at sorting concurrent thoughts, especially when they are wound up. As a result, I am somewhat confused, to say the least. I'm reading Lindsial's thoughts as well as those of Andrial and Donas. And I'm desperately trying to capture Ariel·e's thoughts at the same time. Her thoughts are silent. It takes me a few seconds, but I finally filter out everyone's thoughts. Lindsial is retracing her steps. Donas, Andrial, and Eranba are returning with haste along the path.

I cannot read the spargnarls' thoughts. However, I am once again receiving strange thoughts. These thoughts do not come from my dear Ariel·e. Her thoughts are still un-detectable. These thoughts are not Lindsial's. I would rec-ognize my closest friend's thoughts in a heartbeat. They are not Hannahlo or Zarof's thoughts. What I sense in my mind are sinister thoughts coming from someone or some-thing new.

The threatening thoughts in my mind say, "Well, so much for your merry Group of Seven. It is now one short. Soon it will be the merry group of six, and then five, and so on. Then you, Eva Roblins, will be the only one who re-mains. Once you are alone what will you do? Think about it, Eva Roblins. What will you do when all of your friends are dead?"

As unexpectedly as the thought transference entered my mind, it now becomes eerily silent. I try not to dwell on the thought transference. The safety of our group is first and foremost. Everyone, less Ariel·e, of course, is now as-sembled as a group along the path.

I announce, "Okay, we must stick together. No one leaves the group for any reason without my permission. We will remain in two groups of three. Bratle, you remain with Lindsial and me. Eranba, you are with Donas and Andrial. While it may be my imagination, I believe the path is con-tracting. It appears to be consuming us gradually. Every-one, I want you to be extra alert!"

Turning to face Eranba and Bratle, who look dreadfully worried, I say, "We must get off this path. We do not know how long Ariel·e has been missing. I propose we return to the clearing where we ate our lunch. Ariel·e is our primary concern at the moment. Before long, it could be one of you who go missing. I don't want to lose another of our group." I look at the others one by one. "I insist you truthfully give me your opinions. What do you think we must do?"

"I agree, milady," I watch Eranba's lips reply. "We must return to where we had lunch." Looking at Bratle, he adds, "What do you think, cousin?"

"I also agree with milady," Bratle offers. "I also believe the forest is closing in on us. Look at my foot here." Bratle is pointing to his right foot. "I haven't moved since we arrived a few moments ago. I planted my foot at the very edge of the moss. As you can see, crawling vines now cover it. The forest is slowly consuming us!"

I have to agree. Creepy thorn-covered vines are inching along the forest at a snail's pace toward our feet. They remind me of surface earth's slippery slithering serpents on the hunt for easy prey. The vines on Bratle's foot are now creeping toward his knee.

"I agree as well," Andrial proclaims in his mind. His face is pale. "Whatever happened to Ariel-e must have happened quickly. She may be unconscious. Otherwise, milady, the three of us would have known about her state of affairs immediately. We must find Ariel-e. We must do so with utmost haste."

"You know I'm with you," Lindsial's thoughts convey. She shakes her leg in disgust as a vine creeps up her thigh. She says aloud, "I know what you are thinking, milady. We have journeyed less than one day, and already we are retracing our footsteps. Nevertheless, there is no other way. We must go back over our steps. Perhaps we will discover Ariel-e along the way. A sinister enchantment brought this part of the forest to life. I know you can feel its dark magic as well. There is something terribly menacing behind this dark magic. Of that, I am certain. If we do not draw back, we die."

I whisper, "Okay, we have made our decision. Let's get the heck out of here before these vines choke us. Eranba, you, Donas, and Andrial lead the way. Do not travel so quickly that you move out of our sight. Bratle, please follow behind Lindsial and me. Lindsial, I want you in front of me." I add via telepathy, "If anything were to happen to you, Lindsial, I would want to die. I know you disagree with me. You want to follow me, but you must be in front of me. I insist on it."

Our worried group hurries to the clearing where we ate our midday meal. As we hasten, the path continues to squeeze us little by little. Moss appears out of nowhere, falling from the trees onto our heads. The creeping vines appear to be alive! They intentionally reach out to grab at our legs. That causes us to trip as we rush through the forest.

Low-hanging tree limbs grow ever closer. If we bend down any further, we will be crawling on all fours. This portion of Fogreia was enchanted by some evil spell. Although I have no proof, I would bet the Evil One, Zarof, has something to do with the malice in this portion of the forest.

In less than an hour, our path is impeded by dense thickets. Bratle and the two male elves have to hack feverishly with their swords to keep the undergrowth at bay. The spargnarls' hacking of the underbrush makes the going a bit easier for those of us who follow, although it slows our pace considerably.

I convey to Lindsial details about the thoughts that entered my mind after we discovered Ariel-e was missing. I tell her the sender is someone other than Hannahlo and the Evil One. I explain its sender said its intention was to reduce our group one by one until only I remain.

Lindsial's thoughts reply, "Hopefully, whoever they are, they aren't too far away so we can rescue Ariel-e fairly soon. And let me tell you this, Eva. I will breathe my last breath before I will permit anyone or anything to harm you. I love you too much. Plus, you are too important to the Isle, perhaps to the future of the surface world as well."

All of a sudden, Lindsial, Andrial, and I are aware of Ariel-e's anguished thoughts and whispered words. "Milady, I have been seized by *areneus*. That is what they call themselves. They are huge spiders. They make the webs strewn along our path. I am high up in a tree far off of the path. An utterly sickening sticky web imprisons my body.

"The cluster of dense trees in which they have trapped me is surrounded by an open meadow of sorts. I can see it through the trees. I was struck unconscious. Then again, they may have injected a sedative into me with their stingers. I am groggy and have a ruthless, biting pain between my shoulder blades. My face feels as if it's on fire. They struck me from behind. There was nothing I could do. It happened too fast. I am sorry.

"There are at least two dozen of these hideous creatures. They have my sword and spear. I am defenseless. They do not know I can communicate with you, at least not yet. The morning's rain refreshed my core. I can remain here for a few more days without further replenishment if necessary.

"The areneus speak in a tongue similar to elvish. I overheard their leader Mortaknom talking to another areneus. Mortaknom intends to eliminate each of us one by one. He believes by doing so he can torment the one he really wants. That is you, milady Eva. Without doubt, I wish to be rescued as soon as possible. However, my dear princess, my primary concern is you. I have a plan. I will now be silent vocally and tell my dear princess and sweet Lindsial the plan I have in mind."

CHAPTER TWENTY-FIVE

INDISPUTABLE EVIDENCE

Meanwhile, on surface earth, members of the United Nations General Assembly are settling into their seats. It has been over a decade since the U.S. Secretary of State delivered his infamous presentation to the General Assembly. He had delivered a skillfully orchestrated PowerPoint presentation detailing *indisputable evidence* of a country's development of nuclear, biological, and chemical weapons. Included in the presentation were troubling slides of advanced weapon's delivery systems.

Based upon this indisputable evidence, the United States went to war. Historical facts proved everything the secretary of state said that day was bogus. The former U.S. Secretary of State's infamous presentation is fresh in the minds of those assembled in the great hall. Those in the audience are justifiably skeptical of the scheduled presentation. They are also decidedly cynical of the presentation delivered to them this morning. Many believe what they are about to hear this afternoon is nothing more than American war-mongering.

As the President of the United States enters the Assembly, only half of those in attendance applaud. Fewer rise to their feet. The United States' credibility in the world's standing has ebbed over the past decade. The respect, admiration, and the aura it once garnered as the freest democracy on earth are no more. It may be the most powerful nation on earth, but its influence is open for discussion.

Now that he is standing behind the podium, the President begins to speak. "Ladies and gentlemen of the General Assembly of the United Nations - I come before you today, not merely as a leader of a country but as a fellow human being. I ask you to consider the course of action my country members delivered to you this morning. They provided you with indisputable evidence we might soon confront the most dangerous adversary in the history of our world. Ladies and gentlemen, to put it in the simplest of terms, we must eliminate the threat that lies beneath the sea.

"Many of you remain skeptical of our proposed course of action. I share your concerns - the destruction of the ancient Isle of Spardom is something we do not want to do. On the other hand, the impending threat is rapidly gathering strength. Our very existence as sovereign, peaceful nations could depend on what we agree to do. Let me assure you - we must confront this threat. We must do so as a coalition of willing nations.

"I have been told many of you still question the Isle's existence. You are skeptical the Isle, one-third the size of Australia, can exist one thousand fathoms beneath the sea. Allow me to say, the Isle does exist. After I finish speaking, others will follow to provide further proof of the Isle's existence. They will also provide indisputable evidence of the threat that dwells on the Isle.

"Whether you ultimately trust or distrust facts presented of the Isle's existence - they are secondary in importance to destroying the evil that lurks within the Isle's protective bubble. Ladies and gentlemen, we are talking about a threat that will make all the combined wars in history seem like child's play. We are talking about human beings of every religion, every culture, and on every land becoming enslaved by one · one whose sole purpose is to rule the earth.

"Our cities and cultures destroyed · our ways of life subjugated to the whims of one who is all powerful · the future of our grandchildren put into jeopardy. I can see many of you are shaking your heads. You are probably thinking, impossible. I once thought so myself. It is impossible a living and thriving land could exist deep beneath the sea. It is likewise impossible that mankind's deadly enemy could dwell on the Isle.

"Trust me when I say the threat is real. It is a clear and present danger to all mankind. We have indisputable evidence of the threat. Let me assure you ladies and gentlemen, as the President of the United States I am prepared to act unilaterally. I will risk all to protect my fellow countrymen. I would rather have the support and blessing of the entire world. The evil of which I speak is not going to affect one country. It is going to have an effect on us all.

"As further proof of my country's resolve, I must tell you this. My country, working in concert with others, arranged to send a team of highly specialized volunteers to confront the Isle's threat. Unfortunately, our plan went astray. As a result, we doubt the team will achieve our intended goals. While we have every reason to believe the team arrived on the Isle, they are unaware of their mission.

"I pass on my regrets we did not include this body in our plans at the time. I take full responsibility for my country's actions. I ask you to forgive us our mistake and to move forward · to eliminate the threat to mankind.

"In closing ladies of gentlemen of the General Assembly of the United Nations, I implore you to work together over the coming months. We must reach consensus to counter the evil on the ancient Isle of Spardom beneath the sea, even if that brings about the Isle's destruction. Thank you."

CHAPTER TWENTY-SIX

WHAT IS SHE UP TO?

Cindy Wickham and Admiral Shelly Jones are in Cindy's office at CIA headquarters in Langley, Virginia. They recently returned from attending the President's speech to the General Assembly of the United Nations. Their mood is somber.

Cindy is sitting behind her desk. Her desk nameplate reads, *Cindy Wickham - Deputy Director National Clandestine Service Central Intelligence Agency.* Along with mementos and other knickknacks, a photograph of a much younger Eva Roblins sits on her credenza. As she shuffles through a mound of classified folders in her inbox, Cindy says, "Well, Shelly, do you think they bought it?"

Admiral Jones is adding another teaspoon of sugar to her coffee. She replies, "I doubt it. Granted, the President made some good points. I'm confident the follow-on presentations will dispel any doubts others may have about the Isle's existence. However, those in attendance don't have long-term memory problems.

"As you and I know all too well, Cindy, we blew it when it came to WMD in Iraq. Look what happened there - not to mention what is going on with the Islamic State and Levant in Syria and Iraq. Now the United States is in another war in the Middle East one that will last decades. Given our past mistakes, I seriously doubt the UN representatives will think we have overwhelming intelligence to suggest this most recent threat is real. In addition, there are plenty of dangers afoot in Eastern Europe with Russia arming and financing the rebels in Ukraine. We have our hands full, let there be no doubt about it."

"Darn," Cindy says with a long, drawn out sigh. "If only Eva and the others had allowed us to brief them. I am certain Eva would have realized the importance of the mission. Knowing her the way I do, once she knew the truth she would have volunteered in a heartbeat. However, you and I know there was no way that I was going to allow Eva and her team to enter General Powers' unproven UTD. That's the reason Kristopher and I worked together to have Eva employ her spell. But she was supposed to use her spell *after the briefing, not before!* Goodness! Why is that girl so stubborn?

"For crying out loud, Shelly, we're not certain Eva and the others are even on the Isle. They could have landed in the middle of the ocean. They could be dead - Lord I hope not! I love Eva as much as I love my daughter. Whatever happened, we may have lost our best chance at beating this thing. And I may have lost someone I love very much!" She sighs.

"Aw, don't go saying that Cindy," Shelly whispers. "You have told me on more than one occasion about Eva and her pigheadedness. I will gamble next payday's paycheck she's on the Isle. If she's there, she will ultimately figure out what she has to do. She also has that Lindsial elf with her. That elf is one sharp cookie, smarter than anyone I have ever encountered. I'm confident Lindsial will know what to do, even if Eva is hesitant or doesn't figure out on her own what is happening. Something tells me the two of them working together will accomplish their mission.

"Besides, the elf mermaid, Ariel-e is as sharp as she is

beautiful. Her inquisitiveness and daring attitude inspire me. And there's Donas, who is as cunning as anyone at the Pentagon. Finally, there's Andrial. That elf has eyes of a hawk and hearing ability of an owl. I'm certain the five of them working together can make things happen for the better."

"Perhaps you're right," Cindy says with a sigh. "I only hope the UN Security Council comes up with something better than we have to offer. I would hate to see us set off unilaterally against the Isle. I seriously doubt we could damage the Isle, short of a nuclear detonation, but why risk it? But darn - I do believe that is what the President is thinking. He will have the United States go it alone once again.

"The Isle is innocent as it sits on the ocean floor. It's not hurting us. The thing inside is what we fear. And yes, the more I think about it, the more I know Eva and Lindsial and the others will figure out what to do. Eva has never let me down in the past. I doubt she will let me down now. I only hope she does not hate me for what happened at the transporter site."

Shelly says, "I doubt Eva could ever hate you, Cindy. After all, you treated her as a daughter after her father died. You raised her as your own when she was in her senior year of high school. You combed her hair. You removed her fears, and you wiped her tears. For goodness sakes, you even dressed her prettily, something she could never afford to do before. Yes, I know the story, Cindy. I know how much you love her. I think Eva will figure out this entire mess. She will figure out a way to defeat the enemy. I'm sure of it."

"I sure hope so," Cindy says as she nods her head in agreement. "I took care of Eva when she was a minor and when she worked at the Newspaper. I served as her surrogate mother and supervisor. So I have firsthand knowledge of her amazing attributes. I also know she has a supernatural sixth sense, more powerful and mysterious than anyone could imagine. Being partially deaf myself, I can fully appreciate what that sixth sense entails. All the same, I know her sixth sense is amazingly strong.

"After I landed my first job at the Agency, I worked to get Eva to join the team. Let me tell you, it took some convincing. Fortunately, for the CIA she agreed in the end. Now, only one question remains. What is she up to on the ancient Isle of Spardom beneath the sea?"

CHAPTER TWENTY-SEVEN

WE ARE A TEAM

It has taken more than two hours to reach the clearing where we had our lunch. Our movement along the path was exceedingly difficult. Everything appeared as if it wanted to impede our progress - sticky spider webs, falling tree limbs, crawling vines, hanging moss, nasty, nasty, nasty. Several hours ago the seven of us were happy as we trudged through Fogreia. The only thing bothering us was Bratle's story about morgalps. Now Ariel-e has gone missing. Everything changed from good to bad so quickly!

After eating a quick snack, the two male elves and the spargnarls take defensive positions on the perimeter of the clearing. Lindsial and I are standing beneath the sheltering stone overhang next to our midday meal campfire. We are discussing Ariel-e's plan. Ariel-e's plan seems simple enough. We proceed to the spot where we enjoyed lunch. Done - we're already here.

Donas should pre-stage ahead of us to the area where Ariel-e is being held captive. Via her thoughts, Ariel-e provided Lindsial and me with a detailed description of her surroundings. The creatures imprisoned her in a clump of a

few hundred or so very lofty trees. A spacious green meadow surrounds the trees. Ariel·e is in a nasty web, suspended between two trees. Donas should not have much trouble
finding her.

Donas said he was confident his amazing speed will
keep his approach well-hidden from the areneus. His only
problem will be staying out of sight while awaiting our ar-
rival. It will be then while he is waiting for us to arrive,
that he will be the most vulnerable.

Ariel·e's plan also proposes that Donas provide Lindsial and Andrial a general description of his location. He
will do this by whispering his thoughts. Then Lindsial
should turn invisible. Holding Lindsial's hand while the
two of them walk, Andrial will also be invisible, thus undetected by the areneus. They will proceed to Donas' location,
hopefully, where Ariel·e is being held captive.

Meanwhile, according to Ariel·e's plan at least, the
spargnarls and I shall remain in the well-defended clearing
where we are at present. Ariel·e is confident the
spargnarls' strength and my powers will be more than
enough to overwhelm the areneus should they decide to attack. Large, protective boulders surround the clearing.
There are many places to take up defensive positions along
the tree line. All the same, it is doubtful the areneus will
even come to blows in the clearing. We suspect they prefer
the relative darkness of the trees to wide-open, sunlit clearings where we are standing right now.

Despite the brilliance of Ariel·e's plan, one serious im-
pediment remains. I don't like it - and I'm not going to see
it to fruition. I convey to Lindsial, "There is no way I'm going to allow you, Andrial, and Donas to confront those creatures on your own. Ariel·e is unable to help herself which
leaves you three to battle the spiders. All the while Eranba,
Bratle, and I are to remain here in a purely defensive position when we could be helping. Besides..."

"Eva," Lindsial's thoughts interrupt, "You told me what
the areneus' leader Mortaknom said. He intends to eliminate the six of us one by one until only you remain. His

primary conquest is you, Eva. I seriously doubt he cares about eliminating the six of us. If he can get to you first, he probably won't give us a second glance. You are his prima-ry quest, Eva. There is no way I am going to consent to you being in harm's way. I implore you to allow us to follow Ar-iel-e's plan. Remain here with Eranba and Bratle where you will be safe - please?"

"Lindsial, I appreciate your concerns. As I said, I will not allow the three of you to do my fighting. I am not stay-ing behind in relative safety. If any of us is to die in battle, then we shall die fighting alongside the others. We are, af-ter all, a team, the Group of Seven. Perhaps Ariel-e's plan is not her own. She may be under duress. What she com-municated might be a trap to isolate the spargnarls and me from the rest of you."

"I never considered that possibility," Lindsial conveys. "Still I am concerned for you Eva. It is you who they want. I just know they will do anything to capture you. I worry about your safety more than my own."

I place my hand on Lindsial's shoulder. I continue my thought transference. "I know you do Lindsial. You know I feel the same way about you. Please allow me to be com-pletely frank. I firmly believe I am the target of everything evil on the Isle, so there is no escaping it. If it is not Mortaknom and his areneus, it is the Evil One and Parston. They want me for whatever reasons their twisted minds can suggest. Then tomorrow or the next day, next week, or next month something else will want to harm me. I might as well face their evil ways as they present them-selves to me - one by one. To do this, I must have my team behind me. Does that make sense?"

Lindsial nods her head. She rises up on her toes to place a kiss on my cheek. She smiles and says aloud, "It makes sense milady. I still worry about you. I want you to know that. Do you have a plan?" I nod. I call for the male elves and the spargnarls to move closer. It is time to go on the offensive once again.

CHAPTER TWENTY-EIGHT

THEY VANISHED BEFORE OUR EYES!

"What do you mean they have left the clearing?" Mortaknom screams at Portrang. "Are you certain you even saw them in the first place? You are not lying to me, are you?"

"No, I am not lying to you sir," Portrang cries. He looks at his partner for support. His partner says nothing and looks away.

Portrang says, "Simpelto and I had them under observation at the place where they ate earlier. The spargnarls and the two male elves were in the trees, presumably in defensive positions. The two female elves were facing each other as they stood close to their lunchtime campfire. It was as if they were talking or something. But I did not hear any words, which surprised me. They were simply staring at each other and nodding their heads and stuff while the others hid in the trees. The others in the trees seemed to be waiting. It was if they were waiting for something to happen..."

"What do you mean?" Mortaknom snarls. "You make it

sound as though the two female elves were talking too silently, that you could not hear them. I know your hearing
is very sensitive. That is the reason I sent you two to spy
on them. You should have heard something if they were
talking, anything. I do not care how close they were as they
stood. You need to re-tune your sense of hearing. Couldn't
hear any words - rubbish! Tell me what happened next."

"Well, sir," Portrang says, "The elf with the red hair
placed her hand on the younger female elf's shoulder. She
continued to stare for the longest time. Just like before she
said nothing. I know this for a fact because she did not
move her lips.

"'Then the younger elf nodded, stood up on her toes a
bit, and kissed the redheaded elf on her cheek. The smaller
elf finally said something aloud. She said, 'It makes sense
milady, but I still worry about you, I want you to know
that. Do you have a plan?' That's when I smacked Simpelto
in his side, sir, for him to pay attention. It was because we
would soon know of the redheaded elf's plan.'"

Portrang shrugs his shoulders and says, "It was fairly
odd, sir. It was almost as if the two female elves were having a conversation in their minds! I know that is not possible. Would you not agree with me Simpelto?" This time his
partner nods his head in agreement.

Mortaknom nods his head as if he also agrees, although
he does not. He is not surprised at the elves' behavior. He
presumes the redheaded elf, the one they call Eva Roblins,
has uncanny magical powers that might include telepathy.
That does not explain how the younger elf can communicate without using speech. Perhaps the princess elf was
simply moving her lips while the younger elf read the
words as they formed. Then again, perhaps the younger elf
is deaf or voiceless. Who knows? Maybe it was a one-way
conversation. "Go on, Portrang," he orders.

Portrang says, "The redheaded elf called everyone together into a semi-circle. She began talking. I saw her lips
move. But I could not understand a word she was saying. I
could not hear a thing - nothing! There was too much back-

ground noise."

"Not again! Are you two deaf?" Mortaknom hisses. "Why could you not hear a thing, what background noise?"

Portrang says sheepishly, "The smaller of the two female elves who asked what the plan was removed herself from the group. What she did next was weird - she started singing loudly. Her singing was so loud it hurt my ears! She began to dance and to twirl around in circles! She was acting bizarre like she was crazy or something. I was shocked, sir because it was she who had asked about the redheaded elf's plan! There she was, not even listening to the very plan about which she had asked!

"Simpelto and I just looked at each other in disbelief. We were completely stunned with the smaller of the two female elf's spontaneous weirdness. She is crazy, sir. We have to keep a close eye on that one. She's strange and probably dangerous as well."

It was a diversion you simpleton's, their leader thinks to himself. She knew you would be distracted by her singing and shenanigans. She is telepathic. That is the reason she did not need to be close to the others when Eva Roblins discussed the plan. But enough of this nonsense - he barks, "Then what happened?"

"After a few moments, the weird dancing and singing female elf rejoined the group," Portrang says. "She took the redheaded female elf's hand in her right hand and the light-skinned male elf's hand in her left hand. Then..."

"Hold on," Mortaknom orders. "What was the dark-skinned elf doing? Why was it the younger female elf did not clasp his hand as well?"

Portrang cringes as he submissively replies, "I was about to mention him, sir. He disappeared, sir. The dark-skinned elf vanished into thin air. One moment he was there. The next he was gone! His shadow remained on the ground for a blink of an eye. Then it disappeared as well. We both saw it. It was like magic!" He looks to his partner for support. Simpelto nods his head in agreement.

"What happened to the two spargnarls?" Mortaknom asks angrily.

Portrang says sheepishly, "They stood facing the red-headed elf. Then they vanished, sir. Except no brief shadow remained behind like when the male elf had disappeared. A moment later the two female elves and the light-skinned male elf vanished as well sir, again - right before our eyes! They were holding hands, then poof! - They vanished!

"We remained hidden for a while, not believing what our eyes had seen. We were also hoping the enemy would return, but they never did. I swear to you. They vanished before our eyes! I am sorry we failed you in our mission to keep an eye on the elves, sir."

Mortaknom slowly shakes his head disapprovingly at Portrang and Simpelto. He nods to an areneus standing behind the pair of scouts. Both Portrang and Simpelto feel a sharp sting on their hind quarter's seconds before they collapse to the ground writhing in pain.

CHAPTER TWENTY-NINE

THE ARENEUS

Lindsial, Andrial, and I are trudging hand in hand through knee-high grass. The going is difficult, to say the least. We keep tripping. We can barely stop ourselves from falling let alone keep our hands tightly clasped to Lindsial's hands. Let me tell you, being invisible while holding another's hand is no easy feat. This is especially true when you're invisible for the first time in your life and scared out of your wits. Eranba and Bratle are also invisible. They are a few steps behind us. They are making a loud racket and flattening the grass as they walk.

"Are you certain you can manage with the two of us holding your hands?" I ask Lindsial via thought transference.

"I am okay for now, yes. But let me tell you. I thought it was rough from time to time being blind and invisible. With you two on either side of me, my echolocation is all whacked up, to say the least. I'm just glad you're here to navigate for me. Otherwise, I would have already fallen flat on my face a dozen times or more." She whispers to the spargnarls, "Eranba, are you two okay?"

"Yes, elfin Lindsial, Bratle and I are fine," Eranba replies in a whisper. "I only wish being invisible would make us quieter. We do not want to endanger our dear princess and you and Master Andrial with our noise."

"Don't worry about us, Eranba," Lindsial says softly. "Just make sure you keep up with us. If our lady Eva were to lose you, she could not make you reappear. She must be looking directly at you, or rather where you are standing before she can turn you visible. She will turn you both back to your normal selves when the time is right. Until then, please keep up with us."

As you know, I sensed in my mind every word Lindsial said. She's right. If I were unable to locate Eranba and Bratle, Lord knows what they would do. They'd be stumbling around invisible for the rest of their lives. I convey to Lindsial, "Thanks. It irks me I cannot sense what the spargnarls are saying. It irks me even more I have to look at them straight on to make them visible once more."

"And you?" Lindsial conveys to me. "How are you faring, Eva, now that you are invisible?"

"It is a lot better now. I am still slightly sick to my stomach. I was pretty lightheaded at first. Happily, the dizzy sensation is no more. I wonder why Eranba and Bratle did not experience the same symptoms as me when I turned them invisible."

"I am not certain," Lindsial answers. "Maybe it's due to the quality or pureness of your invisibility power. It is much superior to mine."

"Perhaps," I offer, "Or spargnarls are not prone to the same ailments such as dizziness like us elves." Turning my attention to Andrial I say aloud in a barely audible whisper, "Andrial, how are you feeling?"

Andrial tells me in his mind he has the same symptoms as I am experiencing. All the same he is more worried about Ariel·e than for his own physical condition.

"You know," I convey to Lindsial, "It's baffling. I can see you, Andrial, and everything else while I am holding your hand and invisible. Although I must say, everything is hazy like mist surrounds each object. Despite the haze, I can see things okay I guess. On the other hand, I cannot see Eranba and Bratle, now that they're invisible. For some strange reason, they can see us. Why do you think that is?"

Lindsial conveys, "My invisibility powers are an abnormality of physics. Your invisibility powers are extraordinary magic. They defy the law of physics since they come from a magical spell. Least I presume that is the case. You can see me and Andrial, and Andrial can see you. That is because you are an extension of my physical being while we hold hands.

"Eranba and Bratle are not connected to you physically. They are under your spell. As to how and why they can see you yet you cannot see them that I cannot explain. Maybe someday you'll be able to see something you render invisible. Let us just be glad they can see us. Otherwise, we would be in a terrible mess for sure. They would have trampled us to smithereens by now. Goodness, but they sure are noisy. And, will you look at the way they're trampling the grass!"

Andrial's anguished thoughts suddenly enter Lindsial and my minds, "They have spotted us! They know we are here! One of them scurried off to tell their leader something unseen is moving through the grass."

"How in the world did they discover us?" I exclaim in a soft whisper.

Lindsial looks over her shoulder. She replies via telepathy, "Like I said, it is either the racket Eranba and Bratle are making or the telltale path they are creating through this tall grass, almost certainly both. Spiders have a keen sense of eyesight and hearing." She abruptly changes the subject. "Look at that clump of trees ahead. It comes as no surprise they picked that locale to hide Ariel-e. It is completely surrounded by this wide meadow. Anyone can discover another's approach."

I whisper out loud, "Everyone, I want you to stop! Eranba and Bratle, come to stand directly in front of me. Once you are in front of me, tell Lindsial in a whisper. Do not turn around. Keep your backs to us. I want it to appear you are going in the same direction we are heading. I will turn you visible once more.

"Once I tell you, start walking slowly. Continue to make a commotion and tramp down the grass as much as you can. We will follow in your footsteps. If we are lucky, the areneus will think you are two random spargnarls out for a walk. We might trick them into thinking you are not part of our group."

As I consider what I just told the spargnarls to do, I add, "I seriously doubt the areneus will attack two lone spargnarls. They are after me, not you. Besides, I suspect areneus are unable to venture outside of the forest during the day. I believe you will be quite safe this far from the trees.

"Lindsial and Andrial, this pertains to you. When I give the order - on the count of three, I want you to let go of each other's hands. At that precise moment, I will turn Andrial invisible once more.

"Andrial, I want you to leave our group when you think it safe. Attempt to infiltrate the areneus' defense if you can. Keep Lindsial and me apprised of your progress and of what you see and hear. Once our regrettable business is over, and we have defeated these creatures and rescued Ariel-e, contact me so I can turn you visible. Remember, I cannot see you after I turn you invisible. Make certain you find me."

Now I address my closest friend. I say, "Lindsial, please remain with me holding my hand as we follow in Eranba and Bratle's footsteps. I will remain invisible as long as I think it prudent."

I add in a soft whisper, "Okay, this is for everyone's information. Donas should see Eranba and Bratle once we are closer to the treeline. I expect he will direct our offensive and defensive actions via his thoughts. Ariel-e may also see us. We should expect her to offer advice as well. Bear in mind, we do not know if she is under a spell.

"As soon as the battle begins, if there is to be one, each

of you will find yourself on your own. It goes without say·ing · your initial concern is self-defense. Your second con·cern is rescuing Ariel·e and anyone else who may be captured or injured during the battle. Now, does everyone understand his role?"

I watch as Lindsial and Andrial nod their heads. Lind·sial tells me via thought transference the spargnarls un·derstand what they are supposed to do.

Eranba and Bratle are now plodding slowly toward the clump of trees as before, flattening the grass as they go. The only difference is they are now visible and walking ahead of us. They amicably chat as they walk, acting as if they do not have a care in the world. Lindsial and I, still invisible, are following closely behind.

Andrial, who I rendered invisible a split second after he released Lindsial's hand, has already departed. He scamp·ered away unnoticed onto a grouping of rocks adjacent to the tall grass. He says he is walking undetected close to the tree line. He is also updating Lindsial and me of what he sees and hears.

Donas' thoughts enter Lindsial and my minds. "I see the spargnarls milady. They are walking toward the trees, still a good distance away. I do not see you milady, Lind·sial, or Andrial. The areneus lookouts are not paying Eranba and Bratle much interest. By the way, I have seen our dear Ariel·e. She is hanging in a web. Three areneus guard her. She is conscious, in poor shape it looks, but awake.

"As best as I can tell, the only offensive weapons pos·sessed by the areneus are crude clubs and strange-looking stingers at the back of their abdomens. Each areneus is ca·pable of holding a club in each of his eight claws as he walks. I counted a total of twenty-two areneus. There may be more. The majority are in the trees. A few are placing sticky webs near the ground. Their webs are traps. I am sure of it. Two areneus are motionless on the ground be·neath me. They have not moved in quite a while. By the position of their bodies, they may be dead."

Addressing me, Donas offers, "Milady, my suggestion is Eranba and Bratle ultimately separate. One should proceed to the left, the other to the right. Perhaps they should shake hands before they separate as if they are innocently saying farewell. If we are lucky, the scouts will think Eranba and Bratle are two random spargnarls returning from a hunt who are about to go their separate ways. After all, this forest does belong to the spargnarl tribes. With a bit of luck, the areneus will suppose the spargnarls do not belong to our group."

"Goodness!" Lindsial conveys to me via telepathy. "Donas is cunning. I think his plan may be crazy enough to work. What do you think?"

I do not answer. I immediately whisper Donas' plan to the spargnarls adding, "As soon as we exit the tall grass near that large mound of dirt over there, you two split up. Good luck."

"Sorry, Lindsial, I did not reply," I convey. "There is not a moment to lose. Now, please listen to me carefully. Try not to interrupt because I know you will want to. As soon as Eranba and Bratle shake hands and split up, I am going to unclasp my hand from yours. Precisely when I turn visible, I want you to go into the clump of trees, which is to your left. Once you arrive at the trees, assume offensive and defense postures. Remain invisible. When you think it safe, I want you to seek out Ariel·e using your echolocation. Remain by her side for as long as you can. She is your number one priority, second to your safety, of course."

Lindsial tries to interrupt my thoughts. I anticipated this. I easily wave her thoughts away with my own. My thought transference is now a great deal stronger than hers. There is nothing she can do.

I convey, "Please do not try to interrupt, Lindsial, please. Ariel·e is defenseless, and she is groggy. The last thing I want is for Mortaknom to use her as a sacrificial bargaining chip against us. Keep yourself safe, but do everything you can to protect her." Then, trying to call up a bit of levity I add, "Besides, she is probably one of the two most beautiful elves in this world second to you, of course. I do not want anything to happen to her, or to you. In addition, we surely do not want to lose her cooking ability. Eranba tries his best, but his food tastes like morgalp mush."

Now I allow Lindsial's thoughts into my mind. "But Eva, you will be visible and by yourself. The rest of us will undoubtedly partner up as things progress - the two spargnarls, Donas and Andrial, Ariel-e and me. You will be on your own. I simply cannot allow it, Eva. I cannot!"

I convey, "I am sorry. I do not see any other way to approach this. Ariel-e's freedom is our quest. Our individual well-being is secondary at this point. Unlike her, we are unguarded, and we can fight, at least for now. Ariel-e is totally helpless and completely defenseless. Right now, she needs us more than ever. She saved my life when we were battling the spargnarls. If not for her..." My train of thought stops. I change the subject. "Besides, my dear - I have been in worse predicaments on surface earth. My tactical training and intuitive sixth sense will keep me safe. I also have my magical powers. As we discussed earlier, as soon as you see my fireball high in the air, attack."

Lindsial conveys, "But milady, I..."

Eranba and Bratle are shaking hands. Before Lindsial can finish her thought transference, I let go of her hand and become visible. I convey, "You be safe my dear. And remember, I love you. Now leave with no hesitation and take care of Ariel-e. Be off with you - go!"

As she scampers into the forest, Lindsial tells me she loves me as well. I cannot sense what she says. There are too many thoughts entering my mind at the same time. Donas and Andrial's thoughts are screaming that I am visible. Mortaknom is yelling obscenities at his lookouts. Ariel-e's thoughts are telling me her guards think an attack is imminent.

My private thoughts are also running through my mind - when in tarnation am I going to learn to sift through others' thoughts as they enter my mind at the same time?

Hopefully, it'll be soon. Otherwise, I'm going to go bonkers! Also, I might miss something important!

I stand motionless near the fringes of the trees. I am in plain view for anyone or anything that cares to look at the green meadow. I appreciate I am taunting Mortaknom as I stand alone in the open. Taunting the areneus has been my plan all along - to get Mortaknom so emotionally irritated he makes mistakes. The more mistakes he makes, the easier it is for us to rescue our precious elf mermaid, and if we have to go to battle, defeat him.

I also want to buy time for the others to get into position. I appreciate fortune is on the side of the areneus from tactical and defensive standpoints. They certainly have strong protective positions. They almost certainly have set numerous traps with their sickeningly sticky webs. They are familiar with the territory. They also have the advantage in numbers. More notably, they are holding Ariel-e hostage as leverage against us.

Added to our fix, we do not know the surroundings. We are proceeding into battle as good as blind. We need to be equally on offense and defense as we try to free Ariel-e and fight our way to triumph. These facts place us at a disadvantage but, in my opinion, only to a lesser degree.

To our advantage, the creatures do not know of Lindsial and Andrial's whereabouts since the elves are invisible. They will never suspect the two invisible elves are in their midst. They do not know the location of Donas. They may never spot him at all. He is that quick. If the creatures suppose the two spargnarls do not belong to our group that may also work to our advantage. Spargnarls pretty much look the same, with the exception of Eranba, who has no gnarls on his body. If we are lucky, the spargnarls could very well be our ace in the hole.

Now I'm focusing my thoughts on Mortaknom. I doubt he can read my mind. Just the same, thinking to myself - and sort of to him - helps to calm my nerves. Yes, Mortaknom, your areneus may have eight club-wielding legs, stingers, super hearing, and keen eyesight. You may have an army of areneus at your disposal. Your clump of trees serves as your defense. I doubt, however, you are as smart as us. I am equally certain you do not know of my powers. Plus, I suspect you do not know of the incredible skill, courage, and powers of my team members.

Also, I can read your thoughts although I doubt you can read mine. For this reason, start thinking, Mortaknom you dimwitted fool · tell me what you intend to do! Let me read your thoughts...

As I patiently wait for Mortaknom to say or do some·thing, my thoughts go off on another tangent. If Mor·taknom wanted to reduce the Group of Seven's number to six and so on and so forth, our beloved elf mermaid should already be dead. I am Mortaknom's prize, pure and simple. As Lindsial said, she and the others are unimportant. They are plainly in the way. Even so, something tells me Mor·taknom hasn't the stomach for killing innocents. I do not know how I know this. I just do. I suppose he is being forced to confront us. Some power unbeknownst to me is behind all of this. I just know it.

I must try to get Mortaknom off·balance before the bat·tle begins if there is to be a battle at all. I decide to make the first move. I loudly yell, "Hey you, the leader of those who took my friend Ariel·e, I want you to show yourself to me if you dare! Or are you too cowardly to come to me? I am alone as you can see. I am a solitary female elf. Show yourself!"

I am now reading Mortaknom's thoughts in response to my shouts. He is arguing with another, most likely his se·cond in command. I am privy to one side of the conversa·tion only as Mortaknom formulates words in his mind. I am receiving enough information to know he is overly cau·tious. Perhaps he is a coward. Maybe he commands others to go in harm's way while he remains behind in relative safety, barking orders on the sidelines. I have run into his spineless kind before on surface earth.

As he speaks aloud, Mortaknom's mind says, "It is a trick I tell you. We do not know where the other elves are. I seriously doubt the spargnarls have gone their separate ways as innocents. Yes, yes, I know she is standing by herself. Even so, she is the one they call Eva Roblins. Zarof told me himself she was dangerous. He told me I should be careful. Yes, I know she is standing by herself, you moron. I told you that already. But she is dangerous I tell you. How can I be so sure? Well, I cannot. But why risk it? I can only go with the information Zarof gave me."

"Lindsial, can you receive my thoughts and those of Mortaknom's," I ask via thought transference.

"I can read your thoughts easily enough, Eva," Lindsial conveys. "I cannot read Mortaknom's thoughts at all. What's he saying?" I give Lindsial a brief rundown of what I know from the one-sided conversation I sensed in my mind.

Lindsial conveys, "So we can assume the Evil One is behind all of this, to include Ariel-e's abduction. I'm not surprised. Eva, about Ariel-e · I am on a tree limb beside her. She is not aware of my presence as far as I know. I will not risk telling her. Of course, I cannot see her, but she may be battered Eva. She is moaning quite a bit, and she's calling your name over and over. She also seems confused. Perhaps she is sedated. Nothing substantive is coming from her thoughts, except those whispered words as she calls your name.

"Well, I am relieved she is still alive and not injured more severely," I respond. "Stay with her Lindsial. Do not leave her side. If what I have planned works, she will be moved shortly. Stay invisible and be careful."

I'm startled as an areneus suddenly emerges from the trees in front of me. It is a huge, ugly creature with eight hairy legs. Its eight claws on the ends of its legs somehow clutch clubs as it walks. Its green mouthpart fangs are enormous and powerful-looking. They could easily crush a spargnarl let alone a small elf like me.

The areneus stands a little shorter than me, perhaps five and one-half feet tall. I estimate its length as eight or nine feet and its breadth as five feet. Its leathery skin is light tan in color. It is totally unattractive and very scary-looking.

It reminds me of brown recluse spiders I saw as a child. The brown recluse spiders were dangling from rafters in some of the dilapidated, abandoned homes in which I slept. Of course, this arachnid is a gazillion times bigger than those on surface earth.

I'm glad I don't suffer from phobias, such as arachnophobia. If I did, I would probably have rushed out of here more quickly than you could exclaim, "Where's Eva?" I'm telling you - this enormous monster looks mightily ferocious!

Although I am a bit intimidated in its presence, I shout defiantly, "Who are you? Are you the leader? Do you speak Elvish?" I add in a whisper, "Help me out here, Andrial. Tell me what this hideous creature is saying." Andrial repeats in his mind what the areneus is saying aloud.

The areneus standing before me says, "Yes, I speak your language. It is the common language of Fogreia. And yes, I am the leader. I am the proud leader of my species, a noble class of arachnida. We are called areneus."

"What is your name?" I demand.

"I am Chornado, the leader of all living things called areneus in this part of the forest. You and your elves and the two spargnarls who accompanied you earlier today have entered my domain without my consent. Where are the others? I demand you have them show themselves immediately."

I think silently - Ah-ha, you have made your first mistake Mortaknom. I hope it is your first mistake of many.

"You lie," I shout. You are not the leader. I want to speak to your leader and no one else."

"How dare you," Chornado replies angrily. "I am the leader. You will speak to me."

"You are a liar," I shout defiantly. I inch a few steps closer to Chornado. I point my finger at him and insist boldly, "I want to speak to the true leader of areneus. I am Eva Roblins, Princess of Spardom. You are challenging *my* domain. I am the rightful ruler of this Isle, not you, or any man, beast, elf, or a whole legion of disgusting areneus! Now bring me your leader Mortaknom or die!"

With that, Chornado hastily retreats into the safety of the trees. As he leaves, I think to myself *Score one for the good guys.*

I say in a whisper, "I thank you, Andrial, for helping me. I'm woefully afraid I would have made a poor showing by not being able to comprehend what Chornado was saying. I'm able to read Mortaknom's thoughts only. Please convey to me in your mind any other creature's words of import. I thank you once again."

In response to my appeal, Andrial begins repeating in his mind both sides of Mortaknom's conversation with his underling. There is a slight time delay between what's being said and when I receive the information from Andrial in my mind. I am oblivious to this fact.

"I am not going to meet her," Mortaknom says tersely. "Send another. I do not care who it is you send, but tell him to say he is me. She will never know if he is truthful or not. I am too valuable to confront the elf on my own."

"But sir," the voice of Mortaknom's minion replies. "She somehow knows you are our leader - she spoke your name! As you said yourself, the elf is dangerous, perhaps with more dreadfully powerful magical powers than Zarof. I am uneasy about this sir. I do believe the one they call Eva Roblins has the power to defeat all of us singlehandedly. I think Zarof has made a fool of you, sir.

"There is also the question of the location of the other elves, all three of them, Mortaknom. They disappeared a while ago as you know. They could have us surrounded right now, and we don't even know it! I implore you sir, meet the elf. We still have the other elf with which to bargain. Surely the elfin Eva Roblins will not want any harm to come to her."

The conversation is undoubtedly some distance away. I suspect Mortaknom is somewhere in the center of the cluster of trees. I must try to influence the conversation in our favor even if Mortaknom is not close at hand. The sun will set in a few hours. We will lose the element of surprise when darkness falls.

As loudly as I know how I shout, "Why don't you listen to your assistant, Mortaknom? Come out to the edge of the trees and face me. I give you my word I will not harm you. Bring my elf friend Ariel·e along. I want to see she is alive and well. Bring along as many areneus as you want to ensure your protection. After all, I am but one female elf. I assure you no harm will come to you, as long as no harm comes to my dear friend Ariel·e!"

The unknown areneus says, "Do you not see, sir? She can hear our conversation! It is futile to go against her wishes. She is all·powerful I tell you. I implore you to meet her, sir. Take the elf she calls Ariel·e with you as well. You can use the elf to negotiate with her."

A few moments later the areneus ruler, Mortaknom, appears from the darkened density of the trees. Six of his soldiers accompany him. Five of the creatures are clasping a club in each of their eight claws. I count forty clubs in all, not including the three Mortaknom is carrying.

One mammoth, especially fearsome·looking areneus is carrying Ariel·e in his gargantuan green fangs. I flinch as he opens his fangs to deposit Ariel·e in a heap on the ground. Now the areneus slides his body forward. He positions a surprisingly large stinger protruding from the back of his lower abdomen two feet above Ariel·e's forehead.

As far as I know, spiders on surface earth do not have stingers protruding from their bodies. Like the areneus before me, surface earth spiders have chelicerae mouthparts or fangs. The hollow fangs contain venom. I suspect this areneus' venom is contained in its stinger as well as in its chelicerae. Then again, maybe its stinger contains a knock·out toxin of sorts. I seriously doubt its stinger is simply for show.

I stare at Ariel·e's crumpled body. She looks horrible! Blackish·blue bruises cover her face and shoulders. Her eyes are nearly swollen shut. Her mouth is agape. She looks like she can barely breathe without effort. As her chest rises and falls rapidly I believe she is moaning in agonizing pain like Lindsial said.

I feel an uncontrollable rage rising from deep within my soul. It takes all the self-control I possess to keep from lashing out at Mortaknom and the areneus' at his side. I want to destroy them, enveloping them in flames or hurling them through the air. I want to yell *credo auduro, exarmo, or moveo* or any of the spells I have in my arsenal. I wish for them to feel as much pain as my beloved mermaid elf is experiencing.

With tears of hatred welling in my eyes and my words seething with absolute disgust, I ask, "What did - what did you do? What did - what did you do to my friend, Mortaknom? Why - but why is she injured so?"

I read Mortaknom's mind as he says vocally, "Well if it is not Eva Roblins in the flesh. I have heard a great deal about you. I am Mortaknom, ruler of the areneus. I have a proposition for you. If you want your precious friend to live, I demand you come with me. Tell your other elfin friends to show themselves as well. If you do not do as I say, I will have your friend here, the one you call Ariel-e, killed. I assure you - it will be the most gruesome death as my assassin repeatedly thrusts his stinger into her."

I am now pointing my finger threateningly at Mortaknom. I could easily destroy him and his soldiers with a simple thought in my head or a mere flick of my wrist. With the sound of pure hatred seething from my lips, I demand answers. I carefully say, "I - asked - you a question! Why - is - she - injured badly? What have - what have you done - to her?"

As you have certainly noticed, I am infuriated. I need to regain my composure. I breathe in deeply. I quickly add, "If you have caused her any long-term injuries, or worse, Mortaknom, you will regret you ever saw me!"

"Me regret seeing you?" Mortaknom snarls. "Who do you think you are, speaking to me like that? Do not test my patience, pocket-sized elf! My soldiers can overwhelm you without difficulty. It simply takes a quick command from me. Then you will be lifeless alongside your precious elfin friend before you know it.

"As far as the discoloration of her body, the marks will disappear in a few days, perhaps in a week. They are only temporary markings caused by the stunning poison administered by my soldier's stinger. All the same, let me caution you, Eva Roblins. Repeated stabbings by my assassin will result in a tormenting death for your friend, an agonizingly slow death. Your lovely elfin friend will be conscious the whole time as her body screams for mercy. Now give yourself up to me and tell your hidden elves to show themselves!"

At this very moment, I sense Ariel·e is addressing me in her mind as she lies on the grass beneath the areneus. "I am conscious, my dear lady, Eva. I am pretending to be unconscious. I am concerned about my dear princess' presence here. I had thought she would not endanger herself. Despite that, I will assist her as necessary when she gives the word · on the count of three I propose."

"I will as well," Lindsial's thoughts suddenly convey. "I am standing beside the beast that is straddling Ariel·e. I will slice off his stinger with my sword as soon as you give the word."

I am greatly relieved. Knowing Ariel·e is capable of defending herself and Lindsial is next to the assassin makes me hopeful. Perhaps I can talk some sense into Mortaknom and save all of us a lot of grief. Besides, I do not want anyone hurt.

"I will do nothing of the kind," I boldly state to Mortaknom. "Now, you listen to me carefully. You will tell your assassin to move away from Ariel·e. If he does not, I will cut off his stinger with a simple wave of my hand. I will also pierce his underside with frozen spears. Then let us see who dies an agonizingly slow, tormenting death!"

Mortaknom sneers, "You may have a supernatural hearing ability to eavesdrop on others' whispered conversations from a distance. To slice off my assassin's stinger and pierce his abdomen with frozen spears, I think not."

He laughs. "You will have to move much closer than where you stand, Eva Roblins. Before you can take three paces, your elfin friend will be writhing in agonizing pain. A few moments later she will die. Then what shall you have gained? You shall have gained nothing, nothing at all."

"This is getting us nowhere," I convey to Lindsial. "I wish no harm to come to these creatures. I believe they are blindly following Zarof's evil commands, probably due to the threat of force against them. I am going to try one more ploy. If it does not work be ready to spring into action."

I look squarely into Mortaknom's deep black eyes. I deliberately take two steps forward. In response to my move, Mortaknom raises one front leg. He is prepared to signal a command.

In response to Mortaknom's gesture, the assassin purposely lowers his back appendage. His deathly black stinger warningly glows in the late afternoon sun. Its poisonous tip is now poised inches from Ariel·e's closed eyes.

"Do not attempt anything foolish, Eva Roblins," Mortaknom's mind cautions. "One swift command from me and your precious elfin is dead. Now you give yourself up to me peacefully, and tell the others to show themselves!"

"Let her go!" I scream. "It is me you want, not her! Give her to me. Then I will go with you peacefully. I promised I would do you no harm. As Princess of Spardom, my word is absolute. Let her go now! I will give you until the count of three."

As I continue to stare into Mortaknom's dark eyes, I wait for his response. After a few moments, I begin to count very slowly. "One · two…"

"Three!" Ariel·e is yelling at the top of her lungs. She pierces the assassin's soft underbelly with four frozen spears. At the exact moment Ariel·e impales the areneus with her spears, Lindsial strikes the assassin's stinger. She strikes it with so much force it flies harmlessly to its side.

A split second later Ariel·e hastily rolls from beneath

the areneus' collapsing body. She crawls toward me on all fours. The assassin crumples to the ground and thrashes in pain. He will meet his well-deserved fate in a matter of minutes.

Before Mortaknom and his remaining five soldiers can react, Ariel·e is crouching on all fours beside me. I notice out of the corner of my eye as she and Mortaknom stare wide-eyed at the sky. My outstretched left hand is guiding three of Mortaknom's soldiers. The soldiers are flying in circles dangerously high above our heads. I am using my moveo spell on them. I've added a variant to the spell from a charm Lindsial taught me. It is called *volo*. My spell causes the areneus to fly rapidly in endless circles.

Mortaknom's two other soldiers are running around in circles in response to my praetendō (run stupidly) spell. They foolishly laugh and shout as they run. They are now nonsensical idiots and no longer a threat. Even though they clutch their clubs, they are too dim-witted to use them.

I continue to stare at Mortaknom. My mind thinks *credo auduro!* Small flames of fire erupt on all sides where Mortaknom stands. His legs dance in desperation as he tries to avoid the flames that encircle him.

In a flash, I cast my exarmo spell. The clubs he is gripping with his three legs fly harmlessly into the darkened depths of the forest. Now Mortaknom, like his helpless soldiers, is utterly defenseless.

With a simple nod of my head, I cause the flying areneus above us to slam into each other violently. They are now a tan assemblage of twisted legs, (I imagine) anguished screams and flailing clubs. I cast my exarmo spell once more. My spell causes their clubs to dislodge from their claws and scatter harmlessly across the ground.

Despite my furious anger, I have no intention of killing any of them, at least not yet. I will make them suffer and to be humiliated. It may be the only way to get their leader's attention. It is bad enough one areneus is dead. There is no reason for others to die.

I glue my eyes to Mortaknom's deep black eyes. While I stare at the creature, the tumult of flying and running are- neus continues. I cannot help but grin. At this moment, I am using more than one spell at the same time. I have never accomplished that feat before now. I can only assume absolute anger gives me the ability to do so.

"Now you listen to me, Mortaknom," I command. "The elf that cut off your assassin's stinger is standing beside you." I extinguish the flames around Mortaknom's body. "On my command she will slay you as quickly as your as- sassin was cut down." I place my hands on my hips and shout, "Elfin assassin slayer, show yourself to this coward if you please."

Mortaknom backs away quickly as he unexpectedly sees Lindsial standing before him. She is holding her sword with both hands high above her head. She maneuvers the sword's tip until it is inches from Mortaknom's left eye. Lindsial has a scowl of hatred on her face, the likes of which I have seen only once before. It was when Eranba took my medallion in his huge hand. Her image rapidly moves in and out of visibility.

I understand why Lindsial is angry. She is undoubted- ly appalled at the sounds Ariel-e is undoubtedly making as she grimaces in pain on the grass. If Lindsial could see the elf mermaid, she would probably be even angrier. There is no doubt in my mind that Lindsial is ready to strike with no hesitation.

Mortaknom glares at her. He glances at his helpless soldiers flailing in the air and the two ridiculous soldiers running in circles. He takes a side glance at his unmoving assassin. When his eyes move to look at Lindsial once more, she has disappeared. I watch with satisfaction as he shudders.

In a timid, nearly wheezing voice sensed in my mind as cowardly words of anguish; Mortaknom cries, "You gave me your word! You promised me you would do me no harm. Have you gone back on your word? You cannot kill me, Eva Roblins. To do so will stain your name as Princess of Spardom!"

"Oh, my dear Mortaknom," my voice hisses. "I have no intention of going afoul of my word as Princess of Spardom. I will not kill you. I can assure of this. I can also assure you, Ariel·e, and the assassin slayer will not hesitate to do so."

In response to my words, Lindsial reappears. She is now standing to the right of Mortaknom. Her sword is balanced high above her head on the brink of doom. As before, she is ready to strike on my command. Her image continues to fade in and out speedily.

Ariel·e somehow struggles to her feet. Her detestable stare is a mixture of understandable contempt, pain, and anger. She speedily produces a long spear made of ice and hurdles it with brute force in the direction of Mortaknom. The spear's frozen point embeds itself deeply in the soil less than an inch from Mortaknom's front leg. He reflectively scrambles toward the rear with fright and nearly collapses on the ground.

Ariel·e says with obvious hatred, "Trust me, Mortaknom. I purposely intended to miss you with that one. I guarantee the next one will pierce your eye! Then an ensuing spear will pierce your other eye! After you are blind, what will you do? Who will you lead when you are blind?" Having said this, Ariel·e collapses on her knees onto the ground. Despite the severe pain wracking her body, she glares at Mortaknom with odious contempt in her unblinking eyes.

I glance indifferently at the three areneus suspended in the air. I say to Mortaknom, "I can easily release your soldiers from my spell. I can make them fall to the ground in a heap. That will certainly maim or kill them. Or else, I can cause them to float down gently to the ground, safe and sound. As far as your babbling idiotic soldiers running in circles are concerned, I will allow them to remain that way forever. That is unless I decide to release them from my spell.

"The choice is yours, Mortaknom. You are the personal,

firsthand witness to my powers and those of my fellow elves. What you have seen is nothing in comparison to that which we are capable."

"Oh, my dear Eva Roblins, you forget, I have additional soldiers in the trees," Mortaknom boasts. "On my command they will be here before you can escape."

"I have reinforcements as well, Mortaknom," I reply with a mocking tone. "Your soldiers are surrounded by others who also have amazing powers. So what do you say to a compromise, a truce of sorts? You allow us to go on our way unencumbered without cause for further inconvenience. In turn, we will bring no additional harm to you and your soldiers."

I glare at him. Then I say, "Before we go our separate ways, I want you to tell me everything you know about Zarof. I must caution you Mortaknom, hurry with your decision. I am getting impatient. As a feisty redheaded elf, whenever I get impatient horrible things are possible."

Mortaknom fully appreciates his soldiers are unable to defeat us. He remains silent for a few moments. He is contemplating his options that, of course, I can read via his thoughts. What concerns him the most is the intolerable wrath he will have to face from Zarof. His standing in his tribe concerns him as well. He must not lose his fellow areneus' respect. If he does, he will fall out of favor as their leader.

He says, "Okay, Eva Roblins, I agree to a truce and your demands. I do not wish you and your elves further difficulty. Although, I am certain my soldiers could defeat you and your elves in the end."

I offer with a smile, "Do not forget about the two spargnarls and their hundreds, perhaps thousands of spargnarl friends we can summon to aid us. It would be disastrous if they were to fight you. Your entire tribe would be wiped out in no time."

"I see," Mortaknom's thoughts convey. He had forgotten about the two spargnarls. The possibility, of battling hundreds, if not thousands of spargnarls, is unthinkable.

There is no way his species could survive such an on-slaught. The battle would be over in seconds. Of course, I have no means to summon a handful of spargnarls and certainly not hundreds or thousands of the creatures. But Mortaknom does not know that.

He finally says, "As I said, Eva Roblins, I agree to a truce. What do you offer me in return?"

I tilt my head to one side and laugh. With an uncaring shrug, I reply, "I will allow you to live?"

CHAPTER THIRTY

THE GREAT WIZARD'S SIN

Eranba has prepared a stew for tonight's dinner. The stew is a concoction of feral hog, wild onions, stringy greens and mushy tubers. The viscous, lumpy brown paste is barely edible at best, but it will have to do. We need the nourishment. I must admit, it does fill our bellies.

It is fortunate the stew fills our bellies · none of us could stomach a second helping of the mush. In spite of everything, Eranba did give the stew his best shot. So we compliment him on his cooking. All the while we sneak good-natured side glances at each other that silently utter *eww, ugh, phooey and yucky-poo.*

Without question, we prefer Ariel·e's cooking. Yet I expect she will be unable to cook our meals for some time. She is exhausted. She's also in excruciating pain. Her black and blue bruises have spread. They now cover her entire upper body. Dark purple-colored bruises cover her face. In spite of everything, she is alert, and she does her best to join in our conversation around the fire.

Bratle is a novice in the art of Fogreia medicine. He has experience treating spider stings of little spargnarls that accidentally get caught in webs. He is attending to Ar-iel-e's wounds by applying herbal ointments that help to ease the pain.

Mortaknom is across from me as we eat. A handful of areneus accompanies him. I guess the other areneus are his close advisors. We elves and the spargnarls are eating a cooked meal. It may not taste delicious, but it's edible. In contrast, the areneus feast on raw, disgusting-looking hairy rodents of every size and shape imaginable. As I watch the areneus eat their hairy raw meat, I'm thankful for Eranba's stew regardless that it's tasteless and mushy.

At first Mortaknom and I engage in small talk, sort of testing the truce's waters. After a while, he opens up a bit. He begins to tell the areneus' story and how the Evil One, Zarof, has influenced the areneus' very existence. The others in the Group of Seven listen attentively. Even Ariel-e perks up a bit. As she lies on the ground, she turns toward us to listen to what's being said.

This particular family of areneus dwells in the nearby clump of trees. The clump of trees consists of a few hundred lofty hardwoods. The areneus venture into the forest of Fogreia every other day to sling their web traps. After they complete their tasks, they depart the area without delay. They return to Fogreia two days later to harvest whatever game they caught in their webs.

There are thirty-two adult areneus in the family, twelve females, nineteen male soldiers, and Mortaknom. The soldiers guard the clump of trees and serve as lookouts. The females attend to the young. The females also serve as the areneus' primary food gatherers. They sling the web traps and haul whatever they catch back to the clump of trees.

The number of male soldiers includes the two lookouts Donas mentioned. Donas presumed the two areneus were dead. They are alive. Mortaknom had them stunned as punishment for allowing us to depart the clearing unde-tected. One of the two lookouts, Simpelto, is standing be-side Mortaknom. I suspect he is here to obtain additional information about our undetected escape. He is wasting his time. I do not intend to provide any worthwhile information to the areneus.

In addition to the thirty-two adults, there are fifty-five areneus offspring in the family. Similar to spiders on surface earth, the youngsters are proportionate in size to their parents. Just as spiders on surface earth, unborn baby areneus live in egg sacs. Most of the silken egg sacs are hidden in webs and attached to tree limbs. Some female areneus prefer to carry their egg sacs as they travel. Areneus are large, so most egg sacs hold only five or six baby areneus.

Sadly, once a year, the areneus family must surrender nine of every ten newborn baby's as a tribute to Zarof. The areneus and other creatures of Fogreia do not know what Zarof does with offspring he takes as tribute. He may kill the youngsters, turn them into slaves, or simply abandon them to die along the trails of the desert.

Mortaknom says Zarof's sinful practice of collecting young as tribute is his way of intimidating creatures in Fogreia, Abeti, and almost certainly other outlying regions. Certain creatures, but not all, must give up a percentage of their offspring as tribute. Zarof punishes those creatures that do not comply. Sometimes Zarof kidnaps all the females of a species, leaving the species to wither and finally die. He evicts other creatures from their homelands. The evicted creatures are left to roam in strange lands as Wanderers. Some species have suffered worse fates, to include genocide.

Many years ago hundreds of areneus of Mortaknom's family roamed Fogreia unhindered. They were unbothered by other creatures and seldom bothered others in return. They simply caught small game in their webs. Then one year Zarof tried to force Mortaknom to make war with the spargnarls. Zarof almost certainly wanted to reduce their numbers on both sides.

Mortaknom refused. As retribution, Zarof banished the areneus from Fogreia. He forced them to dwell in the small clump of dense trees. He ordered the areneus to guard the clump of trees and surrounding meadow at any cost. If the areneus disobeyed, he would return and kill all of the female areneus. To prove he was capable of his evil word, he slaughtered all but twelve females. Then he took every offspring as tribute, nearly three hundred in all. The areneus family was devastated.

At one point, to prevent Zarof's envoys from taking his family's newborn areneus as tribute, Mortaknom hid some of them. Regrettably, Zarof discovered the ruse. He ordered his envoys to kill every young areneus in the family, newborn and almost fully-grown youngsters alike.

After that horrible episode, the areneus decided it was tolerable to have nine of every ten baby areneus go with Zarof. Anything was better than having all baby areneus slaughtered. Otherwise, like other wretched species that had gone before, the areneus family would ultimately vanish from the forest of Fogreia.

It has been this way ever since Zarof arrived on the scene. The creatures remain within their clump of trees as best as they can. They guard the trees and the surrounding meadow. They suffer the repeated anguish of watching Zarof's envoys harvest their young once a year.

"So you see, Eva," Mortaknom sighs, "We do not have a quarrel with the Princess of Spardom or her entourage. I merely felt compelled to kidnap Ariel·e and to cause trouble because of Zarof's continuing threats against me and my kind. Zarof told me he wanted to capture the redheaded elfin Eva Roblins."

Mortaknom looks at Ariel·e. She crawled closer to the fire for warmth. She is resting her head on my lap. Mortaknom says with genuine sincerity, "I am terribly sorry you had to experience that ordeal elfin Ariel·e. We areneus are a peaceful species. Please accept my apologies."

Ariel·e nods her head slightly in reply. She looks away. She squeezes my hand. I squeeze hers in return three times. Three squeezes of the hand between us elves imply *I love you*. It is a loving, non-verbal idiom that has endured the test of time.

I feel terrible about the areneus' plight. However, there is little I can do. I say, "Thank you for your apology, Mortaknom. I am certain we could have approached this problem in a different, more harmonious fashion. You should have given us the opportunity to do so. But there is no taking back what you did. What do you think Zarof will do in retaliation for disobeying his order to capture me?"

Mortaknom replies, "I do believe it will be my turn to die. I have now disobeyed Zarof two times. He once told me there will never be a third opportunity to disobey him. My only hope is he spares the rest of my family. I now know I should have refused to bother you. I hope you understand. My main concern was the welfare of my species."

"Well, what is done is done as you said," Lindsial conveys to me via thought transference. "I think it outright cruel for the Evil One to reap nine-tenths of the areneus' newborn offspring once a year. Also, for him to have slaughtered the family's females is nonsensical, unthinkably horrible, and unforgivable. What Mortaknom did to Ariel-e, and the anguish he subjected the rest of us to, was similarly unforgivable. Despite all that has happened, and the contempt I feel in my heart, perhaps there is something we should do."

"I agree with you, Lindsial," my mind conveys. "I honestly believe there is something we should do. Look at this setting. A few hours ago we were ready to go full throttle in battle to save our precious Ariel-e. They in turn were prepared to kill Ariel-e and all of you to capture me. Most regrettably, their assassin died. All the same, here we now sit, chatting by the fire as if we're longtime friends.

"What it boils down to is this. The Evil One caused this mess, most likely in collaboration with Parston. Let us face reality, Lindsial. Mortaknom, along with his family, are victims, pure and simple. The Evil One's wickedness is responsible for everything that happened.

"You I both assume we are on the Isle for a purpose, to get rid of Zarof. Let's see if we can capitalize on this slowly budding mutual understanding between the areneus and us. We should try to enlist Mortaknom and his tribe as allies. Perhaps there is something tangible we can offer them in return."

It is at this very moment I decide it is best for Ariel·e's physical and emotional healing to remain in the vicinity of the areneus. Besides, I need to negotiate with Mortaknom, to try and enlist his assistance as an ally. I figure a few weeks delay of our journey should be sufficient.

During our temporary stay, Ariel·e replenishes her core from water the areneus store in tall containers. She does this every day. Doing so helps her to recover quickly. Eranba enjoys helping Ariel·e. He slowly pours water over her head twice a day. In addition to his aid, his naturally agreeable nature immeasurably helps Ariel·e's frame of mind.

As a side note, Andrial regularly makes a crude soap of sorts by combining animal and vegetable oils with salt. Ariel·e had packed the ingredients in one of her many satchels. Andrial adds dried powdery flower petals as fragrance. We are glad that Andrial makes soap. It's important for personal hygiene. More importantly, while the other elves and I do not produce body odor, the spargnarls do. To put it gently, Eranba and Bratle smell horrible if they do not bathe on a regular basis. Eranba, ever conscious of his odor since Donas told him to take a dip in the ocean, showers every day.

To conserve water, probably because he has to haul it, Eranba regularly attempts to freshen up while pouring water over Ariel·e. He looks silly as he maneuvers beneath the stream, large wooden bucket of water in one huge hand, dinky clump of soap in the other. As he attempts his delicate balancing act, soapy water splashes everywhere. Eranba's comical look causes all of us, including Ariel·e, to laugh. In spite of his clumsy showering technique, Eranba is undoubtedly the freshest smelling, cleanest spargnarl in all of Fogreia.

I do not want to camp within the dense cluster of trees.

The wooded area is far too gloomy and foreboding for my taste. Areneus webs are everywhere. As you know, the webs give us elves the creepy-jeepy's. I also want to keep Ariel-e as far away from the areneus as possible.

We are camping in the meadow. A simple lean-to shelter in the middle of the meadow is where we sleep and eat. I am hopeful the meadow's solitude, cool air, and abundant sunshine will aid Ariel-e as she heals.

Donas tends to a robust fire that is situated just outside of the lean-to's entrance. With the exception of Lindsial, Bratle, and me, the three elves and Eranba pass their free time singing and telling stories. They also sharpen their weapons. I am happy to see Ariel-e takes regular naps.

The bruises on Ariel-e's body are slowly fading. I believe she is experiencing considerably less pain. She doesn't make a pain-stricken face as regularly when she walks. Over time, she gradually becomes her usual jovial and optimistic self. Soon she is smiling her attractively magnetic smile. Her beautiful, heart-warming grin is a charismatic beam of light only Ariel-e can produce.

During the second week of her recovery, Ariel-e resumes cooking delicious meals. We are elated, to say the least. Eranba tried to cook tasty meals, bless his sweet soul. Even so, nothing can compare to Ariel-e's delicious entrees. No matter what the menu, Ariel-e's meals always turn out mouthwateringly scrumptious.

You're probably wondering why Lindsial, Bratle, and I are not wiling away our time around the lean-to with the others. The reason is simple enough. Bratle is off on a personal mission on my behalf. Meanwhile, Lindsial and I are spending the majority of our days in discussions with Mortaknom and his advisors. We are trying to secure Mortaknom's loyalty as an ally. He has just as much to lose like the rest of us when it comes to Zarof, probably much more.

Lindsial and I are playing the good cop bad cop routine. She's the bad cop - I'm the good cop. Lindsial does the

squabbling with Mortaknom, and then I throw my comments into the mix as compromises. Lindsial is quite good
at this. She sets the tone of each day's discussion with clev-
erness. Of course, she and I aren't totally fair. We coordi-
nate our actions via telepathy before, during, and after
every discussion. Despite our ruse, my conscience is clear.
We need to teach Mortaknom a lesson and hold him ac-
countable for what he did to Ariel·e. What he doesn't know
won't hurt him.

Mortaknom tells of numerous colonies of large arach-
nids in the forest, such as other species of spiders, scorpions, and chiggers. Since the areneus species is few in
numbers, I realize these other creatures could be useful allies as well. I delicately try to convince Mortaknom that it's
important for him to obtain the others' help as allies if the
need arises. Areneus are on friendly terms with most of the
creatures, except for scorpions called *storngfuls*. Mortaknom says the storngfuls are especially ruthless creatures. We will run into storngfuls in the future.

Bratle's mission on my behalf is to alert his friends
concerning Zarof's mischief-making and the Great Wizard's
quest to capture me. Bratle is to narrate Mortaknom's story regarding Zarof's evil ways. His narration should include how Zarof had tried to instigate hostilities between
the spargnarls and areneus.

Bratle is also to tell of the areneus family's suffering
due to Mortaknom's refusal to initiate hostilities between
the two species. Bratle should request his friends visit the
areneus from time to time. In sum, the spargnarls should
do all that they can to shield the areneus from harm.

I seriously doubt the spargnarls can prevent Zarof from
harming the areneus. However, I feel compelled to try. I
want to ease the areneus' apprehension, since the areneus
are nothing but scapegoats for Zarof's wickedness.

Spargnarls are the most populous, organized, and lethal creatures in Fogreia. They have no quarrel with the
areneus. As you have probably guessed, I have an ulterior
motive for asking the spargnarls to look after the areneus.

It is one more subtle gesture of friendship toward the spargnarls. I am enlisting them as potential future allies against a common foe · the Great Wizard of Abeti, Zarof the Evil One.

It is now three weeks since we first encountered the areneus, and we're ready to resume our journey. Mortaknom offers up his best lookouts, Portrang and Simpelto, to accompany us to the easternmost edge of the forest. It is a gesture of good will. Mortaknom says it is a payment for the injuries inflicted on Ariel·e and the trouble he caused the rest of us.

I ask Ariel·e if the two areneus can accompany us. She says it is okay with her. I readily agree with Mortaknom's offer. It should prove useful to have the two areneus in our company, just in case we encounter other creatures of their kind. The areneus may also prove helpful in enlisting more allies.

I plan for Portrang and Simpelto to precede our main group through Fogreia. Their large bodies will clear spider webs and low hanging limbs along our path. The larger of the two lookouts, Simpelto, offers to carry provisions on his back. He also carries enough water to keep Ariel·e's core replenished for quite some time.

Surprisingly, given all she has been through, Ariel·e readily befriends Portrang. Using a makeshift harness for support, she happily rides on his back at the front of our procession. As she does, she shouts *Howdy do, giddy up* · as well as other funny, Wild West shout·outs she heard while watching movies on my computer many months ago.

I smile as I sense Ariel·e's happy thoughts. I convey to Lindsial, "I am relieved Ariel·e is back to normal. I was worried she would not recover as quickly as she has."

"So am I, as are the others," Lindsial conveys. "It is nothing short of amazing. She also has taken to Portrang without difficulty. I imagine it shouldn't come as a sur·prise. After all, she's one of a kind, with a naturally pleas·ant and forgiving manner. Just look at her, Eva, she is a true gem. She learned that ridiculous cowboy hoot and hol·

lered stuff back in your apartment. It seems so very long ago, doesn't it?"

"Yes it does," I reply with a sigh. "It seems so very long ago indeed."

We are about to reenter Fogreia from the opposite side of the expansive meadow. Before we do, we stop to turn and wave our goodbyes. Every areneus, to include the youngsters, is high up in the trees near the meadow's edge watching us go. They look quite comical as they balance on two hind legs and wave with the other six.

As I wave goodbye I sense Mortaknom's thoughts in my mind, "Farewell, Eva Roblins, Princess of Spardom and true friend of areneus. We wish you and the others of the Group of Seven a safe and successful journey. If you ever need us, we shall not hesitate to be by your side."

CHAPTER THIRTY-ONE

ZIPLIPS AT YOUR SERVICE

The warm weather blesses us as we continue our journey. The air is as surprisingly clean and fresh as it is
wholesome. The forest no longer closes in around us. Although rain showers come and go, it is less humid. This part
of Fogreia is not teeming with lofty, wide-trunk trees like it
was to the west. The trees in this part of the forest are
evenly spaced. Perhaps they were purposely planted. There
are plentiful clearings where we can stop to eat and make
camp. We can feel the sun's warmth on our faces from time
to time in openings in the trees. It is refreshing, to say the
least.

There is little underbrush along the path to slow our
pace. As a result, the going is rather trouble-free. Unlike
our trek through western Fogreia, we are now able to ride
our horses. As we ride, colorful songbirds of stunning colors
of gold, blue, red and green fool around in the trees. Andrial tells me in his thoughts the songbirds begin singing as
soon as they see us approach. He says they are in high
spirits because of the Princess of Spardom's presence.

Now and then I try to discern in my mind the songbirds' melodies. Whatever they are singing makes no sense - at least not to me. The only things I sense in my mind, are *tweets, chirps, cheeps, peeps, chitters, chirrups and chirrs.*

But at least it is something! I take pleasure in knowing I can now sense thoughts from these beautiful creatures' tiny brains - well, at least a little. And it certainly doesn't matter to me if they're bird brains.

Late afternoon is my favorite time of day. It is when the forest is much cooler, and our bodies are geared up to relax, we can finally unwind. As we sit in a tight circle around the campfire, our Group of Seven's friendship bounces to life. We tell jokes, laugh, sing, hold hands, hug, dance and narrate stories - some made up but a good number true.

Despite the loving amity around the campfire, the best part, at least for me, is dinner. I always seem to be ravenously hungry. Lindsial says she believes my hunger pains result from ongoing changes in my metabolism as I continue to transform from human to elf. In any event, eating every mouthwatering meal prepared by Ariel-e makes my day complete.

As we relax on the forest floor at night, we gaze dreamily at Spardom's twinkling stars - except for Lindsial, of course. Seeing as she is blind, I convey to her as accurately as I can what I see in the nighttime sky. She says my descriptions are vivid. She swears she can see in her mind's eye what I am seeing.

As we relax this evening, I notice a pair of shiny green bulbs peering from within a bushy thicket. Perhaps I am too tired from today's hike. I may be seeing things that are not there. I blink my eyes rapidly. I close my eyes and squeeze them tightly. When I open my eyes again, I cannot help but blink my eyes rapidly once more. Do I see double? There are now two pairs of shiny green bulbs!

I slowly shake my head back and forth to clear my vision. I look again. I narrow my eyes to focus on what I'm seeing. Now there are three pairs of shiny green bulbs!

Then a fourth appears followed shortly by a fifth. Suddenly it dawns on me. What I am seeing are not unblinking bulbs. What I am seeing are *unblinking shiny green eyes!*

Now, if it's one thing I have learned since I've been on the ancient Isle of Spardom, it is this. Expect the unexpected to happen when you least expect it. I nudge Lindsial in her ribs with my elbow. She doesn't respond. So I nudge her more forcefully.

She turns her head in my direction. I watch her lips say, "Ouch, milady. That hurt!" As she reads my mind, she conveys, "What is it Eva?"

I purse my lips and nod my head in the direction of the thicket. It's a force of habit to point with my pursed lips. Quickly realizing Lindsial cannot see to where I am referring, I convey, "Over there, in the thicket to our left. Something's at hand."

Lindsial is incredible! Although she cannot see what I see, she somehow knows the thicket to which I refer. She slowly turns her head to the left. She stops her head movement and now appears to be looking directly at the thicket! Of course, since she's blind she isn't looking at anything. Astonishingly, the position of her head gives me the impression she is looking dead-on at the thicket!

I watch in wonder as the expression on her face becomes one of total awareness. I suspect she's using her echolocation to discern shadowy shapes within the bushy undergrowth. The look on her face suddenly becomes one of major concern. By some means, she has located whatever it is that's lurking in the thicket. Incredible!

She pats my knee with her hand a few times. I suspect she is telling me to remain calm and to stay where I am. I try to read her thoughts, but I cannot. I guess she has blocked her thoughts. I watch as she steadily pulls her sword toward her inch by inch.

Now that her sword is unsheathed and in her hand I watch as her lips scream, "Group of Seven, to your weapons!" In a flash, the seven of us snap to our feet, weapons in hand. Except for Lindsial and me, the others are looking around wondering what in the devil is going on.

Lindsial points to the thicket with her sword. "You there, the five of you in the thicket, show yourselves now!" I quickly think to myself · five? How does she know there are five things in the thicket? I didn't tell her what I saw!

At first nothing happens. Then slowly and timidly, one, then another, a third, a fourth, and finally five small crea-tures emerge from the underbrush. The creatures look like miniaturized elves. They stand four feet tall at best. They have elongated elf·looking ears, much longer than ours. These creatures' slender ears just about run all the way to the tops of their heads. The creatures appear to be fifteen to sixteen years of age, perhaps a bit older.

The five of them look identical, except for the length of their hair and caps of different colors they wear on their heads. I cannot be certain, but it looks like there are three males and two females. The two wearing their long red hair in braids are probably females. The males, at least I think they are males, have short bushy red hair. In the flickering light of the campfire, I can barely make out slight wings tucked behind their backs. The creatures look like elf faeries! They may have our dander up right now. However, I cannot help but think these creatures are darned cute! For sure, as I think these thoughts, Lindsial is reading my mind. She nods her head.

One creature wearing a bright orange cap faces Lind-sial to say, "Oh, we are sorry fair lady Lindsial. We did not intend to frighten you. We mean you no harm." The five creatures bow in unison, their caps sweeping off their heads as they hold them in their hands.

Turning his attention to me, the creature in the orange cap says as he bows, "We are at your service, our lady Eva Roblins, Princess of Spardom."

Despite the creature's apparent peace·making gesture, we remain cautious. Each creature has a tiny bow in his or her hand, and a miniature quiver of arrows slung over its right shoulder. In spite of their sudden presence and being armed, I cannot help but smile.

I convey to Lindsial, "They look like diminutive angelic cherubs. Maybe they're tiny cupids. Although they carry weapons, they do not look dangerous at all. I can just imagine one shooting me in the butt with his arrow and wham! I'm falling desperately in love - with whom, I do not know. But it would be fun just the same." Even as she continues pointing her sword at the creatures, Lindsial laughs.

As the creatures and the Group of Seven continue to stare at each other, I decide to get things going. "Hello," I say. "Who are you and why are you spying on us?" I notice the others in my group are keeping their weapons at the ready in spite of my diplomatic overture.

The one in the orange cap says, "We are *ziplips*, milady Eva, Princess of Spardom, and we are at your service." He bows.

Lindsial asks, "What in the world are ziplips?"

The creature responds, "We are fair lady, Lindsial. We are ziplips, and we are at your service." He bows once again.

I cannot help but laugh as I say, "Okay, what exactly are ziplips?"

The creature looks puzzled. He scratches his head. He looks at the other creatures and shrugs. They likewise shrug, their big eyes never blinking. Still scratching his head beneath his orange cap the creature responds, "Our Lady of Spardom, as I told our fair lady Lindsial, we are ziplips. And we are at your service." He bows a third time.

By now the atmosphere is more relaxed. The elves and spargnarls have lowered their weapons. I lower my sword and sheath it. The others do the same.

"Okay, okay," I say with a laugh. "Let me try a different approach. You are ziplips. I'll grant you that. From where did you come and why are you here?"

He says, "We come from the Land of the Unseen my dear princess. The ruler of our land, Hannahlo sent us. She is the fairest and most beautiful of all that live on the Isle - present company excluded, of course." He bows deeply and smiles mischievously.

"We are descendants of the first elves to inhabit Spardom. Others born from our cast evolved over countless centuries, such as you five elves. As elves evolved, their appearances changed. Evil and disgusting creatures such as morgalps are but one example. But all ten elves, which are here around your warm campfire are one and the same. You are taller than us. We are shorter than you. That is the only major difference. Yes, we are ziplips, and we are at your service." He bows along with the others.

"So, Hannahlo sent you," I say. "This is great news indeed. Tell me my dear sir, why do they call you ziplips?"

I watch as the creature responds. His lips do not move. I sense his thoughts in my mind as before. "We are called ziplips because we speak only in our minds."

I look at the others in the Group of Seven. Except for Lindsial, the others are staring at the creature with looks of expectation. They are waiting for him to say something!

Lindsial shrugs her shoulders. She conveys, "Beats me."

Wait a minute, sir," I say aloud. "If you speak only in your minds why could the others hear what you were saying a moment ago?"

"Oh, my fair lady princess," the creature responds, "It is because you wish it to be. Otherwise, we speak only in our minds. Lacking elfin Lindsial and your powers, others cannot understand what we are saying - unless they possess telepathy. You see princess - you are the one who is allowing our thoughts to turn into audible words so the others may hear what we are saying in our minds." As expected, he bows once more.

"Well, I'll be darned," I convey to Lindsial. "I learn something new every day." Addressing the creature, I add, "You seem to know everything about us. How is that?"

"Princess, we have been following you for several weeks now. Hannahlo told us to remain hidden from view until you reached the crossroads in the desert. We did not want to interfere. It is there, at the three paths' crossroads, we intended to show ourselves, to reveal the correct pathway to the Land of the Unseen. I must say, dear princess, your performance with those eight-legged creatures was quite entertaining." He bows.

It comes as no surprise to me when Lindsial interrupts. She has been eager to know what forms of creatures live in the Land of the Unseen. She asks, "Why do you call your realm the Land of the Unseen?"

With a wave of his hand, the creature disappears. I am bewildered at Lindsial's powers once again. She somehow knows the creature has turned invisible. She claps her hands and says jubilantly, "Yeah, more creatures who can turn invisible. Now, this is perfectly cool. I'm going to like these creatures! I'm going to like them a bunch!"

Visible once again, the creature in the orange cap says, "Oh, lady Lindsial. We are not creatures. We are ziplips, and we are at your service." He bows and then he smiles. "Like us ziplips when we turn invisible, the Land of the Unseen is also hidden. Only those who our beloved lady Hannahlo allows to see our land are capable of doing so."

Andrial glances toward me. He gestures in the direction of the campfire. His mind says, "Perhaps we should ask them to join us by the fire. I notice the female creatures are shivering." I see he's blushing as he says this. Perhaps he's taken a liking to one of the two female ziplips?

I say, "Good idea, Andrial. Thank you." Smiling at the creature, or I should say ziplip, I say, "It is getting chilly. Please sit with us. It will be a tight squeeze, but I think we can manage." I glance at Andrial. He's staring at the female ziplip wearing a pink cap and, as I expected, he's still blushing. Lindsial has read my mind. She giggles.

Eranba and Bratle pull a large log near the campfire on which the ziplips can sit. Ariel-e offers them leftovers of the evening meal. The leftovers are piping hot, keeping themselves at just the right temperature in Ariel-e's magical containers. The ziplips hungrily eat in silence. By the manner in which they are wolfing down their food, I bet they haven't had a nutritious hot meal in days if not weeks.

After they have finished eating, I say, "Well, I do be-lieve it's time we get to know you. Please tell us your name and introduce us to your companions."

The ziplip in the orange cap stands and then he bows. "I am Jakebe at our service, Princess Eva Roblins. Han-nahlo charged me with the safety and well-being of my companions." Pointing down the line to the others on his left he says, "This is Cackbe."

Cackbe stands and bows. He sits. Each of the ziplips wears a different color cap. I am glad - otherwise it would be hard to tell them apart, except for their hair, of course. Cackbe is wearing a yellow cap.

Jakebe says, "This is Grantbe." Grantbe is wearing a purple cap. Like Cackbe, Grantbe stands, bows, and he sits on the log.

Jakebe continues, "And this is Shelbe." She stands, curtsies, and like the others, she sits down. Shelbe is wear-ing a pink cap.

Goodness! Did I just detect the exchange of subtle smiles between Andrial and Shelbe? It wouldn't surprise me in the least since Shelbe can read minds. I bet Andrial was thinking about her. I purposely block Andrial and Shelbe's thoughts from entering my mind. I do not want to be intrusive. But you have to admit, this is too sweet!

Jakebe looks at the last elf, and then he says, "And this is..."

Before he can finish his sentence, the ziplip at the end of the log unexpectedly jumps up and shouts, "And I am Clover!" She curtsies two times. Unlike the others, she re-mains standing. Her unblinking shiny green eyes sparkle with amusement. She is wonderfully cute. We laugh good-naturedly. She is wearing a bright green cap.

Donas asks Clover, "Every one of you ziplips has a name that ends in *b-e*. Why is your name different than the others, Clover?"

It is readily apparent Clover has had this question asked of her many times before tonight. With a wave of her hand, Clover's entire body turns a medium green color. Miraculously, four beautiful soft green wings begin to flutter as fine wisps from behind her back. In an instant, she is hovering gracefully above our heads. Now she turns invisible. When she reappears, she is the brightest emerald green you can imagine.

The joy I feel in my heart is wonderful. Never in my twenty-nine years have I seen anything so delicately exquisite and elegantly attractive. Clover is completely, staggeringly, extraordinarily beautiful!

All of us, including the other ziplips, are clapping our hands and cheering. Since she has read my mind as I followed Clover's marvelous feats, Lindsial is elated as well. All of us are on our feet as we give Clover a standing ovation. I am out of breath. I can hardly speak. All the same, I manage to give it a go. I say, "My goodness, I can see why they call you Clover. You turn a beautiful shade of green just like a clover leaf on surface earth. And..."

Before I can continue, Clover offers, "And my darling Princess Eva, unlike the others I have four wings? And they only have two? Yes, I am blessed · at least that is what everyone says. I am the lucky four-winged green ziplip of the Land of the Unseen. I am four-winged Clover. Of course, milady Princess Eva, I am also at your service." She gently descends to the grass and curtsies once again.

I think to myself, and you're different than the others · stunningly unique, standing out amongst the crowd. That makes you special. Plus you are just as spunky as someone else I know. As if she has read my mind, but of course she has not, Ariel-e gestures for Clover to sit beside her.

Ah, my darling, precious Ariel-e. There are now two spunky peas in that attractive, high-spirited, happy-go-lucky pod · you and Clover.

"Well, look here," I convey to Lindsial. "It appears as though the Group of Seven has company. We're now a very large, happy bunch of elves, spargnarls, areneus', and now ziplips. I'm rather glad we are taking a new path. Perhaps Hannahlo can provide us with more details about our Isle and more information about the Evil One. I'm certain we would have been okay traveling along Ariel-e's trail to the Banned Borders. But this detour should serve us well. I'm particularly anxious to meet Hannahlo."

"I'm looking forward to meeting Hannahlo as well," Lindsial conveys. "I'm also looking forward to meeting other creatures like the ziplips. It goes without saying I cannot wait to visit the Land of the Unseen for myself."

CHAPTER THIRTY-TWO

LYNNETTE MCKINLEY -
A TRUE STORY

Over the next several weeks, we encounter no frighten-ing beasts along our path. We see the occasional small rodent scampering on the forest floor. Now and then one of the unlucky rodents is caught. A thin stream of sticky thread produced by one of the areneus' abdomen snares it. Luckily for the rodent, its demise is swift. Whichever of the two areneus snared it devours it on the go.

"The areneus are quite skillful when it comes to food," Lindsial conveys. "When they see something that looks particularly appetizing, there's no hesitation. They simply shoot a thin stream of thread from their spinneret and presto! It's dinner time. But I say *ugh* just the same."

I can't help but laugh. I convey, "At first I was like, you know - *totally ugh!* Then the more I thought about it, I was somewhat intrigued. Imagine us elves walking along hun-grily. Then swish! - A snack of freshly caught meat. We wouldn't have to stop to clean and cook it. Just like the areneus we could eat it on the go. Yummy!"

Lindsial laughs as her mind conveys, "Yuck! That's disgusting, Eva. I guess it has its advantages. Just the same, I would rather eat the meals Ariel·e cooks. Everything she prepares tastes delicious. She also cooks it thoroughly. I don't care what anyone says, I like my meat well done."

My mind responds, "Like you, I like my red meat cooked as well, medium over a charcoal fire thank you. Then again, when it comes to sashimi, give it to me fresh from the sea along with soy sauce and nasal clearing wasabi paste!" I laugh. "Despite their nasty eating habits, we are fortunate to have the areneus along with us." I change the subject. "On a more serious note, I'm thinking back to our first encounter with the areneus. Why do you think I could sense Mortaknom's thoughts? He is a primitive beast, after all."

Lindsial conveys, "I honestly think your telepathic senses are becoming more refined, Eva. I believe you can now read any creature's thoughts if you try hard enough."

"Hmm, I wonder Lindsial. I could not read the other areneus' thoughts, no matter how hard I tried."

"Because you concentrated primarily on sensing Mortaknom's thoughts," Lindsial conveys. "After the areneus kidnaped Ariel·e, you subconsciously zeroed in on the thoughts that caused you the most concern, Mortaknom's. And, of course, at first he was speaking to you in your mind. After that, your mind selectively concentrated to sense Mortaknom's thoughts and his alone. That was because you found out he was the leader, and he was the one who could do Ariel·e and us the most harm.

"If you'll recall Eva, I once said the mind is a powerful instrument. It has a definite will of its own. Never forget that fact. And you, milady, you are your mind's landlord, an extremely intelligent and powerful landlord at that.

"Try to detect other creatures' thoughts such as those of the spargnarls. A word of caution · you must teach your mind to be highly selective. If you do not, you will find yourself overwhelmed with random thoughts from every living creature's brain."

"Goodness, Lindsial. You are a wealth of knowledge, especially when it comes to psychic abilities."

"Thank you," Lindsial replies in her mind. "I learned the principles of telepathy from one of the best · Kristopher. Elves with thought transference abilities on surface earth are extremely rare. While Kristopher's abilities are highly refined, they are nothing in comparison to yours.

"Also, and I have dreaded telling you this up till now, Eva, but here goes. You should try to block your thoughts from me and vice versa. It will take the deepest level of concentration you can summon. You must command your mind to do what you tell it to do. I hope you never have to block your thoughts from me or mine from you. Who knows? Someday you may have to."

"Oh no," I declare in my mind. "I could never block you from my thoughts, Lindsial, never!"

"Hopefully, it never comes to that," Lindsial responds. "It is important for you to try now and then. It could save your life or the life of those whom you love. After all, there are devilish beings that would like nothing better than to seize Eva Roblins' thoughts."

As we continue along the path, I try · in a hit or miss experimental fashion · to sense Eranba and Bratle's thoughts. After deep concentration and repeated tries, I am finally able to read their minds. After more practice, I am successful at reading Portrang and Simpelto's thoughts as well. Now I block out all thoughts in my head and concentrate keenly.

What was that you said, Lindsial, about blocking my thoughts from others? Oh yes, you said I must command my mind to do what I tell it to do. Am I correct?

After Lindsial does not respond, I realize I was able to block her from reading my thoughts. Tears collect in my eyes. My tears reveal more than inner thoughts or spoken words could ever hope to convey. They disclose to me a bittersweet, scary realization. My phenomenal telepathy powers may someday have to shut out even my best friend's mind.

It takes a few more days of practice, but I eventually find myself capable of reading the minds of many of the creatures we see along the way. Of course, I am selective. As you would expect, I do not purposely read the minds of the others in our group. I feel this is pointless eavesdropping and incredibly intrusive.

However, reading Pranzen's thoughts is a delight. She and I have lively conversations as she carries me along the path. I read her mind, and then I talk to her aloud. Our mind-reading and talking routine works out well for both of us. I tell her stories of my times as a photojournalist reporter and as an agent for the CIA. She, in turn, relates stories about exciting places she has visited on our Isle. Although she is quite young, Pranzen has seen much in the short span of her natural life.

Lindsial and her horse Ceria often join us in our storytelling. Lindsial cannot read Ceria's thoughts. Nevertheless, Ceria understands what Lindsial says out loud. Whenever Ceria has something to say to Lindsial, I read Ceria's thoughts and pass them along. The four of us enjoy sharing our experiences. It helps to make monotonous days that turn into lengthy weeks much more agreeable.

Pranzen, Ceria, and I cannot help but chuckle when Lindsial relates funny tales she has heard over the years. Many of her tales are also about fun times she had with her three horses when she was a child. She kept her horses at her grandparents' farm. Some of Lindsial's stories seem too impossible to be true. Others are out-and-out hilarious. A few of Lindsial's stories are somewhat thought-provoking. One of Lindsial's stories is worth retelling. So tell it I will.

This story centers on a day Lindsial, and a group of elves was exploring a cavern. There must have been eight or nine elves in the group. Lindsial believes she was ten years old at the time.

The cavern was considered awfully dangerous because of numerous cave-ins over the years. The elves' parents, including Lindsial's, told the youngster elves never to go into the cavern. Kids being kids and doing what kids sometimes do; Lindsial and her friends explored the cavern just the same. Although Lindsial was blind, she easily navigated the underground chambers using echolocation. The others in her group held torches as they walked. Lindsial smiled as she heard the other elves' gleeful shouts. They were commenting on majestic stalactites hanging like icicles from the roof of the cavern, their calcium tips dripping slimy water.

Huge statue-like stalagmites that grew from the floor likewise brought the elves much delight. The stalagmites were of various sizes and shapes and seemed to grow increasingly larger as the group walked deeper into the yawning deep. As she maneuvered around the stalagmites, Lindsial recalls she was impressed by their girth and height. Her echolocation was working overtime.

The elves explored many side tunnels and sampled clear water from cold fresh water ponds that dotted the floor. The young elves saw numerous markings on tunnel walls. They were ancient markings perhaps, of animals and funny-looking symbols. There were paintings of creatures that may have been crude portrayals of humans.

Oddly enough, the creatures depicted in the paintings looked nothing like humans. They had enormous heads, bulging eyes, skinny bodies, and antennae. They looked like aliens from a faraway galaxy. Of course, Lindsial could not see the markings and paintings, so her friends described them to her.

As the group was eating lunch beside a large pond, a huge gust of wind rushed through the tunnel with a loud *whoosh!* The blast of wind came from a cave-in deep within the never-ending depths of the cavern. The elves' torches, lighted before they entered the cave, were instantly extinguished. The cavern turned pitch-black.

Lindsial's friends started to panic. They could not see a thing. They couldn't even see their hands when they held them right in front of their eyes! To those with normal vision, not being able to see is a horrifying sensation, to say the least.

One of Lindsial's friends started screaming. She cried hysterically, "There is no way we're going to find our way out of the cave in the dark. We're all going to die! Oh why, why did I not listen to my momma?" Soon, all of Lindsial's friends were crying similar words of doom.

Lindsial admits she was as frightened as her friends. Then something occurred to her. She navigated in the dark. To her, everything seeable in life was as obscure as the darkest night imaginable. She could also see things in her perpetual darkness others could not see, merely by using her mind's eyes. She possessed echolocation, so she could also sense things about her as well.

She gathered her friends around her. She told them to try and remain calm. She reassured them she and her best friend at the time, Berlama, would lead the others out of the cavern.

Berlama had an unusual gift. She had an *eidetic memory*. Berlama's extraordinary eidetic memory allowed her to recall visual images with complete accuracy. By combining Lindsial's power of echolocation and Berlama's eidetic memory, Lindsial would guide the group to safety.

Lindsial told her friends she was going to lead the group with Berlama following right behind her. The other elves were to follow in a single file behind Berlama. All of the elves were to hold hands. If any elf encountered a problem along the way, he or she was to shout out immediately.

As Lindsial led the group in the direction from whence they had come, Berlama told Lindsial the last thing she remembered seeing. By means of her echolocation, Lindsial told Berlama what lay ahead. Then Berlama once again sought in her memory where to go next. She told Lindsial to proceed straight ahead, turn left, right, or wherever the group needed to go. The steady sharing of information between Lindsial and Berlama ultimately led to success. It took hours to find their way to the cavern's opening, but they arrived safely.

It was nighttime when they exited the cavern. As expected, their worried parents were gathered at the cavern's entrance. Lindsial recalls there were loads of happy shouts, lots of tears, many embraces, and then the scolding began. Punishment in the form of no playing with each other for nearly two weeks followed.

You have to admit, what Lindsial and Berlama did together to save the other elves is awe-inspiring. For sure, I have known Lindsial to be something special since the day I met her. This story lends further credence to that fact.

The days seem to drag on and on. The eastern portion of Fogreia is lovely, and its mood benevolent, especially in comparison to the enchanted forest to the west. However, it is seemingly never-ending, mind-numbing repetitive scenery - trees, bushes, weeds, thickets, and dirt. My mind is wandering all over the place. I decide to tune into Ariel-e's thoughts. True to form, she is having a great time. I watch with profound happiness as Clover flies above her. Clover is decidedly one clever, super happy ziplip. She manages to keep us laughing during every evening meal - not to mention she is darned cute! What's more important, now my darling elf mermaid has a best friend, equally darling Clover.

It is obvious to me Ariel-e has never been happier. My mind tells me the lovely, happy-go-lucky elf mermaid is singing jovially. She's sings song after song as she rides on Portrang's massive back. The areneus often darts among the foliage, more for happy-go-lucky Ariel-e's benefit than out of necessity. Whenever he does a particularly exciting or daring acrobatic trick, Ariel-e interrupts her singing and shouts, "yippee, hee haw, git along little spidey!"

Wait a minute. I know the song Ariel-e is singing! It is *Whoopie Ti Yi Yo*, more commonly referred to as *Git Along Little Doggie*. I sang the song during a play at assembly as a sixth grader when I attended Public School No. 42 in Schenectady, New York. The song's chorus was my favorite part of the song. How did it go again? Oh, yes, just as Ariel-e is singing it right now!

Whoopie ti yi yo, git along little doggies
It's your misfortune and none of my own
Whoopie ti yi yo, git along little doggies
You know Wyoming will be your new home

Ah, School 42, a fun school in a way, but I had a school year that fills my mind with horrible memories. While I adored my sweet sixth-grade teacher, Mrs. Blair, I had a rough time in the school, to say the least. My rough time was not due to academics. My grades were nearly perfect. I scored an A or A-minus in every subject. I was never tardy. I also had perfect attendance that year. In fact, I think it was the only school year I was not absent for a day or two or more.

I had received certificates for my punctuality and perfect attendance at a school assembly before school ended for summer vacation. I was mightily proud of those certificates. I hadn't received any recognition in school up till then. I remember covering the certificates in plastic wrap. Then I framed them by taping a one-inch wide border cut from a white-colored cardboard gift box.

I still have the certificates in my hope chest. Well, at least I hope they are there - if the Agency arranged for my personal things from my apartment packed and stored after we departed surface earth. Then again, maybe the Agency is footing my apartment rent bill while I am here. Wouldn't that be terrific!

Lynnette McKinley was the name I went by when I attended School 42. I never knew why Papa registered me with an alias at that school. As best as I can figure, Papa had to assume a new identity, at least that year. The reason was most likely due to unpaid rent at the previous town where we lived.

How Papa was able to register me as Lynnette McKinley, I'll never know. My school records undoubtedly said Eva Roblins. Then again, maybe Papa didn't bring my old school records along when we traveled. Oh well, it is but one more of life's strange mysteries that I'll probably never unravel.

That was the only time I had to assume an alias as a child. I am sure the temptation for Papa to do so again was always there. He was forever late paying bills. Perhaps in the end it was too difficult · not to mention against the law · to assume a new identity.

If you'll recall, I also assumed an alias while on as· signment as an agent with the Agency, when Miguel shot me. Let me tell you, having to go by fake names is weird, especially fake names like Gloria or Lynnette. I'm sort of biased toward my real given name, Eva Caroline Roblins.

I was pretty much a nomadic child after momma died. I accompanied Papa as he roamed the northeastern United States in search of work. Papa was a Canadian immigrant. He had no more than a sixth·grade education. He pos· sessed no critical, marketable skills. He worked as a labor· er for minimum wage or for under the counter cash salary. Due to his transitory status, his employment was usually temporary. We moved quite often.

Whenever Papa could find employment in a town, the two of us took up residence for a year or two, sometimes longer. But we usually stayed for only one full school term. Once we arrived in a town where Papa thought employ· ment looked promising, he would enroll me in the neigh· borhood school. School was always close to his workplace.

I attended ten public schools in half as many cities and towns in the Northeast over a twelve·year period. I was fortunate to have never missed more than a few days of any given school year. The exception was the four weeks of school I missed when I had meningitis. Papa made my edu· cation his second priority, right after food on the table.

When we hadn't secured a legal residence in a new town, Papa would select a random street address. By using the telephone white pages, he was able to match up the address and phone number. The real name of the address's resident was never an issue. Back in the day no one paid much attention to such bothersome necessities. As far as it concerned public school officials, a man's word was as good as gospel. After all, the more students, the more federal bucks, so why check?

Copies of utility bills likewise were not required to show proof of residence when I was in school. When it came to a home phone number, Papa would tell the school to call him at work. We never had a home phone all the years I was a child. Besides, it made perfect sense to give his work phone number. He was a male single parent · a rarity back then for sure. He was never at home during school hours. He worked days.

Finding a safe place to live was particularly dicey. Sometimes Papa was fortunate enough to rent *the price is right* cockroach-infested one or two-room shanty. Our rental was habitually in the poorest, most crime-ridden part of town.

Often home sweet home was a leaky and drafty tent at a campsite on the outskirts of town. Then again, our dilapidated van parked in an empty lot was home just as often. We never parked in the same lot two nights in a row unless, of course, it was affordable or free.

I loved our family van. I affectionately called it Betsy, good ole blue Betsy. If you'll recall, mother died in the van one night when the temperature dipped well below zero. She had covered me with her blanket since it was unbearably cold. She was already frail with cancer. Her immune system was near zero. She plainly froze to death that night.

I'll never forget Papa bargaining with the mortician to lower the price of burying my mother. Her final resting place is in a commoner's grave near Tonawanda, New York. I visit her now and then to say hello. I was seven years old when my mother died. I miss her dearly.

Despite that single, truly sad recollection, riding in good ole blue Betsy holds for me the dearest and sweetest memories. I'll never forget when we sang, laughed, picnicked, told jokes, played road sign bingo and license plate alphabet games.

Before my mother died, and I was able to sit up front with Papa, I sat in the middle of the seat behind them. I can remember yelling over and over, "Trash, please." It was my empty-headed way of asking one of my parents to throw my soda cup, candy wrapper or whatever in the trash. Let me tell you, that two-word phrase drove my parent's nuts!

When I said ill-mannered things like, "trash please," or responded with a "huh," or "what," or forgot to say please and thank you, or picked my nose, gross things like that, Papa would gently scold me. He would say, "Eva, how many times have I told you? *Don't be the example, set the example!"* I disliked that phrase when I was a child, probably because I didn't understand what it meant. But now that I know what it implies, I believe it pertained to me exactly when I was a child. As an adult, I always try to set the example in everything I do. Being the example doesn't cut it.

Driving through the countryside looking for the next night's cheap stay in good ole blue Betsy was outright fun, at least for me. That van took us camping to the bay many summers. We would fish, catch crabs, run around without shoes, explore the woods, climb rocks and hide in trees. We once picked up numerous bags of discarded beer bottles and soda cans. We also built a stairs of sorts on the beach after a hurricane wiped out the real ones.

The other campers at the campground were a funny lot. We called them Shoe-bees. Unlike us, who never wore shoes, even in winter, Shoe-bees wore shoes all year long, even in summer! Shoe-bees were clumsy camping wanna-be's - shoe-wearing busy bees who seemed more wound up than they should have been.

They scurried here and there breathlessly whooping and hollering, saying brainless things like, "Look at the lake!" (It was a bay); or "Oh, my goodness - a shark!" (It was a dolphin); or "They closed the bathhouse!" (So go pee behind a tree like us); and "The fish took my bait!" (It was a crab).

One group of campers was well-seasoned like us. They weren't obnoxious Shoe-bees like the others. There were five kids and a father in their family. If I remember correctly, there was an older girl named Shelly, three boys, named Ed, Josh, and Jay, and a little girl they called Liz. They lived in an ugly greenish-yellow pop-up camper that leaked. They also had a variety of tents.

Shelly was a talented artist. She took long jogs on the five-mile bike trail. Ed was a skateboarder. He loved to skate at three o'clock in the morning. Josh played a lot of video games inside his tent when he wasn't catching sharks. Despite his small stature, Jay could cast the bait net with ease. One time he landed a big red fish. And the little girl Liz ran wide-eyed all over the place following in her older siblings' footsteps. They were cool campers. Like us, they had camped for months on end and returned during the summertime year after year.

They also thought the Shoe-bees were inferior to us more seasoned, tested, tried, and true campers. After all, at one time we had camped for eleven months! Indeed, summertime camping at the bay was wonderful. And we owed it all to good ole blue Betsy.

When she finally passed on, good ole blue Betsy had over three hundred thirty thousand miles under her hood. She was still coughing and sputtering down the road of life, only barely, when I neared my eighteenth birthday.

It was a sad day indeed when Cindy told me of Betsy's imminent passing. She had said, "Honey, it'll cost twenty times as much to repair Betsy than she's worth. She's unsafe. Her windows won't open. Her rear door won't close properly. Her blue paint is flaking like she has a disease, and her engine is shot. I'm afraid she goes to the junkyard tomorrow."

Cindy had added an offering of sorts for taking away my last childhood belonging. "Eva, whatever money we get you can keep." The payoff was the first one hundred dollar bill I ever held in my hand. It was a mixed blessing. Yes, good ole blue Betsy is now recyclable scrap - yet her memories remain fresh in my mind as if she is still brand-spanking new.

Oh, Papa, I miss you so much. Thank you for not keeping me in School 42 past the sixth grade. School 42 where fellow students in my class, mostly boys, would pretend to inoculate themselves with their imaginary X-29 vaccine. They had done this before they handled anything I, or I should say my alias Lynnette McKinley, touched. They also administered X-29 after they accidentally brushed by me.

I must admit, it was terrible knowing that so many of my classmates despised me. I never did anything to them, nothing at all. It's just that I was the new kid on the block and different, in hair color, mannerisms, and the way I dressed. To be honest with you, I dreaded waking up each weekday morning. I would fend stomach aches, headaches, backaches, anything to keep from going to school. Of course, Papa saw through my daily made-up sickness tricks, and I never missed a day of class.

But let me tell you, I hated being in school. When I had to recite something in the front of the class, students would stick their tongues out at me, snicker, cross their eyes or mouth f-you's. It was completely horrifying to be in a class of twenty-five fellow students knowing that everyone loathed me. Even kids from other classes made fun of me. When I walked in the hall, others would move to the other side. I sat at a table with my crumpled brown paper bag all by myself during lunch. If someone had to sit at the same table as me for whatever reason, they would not talk to me. It was a ghastly year of school.

I hope you or someone you know never has to undergo similar abuse and harassment. If you know of someone subjected to bullying, do something about it. As you know, I managed to survive. I become much prettier and better dressed. I landed well-paying jobs that enhanced my self-esteem. Others in this Internet social media day and age that are bullied may not have the same conviction as me. What's more, they may do the unthinkable. They may seek to end it all to escape the intolerable suffering. Whether you're young or young at heart, speak out and do something to help them before it's too late.

Please allow me to talk more about the X-29 garbage. Administering the pretend X-29 vaccine was a simple process. All it took was the telltale click of a plastic ballpoint pen and an ink dot on one's hand. It didn't matter how a student gave himself the imaginary vaccine. As long as one pretended inoculation against Lynnette's deadly, infectious disease you were good to go. Let me tell you, I would sit in the back of my row and cower every time I heard the telltale clicks of many pens in the room as we prepared to pass papers forward. Tears come to my eyes even now when I think about it.

Writing the symbol X-29 on one's hand also served as an inoculation of sorts. Doing so was better than the click of a ball pen and a dot on one's hand. It would protect one from Lynnette's disease the entire day, or at least until Mrs. Blair saw the marking. Then the student was forced to wash the symbol from his hands in the bathroom.

Although Mrs. Blair had no idea what X-29 signified, writing on one's hand back in the day was not allowed. Students were renowned for writing test answers on their hands and arms. They probably still do the same today.

A few of the most hateful boys and girls were more daring than the others. They would pretend to render themselves permanently immune to Lynnette's (my) pretend sickness by writing X-29 in red ink on the back of their hands. That was a profoundly bold act. Mrs. Blair forbade use of red ink in the classroom. It was reserved exclusively for Mrs. Blair's marking of test papers. Students caught with anything having to do with red ink suffered severe consequences.

Class bullies not only ridiculed me with their insensitive X-29 rubbish, they also poked fun at my careless-looking appearance. Eva Roblins, a.k.a. Lynnette McKinley was underprivileged and also poor, to say the least. I wore hand-me-downs Papa would find at the thrift store or neighborhood yard sales. Even Goodwill stores were too expensive for Papa to shop. Christmases and birthdays were sad affairs, although I never complained. I was content with the least amount of inexpensive gifts.

I was elated one year when I got a used Barbie doll and tattered Barbie clothes for Christmas. I was equally excited when I got a drawing pad and broken Crayola crayons on my birthday. It was a particularly good year if memory serves me correctly. Most of my toys were discarded by others, broken, scratched, with bite marks and missing parts. But to me they were priceless.

Being poor and alone makes you appreciate what others who are more fortunate take for granted. Every possession, no matter how small, insignificant, cheap, banged up, or frayed, somehow brings loving joy to your heart. Just like the wonder of life, you learn never to abandon it, no matter what.

Since I lived most of my days out of good ole blue Betsy or in a tent, I was seldom able to shower. When I was in grammar school, my fingernails were dirty more often than not and my hair greasy, grimy, and uncombed. Like I said earlier in this story, I was a childlike pigpen. Fortunately, my appearance improved as I matured.

I had developed a nervous twitch in sixth grade that consisted of moving my head to the right as though I was trying to get my ragged bangs out my eyes. This twitch would occur every few seconds. Incessant bullying, name-calling, and constant X-29 inoculations by classmates to protect against my pretend, infectious disease undoubtedly caused it.

Children would mimic my twitch behind my back. But I somehow knew they were making fun of me. I wouldn't even have to look at them to know. My sixth sense was already close at hand even at an early age. Happily, my twitch disappeared somewhere around the middle of seventh grade. It should come as no surprise. There were plenty of minorities in the new school I attended in seventh grade. Because of my uncommon red hair, I was part of the minority. I seemed to fit in satisfactorily and received considerably less bullying.

In sixth grade I sported glasses taped on the bridge. My glasses were ridiculous-looking. My glasses also included fine spider-like cracks all around the lens' edges. I had dropped them while I played hopscotch, and afterward stepped on them. I hadn't yet lost my hearing. Thus, I cringed when I heard *crunch, scrape, and scratch!* Papa had no extra money to buy replacement glasses. To tell you the truth, I looked hideous. Somewhere around my first year of high school, my astigmatism corrected itself. Thankfully, wearing glasses was no more.

As I mentioned earlier, I also received hurtful taunts about my pale skin, numerous freckles, and unkempt bright red hair. As you know, the insensitive taunts followed me all the way into high school until that glorious day as a junior I knocked Francis on his butt. Little did I know at the time - when my classmates called me an elfin heroine - I would become an elf on my twenty-ninth birthday!

I transferred from Public School 42 a few days before summer break. On my last day of school, I left a poem that I wrote on Miss Blair's desk. Perhaps Miss Blair read the poem to my classmates. I knew I wasn't returning, so I didn't need to worry about revenge from my classmates. The poem, *I'm Sorry* is located at the end of this novel. I've included it along with another poem entitled *Carrot Top*.

Yes, those were rough times, Lynnette McKinley. Now that I've told your story I hope you can finally rest in peace. God bless you my dear.

CHAPTER THIRTY-THREE

SOMEONE HAS TO DIE TONIGHT

I suddenly sense Ariel-e's repeated shouts in my mind. I flinch. I should not have allowed her to ride so far ahead of the group. I must get to her, now! I urge Pranzen to take off at a gallop. I convey to Lindsial, "She's in trouble again, Lindsial! I was daydreaming about my past. I should have paid more attention to what was going on here. Darn, what was I thinking?"

Lindsial laughs as Pranzen and I bolt ahead. As we pass Lindsial at a gallop, I call back to her aloud, "What is so funny?"

Lindsial conveys, "Oh, Eva, Ariel-e's not in trouble. You probably missed the part of her excitable screams when she said we reached the end of Fogreia. She says she sees the desert up ahead. We are almost at the boundary of Fogreia and the Land of Abeti."

I tug on Pranzen's reigns and shout, "Pranzen, please slow down and let's head back to Lindsial. Thank you." As Pranzen trots back to Lindsial, I convey, "Oh, do I feel silly now. I should be more careful than to allow my thoughts to

distract me. The others must think I've gone crazy, galloping off like that."

Lindsial's mind conveys, "I wouldn't worry about it,
Eva. I read portions of your thoughts. I cannot blame you
for being distracted. Some terrible things happened to you
as a human child. I feel so badly for you. I am deeply sorry
- you deserved so much better.

"As far as it concerns the others, they have no clue why
you started galloping away. Perhaps they think you are excited as they are that we're finally leaving Fogreia. Just
the same, I must come clean by saying this. I bet you
looked as amusing as you galloped ahead as you say Ariel-e
looks on the back of the areneus. All that was missing was
the *hee-haw and giddy up!*" She laughs.

I have to laugh when I think of how silly Ariel-e looks
as she rides on Portrang's back. I convey jokingly, "Thanks
a lot, Lindsial, for the vision of my awkward riding skills I
will forever have in my mind. About my childhood, my
dear, thank you just the same. It's okay. I lived through it.
The experience made me a better person - well, elf."

As I look ahead to where Ariel-e is, I question in my
mind, "So we have reached the end of the Forest of Fogreia,
and we're almost in the Land of Abeti, eh? I wonder what is
in store for us in the coming days and weeks."

Despite my question to Lindsial, I already know what
is in store for us. I have dreamed the last several nights
what will happen shortly to the Group of Seven and our
ziplip and areneus friends.

"Only time will tell," Lindsial conveys. "As far as we
know, this is the Evil One's territory. We must be on our
guard at all times."

We set up camp at the edge of Fogreia a few yards into
the sandy loam of the Land of Abeti. We are enjoying ourselves as we wolf down but one more tasty meal prepared
by our cheerful chef, Ariel-e. Donas, who had sprinted from
the forest a while ago to scope out the immediate vicinity of
the desert, has just returned. He says he has good news.

"There is no noticeable danger ahead. I saw a well-traveled path that seems to head due east in the direction of Magigro and the Banned Borders. I suppose it is the one Ariel·e pointed out to us months ago. I also saw large paw prints, almost certainly from medium·sized beasts of prey. I saw evidence of many two·legged animals as well, possibly morgalps. I cannot be certain. I have never seen a morgalp's footprints. In any event, I believe foraging animals are plentiful. We should have abundant game for food along the way."

Lindsial conveys to me, "Something other than morgalps could have made those two·legged footprints, maybe predators that frequent the path. Let us hope Donas is right. I believe we can deal with morgalps if there is but a small number of them. Other two·legged creatures that we do not know about worry me more."

Andrial is scanning the desert. He says he also detects no signs of peril in the immediate vicinity of our intended path. He sees a few birds and small animals here and there. He hears distant cries of creatures he cannot recognize. Thankfully, nothing menacing enters his senses at this point.

Jakebe and his fellow ziplips are flitting around here and there as they fly. They are scouting the desert's immediate surroundings for any signs of trouble. Sometimes they are visible. Other times they vanish for minutes on end. It makes no difference to me. I can read their thoughts. They are comical when they speak with their minds. They try to outdo each other as they report to Jakebe what they find or, should I say, what they do not find. Happily, they also have nothing troublesome to report.

As usual, Clover is sitting beside Ariel·e as the other ziplips flit around in the sky. The two of them are chatting away excitedly as if they have met for the first time. Also, Shelbe seems to spend an inordinate amount of time hovering above Andrial. I have to wonder if a close friendship is in the making. I can only hope so since Andrial and Shelbe are two incredibly sweet elves. As I said earlier, I blocked their thoughts, so I have no clue what they are thinking.

Now Portrang and Simpelto are saying their goodbyes. They are unable to venture into the desert. Without the protection of Fogreia's trees, they are at risk. Ariel·e takes one of Portrang's massive claws into her small hand. As they shake, I cannot help but feel mixed emotions. Despite her horrible suffering at the hands of the areneus, she has shown incredible kindness toward the areneus from beginning to end. In turn, Portrang was especially helpful. He was a jewel of strength for Ariel·e's speedy recovery.

As I say goodbye to the two areneus, I ask them to tell Mortaknom we will send word if we need his help. I also thank Portrang and Simpelto for being kind to us, especially to Ariel·e, during our final journey through Fogreia. Despite our goodbyes, I'm positive Portrang, Simpelto, and some of us in the Group of Seven will cross paths in the future.

The sun is setting beyond the trees of Fogreia. The twelve of us are sitting around the campfire, our backs to the forest. I ponder the vast wasteland below. Unlike the lush forest of Fogreia, which sits on a plateau, the desert is lowland of endless sand. The barren region is magnificent. Tall hills and deep looking valleys dot the scene at random. It is difficult to distinguish where the dull grayish sands of the desert end and where the deep brown·colored valleys begin.

In direct contrast with the desert floor and valleys, rolling hills are sprinkled here and there with what looks to be light green foliage. I imagine the scraps of green are desert scrubs competing for the desert's paltry nighttime moisture. When I squint, I can also make out tiny patches of bright green far off on the horizon. The setting sun highlights the patches' vividness. They look like small oases.

In his mind, Andrial confirms there are many plots of land that undoubtedly hold fresh water springs and foliage of some sort. He can make out patches of small trees and clumps of bright green bushes within his view.

I repeat what Andrial said to the others. Knowing

there are springs in the desert is good news, especially for Ariel·e. She says she will be able to replenish her core fre·quently as we travel through Abeti.

The air to our backs at the edge of the forest is cool and damp, much cooler than the intermittent desert breeze. Even at this late hour, perhaps a half·hour before sunset, the desert breeze from the east is markedly hotter and dri·er.

I see bright flashes of lightening on the horizon to the north. Donas suggests it may be heat lightning. Andrial offers in his mind what we are seeing may be a storm. He says the flashes of lightning are followed now and again by echoes of sounds like thunder. The others cannot hear the thunder. It is too far off in the distance for their hearing to detect. For sure I cannot hear the thunder, no matter if it is way out there or right above my head. Lindsial repeats aloud for the benefit of the others what Andrial has just said.

Andrial's thoughts once again enter Lindsial and my minds. His thoughts urgently exclaim, "I think I hear mor·galps! Their howls are coming from the northern and southern parts of the forest." He pauses for a short time to listen keenly. "Their howls are also coming from the wil·derness below." He points to the north, to the east, and then to the south. "I could be incorrect, but it appears as though the three groups are answering one another."

I say aloud to Andrial, "Is there any way of knowing how many there are?"

Andrial shakes his head as his mind responds, "I have no idea. The sounds originate a good distance from us."

At the very moment Andrial replies, Donas thoughts say, "Knowing how many there are of what, milady?"

I smile, and then I reply, "I am sorry. Andrial just told Lindsial and me via his thoughts he hears morgalps. Their sounds are coming from the forest and also from the desert. He says their cries are a good distance away from our loca·tion."

I stand and say, "Eranba and Bratle, Donas and Andri·

al, collect bunches of firewood if you please. I want to create a larger fire. We will remain close to our smaller campfire tonight. If something comes in the night, I want to be
able to see it clearly. A larger fire will serve us well in that
regard." I briefly inspect our surroundings. I point to a
clearing to our right that is a safe distance from the trees.
"Put it over there. Collect plenty of spare firewood as well.
We will want to keep the fire blazing all night."

Lindsial looks in my direction and conveys, "I find it
rather interesting, and I must admit a bit frightening as
well. Tonight is the first time we have had any inkling of
morgalps. Here we sit on the edge of Fogreia and Abeti
while morgalps decide to show. It seems rather peculiar
don't you think? I wonder how Andrial knows for certain
the howls he is hearing are from morgalps. Perhaps he has
heard them before, but he never told us. "

"I wonder as well," I reply. "Why not ask him?" I say
my credo auduro spell in my mind. A blazing bonfire results from my thoughts.

I read Lindsial's thoughts as she asks Andrial if he had
detected any signs of morgalps prior to this evening. Andrial's mind responds he has not. "Then how do you know
they are in fact morgalp's?" she inquires.

Andrial's mind replies, "It is quite simple, lady Lindsial. They mingle their creepy howls with words I can understand. They are speaking Elvish. If you will recall,
Bratle said morgalps howl as animals. However, they
speak the Elvish language."

Lindsial then asks Eranba and Bratle if they had noticed any signs of morgalps when we were in the forest.
They also respond to the negative. With a serious look on
his face Bratle offers, "My dear elf Lindsial, there is a full
moon tonight. Perhaps the morgalps' animation is due to
that. Otherwise..."

"Otherwise, what - what do you mean?" Lindsial asks
with breathless uneasiness. She is afraid to know what he
is about to say. Something in her heart tells her terrifying
danger is in the works.

Lindsial undoubtedly has read some of the thoughts running through my mind. She comprehends a bit of what I know - grave danger is afoot. I haven't allowed her to read from my thoughts all the details that I know. I will let her know everything that I know when I tell the others.

As he stares out to the desert, Bratle says nothing for a moment or two. Then, with noticeable worry on his face, he answers gravely, "Otherwise, they know we are here, that we are not well-defended. They may also know we are in the open. Something or someone is guiding them. How else would they know we are undefended in an exposed place? My dear elf, Lindsial, we should be especially alert tonight like never before. An assault from morgalps that comes from more than one direction will be extremely hard to defend, particularly at night."

If the morgalps attack during the hours of darkness, Donas' incredible swiftness is of no use to the group. For this reason, he has positioned himself high in a tree. He is our lookout.

Andrial is sitting on a tree stump some distance from the group. He is carefully listening for further signs of the morgalps. He has not heard them since the sun set.

The ziplips are also high in the trees. Since they can fly and turn invisible, they are not in any danger. Their arrows will be put to good use if the need arises.

Lindsial, Ariel-e, and I bundle in our cloaks. We huddle together next to the smaller of the two blazing fires. The spargnarls are sitting with us. They have just returned from the outskirts of the forest. They do not concern themselves with the sudden chill that has descended on our camp. Their hides are as thick as leather. Their leathery skin keeps them comfortably warm.

As we sit in a circle around the fire, our eyes nervously scan the darkness. The larger of the two fires is roughly thirty feet away to the right of our smaller campfire. Its flames cast creepy shadows on the ground and the nearby tree trunks. Its darting flames seem to grow weaker as they lick the now bitterly cold air.

"Goodness, it certainly did get unpleasantly cold," I say aloud. "I have read about deserts being super hot at night and very cold at night. I expected it would be a bit warmer where we sit. After all, we are camping right next to the forest."

Bratle's thoughts enter mine as he speaks. "Milady, Eva, the periphery of the forest is now as cold as it is here. I have never known the forest to be this cold. I do believe it is a disturbing sign of warning."

I nod my head and smile. No one, not even Lindsial, knows what I know. All the same, as I said, I am somewhat certain Lindsial has detected a few thoughts in my mind. For instance, I know for sure we will meet Hannahlo to-night. When exactly or how she will show, I do not know. I only know what my claircognizance powers are telling me, nothing more. Hannahlo will appear after the moon is at its highest in the sky. She will arrive after the morgalps attack the twelve us from three sides.

It is time to tell the others some of what I know. I hope my voice is loud enough for Donas to hear me from his perch in the trees. The ziplips can read my mind, so wher-ever they are, they will know what I am saying.

I stand with my back to Fogreia. I tell the others to remain seated. "Everyone," I say aloud, "We are going to be attacked by morgalps tonight. The attack will come from three directions. Please do not ask me how I know this. I just do."

I point to the darkened desert. "The largest group will come from the east, from the desert. Another group will come from the south to our right. The third group will come from the north to our left." I sweep my hand left to right, north to south along the horizon. "We will be attacked from all three directions with our backs to Fogreia. We will be outnumbered by at least twenty to one.

"We are being flanked as I speak. Morgalps are now flanking us to the north and the south. There is but one es-cape route · through Fogreia. If we try to escape through the forest, the morgalps will ensnare us. They set deadly booby traps along the forest's path. The traps are not designed to maim. They are designed to kill instantly.

"I suggest we remain here and fight. To be honest with you, I do not believe we have any other option. The battle will be hard, but we should prevail. Some power will come to our aid this night. This power should help turn the tide of the battle in our favor. Again, please do not ask me how I know this. I just do."

Suddenly, a foreign thought enters my mind. As it does, I nearly lose my train of thought. It says *someone has to die tonight.*

Shivers run up and down my spine. I'm suddenly scared to death! From where did this thought come? It is the strangest, most terribly frightening foreign thought I have ever sensed! I fight off the sudden urge to scream aloud. In some way, I manage to maintain my composure. I must remain strong. I do not wish to frighten the others.

Even with my most concentrated efforts to discard it, the thought continues unabated over and again in my mind. *Someone has to die tonight. Someone has to die tonight.*

Despite the sinister thoughts tormenting my mind, I manage to continue speaking to the others. "I do not know anything more about this power. I have no idea in what form it will appear. I do know this much. Its presence will not provide us a guarantee of success. We will have to fight the fight of our lives. So my dear friends, you now know what I have known for a few days. Please try to get some rest. Our enemy will not attack until past midnight. That is at least half a dozen hours from now."

As I sit down on the log, the ominous thought continues to assault my mind. It's tormenting me! *Someone has to die tonight. Someone has to die tonight. Someone has to die tonight!!!*

I immediately block all thoughts from entering my mind, to include Lindsial's thoughts. By the sad expression on her face, I can tell she knows I am blocking her from my thoughts and blocking her thoughts from entering my mind. She manages to smile, despite tears welling in her eyes.

She knowingly nods her head. She undoubtedly believes I am trying to focus all of my clairaudience powers on one entity's thoughts. In reality, I am trying to dispose of these foreign, terrifying thoughts that are trying to enter my mind. They are making me scared as ever! I throw her a kiss and manage a meek smile. Once again, Lindsial amazes me with her power of echolocation. She smiles and then she blows me a kiss in return.

I try to appear as calm as I can in front of the others. I wrap my cloak tightly around me. Using my satchel as a crude pillow, I lie down on the ground on my back. I close my eyes. Lindsial lies down beside me to my left. Ariel·e lies to my right. I slip my arms around their necks. As their heads come to rest upon my chest, I hug them to me tenderly. We often sleep next to each other like this to keep warm on chilly nights. But tonight is different, at least for me. My heart is breaking. One of the Group of Seven will die tonight. And now · thanks to the foreboding thoughts in my mind · I know who it will be. *Someone has to die tonight.*

The stealthy morgalps noiselessly converge upon us. They are advancing from three directions, exactly as I had anticipated. For some strange reason I cannot explain, I can see them in my mind as they approach. Morgalps are hideous creatures, just as Bratle described the beasts months ago. They are deathlike silent as they walk on their massive hind legs. They noiselessly drag their long tentacles behind them as they walk. Their faces are oddly hostile-looking, full of contempt and hatred.

I can see in my mind the large group as it converges in the east, the desert. A while later I can see the group as it approaches from the north. A few moments later I can see the group that approaches from the south. Then it dawns on me. I am once again the bird flying through the air!

I open my eyes to look skyward and yes, there it is! It is barely visible in the darkened sky, but it is there. There is no doubt in my mind. I can see in my peripheral vision that the bird is flying in circles up high. When I look at it directly, it immediately flies to the horizon out of my view.

Now I know what is taking place. I can *transfigure!* That means I can change my appearance outwardly into the large white bird as it spies on the morgalps approaching from three sides! I am certain of one thing that has been nagging me for many months. *I am both elf and bird!*

I didn't realize this phenomenon until now - now that we are once again in the open - on the edge of Abeti. But enough of this - there are more important things to consider at the moment.

I can foresee the morgalp's intent but only to a small degree. Since I can see them as they approach, I know there are many of the beasts, perhaps one hundred fifty, possibly more. I sense they have two objectives. Their first objective is to capture me. That ambition is without a doubt Parston and the Evil One's doing. The second objective is to rid the Isle of kindhearted elves like Lindsial and the others. In the morgalps' eyes, we elves, to include the ziplips, are disgusting freaks. It goes without saying, morgalps hate spargnarls.

It is close to midnight. I have been thinking about the impending battle for over five hours. Through my bird's eyes - let me tell you, it will take some time to get used to this incredible power - I continue to watch the three groups as they draw nearer. Obviously, I did not sleep a wink.

Startling Lindsial and Ariel-e, I suddenly sit up and shout, "Andrial, can you see or hear any of them?" His thoughts respond in his mind, "Not yet, milady. I cannot detect a thing."

I rise to my feet and shout again, "Okay everyone, and listen up. Andrial cannot see or hear the morgalps approach. They are very stealthy. However, I know they continue to press forward. There are at least one hundred fifty of them, perhaps many more. They are coming at us from three directions as I foresaw. Trust me when I say this - I can see them in my mind!

"At the start of hostilities the morgalps' aim is to attack from the desert, which is to the east." I point to the
desert. "The opening attack is nothing more than a trick. It
will consist of no more than a dozen morgalps. Its intent is
to divert our attention away from the north and south. A
follow-on, larger attack from the east will happen soon after that. I'll speak to this larger attack from the east in a
moment.

"Shortly after the initial misleading attack from the
east, they will send in a group from the north." I point to
my left, to the north. "This attack should number two doz-
en morgalps. It will be a powerful assault. Like the initial
small attack from the east, it is a diversion. Its purpose is
to confuse our posture and split our defenses.

"The force from the south is another diversion." I point
to my right. "This group, probably a dozen morgalps, intends to hit and run. That is to say - they will attack vigorously. Then they will pull back. A few moments later they
will return. Again, this is to divert our attention from the
larger attack, which will be from the east.

"The initial attack from the east and the following sim-
ultaneous attacks from the north and south will be substantial. We're looking at roughly fifty morgalps in the first
three attacks. Considering there are twelve of us, they will
outnumber us better than four to one. That is nothing in
comparison to what will follow. The second attack from the
east may be overwhelming. We can expect over one hundred morgalps, maybe more, to assault us from the east
during the second attack.

"Donas, come down from your perch as quickly as you
can and gather as many arrows as you can carry. Then return to your perch. With the exception of Lindsial, who will
be invisible and able to fight at the outside edge, arrows
will be of no use to those of us fighting on the ground tonight. Our fight will be nearly hand-to-hand. Donas, use
your arrows judiciously.

"Jakebe, you and your team please give Donas a hand
collecting arrows. Ensure you and your fellow ziplips posi-

tion yourselves to provide early warning of any impending attack. Once the attack begins, please feel free to let your arrows fly. I know you are not in danger high in the sky, but stay safe just the same.

"Andrial and Ariel-e, I want you to assume a defensive position facing the north." I point to the left of our campsite. "Your quickness and sword skills will be neces-sary to ward off the attack. It will be a brutal assault with two dozen morgalps, perhaps a few more.

"Eranba and Bratle, I want you to position yourselves to the south." I point to my right. "The attack should be ir-regular at best, a few morgalps here and there - a classic hit and run tactic. As such, you should be prepared to as-sist me and the others as you can.

"Lindsial, please become invisible and remain along-side Andrial and Ariel-e. As I said, we will be attacked from three sides simultaneously. For this reason, stay flex-ible. Assist Eranba and Bratle as necessary. Stay on the perimeter of the battle if you can. Your ease of movement on the periphery will give you a better perspective of the morgalps' attack. It will also allow you plenty of room to launch your arrows successfully. And don't hesitate to use your sword.

"I will face the opening attack from the east. As I said, the first offensive will be relatively small. The second at-tack from the east will be vicious. It is then I want all of you to unite in the center of our group, about where the smaller campfire is. We may eventually find ourselves fighting alongside each other back to back, side by side.

"The initial attack will occur in less than a half-hour. An unknown power will come to our aid during the final phase of the attack. As I said before, I have no clue what this power will be. I just know it is coming. Stay vigilant and remain together in teams as I have instructed.

"Well, that's about all I can tell you about the events that are about to unfold. Keep the faith. Always remember, I admire you. I am proud to call you my dear friends. Most of all, I love each of you very much."

I sit down on a log. Like the others, I'm frightened. I've been frightened before, but nothing like this. The combined forces of morgalps outnumber us better than twelve to one. Those are pretty lopsided odds, to say the least, and definitely not in our favor.

Of course, there is this foreboding premonition I sense in my mind. *Someone has to die tonight.* It says over and over one of our Group of Seven is to die tonight. I am in a dilemma I never thought I would ever have to face during my lifetime.

Maybe I can somehow change the course of destiny. Can I save the life of one while possibly risking the life of another? Can I change the future to keep one whom I love from dying? Should I even try?

I already know the answer to these questions. I'll try with all the strength and cunning I can muster to save a life tonight. I'm scared just the same. I may fail and foul things so badly I will put other's lives in danger. In fact, I may kill us all!

The morgalp's nearness will be quite eerie for me, to say the least. I will be unable to hear their growls or spoken words. I can accept that. I doubt I will be able to read their thoughts. That realism causes me much worry. I will have no clue what the morgalps are saying *or thinking*.

Not being able to read the morgalps thoughts makes sense. Yes, the creatures are hideous-looking. I've seen them from my high in the sky bird's-eye vantage point. Despite everything, elf blood runs through their veins. So, they certainly possess gifted intelligence. That means they may know how to block their thoughts. That is the only plausible explanation as to why I haven't sensed their thoughts up till now.

Another fact causes me worry. No authority figure is leading the morgalps as far as I know, at least not at this point. Surely, the morgalps have been given tactical orders. How else to explain their stealthy silence as they approach from three directions? How else should they know straightforward, but workable tactics that include rudiments of surprise and diversion?

There is a possible answer. Some force as equally pow-erful, or perhaps even more powerful than me is in charge. And maybe, just maybe, this powerful, astute force is blocking me from reading its thoughts. Luckily, something has allowed me to know what is about to happen. I have gleaned enough information to prepare ourselves.

I'm suddenly on my feet. I shout, "Here they come!" My heart sinks as dozens of morgalps appear in the desert to the east. Then I cannot help but smile. The morgalps are struggling to climb the bank. The morgalp's struggle up the bank is one defensive element I had overlooked. We have the high ground advantage!

I yell at the top of my lungs, "Donas, Andrial, and Jakebe! I know there's not much light, but see if you can pick them off as they climb the bank." Just as I say this, I have an idea to send bursts of blazing flares high into the sky. It works! I've illuminated the front line with my spell!

I convey to Lindsial, "Stay invisible. Feel free to let your arrows fly."

She responds via thought transference, "No problem here, Eva. We still have plenty of arrows at our disposal here on the ground. I am picking them off as best as I can."

Just as she says this, I watch as morgalp after morgalp rolls down the embankment. Arrows are sticking out of their chests, their necks, and their heads. Given her blind-ness, Lindsial is not as accurate with her arrows as the others. That's because her echolocation does not discern objects as far away as the eye can see. Still, she manages to strike morgalps that are near. I shout words of encourage-ment, "That's the way to go, Lindsial, Donas, Andrial, Jakebe and the rest of you wonderful ziplips!"

Ariel·e's excited thoughts now enter my mind. She says, "Here they come, Andrial. Get ready!"

I look to my left. Sure enough, morgalps are springing up the bank toward Ariel·e and Andrial.

With a wave of my hand I send flames across the ground. My intent is to create a line of glowing flames directly in front of the morgalps as they approach. I do not want the flames to stop the beasts in their tracks. I want the flames just high enough to slow their pace. That way they will be easy picking for our arrows. It seems to work.

Even so, many morgalps make it past the semi-circle of flames. Ariel·e and Andrial are in close quarter combat with the enemy almost immediately. It is rough going for them. The morgalps have the reach advantage with their lengthy tentacles.

"Milady, Eva," Eranba's mind conveys, "They are com·ing at us too!"

I glance over my right shoulder. I watch as a few mor·galps approach from the south. The southern embankment is not as steep as the other two. These morgalps easily as·cend the hill. Just as the spargnarls engage the morgalps in close quarter combat, I am forced to look away.

Six morgalps have broken through the line in front of me. They rapidly enclose me in a twisted mess of ghastly-looking rubbery appendages. My mind screams *moveo!* Two of the morgalps release me. They slide back down the bank to disappear from view. Their sickly appendages coil around them as they roll.

I remain ensnared by the other four. I pull and tug and try with all my strength to release myself from their grip. I feverishly hack at their tentacles with my sword. One re·leases me, his black blood spurting in all directions includ·ing on my face and hands.

Then my mind yells in Fortunomy *praetendō release me!* It works! The three morgalps release me from their grasp. They stand before me mystified at having just re·leased me from their grip.

I thrash at them with my sword. Even though they cannot entangle me with their tentacles, they can still ward off my blows. I manage to cut off one morgalp's ap·pendages with a single downward slice of my sword. I then watch as the two remaining morgalps fall face forward to the ground dead. Lindsial! The invisible elf has slain them with her sword!

The morgalps continue advancing. As we battle the morgalps in close quarters, it is difficult to keep our footing. At least two dozen morgalps are lying on the ground. Most are lifeless, arrows sticking out of the bodies. Others have large, wide open wounds.

As they thrash about in pain, sticky, putrid-smelling black blood spurts in all directions from their severed appendages and legs. As I glance about, I feel depressed. The ongoing carnage is one more bloodbath that should not have been. Why, oh why do some creatures here on my beloved Isle want me to see me dead?

There is no time to dwell on the bloodshed that surrounds. I sense Ariel·e and Andrial have had to back away slowly toward the center of our group. It is obvious the morgalp's are giving Ariel·e and Andrial a real problem. The two elves are experts with their swords. However, the morgalps' long appendages and sheer numbers are hard to manage.

I am sending spell after spell down the bank in front of me to stop the morgalps in their tracks. If more morgalps manage to climb the hill, they will swiftly overrun us. All the same, I continue to assist the others as best as I can. I hurl a morgalp here or there away from the others with my moveo spell or cast a praetendō spell. My primary focus, simply because it contains countless morgalps, is the assault facing me to the east.

I set many morgalps on fire. I trap others within flaming circles caused by my credo auduro spell. When I can, I compel others to float helplessly in the sky.

Donas has run out of arrows. He only can shout warnings when he sees something is about to happen. Thank goodness he has the foresight to bark defensive warnings. He has saved me on more than one occasion as I've read his warnings in my mind. I suspect he has also saved some of the others.

I am relieved when a morgalp falls near me without any visible cause why he fell. I know dear invisible friend, Lindsial is next to me. She is stalking the morgalps one by one with her sword. I have been almost overwhelmed by morgalps that have managed to climb the bank. I readily recognize Lindsial has also saved me on more than one occasion tonight. She is the embodiment of a courageous warrior.

I glance to my right. I cannot see Bratle! His cousin continues to battle the morgalps. Eranba's heavy sword is expertly slashing at the enemy. I shout, "Eranba, tell me - where is Bratle?"

I read his mind as he responds, "He is behind this log next to me, milady." He gestures with his head to a massive log. "A morgalp somehow seized his sword and cut his foot. Bratle is unable to stand. He banged his head on a log when he fell. I think he is unconscious."

Someone has to die tonight. No, I think to myself. It is not Bratle who dies tonight. It is another. Was the vision I saw in my mind incorrect? Did I somehow change the future by posting Bratle alongside Eranba to the south? My first thought had been to post Bratle alongside Ariel-e to the north with Andrial and Eranba to the south. Will my actions cause Bratle to die? Then again, have I caused two of us to die tonight? Enough of this, there is a battle going on! I redirect my attention to the desert.

I stare in horror. Then I consider. Wait - what is that? No, it cannot be. There is no way - scorpions! Could Hannahlo actually be... a scorpion?

As you know, my forewarning of tonight's battle included a premonition of meeting Hannahlo. I imagined Hannahlo to be a lovely creature with eye-catching features, flowing hair and graceful limbs. Jakebe even said Hannahlo was - he had tactfully added, second to me - the most beautiful of all on the Isle. Surely Hannahlo isn't one of the monstrous scorpions crawling up the embankment toward me. At least I hope not!

It's not that I consider scorpions particularly unattractive, quite the opposite. I suppose they're okay when it comes to their appearance - if you're a scorpion that is. They're a whole lot better to look at than other creatures of the arachnid class, for example, spiders, ticks, chiggers, and mites. It's just that, at least to me, scorpions aren't the most charmingly gorgeous creatures in the world.

The creatures crawling up the bank are similar to scorpions on surface earth except for their size. They are as life-size and powerful-looking as lions! Like on surface earth, these scorpions have eight legs, grasping claws called pedipalps, and tails that curve forward across their backs. They also have stingers at the end of the tails.

About one out of every forty species of scorpions on surface earth has venom in their stingers. That venom is deadly to humans. I guess we can apply that same ratio to elves. So, of one thousand-plus known species of surface earth scorpions with stingers, one out of forty with poisonous venom in their stingers doesn't sound terribly dire. Just the same, I'd bet anything these scorpions' venom is lethal to elves. If it's not lethal, why are the scorpions here?

Now I seriously doubt Hannahlo is a scorpion. The fifty or so scorpions climbing the bank are being mounted by the struggling morgalps. I am about to shout we have a new enemy when Donas' thoughts enter my mind. He has already informed the others.

Since a new threat has come about, I block others from reading my thoughts. I do not want unfamiliar snooping beings with telepathic powers to pry into my thoughts. I continue to receive incoming thoughts on a case-by-case basis.

I sense agitated shouts from Ariel·e, Andrial, and Eranba. I can only imagine they are twisting and turning to avoid capture as they slash at the morgalps' tentacles. There is little I can do to aid them. I am too busy here on the crest of the east bank. I am sending spell after spell into the throng of beasts. I'm just glad Lindsial is somewhere beside the others and me, slaying morgalps with her sword as quickly as she can.

The morgalps keep coming. The scorpions seem impervious to fire. The eight-legged beasts crawl unhindered through my walls of blistering flames.

We battle the enemy ferociously and courageously. I quickly realize our gallant efforts aren't going to be enough. We are losing the battle. Then I speculate. Where is the power that I foresaw? Will it arrive in time? Will it arrive at all?

Donas and Bratle's skills are no longer an asset to our defense. The five ziplips have run out of arrows. That leaves Lindsial, Ariel-e, Andrial, Eranba, and me to fight countless creatures coming at us from three sides. We are slowly inching closer and closer into a circle. It is only a matter of minutes before the circle tightens like a noose and strangles us. Then all means of retreat will be gone.

Suddenly, now hardened, normal-shaped rocks we carried from our original campsite slice open our satchels. They fly here and there through the night slicing morgalps in two. I am elated! The others are as excited as me. I can sense fiercely happy whoops and hollers. Even though they bounce off the scorpion's thick hides, the rocks are slaughtering the morgalps!

Then, as suddenly as they appeared, the rocks plummet lifeless to the ground. A dazzling white light that miraculously appeared from the heavens killed them!

Zarof - it must be Zarof! The evil wizard somehow killed our benevolent rocks with a spell! Or else, as I somehow suspect, he cast a curse on them when we were in the forbidden part of the forest when we initially met the areneus! That was the only time we did not have our satchels in our possession. We had left them behind where we rendezvoused after the areneus kidnaped Ariel-e. We didn't retrieve them until hours later.

The scorpions are tough creatures. Not only are they resistant to fire, they also tolerate blow after blow of the sword on their hard-shelled bodies. My spells seem to be the only effective weapons we have against them. I send some tumbling down the hill. Others I send helplessly into the air where they swirl around without purpose. As a result of my praetendō spell, many scorpions walk ridiculously in circles, their stingers thrashing harmlessly at thin air. Despite my best efforts, there are far too many crea-tures for me to deal with at once. It is as if the scorpions' ranks are inexhaustible. The morgalps numbers are also multiplying.

For whatever reason, I was unable to see beyond the initial phase of the battle as far as it concerned the enemy's strength. My estimate of one hundred fifty morgalps was too conservative. That estimate clearly addressed the ini-tial onslaught and nothing that followed. Now, there must be over two hundred morgalps!

I come to a decision. Before all hope runs out, I will use my finishing tactic. It may be our only chance if we are to live to see tomorrow. I will have to turn Ariel·e, Donas, Andrial and the two spargnarls invisible. Then I will hope for the best as they disappear to safer ground. When it comes to my escape, I will leave that in Lindsial's hands. I will ask her to clasp my hand in hers so we can turn invisi-ble to escape as one.

I use my moveo charm to dislodge the largest of the two fires and the steaming hot soil beneath it. I am indescriba-bly irritated, so I hurl the enormous flaming mess at a large group of morgalps advancing toward me. Their bodies vaporize where they stood.

I tell Eranba and Andrial to drag Bratle to the spot where the large fire was a split second ago. With the ground beneath it gone, the cratered area is as cool as the surrounding sand.

I whisper to Ariel·e, "Stay by my side if you please. I can use an extra hand while I cast a few defensive spells. Whatever you do, Ariel·e, you must stay by my side. Do not, I repeat, do not move from my side. You must do as I say. Do you understand?" I read her mind as she replies, "Yes, milady."

Using my moveo spell, I relocate Donas from his perch in the tree to the exact spot where the blazing fire was. I ignore his anxious shouts of protest. If he were to sit in that tree unaided the attacking beasts would ultimately kill him.

I use my labor lapsus spell to slide Bratle's sword across the ground. When I see the Bratle's sword is at Donas' feet I yell, "Donas take up Bratle's sword. Protect yourself, Bratle, and the others as best as you can!" Unlike his slow nighttime gait, Donas' hand remains quick at night. He immediately slices at morgalp tentacles that draw too close to him and the others.

The enemy's noose continues to tighten. I remain hopeful as it concerns our escape. Everyone is now beside me. I assume our invisible warrior, Lindsial, is beside me as well. Although the elves, Eranba, and I continue to fight bravely, it is time to retreat.

I whisper to the elves and Eranba, "I want you to listen carefully. I'm going to turn all of you invisible. That way you can be out of harm's way like Lindsial. What they cannot see they cannot harm. After I turn you invisible run like heck away from here. Stay together as a group as best as you can. Eranba, carry Bratle on your back. Andrial, you do the same with Donas.

"Ariel-e, you are in charge. Please be extra careful and guide the others as you see fit. Regroup to a safe area. Find me when things quiet down a bit. I will then turn you and the others visible once again."

I whisper, "Please stop arguing with me in your minds. My mind has enough problems right now. I love you all, and I will see you soon. Get out of here now!"

Without any further ado, I turn the elves and spargnarls invisible as a group with my invisibilis spell. For the moment, I continue to face the onslaught by myself. As I do, dozens of morgalps and countless scorpions move closer to me. As they begin to merge in front of me, they look like a huge mass of mad creatures. I cannot help but wonder why they are intolerably hateful. We have done nothing to harm or irritate them.

I persist in hurling spell after spell at them. I send up an enormous wall of fire. It burns many hapless morgalps to a crisp. Despite my efforts, the scorpions keep on moving toward me through the flames. A few lucky morgalps that survived the flames also move toward me. With a sweeping wave of my hand, I move the entire encircling mess of crea-tures forty to fifty paces away from where I stand.

But they quickly regroup and gradually advance. Now, with my back to a tree, the creatures surround me on three sides. They are but ten yards away from where I am stand-ing. I can only hope my invisible friends have had enough time to escape. I know time has run out with not a second to spare. I enact the ending phase of my plan.

"Lindsial," I say in a whisper, "Please take my hand in yours so you can turn me invisible. Then let's get out of here!"

Nothing happens. Lindsial does not reach out to take my hand! I stare speechlessly and in paralyzing panic at a scene outside the perimeter of encircling creatures.

Morgalps are being slain by some invisible force out-side the ring! It's Lindsial!

I suddenly feel weak. I can feel all the color from my face drain to monochrome white. What is more, I now re-member · I intentionally blocked others from reading my thoughts when the scorpions arrived. That included Lind-sial! When the others protested after I had turned them invisible, I also blocked others' thoughts from entering my mind.

My dear, invisible elfin friend battling outside the pe-rimeter of the encircling creatures has had no inkling of what I planned to do! I can see she is trying to reach me. Morgalps are falling as quickly as she can eliminate them.

Without warning and before I can react, ten or more morgalps suddenly appear from the forest. They reach from behind to clasp me in their tentacles. I squirm helplessly. I continue to fight back with my spells. Some of the morgalps holding me fly high into the air. Others release me from their grasp as they catch on fire. But more of the creatures keep on coming, reaching out with their tentacles to grab me!

Now fifteen or more morgalps hold me in place with their rubbery appendages. I watch horror-struck as a solitary storngful scorpion unhurriedly advances toward me. He positions his stinger to end it all. I immediately know my premonition was one hundred percent correct.

Someone has to die tonight. Someone has to die tonight. Someone has to die tonight!!!

I unblock my mind and say aloud, "Lindsial, they have me surrounded! I cannot get loose!"

As she reads my now unblocked anguished thoughts, Lindsial's tormented screams enter my mind. "Eva, what have you done? My god, Eva! Oh my god - what have you done? No Eva, no, no, no! Are the others by your side? Try to use your spells! Try to escape from their tentacles. I think I'm getting closer to you Eva. I will be by your side before long. Use your spells now! My god, Eva! Fight them!"

It is too late for me to respond. I am overwhelmed with panic. I cannot think clearly. The morgalps hold me so tightly I cannot breathe. One morgalp's tentacles encircle my neck. Its tentacles slowly squeeze. It's choking me! I feel as if I am about to lose consciousness!

My eyes widen in terror as the scorpion's stinger begins to slash at my breasts. His stinger slashes again and again and again! My entire body shudders wildly with the most excruciating pain imaginable. Even Miguel's revengeful bullet did not hurt as much as this unbearable pain!

I somehow sense the morgalps anguished cries in the ancient Elvish language of Fortunomy. The morgalps suddenly release me from their grasp. I fall to my knees, and then I collapse to the ground. I stare horror-struck at the blood gushing out of my chest. I cry out, "Oh my god, I'm dying!"

As I hurriedly slip from consciousness Lindsial's tormented cries enter my mind. "No, no, no! My god, Eva - you can't leave me - no! Oh, Eva, no! I love you!"

At the same time the air rushes out of my gaping chest wound, I somehow manage to reply in a barely audible whisper, "I love you too, Lindsial. Goodbye."

CHAPTER THIRTY-FOUR

THE ELF PRINCESS IS DEAD

King Parston is screaming at Felcio. "You stupid imbecile, you poor excuse for a lowlife wannabe great sorcerer! You are a disgrace to your noble father's memory. To think your father's greatness runs through your veins - hah!

"I told you I wanted the one they call Eva Roblins taken alive. Yes, the medallion's magic is extraordinary. I know that. I told you I wanted the elf taken alive! The Isle's true power was within her heart and mind. That power has vanished. Because she is dead - the elf princess is dead! Explain yourself, Felcio. Why did you disobey my command?"

Felcio is about to answer when Zarof says, "Your Excellency, the elfin's demise is mostly my fault. Agreed, Felcio has to share in the blame for the attack on the elf and her followers. It was he who summoned the storngful scorpions to assist the morgalps.

"However, your Excellency, I am afraid the morgalps under my control were brazenly overzealous. They failed to prevent the scorpion from assaulting the elf. They held her firmly in their tentacles as the storngful struck at her heart again and again. Quite frankly, the storngful scorpion acted instinctively - it did not know any better. It was unaware the morgalps' mission was to take the elf alive."

King Parston turns away from Zarof to look with disgust at his troll sorcerer. The condemnation in his voice is apparent. He screams, "Why did you summon those hideous scorpions, Felcio? You know they cannot be trusted to act sensibly when excited. The storngful clan is undoubtedly the most primitive of all scorpions. You should only call on storngful's as a last resort. Why, of all the creatures on the Isle, did you summon the storngful's to assist the morgalps?"

"Well, my lord," Felcio replies timidly, "It was obvious that the elfin Eva Roblins and her comrades were defeating the morgalps. She somehow knew of the morgalps' tactics. She had positioned her defenses accordingly. She is, or should I say was, a remarkably powerful sorceress. I have never witnessed such paranormal magic.

"Even though his lordship Zarof summoned morgalp reinforcements, I felt it prudent to have the storngful's aid the morgalps. The storngful's are as you know, impervious to flames, while the morgalps are not. The elfin's flame spell would have surely triumphed over the morgalps in the end. The other elves also have mystic powers, my lord. Plus, the ziplips were..."

"Enough of this rubbish, Felcio," King Parston proclaims. "You brazenly disobeyed my orders when you introduced the storngful's into the battle. I'd be satisfied to have the entire so-called Group of Seven survive, to tell the tale of the battle. I'd be content to see only one or two of Roblins' soldiers die. I'd been satisfied simply to tire them, to learn of their stratagem to my benefit.

"I wanted the elf Eva Roblins taken alive. You knew that! You have finally overstepped your bounds, Felcio. I am sick of looking at your disrespectful, disobedient, two-headed, four-armed revolting form. Get out of my sight before I have you banished to the dungeon."

King Parston turns to Zarof. "How could you have allowed this to happen? You told me you were keeping an eye on the battle. Tell me in your own words what happened, Zarof. How did things go so terribly wrong that the elf ended up dead?"

Zarof relates the battle from beginning to end. He tells how the supposed Princess of Spardom had somehow known of the morgalps' plan. She had positioned her defenses in such a manner her underlings could deal with the morgalps attacking from the north and south. He also narrates how the female elf had positioned herself to face nearly single-handedly the morgalps' assault from the east.

Zarof also speaks of some unseen force within the Group of Seven's midst that, by some means, felled many morgalps. Speedy arrows along with deadly slices of an invisible blade struck fatal blows to many morgalps, especially those that came too close to the elfin princess.

He tells of ziplips high in the air shooting their arrows at any morgalp that managed to draw near the elfin princess. He narrates the swiftness and expertness of both elves and spargnarls as it related to their sword skills.

He tells King Parston how, when the storngful scorpions entered the battle, the redheaded elfin would effortlessly throw many of them back down the embankment. How she would force others to float in the sky while others would pointlessly dance around in circles, their stingers thrashing harmlessly at the air.

He tells how she made raging rings of fire that completely enveloped storngful's and morgalps. While the storngful's easily walked through the blazes, the morgalps were helplessly trapped within the rings of fire. He mentions the look-alike rocks the elves had gathered near the forest edge before they left the shoreline. He relates how he had told a forest wizard to hex the rocks when the elves were distracted by the areneus months ago.

Zarof goes on to describe how the princess elf gathered everyone near her in the center of the battle. Then amazingly she turned the two spargnarls and other elves invisible. He ends by explaining to the Monarch of Magigro how the morgalps seized the elf in their tentacles before the final blow.

Zarof concludes his story saying, "That, your Excellency, is when my plan to carry out your orders to take the elf alive when awry. The scorpion appeared out of nowhere. Without notice, it thrust its stinger five or six times into the elf's heart. The horrified morgalps straight away released her from their grip. The elf collapsed on the ground in a widening pool of her blood, dead."

"Were you able to listen to her thoughts via telepathy?" King Parston asks. "Did she say anything of significance before she died? Did she mention anything that can be useful to us?"

"I could not read her mind during the final portion of the battle, your Excellency," Zarof says. "I am ashamed to say her powers were too strong at that point. I could not penetrate her mind. That has never happened to me prior to the battle with Eva Roblins and her followers."

"Not that it matters now," King Parston says, "Do you think she was able to read *your* mind? Did she know of *your* objective? Did she, let us say, know about you and me and our alliance?"

Zarof replies hesitantly, "I am not quite sure, your Excellency. As I said, she seemed to know of our plans beforehand. On the other hand, perhaps she was lucky. After all, she was an agent of a secret spy organization on surface earth. She undoubtedly had tactical training.

"Then again, the expanse of the desert to the east is much greater than that of the north and south. It would make sense to position one's defenses accordingly. To answer your question, did she know our objective? No, I do not think she did. I also doubt she knew anything concerning you and me and our alliance."

There are some parts of the battle Zarof does not mention to King Parston. He is wondering if the so-called Princess of Spardom was able to read *his* mind. Perhaps she knew of *his* objectives beforehand. Her defenses were far

too accurate in respect to his attack plans. More disturb-
ingly, she obviously possessed powers equal to his, maybe
superior in some respects.

*It does not matter, Eva Roblins, supposed Princess of
Spardom. You shall not trouble me any further. You are
dead. I only wish we could have met personally. I would
have taken you as my prize - my bride, my queen sitting
next to the immortal Zarof, King of Spardom.*

"What about the medallion, Zarof," King Parston asks.
"Did you find the medallion? Were the morgalps able to
take it from her after she died?"

Zarof replies, "No, your Excellency, we found no trace
of the elf's medallion."

King Parston's looks skeptical. He says, "I see, Zarof. If
the medallion was not on the elf and if it was not detached
by the stinger, where do you think it is? Please be truthful
with me."

Zarof replies matter-of-factly, "I believe it is with the
Group of Seven's second-in-command, your Excellency."

Zarof is lying about the medallion. He does not know if
the second-in-command, Lindsial, has the medallion in her
possession. However, he must say something - anything to
appease the king, to keep the king from suspecting Zarof is
in the wrong. Otherwise, the king will believe he is as useless as the king's underling Felcio. Of course, he is not useless. He is much more powerful. All the same, he must stay
on good terms with the king.

The alliance between Magigro and Abeti is too important to allow anything to jeopardize it, at least for now.
Zarof's forces are too few and too weak at this point. There
is no way he can face up to the Fortress of Magigro and its
countless two-headed trolls. He needs to increase his
strength. He also needs more time. Then there is the larger
quest, the quest to rule the world.

The medallion was not found. Plus, the princess' body
vanished. Zarof speculates that elves' bodies are spirited
away when they die. Like the King, Zarof also wanted the
elfin princess taken alive. He wanted her to open the magi-

cal Enchanted Gate. There are more disturbing facts which Zarof has reflected on before tonight. He decides to keep those facts from even entering his mind.

"Who is this second-in-command to whom you refer," King Parston asks.

"She is a mere child, a young female elf," Zarof replies. "Her name is Lindsial. She has exceptional sword and archery skills. The others will unquestionably follow her lead."

King Parston asks, "Why is this youthful female elf, this so-called Lindsial trying to lead others?"

Zarof's face is expressionless as he lies once more. "She is destined to fulfill the supposed Princess of Spardom's dying wish - to remove you from the throne."

CHAPTER THIRTY-FIVE

CENTAURS - UNICORNS - TILBELLS

Is it not strange how you can be in a dream, just to wake up and believe the dream was real? You go through your normal paces of everyday life, working, attending school, fooling around with your friends, watching television, exercising, surfing the Internet, or playing a video game. Maybe you attend to your garden or occupy yourself with a fun hobby. Perhaps you stroll up to the summit of the next hill because you have never been there, and you are curious what wonders lie beyond.

And that vision you dreamed · the one that felt so real, it somehow, by some means, in some strange fashion stays within your mind. It is as if you desperately want it to be real, for it to never go away. That is the kind of vision I am having at this very moment. I am being lifted up weight· lessly from a triumphant multitude of repulsive creatures whose only aim is to end my life.

Suddenly, marvelous creatures, that I used to read about in fairytale picture books as a child, appear before my eyes. They are centaurs and unicorns, stupendous crea·

tures of fascinating legends that survived natural disasters, human wars, disease, famine, and scorn. They carried on over the millennium and lived to tell their electrifying tales.

Dashing male and female centaurs led by a particularly fearless centaur they call Nicolas - their flowing lengthy hair of brown, their skin lightly tanned, with muscular arms holding deadly swords. They slay beasts that fall in heaps similar to throwing away filthy filth flung from a spade.

What's more, there are feminine unicorns, extremely elegant, amazingly beautiful one-horned, pure-white, sandy blonde-haired creatures forged from the flawless molds of nature's chastity. They are silent creatures. They dash through the mix, scattering bodies hither and yon with a simple nod of their head. They have, but one quest - to make way for the most magnificent creation that has ever lived, the captivating, beautiful E-mah.

E-mah, maidenhead of all unicorns, touches her horn to my exposed, gaping chest wound. I am at once free of hurting. Her mesmerizing hazel-gray kindly eyes seek my eyes wrapped in death's grip. I watch her lips as they move.

"All will be okay, Princess Eva. Please trust me when I say this. You were so fearless as you stood alone before the beasts. You are pure. Life's joy and vibrancy will enter into your being yet again. You shall never grow older, always staying as you are today - vivacious, gorgeous, wonderfully alive, and clean."

Standing next to E-mah is another indescribably beautiful creature, Hannahlo. Hannahlo just as I pictured her, with flowing reddish bronze hair that catches the moonlight like sparkles of lavender. Her light brown eyes stare into mine as loving teardrops caress her pretty, unblemished face. Is it really you, Hannah? Are you my childhood friend of long ago?

Next to Hannahlo is Nicolas, the handsome leader of the centaurs. He is strikingly eye-catching handsome and extremely intelligent. He has massive shoulders and bulging muscles. Surprisingly, given his age - he's perhaps eighteen years old - he sports a charming, short-cropped beard. He kneels on all fours next to me, his head close to mine, his hands clasping mine tightly. His interesting brown eyes stare into my unblinking eyes. I can barely see his lips as they move in the translucent mist that encircles my body.

His compassionate, reassuring words form on his lips saying, "You will be okay, my dear princess. We ask your pardon for not arriving sooner. Even so, all will be all right. Please trust me when I say this. We will carry you and the others to shelter and salvation."

Standing next to Nicolas is the beautiful centaur S-Shea. She will gently bear me to recuperation. Her gorgeous, long brown hair and searching brown eyes meet mine. I read her lips, as they say, "It will not be long now, my dear princess, Eva, darling jewel of Spardom. Soon you will be safe. Soon you will rest. I will carry you to your new life, a life that will bring great tidings and untold happiness to the entire Isle and to surface earth."

Suddenly I bear in mind, Lindsial, my dearest friend, whom I love more than anyone. Was Lindsial the one that died? Was she the one who perished as we battled our enemy on the crest of Abeti? She was by herself as she battled countless morgalps on the periphery of the gathering. She was all alone fighting the seemingly unstoppable, ruthless enemy. She said she was trying to come to me. Did I unwillingly sacrifice her life for the sake of another?

She was not supposed to die - it was another who was supposed to die. At least that is what I saw in my mind as the premonition said over and over - *Someone has to die tonight. Someone has to die tonight. Someone has to die tonight!!!*

I had turned the one that was supposed to die invisible with the others. Perhaps I had saved a life, after all. And, of course! Lindsial was invisible as well. She must have survived! All the same, my premonition had warned me - do not tamper with fate. Do not try to change the future. If you try to alter destiny, dreadful things may result. Oh Lindsial, how can I ever forgive myself? Did I sacrifice you for her?

Someone has to die tonight... Someone has to die tonight...

All of a sudden my dream ends. I open my eyes. Standing to the side of me is my darling angel, Lindsial. She has closed her sightless eyes tightly. Her hands are folded in front of her face as if she is praying. She is trembling from head to toe. A torrent of tears runs down her cheeks.

With a slight gasp, I whisper softly, "Oh my god, Lindsial, you are alive!"

Lindsial rushes to me when she hears my voice. She falls into my arms and embraces me so forcefully I can scarcely breathe. As I hold her in my arms, I cannot help but feel sorry for her. She is shaking hysterically. Sob after sob convulses from deep within her soul. Her nonstop tears shroud her lovely face.

After a few moments, I gently ease her away to stare into her beautiful light blue unseeing eyes. Although Lindsial may be eons older than me, I do not care. She is my precious. She looks like a twelve-year-old child, a younger sister perhaps. She could even pass as my daughter. No matter, she is alive, and I love her more than anything! I kiss her left cheek and then her right. I pull her lovingly to me once more. We embrace for the longest time.

She gently pushes away from me. Her unseeing eyes seem to stare into mine. Her lips move. "Eva, darling, unblock my thoughts from you and yours from me if you please. You blocked them once again after you said goodbye on the battlefield."

I immediately do as she asks. She is still shaking uncontrollably. I pull her to me again. I hug her as if I will never let her go. As we embrace, she conveys via telepathy, "You were dead, Eva. Oh my god, you were dead! You sacrificed yourself to allow the others to live. Oh, Eva, it was horrible. I tried to reach you, but I could not battle through them in time. The others told me ten to fifteen morgalps held you in their tentacles. Then a storngful repeatedly slashed at your breasts. Andrial said blood gushed from your wounds, Eva. He said you fell where you had stood. Oh my god, Eva, you were dead! The others told me the blood from your wound stained the ground where you lay. They said it was utterly dreadful!

"I continued to hack at the enemy with my sword. But I knew I was too late. Then they were upon me. They could not see me, but they knew I was in the thick of their masses. So they began to strike out at me without purpose. Then, thankfully, E-mah and Hannahlo appeared."

I gently push Lindsial away to look at her. I say out loud, "Two things, Lindsial. How are Ariel-e and the others? Did all of them make it? Is Bratle okay? And this creature E-mah you mentioned - who is E-mah?"

Lindsial laughs and says, "I see you haven't changed. Two questions - that is like four questions." She laughs again. "Yes, the other elves and spargnarls are okay. Bratle is fine. He should be able to walk in a couple of weeks. He may have to remain behind as we journey.

"E-mah is the unicorn who brought you back to life. My goodness, Eva, she has powers that are as astonishing as yours. The others say she is extremely pretty, Eva, unbelievably gorgeous! They say she is probably the most beautiful creature they have ever seen. Her eyes are hazel gray, her long hair sandy blond. They say she looks like an angel, Eva, she honestly does. She is only twelve or thirteen years of age, but she is extremely intelligent and so very sweet!

"And oh, you mispronounced her name, Eva. You do not pronounce it with a hard *e*. You pronounce it with a soft *e*, just like on surface earth - *e-m-m-a*. Gosh, Eva, the others swear she is the most attractive, elegant creature imaginable, even more so than Clover. She has the utmost brain power and astonishing magical powers!"

"E-mah is a unicorn?" I ask in disbelief. "Unicorns live? And she's more elegant and attractive than Clover? Wow, she must be something else!"

"Yes, E-mah is a unicorn, Eva. And yes, she's everything I said. Now hush for now and bear with me as I tell
all. I could sense that you were lying on the ground. You
were dead, Eva - you were dead! I could read the other
elves' thoughts. They were a good distance away from the
fray, standing on a knoll that overlooked the battle.
Eranba and Bratle were with the elves, out of harm's way.
Andrial was narrating in his mind everything that was
happening. Even though they were out of harm's way, the
others were crying Eva. Like me, the others thought you
had departed forever!

"Jakebe and the ziplips were flying above the carnage.
They had run out of arrows; yet they were hitting morgalps
with their bows, rocks, sticks, anything they could find.
Like those of us in the Group of Seven, they were crying
hysterically. Jakebe told me Clover turned invisible and
actually hovered above your body, Eva. She was striking
out at the morgalps as they attempted to move you. She
repeatedly stabbed morgalps with an arrow she found on
the ground. She would not let them touch you. She is devoted to you Eva, and so fearless, courageous, and sweet.

"Oh, Eva, I knew there was nothing I could do for you. I
could not decide what to do, so I began to back away. Let
me tell you this, my heart was breaking. I was crying uncontrollably. I wanted to leap into the heart of the enemy
and come to blows over your body until I lay lifeless by
your side. On the other hand, I knew our friends would
need me once you were not here. It was then the unicorns
and centaurs and Hannahlo appeared."

"Wait a minute," I say. "Centaurs and even more unicorns appeared? From where in the world did the centaurs
come? About Hannahlo - who or what is she? Is she a centaur or a unicorn. Or is she something else entirely?"

"Hannahlo is an elf, Eva, and a strikingly beautiful one
at that. Now hush will you? I will get to everything momentarily if you will stop interrupting."

She smiles and continues telling her story. As she does,
little creatures, both male and female, in dark blue shirts

and pants serve our lunch. I feel strong enough to sit up in bed. Lindsial sits beside me. She will talk nonstop for several hours.

Let me tell you about these little people. They look like dwarfs, only shorter. If I was standing, they might come up to my chest. That would make them roughly four feet tall. They are darling diminutive creatures with pink faces, long noses, and whiskers on their chins. Even the females have whiskers. The only noticeable difference between the sexes is the length of their hair. The males have short hair similar to human crew cuts. The females wear their hair in long braided coils that run the full length of their backs.

Lindsial tells me the charming creatures are called *tilbells*. Tilbells are descendants of dwarfs that once lived in the Hidden Valley. After the Grand War, they became Wanderers. They now live in Hannahlo's Kingdom, the Land of the Unseen. They are noble warriors and incredibly strong and nimble for their small size. Their weapon of choice is the ax.

From what the others have told her, Lindsial relates how the centaurs, led by the incredibly attractive and brave Nicolas, appeared out of nowhere. The lovely centaur S-Shea was by Nicolas' side. The two of them came galloping with the other centaurs slashing with their swords, one in each hand.

Then the unicorns appeared. With one touch of their horns to the armored, thick crust of the storngfuls, the creatures shriveled away to nothing. When the unicorns touched morgalps with their horns, the morgalps shriveled away to nothing just like the storngfuls.

Once the centaurs and unicorns were on the scene, the battle quickly collapsed. The surviving storngfuls and morgalps scampered to disappear into the night. Immediately after that, a beautiful creature appeared from the north. She galloped up the sloping hill with a rider.

The galloping creature was E-mah, queen of the unicorns. Hannahlo was her rider. As Jakebe had said, Hannahlo rules the Land of the Unseen. The gracious young E-mah rules over the land of pureness called *Clarity*. Clarity encompasses the Hidden Valley, Lake Namoni, and the region on our map entitled *Unknown*. The extreme western portion of Clarity, the Unknown area, is entirely surrounded by seemingly impenetrable majestic mountains. I presume the Enchanted Gate lies to the northwest of the Unknown area, the area on our map that reads *Unexplored*.

Interestingly, there are no known male unicorns on the Isle. All of the unicorns are females. Since they are pure and their lives never-ending, their species should live on forever. The unicorns number exactly forty-two. By their look, all of the unicorns are youthful, anywhere between ten to sixteen years of age.

Conversely, the centaurs consist of all ages of males, females and, of course, little centaurs. The centaurs' number constantly changes with births and deaths in the colony. At present, they number six hundred twenty-four. Nicolas has been their ruler for the past four years. At eighteen, he's the youngest centaur that has ever ruled the others. He is courageous, outgoing, intelligent, well-liked, and respected by his clan. His assistant is the lovely S-Shea. She carried me from the battlefield to here. Like most benevolent creatures on Spardom, S-Shea is young-looking. She is perhaps fifteen years of age.

As Andrial told it to Lindsial, once E-mah arrived at the battle, she immediately walked over to me. Hannahlo slid off her back and stood next to E-mah. E-mah studied me for a moment. With a nod of her head, she said to Hannahlo, "She is pure. I shall bring her back to life."

Kneeling on her front legs, E-mah touched her horn to my wounds. In a matter of seconds, my blood, that had saturated my clothing and seeped into the ground began to reenter my wounds. Shortly after that, I moaned and started breathing. My eyes were open the whole time. My heart had stopped its beating, but my mind was still alive. My eyes were still seeing all. In essence, what I had thought I had dreamed was real.

So there, you have it. Fairy tales can come true, and dreams can turn into reality. And yes, stunningly gorgeous unicorns like E-mah live - along with itsy-bitsy dwarfs called tilbells and centaurs with flowing brown locks such as Nicolas and S-Shea. Moreover, one of the most beautiful creatures on Spardom lives as well, elfin Hannahlo.

We decide to eat our lunch before it gets cold. During this lull in Lindsial's story-telling, I ask via telepathy, "Lindsial, where is our beloved elf mermaid, Ariel-e?"

Lindsial conveys, "Oh, she is down the corridor with the others. E-mah returned her and the others visible shortly after the battle ended. I cannot sense that Ariel-e is speaking, and I cannot read her thoughts. She may be asleep. Why do you ask?"

As my eyes begin to water Lindsial grabs my hand. She is reading my mind. She seems to stare at me questionably as tears begin to well in her sightless eyes once more. I stare into her unseeing eyes and say aloud, "Yes."

Lindsial's mind slowly conveys, "So it was Ariel-e who was supposed to die? You foresaw it. You wanted to change the future so she could live. Oh my goodness, Eva, you deliberately sacrificed yourself for her. The other elves and I have known Ariel-e what seems like forever. We love her dearly, just like you. And you saved her! You are the most courageous elf I've ever met! I love you so much!"

Lindsial buries her head in my shoulder and sobs uncontrollably once more. As I hold her closely, I continue to recount my actions on the battlefield. "Lindsial, that is why I called everyone together, including you. At least I thought I had called you using telepathy. I wanted all of us to leave as a group. More than ever I wanted Ariel-e beside me. I even told her to not leave my side under any circumstances. I needed to save her from harm. Once I turned her invisible with the others, I knew she was safe, that I had tricked fate.

"Yet I forgot I had blocked my thoughts. I had blocked you and others from my thoughts when the storngfuls arrived. I wanted to protect you and the others from harm. It was obvious I made a terrible mistake, blocking my thoughts. When I saw morgalps being slain by some invisible force beyond the edge of the encroaching creatures, I knew it was you, Lindsial. It was then I could see everything clearly in my mind.

"My premonition had warned me. It said I should not try to change the future. It had said, explicitly; *someone has to die tonight*. I tried to change that fate. I had saved Ariel·e. But by doing so, I immediately knew someone was going to die. It was I who had to die."

CHAPTER THIRTY-SIX

EXITUS SPARDOM DIRECTO

Over a month has passed since I died beneath a full moon on the fringes of Abeti. I cannot believe I was unconscious for nearly two weeks after I died on the battle-field. My dearest friend Lindsial and beautiful E-mah are the only visitors I have been allowed to have up to this point. E-mah wanted to ensure I made a complete recovery.

At first she was hesitant even to allow Lindsial by my side. Lindsial made such a commotion, in the end E-mah had no other choice than to concede. Lindsial has been by my side from the beginning, from the very moment I passed on until now. She slept and ate in my chamber and sat by my bed for two solid weeks. During the past two weeks, she has been my side the entire time as well.

E-mah tells me it takes at least three weeks to restore a formerly deceased living thing to full vitality. The numerous scars, where the storngful slashed me, will eventually fade until they are barely noticeable. Although she brought me back to life, as hard as she tried, E-mah was unable to restore my hearing. It seems I will be deaf forever. All the same, she was able to fix a little something in my mind so I can now comprehend Hannahlo's thoughts.

According to E-mah, Hannahlo's thought transference ability is somewhere between auditory and telepathy. That is why Hannahlo and I couldn't connect via thought transference in Fogreia. It has something to do with a serious injury to Hannahlo's brain she suffered many years ago. Fortunately, for E-mah and me, we have normal thought transference ability - that is, if you can call what we have as normal.

Most amazing, and this I cannot grasp for the life of me - with E-mah's touch of her unicorn horn I will never grow a day older. I will be twenty-nine years of age until the end of time. Staying at my present age is not to say I am immortal. I can still die - again. It's just that I cannot die of natural causes. Only if someone or something kills me will I die. I hope that never happens again. Dying is not a pleasant occurrence by any stretch of the imagination.

E-mah tells me Lindsial, Ariel-e, Donas, and Andrial certainly were reborn when they were youngsters. She says that is the only logical explanation how they lived as unchanging youngsters through the ages. She supposes they were brought back to life to live forever at the exact age they were when they perished. To my surprise, she has no clue how the other elves in my Group of Seven had life restored to them. She is the only unicorn on Spardom with powers to restore life. She is positive she did not bring them back to life.

Of course, Queen April had such powers. All the same, there is no record in Chronicles that the queen ever used her magic to restore life. Then again, perhaps she did. There were a few unicorns on surface earth many centuries ago. E-mah says a gifted surface earth unicorn may have completed the rebirth process on the four elves.

I ask E-mah why the elves do not seem to know they were reborn.

She says, "If they had life restored to them they are powerless to remember. It'll be the same with you at some point, Eva. Someday you will forget that you died and that

I brought you back to life. It is a spin-off of the unicorn's gift.

"The breadth of unicorns' powers is not something the world should know. Creatures eventually fail to remember at some point in their lives that we assisted them. In fact, unless they are around unicorns continuously, in the fullness of time creatures that we aided will cease thinking about us.

"That's the way it was on surface earth many centuries ago. Humans continuously hunted unicorns for our horns, so we began to hide from them. The longer we were absent from humans our way of life in their minds turned from reality to legend and then to myth. Now we are nothing more than a fantasy in human youngsters' fairy tales."

E-mah says the unicorn horn is capable of amazing things. These include returning the dead to life, restoring polluted water to drinkable liquid and healing wounds. When it comes to living things, only the purest of any species can be treated. Most creatures treated by unicorns are toddlers, youngsters, teenagers, and the purest of adults. Others are left to die. She also says, unless a unicorn loses its horn, it cannot depart this life. Having a horn severed from a unicorn's body rarely happens.

I cannot thank E-mah enough for coming to my rescue, for bringing me back to life. I have never been afraid to die, and I don't worry about it too much. Besides, I know I have important things to do on the Isle and perhaps on surface earth as well. More importantly, I do not want to lose the closeness I enjoy with my friends.

At last I am introduced to Hannahlo. Many amazing things have happened to me since Mustache Bobby delivered the package to my door on surface earth nearly a year ago. What I am about to share with you is undoubtedly the most amazing miracle of all. It happened many years before my twenty-ninth birthday. Perhaps it is best narrated by Hannahlo in her words.

"Yes, Eva, I am the very same Hannah you talked to as a child. If you will recall, you were playing with a raggedy doll in a rundown shack in Schenectady, New York on surface earth. You were nine years old at the time. You were talking to yourself as children often do when they play with dolls, soldiers, and other lifelike toys. You looked up at the yellowed flaking ceiling. You said to no one, in particular, 'Hello, my name is Eva. What's your name?'"

"'Of course you answered your question. You said, 'I am Hannah. It is a pleasure to meet you. Do you mind if I play with you? Can I be your friend?'"

"You answered your newfound friend Hannah readily and you wholeheartedly agreed to be her friend. Although I was here below the ocean on Spardom ruling the Land of the Unseen, I was with you on surface earth. Of course, you could not see me. In your mind, you could sense my presence although you presumed I was make-believe.

"You undoubtedly do not know this - I have a psychic ability called *bilocation.* It is the gift of being in more than one location at the same time. I was with you on surface earth at the same time I was here in the Land of the Unseen."

She winks at E-mah and says, "And soon you will meet another who has bilocation abilities, plus many more abilities and powers that will augment your amazing paranormal skills."

Hannahlo continues her story. "Immediately following the disappearance of the original Princess Eva, the Islanders modified the Chronicles. The change in the Isle's laws stipulated any child or heir of Queen April and her husband would have a guardian angel. The guardian angel was to look after the child no matter what. As a descendant of Queen April, you were destined to have a guardian angel.

"You often called to me during your dreams. We soared together to distant lands in your imaginings. We explored secret caves, climbed the steepest hills, and fought made-up wicked fiends. When you were wide awake, we played, sang, skipped, jumped, and even roller skated together. We told stories, and you read to me from your fairytale book.

"As you matured, you called my name less frequently. I was there beside you just the same Eva, always ready to help ease the pain - to give you strength. I was close at hand and by your side the three weeks you were in a coma. The day you discovered you were deaf you called my name. It broke my heart to see you in such a state of mind, Eva, it truly did. I have remained by your side since the day we met.

"In fact, Eva, I was by your side long before you first called my name. Since your birth, I have known you were destined to be the Princess of Spardom. I have been your guardian angel all these years, and finally - finally I have the distinct pleasure of meeting you in person at last!"

I can hardly believe Hannahlo's story. I am also a bit confused. I say, "But Hannah - I mean Hannahlo - how is it you are so young? You still look as though you are ten or eleven years old. I have aged twenty years since we first met in my imagination. You still look the same today as I thought you looked back then. How is this possible?"

Hannahlo glances at E-mah with a smile and says, "My dear Eva, I am reborn. I perished more than a century ago. I was a little elf, eleven years old to be exact. I was climbing a hill, tripped and fell many feet. I hit my head on a rock. E-mah happened to walk by my lifeless body. I was young and, of course, pure. She brought me back to life. My savior, E-mah and I have been the closest of friends ever since."

E-mah moves to stand beside Hannahlo. She rubs her mane against Hannahlo's shoulder. Hannahlo tenderly hugs E-mah's neck and kisses her on the forehead.

It is rather peculiar sitting beside Hannahlo. Hannahlo has been my only true friend for nearly twenty years. I have known her nearly all my life. However, we just met face to face today. She looks today just how I thought she looked when I imagined her in my mind as a child. Of course, no one can take the place of Lindsial when it comes to my love. On the other hand, Hannahlo has a very special place in my heart. She is my guardian angel, and I love her dearly. I owe her my sanity, well-being, optimism, and capacity to love. She is truly an angel.

I accompany E-mah and Hannahlo on a short tour of a small portion of the Land of the Unseen. Lindsial is with me. I vow to never again let Lindsial out of my sight. I am still rather weak as I walk. I lose my footing quite often. Lindsial prevents me from falling as I lean on her for support.

The Land of the Unseen has a suitable name. It is a cavernous grotto that lies beneath the desert, hidden from view from all but its inhabitants. The sole entrance to the land is via a small fissure in a desert hilltop.

Hannahlo compares her domain to Queen April's protective bubble that surrounds the entire Isle - except the Land of the Unseen is underground. No creature can venture into the Land of the Unseen without Hannahlo's permission. It is a secret place far below the desert, hidden from the rest of the Isle. Desert plants and animals miraculously thrive due to its self-sustaining artificial light. Edible plants, vegetables, fruit trees, and a meadow flourish as well. There is also a large lake called *Serenitas*.

Serenitas is icy cold with clear fresh water. It is full of fish and other freshwater creatures. Hannahlo explains the lake was once as salty as the sea. Centaurs, elves, ziplips, tilbells, and other Wanderers were forced to drink from the few streams that crisscrossed the land. It was not until Hannahlo befriended the unicorns nearly a century ago that the lake became fresh water. She smiles at E-mah when she tells me how the unicorns' magical horns transformed the lake into fresh water. E-mah smiles, and then she nods her head.

Please allow me to tell you about the chunky, funny-looking feathered fowl that live in the land. They remind me of chickens on surface earth as they peck away at the ground within large, wooden-fenced areas. These creatures are called *cathoos*. Like chickens on surface earth, female cathoos lay eggs.

Unlike chickens on surface earth, both sexes of cathoos

crow loudly. Instead of the familiar *cock-a-doodle-doo* like on surface earth, I'm told these creatures scream, "Cathoo - cathoo - cathoo." In addition to providing eggs, cathoos supply fresh meat for the inhabitants of the Land of the Unseen.

After my brief scenic tour of a small portion of the Land of the Unseen, E-mah and Hannahlo take me to visit the rest of my Group of Seven. E-mah delayed this final step in my recuperative process as long as she dared. She wanted to ensure I was strong enough. Given my persistent nagging the past few days, she finally consented, and here we are.

You can only imagine the excitement on everyone's faces now we are together once more. After kissing Bratle on his cheek, I inspect his wound. It is healing nicely. A portion of his right foot is missing, detached at the bone. It will be a while before he can walk. Despite the unicorn's treatment of his severe wound, he will walk with a limp for the rest of his life.

E-mah explains, while the horn of a unicorn can fix wounds and even breathe life into the unblemished dead, it cannot reattach severed limbs. I already know Bratle will be unable to journey with us in the future. I have seen it in a dream. Thus, the Group of Seven, as we know it today, will be no more. I'm keeping the particulars of this inside information to myself. You'll just have to wait until later to learn what happens next.

Ariel-e looks as beautiful as ever. I kiss her cheeks over and again. As she and I embrace, I glimpse at her left thigh. E-mah repaired a large gaping cut that ran the full length of Ariel-e's upper leg. Ariel-e had cut herself when she slashed at a morgalp with her sword. The morgalp was right behind me at the time. Once again, Ariel-e had saved my life. E-mah says Ariel-e's cut will heal nicely and leave no scar. Knowing that the scar will disappear brings a smile to my face. After all, to me, the charismatic, truly lovely elf mermaid is as perfect as the most precious pearl.

When I see Donas and Andrial, my heart leaps with

joy. I hug them both and kiss their cheeks repeatedly. They also have an assortment of scars on their bodies. The most noticeable scars are on their forearms where they slashed themselves when hacking at morgalp tentacles. Their scars will eventually disappear as well.

Astonishingly, Eranba doesn't have a scratch on his body. I am happy. He is too sweet, caring, and handsome. Even though he is different than his kind, his gnarl-less body will continue to be noticeably beautiful and perfect. He bows before me. As he does, I kiss his huge forehead. Then he and I hug for the longest time. I can tell he continues to bathe often. He smells like perfumed roses.

Later in the evening, after a delicious dinner and the others have departed to their quarters, Lindsial, E-mah, Hannahlo and I gather around the dinner table. The ruler of Clarity, E-mah, stands next to our table as the rest of us relax on a long bench. Our telepathic conversation is serious.

E-mah provides further details of the Enchanted Gate. She explains it is an unexplored, mountainous land full of enchanted forests, unusual beasts, and magical wonders. She says she believes it is where Queen April lived when she ruled the Isle of Spardom.

E-mah says if I am to defeat the Evil One, I will first have to visit the land that lies behind the Enchanted Gate. She says friendly creatures of Abeti, the Land of the Unseen, Clarity, Fogreia, and the Banned Borders, may be beneficial allies. However, my true destiny lies beyond the Enchanted Gate.

Whether powers, which lie within the gate are mystical, physical or practical, E-mah does not know. She only knows what she has heard from legends passed down through the generations. The Enchanted Gate is where I will find my purpose and the powers to achieve my goal.

After our long-lasting discussion, Hannahlo takes Lindsial, E-mah, and me to the hilltop entrance of the desert above the Land of the Unseen. The nighttime view in the desert is truly amazing. I gaze at the night sky. I see

Spardom's stars, the moon, and yes · I can also see the lightning storm to the northwest. The surrounding scene is breathtaking, to say the least. I describe to Lindsial in great detail what I am seeing.

E-mah points in the direction of the lightning. She says via telepathy, "See that? Those flashes of light are not lightning, Eva. Humans on your surface world cause the sources of light. What you see are exploding bombs, missiles, and depth charges. It has been virtually nonstop for just about two months now.

"They are trying to destroy our world, Eva. While I seriously doubt they can do much damage, it is too risky for the bombardments to continue. You, Eva, Princess of Spardom, you are the only one who can stop their bloodthirsty evil."

"Oh my goodness," my thoughts convey. "This is horrible news! I bet it is my country that is doing this to us. I would not put it past those dimwit politicians. How do I stop it, E-mah? I am here, and they are up there on surface earth."

E-mah conveys, "In a little while I will tell you what you need to know. But first, there is someone I want you to meet." She winks at Hannahlo. Hannahlo winks in return.

My inquisitiveness is driving me wild. I'm wondering what's going on between E-mah and Hannahlo. I notice that this is the second time the two of them have shared winks and knowing glances. Am I about to meet that special someone who has bilocation abilities Hannahlo mentioned? If so, my claircognizance skill is temporarily suspended. I have no prior knowledge of what is going to happen. Perhaps the all-powerful E-mah is somehow blocking my insight as it pertains to this unknown entity. Needless to say, I am very excited.

Lindsial, E-mah, and I follow Hannahlo the length of an extensive labyrinth of twisting tunnels until we reach an open cavern carved into a large arena. Inside, beneath the artificial light caused by Hannahlo's magic, strange-looking creatures engage in, what looks to be, warfare schooling of some sort.

Of course, there are a few recognizable creatures as well. Male and female tilbells are practicing with axes. They are attacking straw-stuffed dummies. Ziplips fly here and there as they shoot arrows at targets suspended from the ceiling. There are also unicorns dueling with their horns and centaurs engaging in target practice. Some centaurs duel with sword and shield while others practice shooting arrows at targets. A few centaurs are throwing spears at straw targets leaning against the stone walls. Crudely painted images that look like trolls are on all of the straw targets.

Then there are the strange creatures I mentioned, the likes of which I have never seen in my life! There are dozens of horned, two-legged, green-colored hairy creatures. They are called *pormitios.* They resemble monkeys on surface earth, except they do not have tails. They are swift as they scamper to and fro on the ground shooting arrows from tiny bows.

There are a dozen or so odd creatures called *dortons* to go along with the pormitios. Unlike the small pormitios, dortons are huge, two-legged beasts, perhaps twenty feet tall. They are gray in color, with broad backs and gigantic muscles. They look like they are grunting and groaning as they lift extremely large boulders similar to weights above their heads. I imagine dortons are employed to carry heavy loads or to break stuff, possibly massive walls of a troll fortress.

There are also small creatures that resemble black crows on surface earth both in color and size. They are called *cromkins.* The cromkins must number in the hundreds as they flutter as one huge black gathering in the back of the cavern. As they fly, cromkins tilt their wings to reveal two claws, which allow bursts of fire to escape. Large explosions result from their bursts of fire, crumbling the cavern's walls bit by bit.

E-mah explains cromkins are in combat training like the rest of the creatures in the room. The cromkins' activity also serves one other item of importance. They are slowly expanding the arena as the walls crumble beneath their fiery blasts. I watch as tiny tilbells sweep up debris on the cavern's floor once the cromkins leave the area to regroup. A few dortons haul the debris away in huge wooden containers that resemble wheelbarrows on surface earth.

In the middle of all of this strange, busy activity, two identical young female elves are dueling with swords. Three additional elves, identical to these two, are shooting arrows at moving targets suspended from the cavern's ceiling. The five elves' appearance is impossible to tell apart. They look like matching quintuplets born of one mother.

Now, before my eyes, two additional identical elves suddenly become visible to my left. These two elves are standing in front of a stationary target and throwing spears from a distance of at least twenty paces. Their accuracy is absolute. They hit the heart of the target nearly every time.

I look from left to right, counting as I go - and now I see nine identical elves! The two extra elves, that suddenly appeared, are throwing knives at a target to my far right. Something is out of place as it concerns these elves. It's as if they are multiplying before my eyes!

Lindsial has read my thoughts. She conveys, "Beat's me, Eva. I also have no idea what's happening here. At the start, I was able to make out five elves, just like you. By what I sensed in my mind, they seemed to be the same size, shape, and density. They appeared to be identical. Then I detected two more. Now, by using echolocation, I sense two more elves, for a total of nine elves that appear to have identical characteristics! I agree - it's as if they are multiplying!"

I look guardedly at E-mah and Hannahlo. They are laughing. I sense in my mind E-mah's words as she says aloud, "Talya-cee," please come here to meet Princess Eva and Lindsial."

Astonishingly, the nine elves ascend into the air at the same time. As they hover in midair, they unite as a group, form a straight line, and then slowly descend to stand before us. I notice they left their weapons behind, probably to put Lindsial and me at ease. I couldn't be more mistaken!

All of a sudden, the nine identical-looking elves reach out with their right arms at the same time. Their weapons miraculously become visible in each of their hands! One second the weapons were scattered on the cavern floor, the next second the weapons were in the nine elves' hands. I didn't see the weapons move through the air!

You must admit, my labor lapus spell is awesome. I can move objects from one place to another with my spell. All the same, the objects are visible the entire time. But this phenomenon, I just witnessed, is totally cool - to move objects from one place to another without their being seen is startling! What's even more unbelievable is the fact that nine lookalike elves moved nine objects at the same time!

E-mah's thoughts enter my mind once more. She conveys, "Eva and Lindsial, this is Talya-cee; Talya-cee, Princess Eva, and Lindsial."

I'm once more utterly confused. I can read Lindsial's mind - she's just as confused as me. E-mah introduced the nine elves as if they were one and the same.

Now, unexpectedly, only one Talya-cee is standing before us! The eight other identical elves disappeared into thin air along with their weapons! I laugh as Lindsial takes a step backward. She is as surprised as me. She sensed the same phenomenon with echolocation as I saw with my eyes. Nine elves turned into one! Her mind conveys, "What in the world..."

The one remaining elf standing before me reaches out with her hand to clasp mine in hers. She eagerly shakes my hand. I read her mind as she says audibly, "Milady, Eva, Princess of Spardom, it is an honor to meet you at last. I am very happy you are finally out and about. I am at your service." She curtsies.

Taking Lindsial's hand, she says, "Elfin Lindsial, I have heard so much about you. Thank you for taking care of our beloved princess. It is a pleasure to meet you as well." Lindsial smiles, but she says nothing. She is awestruck, just like me.

The elf standing before us is exquisite. She has long brown hair and brown eyes. Her skin is a light olive-skinned color. She is tall and slender. Her eyes sparkle with amusement as she beams a charming smile. She is a cheerful elf that is certain. Talya-cee is as young as the other elves in my group. She is, perhaps, thirteen years of age. I wonder if she is reborn like Hannahlo and the other elves in the Group of Seven.

I look at E-mah, and then I look at Hannahlo. I laugh. "Okay," my mind conveys. "What's going on here?"

As an afterthought, I look at Talya-cee and say aloud, "Oh, I am sorry. It is a pleasure to meet you as well Talya-cee. Please excuse Lindsial and me. We are a bit dazed by all that has just happened. First there were five of you, then seven, then nine, now only one. It's too amazing to grasp." I laugh, adding, "I'm so bewildered I can't even think clearly!"

E-mah conveys in her mind, "Eva and Lindsial, what you just saw and sensed a few moments ago was Talya-cee and only our precious elfin Talya-cee. As I mentioned earlier, she has bilocation skills, just like Hannahlo. However, Hannahlo's are not as pronounced as Talya-cee's bilocation skills. Hannahlo can only be in two places at once. Such was the scenario when you were a child, Eva. Hannahlo was with you on surface earth while she was also here in the Land of the Unseen.

"On the other hand, Talya-cee can split her being for a total of nine distinct beings in nine separate places all at once. Since she can be in nine places at once, her nine individual entities can do nine completely different things. I suppose one could say her incredible skills are *multilocation* vice bilocation."

E-mah has read my mind. She laughs and conveys, "And yes, Eva, you are right. Like human myths on surface earth regarding a cat having nine lives, to be sure Talya-cee also has nine lives. Her powers make her a formidable opponent for any potential adversary.

"As far as it concerns her retrieval of weapons, she has an *apportation* power. This power enables her to teleport, or move, objects at will to each of her nine entities. She can do this quickly and with complete invisibility.

"As you can see, Eva, Talya-cee does not have wings. All the same, you saw her nine entities fly. They flew thanks to her *levitation* skill. Finally, like the rest of the elves born in the Land of the Unseen, Talya-cee can become invisible. I am pleased to say Talya-cee has volunteered to accompany you on the next phase of your journey here on Spardom."

In response to what E-mah conveys in her mind, Talya-cee curtsies and says aloud, "I am looking forward to accompanying you on the next portion of your journey on our beloved Isle."

I think to myself, and yes - Talya-cee is telepathic as well. She's just one more amazing elf of the many incredible creatures I have come to know and love on Spardom.

E-mah says, "There are two more elves I would like you to meet. Their names are Estefany and Jade. They are secretly doing some spying for me, so they are unavailable right now. Estefany has remarkable abilities and Jade, while very young, has magical powers that mirror yours. Trust me when I say they will be with you on the next portion of your journey."

E-mah winks at Hannahlo. Hannahlo winks in return. Naturally, I am wondering what is going on between the E-mah and Hannahlo as it concerns Estefany and Jade. I, along with you, will found out soon enough - in the sequel to this story.

A week later the elves, spargnarls and I are relaxing on the same hilltop where E-mah, Hannahlo, Lindsial, and I sat. With the exception of Lindsial, we gaze at the stars as they twinkle brightly in the heavens behind a sliver of the quarter moon. We also see flashes of light. The flashes now appear from the northeast, having moved from the northwest the night before. Despite the breathtaking scene, I know our view of Spardom's stars, the moon, and the flash-es of light will soon disappear. Shadowy clouds are rapidly gathering from the south.

I am suddenly conscious of Lindsial's thoughts entering my mind. She conveys, "Milady, Eva, what is it? I have this feeling you are thinking of something odd. It is as if you are blocking some of your thoughts from mine. All the same, you are allowing me in your mind a little so that I know something is amiss. It is as if you are putting me on my guard. Are you okay? You're scaring me like you did before the battle with the morgalps and storngfuls."

Without looking at Lindsial, I convey via thought transference, "I will explain everything shortly, Lindsial. Now, I want you to listen carefully. When I tell you to take my hand, immediately do as I ask. Will you do that for me, Lindsial, will you?"

"Of course, you know I will," Lindsial conveys. "But why, what is wrong? I am frightened, Eva. Please tell me what is going on. I am afraid for you, Eva."

I squeeze Lindsial's hand three times. I'm telling her that I love her. I do not want to reply audibly or via telepa-thy. I need to concentrate. What's more, I do not want to foul things up like I did on the recent battlefield. Every-thing must go as planned - everything must be in the same order as my forewarning. I cannot depart from what I saw in my mind.

I sense Eranba's thoughts in my mind as he suddenly shouts, "What are these things?" He reaches out with his hand.

I anticipated Eranba's outburst. I have witnessed it a few times before in a recurring night-after-night dream. What is happening now is like a dream come true. I look skyward and say with a grin, "Why, they're snowflakes, Eranba. And look! There are millions and millions of snow-flakes. They are wonderful. Snowflakes fall for many days and nights in certain places on surface earth. They appear in the season called winter. I make snowmen and snow-balls with bunches and bunches of snowflakes. I hurl the snowballs at trees. Have you not seen snowflakes before tonight?"

"No, we have not, my dear princess," Bratle softly answers for his cousin. Bratle's look is one of trepidation. I read his mind as he looks at the others and says aloud, "We have not seen such things in our lifetime. To be honest with you, nothing of the sort has happened on the Isle before, except when..."

"Do go on, Bratle, except when...?" I ask softly. Sooner than he can even outline his thoughts in his mind, I decide to answer for him. I know what he is going to say. My saying it for him will not change the future. "Yes," I say calmly. "The only other time snowflakes fell on the lower altitudes of the Isle is when the little girl Princess of Spardom disappeared, am I correct?"

Bratle manages to stifle a cry with his reply. "Yes, milady, legends say snowflakes fell that very night, and for weeks after that! The Isle became so cold and sad. The sun and the moon hid behind clouds for many months. All of Spardom was mourning the princess' disappearance. Snow covered everything on the Isle for a very long time."

I nod my head and smile. Yes, I have dreamed this exact scene for several nights now, to include the precise words spoken tonight by Eranba and Bratle. In my dream, I was sitting here surrounded by my amazingly daring Group of Seven friends beneath the stars and moon that abruptly turned to snow clouds. If my dream is one hundred percent accurate, Ariel-e will speak in a few moments.

I have had other dreams too. Thanks to my dreams, and having learned E-mah's powerful spells, I now know how to defeat the Evil One. My knowledge to defeat Zarof includes overwhelming those who conspire with him. These include Parston, Felcio and their army of trolls, and many others, some of which we haven't even met. To defeat our enemy will take both time and luck. However, this is not the time to confront the Isle's evil. More important issues are at hand, issues I must face up to on surface earth.

Like the redheaded girl princess who disappeared

many eons ago, a fully grown, feisty redhead who is twenty-nine years old will vanish as well. Unlike the little princess of long ago, I will return. I will return soon. I am certain of this. I have seen it in my mind and my dreams.

I feel badly for the others as they fearfully watch my presence gradually fade before them. As the snow continues to fall heavily from Spardom's heaven, my presence is nearly gone. I am pretty much a see-through spirit. In a few moments, I will disappear entirely.

In my mind, I can sense Ariel-e's gentle whisper, "No, milady, Eva, no. I beg of you, do not go, please? I could not bear being without you." Tears are streaming down her face. I place my barely visible arm around her shoulders and hug her to me.

I take her hand in mine. As I do, I shake my head slowly and smile. I say, "It is okay, Ariel-e. Do not cry. I will return. I promise you. You are more special to me than you know. I need for you to know that. Ask E-mah to tell you what happened before I perished on the battlefield. Then you will know, my sweet Ariel-e, you will know how much I love you. And love you I always will."

Looking at the others, I slowly say, "I am so sorry I must away. It is because of the flashing lights you saw to the northeast before the clouds came into view. The display of lights is not of our Isle. It is not natural. It is manmade. It is from surface earth. I must bring it to an end. I do not believe it will harm us. At least I hope it does not. In spite of this, its objective - the reason it is happening in the first place - is of more concern to me than its show of brilliance in our night sky.

"While I am away my loyal friends, remain here. Stay here in the Land of the Unseen with those who will protect you and care for you. You deserve a rest. There is much to learn from the elves, ziplips, centaurs, tilbells, and the visiting unicorns. Try to enjoy yourselves while you can. When I return, some of us will journey anew. Our next journey will take us north instead of east. We must learn of many things that lie in the unexplored land, the land they call the Enchanted Gate."

Before I completely fade from view, I nod my head slightly. I smile one last time and say softly, "I love each of you dearly. I am very proud of you. Be safe and trust me when I say, I shall return." I blow them a kiss one at a time.

I squeeze Ariel‑e's hand three times · *I love you*. She manages her warm, charismatic smile despite the stream of sad tears flowing down her lovely face. She squeezes my hand four times in response, *I love you, too*.

At last, in a barely audible whisper, I say to my dear friend, "Lindsial, please take my hand." As Lindsial takes my hand in hers, I think silently to myself, *exitus Spardom directo*.

CHAPTER THIRTY-SEVEN

THE OVAL OFFICE

It is a crisp winter day when I enter the Oval Office of the President of the United States. I am wearing the lengthy, white hooded elfin robe Eranba sewed for me. It has been nearly nine months now since he sewed it. It still looks brand new. I am also wearing white leather boots, compliments of my bedroom closet here on surface earth. There are at least four inches of wet snow on the ground, and more is falling. The fact that there is snow outside gives me more goosebumps than being here in the office of the most powerful man on surface earth.

A handsome Marine is holstering a sidearm. He snaps to attention beside me. I watch as the Marine's lips say, "Mr. President, as you know the metal detector repeatedly alarmed, as did the handheld wand. However, she carries no weapons on her person. The only thing made of metal is this. It is not harmful, sir."

He hands me my medallion. The Marine continues, saying, "Sir, she has undergone a cavity search by a female secret service agent. She was x-rayed as an added precaution. She is good to go, sir."

The Marine glances at me sheepishly. He forces an apologetic smile. I read his mind as it says, "I am truly sorry to have put you through this, ma'am - so terribly sorry. You're too pretty to carry anything dangerous."

As I put on my medallion, I return the Marine's smile and whisper, "It is fine, Sergeant. You were doing your job, as uncomfortable as it seemed to be. Thank you just the same." I smile again, and then I add, "And thanks for the compliment, too. It has been a long time since someone called me pretty."

The Marine looks at me in astonishment. He neither says nor thinks anything in reply.

As I stand in the doorway, I watch the lips of the United States President as he says, "Thank you, Sergeant, you are dismissed." Then looking at me with a spurious smile only a practiced politician can craft, he adds, "Welcome, Miss Roblins. Do come in and have a seat."

As I walk to the President's desk, everyone but the President stands. I recognize some of those in the room. Cindy is here, as is the Chairman, JCS, General Fuller. I used to think Fuller was a pretty cool guy. Not anymore. The jerk threatened to have us tranquilized!

The Vice President of the United States, Jerry Mateo, is sitting in a chair to the right of the President. The President's Chief of Staff, Joseph Bean, and National Security Advisor, Teresa Sampson, are sitting on the couch. As I continue to glance around the room, I flinch. My good ole pal General Powers is here!

In addition to the President's advisors, the Oval Office is full of politicians, perhaps nine or ten. I recognize a few of their faces. I cannot remember their names. I have been away from surface earth too long. Besides, their petty, political nonsense is far below me at this point in my life.

I stand in front of the President's desk. I watch as his lips say, "Please have a seat. Can I get you a cup of coffee?"

"No, Mr. President. I would rather stand," I reply. "I do not want a cup of coffee. Thank you just the same."

"Now, Miss Roblins, we do not have to start this discussion on the wrong footing. The President of the United States is offering you a chair. Will you not oblige him by taking a seat?"

"No sir, I would rather stand."

The President rises from his chair. He says, "As you wish." He turns to face the window overlooking the manicured White House grounds. I look over his shoulder. It is a gorgeous day. Glistening white snow is everywhere. I am envious of the president's view from the Oval Office. I cannot wait to clear out of here to play in the snow and hurl snowballs.

I begin to read the President's mind. With his back toward me, he is mocking my deafness as he speaks aloud. He knows I am deaf. His audible mockery is his way of scoring points with his advisors and the other political cronies in the room. He needs to show everyone he is in control, even if it means insulting a deaf woman. He is also trying to keep me on the edge. I cannot believe he is trying to keep *me on the edge* - what a laugh!

My thoughts spin deviously. Okay, let's you and me have at it, Mr. President. I was hoping the two of us could have an amicable conversation. It is obvious you want to play hardball and get dirty. I'm game. Batter up, as they say.

"Sir," I ask in a loud voice, "May I ask why you are speaking to me with your back turned? Has no one had the civility to tell you I am deaf? I would appreciate the courtesy of you facing me if you wish to talk to me. As you probably know, I can read lips."

I read the President's mind once more as he continues looking out the window. I have him riled up. Good. He is no longer speaking. However, he is thinking. His thoughts say, "You pint-sized arrogant snot. I will address you any way I want. I don't give a damn if you're *deaf, dumb, and blind*. I ought to have you thrown out and have you shot for speaking to me like that!" He turns to look at me. He is pretending to smile, although his face is one of obvious disgust. He gets ready to speak aloud.

I say as nonchalantly and calmly as I can, "Mr. President, I would appreciate if you did not refer to me as - and I quote - *a pint-sized arrogant snot.* Plus, one would expect the President of the United States to be more understanding when it comes to a citizen's deafness." Raising my voice at least one more decibel, I add, "And how dare you say you do not care if I am deaf, dumb, or blind. Furthermore, of all things, that you should remove me from this room, so you can have me shot!"

The President's jaw drops in alarm. He, as well as the others in the room, is flabbergasted. Although I have not heard the others' gasps, I can read their minds. The President's advisors and others in the room are appalled with what I have just said. It is unthinkable for the President to think such thoughts, especially in the sacred Oval Office. Cindy, who, without her hearing aid is clinically deaf, is roaring mad right now.

"That is right, sir. I can read your thoughts. I can also read thoughts of every other person in this room. At this very moment, your advisors are stunned. They should be. Your advisors and the congressmen and congresswomen in this room cannot believe what just crossed your mind. For this reason, Mr. President, do not imagine you can threaten me. I will know every move you make, every thought you think, and every suggestion you have before you can create it."

The President slumps into his chair and stares. He is scowling. I stand unmoving. My stare is impassive. I cross my arms in front of me.

"Okay, Miss Roblins. Let us have an honest discussion. I summoned you here..."

I interrupt him with a smile, "You did not summon me here, Mr. President. Others simply asked I come to see you. I came on my own accord. You are incapable of telling me to do a darned thing, Mr. President. I could walk out of here if I wanted to. And you could not stop me."

The President slumps back in his oversized leather armchair. He howls, "How dare you talk to me like that,

Miss Roblins." He reaches out to bang his fist on his desk. "I am the President of the United States. You are an employee in my charge as well as a citizen of the United States. You will not speak to me in such terms! I am head of state of this great nation of ours, and I demand your respect! I have earned it!"

Shrugging my shoulders I reply, "Mr. President, I am no longer an employee of the CIA. I quit." I turn to look briefly at Cindy. I smile, and then I add, "Ms. Wickham, you will have my resignation on your desk first thing in the morning." As an afterthought, I say, "You're looking well, ma'am. Please give my regards to your family."

Turning to look at the President I say, "Although I remain a citizen of our great country, I am your equal, Mr. President. I am Princess of Spardom of the ancient Isle beneath the sea. Therefore, I would appreciate it if you do not speak to me in such terms. As an equal head of state of a great land, I deserve *your* respect. I do believe I too have earned it!"

The President reaches across his desk. He points his finger threateningly. "Do not think for one moment I cannot have you removed with force from this office, Miss Roblins. You are in my office, my territory, my domain. I will not allow you to speak to me in that tone of voice in front of my advisors and members of Congress. Is that clear? Now sit down!"

"I will not sit down, Mr. President. And you are powerless to do anything about it." As I say this, the President's ink blotter begins to move across his desk. He quickly grabs it to clutch it tightly in his fist. In response to my little show of magic, I can detect renewed gasps from his advisors and others in the room. Good! There're at least twenty witnesses to what I am about to do next.

The picture frames on the President's credenza fall one by one flat on their faces (hopefully with a loud crash). I'm enjoying myself too much. So I continue showing off my magical powers.

The President's pen lifts itself from his desk and begins

scribbling on a notepad. Now the Oval Office lights flicker on and off. Papers in the President's in and out boxes fly through the air. The inbox papers are now neatly stacked in the outbox and vice versa. I make the President's nameplate disappear. A few seconds later it appears on his credenza. Finally, to the alarm of everyone in the room, the very chair the President is sitting begins to rise slowly into the air.

Having made my point, with a wave of my hand, I return the picture frames to their original positions. I switch the contents in the desks in and out boxes. The pen ceases its scribbling. I set the president and his chair back on the carpet. I return his nameplate.

This insensitive human being will not intimidate me. Too much is at stake. Besides, he called me a pint-sized, arrogant snot! I hate it when people call me names! He has a reputation as being a bully. Well, he won't bully me, I guarantee it!

"Hah, nothing but cheap parlor tricks," I watch the President's lips hiss. "You cannot frighten me with such pretend, magical nonsense."

Despite his valiant words, I notice his upper lip is trembling, as is his hand. He is clutching the ink blotter so tightly his hand is five shades of white. Maybe he will throw the ink blotter at me. Oh, he better not. Then I will show him some super cool cheap parlor tricks!

I remain standing. With a smile, I say, "Mr. President, I do believe you are a charitable man. All the same, I do believe your advisors are steering you in the wrong direction." I slightly turn so I can see the others. I snap my fingers, "Like your Chief of Staff." The president's Chief of Staff suddenly disappears. I snap my fingers again and say, "And your National Security Advisor, a woman whom I never liked." Teresa Sampson also disappears.

I snap my fingers a third time. "And there's the Vice President of the United States." The Vice President disappears just as the other two. For theatrics, I add mockingly, "Oops, there goes your successor to the Presidency."

Now you and I both know I should not do it. However, you know I cannot resist. After all, I will never again be bullied, and I vowed to get my revenge. I say, "As far as it concerns your bigoted, foul-mouth, sexist Universal Transporter Device coordinator..." I snap my fingers. With a look of absolute horror on his face, General Powers gradually floats in the air through the room until he is standing five feet beside me. The others in the room are shocked.

At about six-foot-five inches, the General towers over me. Nonetheless, I stare up into his frightened, bulging eyes. I say, "I can't believe you called me at the transporter facility - and I quote verbatim - a brainless, arrogant civilian sand crab, low-life, and redheaded, freckle-faced stupid idiot! Then you called me an obnoxious idiot! And oh yeah, did you ever ask Ms. Wickham out for the date you were thinking about, you sexist, obnoxious, married moron, poor excuse for a gentleman?"

General Powers' face turns pasty white. I say, "Yes, you do remember what you said about me in your mind and how you were drooling over Ms. Wickham and how much you liked us female elves' butts, don't you? Well, General, I admit it. I am obnoxious at times. I guess I am also your worst nightmare. Get out of my sight, if you please." When I snap my fingers, the General disappears.

I turn to face the President. He is now dreadfully troubled. His lower lip is trembling. His face is pale and the hand holding the blotter is shaking uncontrollably. I wonder if it shakes because he is angry, or because he is scared. I suspect the latter, as heartbreaking as it is to consider.

"Miss Roblins, would you please return my advisors?" The President's lips say purposely. I turn once more. With a snap of my fingers, the first three reappear. Then I allow General Powers to reappear. He's on the floor next to the couch he was sitting before I toyed with him. Or should I say messed with him? I watch with satisfaction as he scrambles to take his seat on the couch. All the while he stares at me. His eyes reflect both hatred and terror.

I immediately turn around to face the President. I do not want to see his advisors' faces. It is bad enough I can read their thoughts. They are frightened. I cannot blame them. The first time I held Lindsial's hand and turned invisible, I was petrified. I nearly passed out. I was nauseous for hours.

These folks are better off. I doubt they'll feel nauseous since, as Lindsial had said, my invisibilis spell is somewhat pure. To be honest, I sort of feel sorry for the President's advisors, not too much mind you, just an itsy bitsy little bit.

The President says, "Miss Roblins, I appreciate your powers. However, let me be frank with you. While those of us here in the Oval Office are unarmed, there are dozens of armed Secret Service and Marines in the White House. I can summon them in a heartbeat. Sergeant Edwards is right outside my door. I also have this." He gestures to an area on the left side of the lower portion of his desk. I presume there is a panic alarm button there.

"Mr. President, I am a kind elf," I respond. "However, I caution you in return. With a mere flick of my wrist, I could take out the 14th Street Bridge from here if I wanted to. With a snap of my fingers, every Marine, who enters into this room, would be unconscious before he knew what hit him. You sir and all the Marines in this great country of ours could not do a darned thing about it.

"You see, sir, while I am on surface earth I am untouchable. You cannot injure me. You cannot kill me. Thus, you cannot intimidate me." I'm lying, of course. I can be killed anywhere I walk. But what the President doesn't know...

Because I am enjoying this much more than I thought I would, I add, "As far as Sergeant Edwards is concerned, he will not shoot me. I read his mind when he said I was pretty."

I smile briefly, and now my mood turns serious. "But enough of this tit-for-tat chitchat, Mr. President. Please allow me to be frank with you. At this very moment, dozens of your ships, submarines, and planes are attacking my Isle with missiles, torpedoes, and depth charges. My countrymen, Mr. President - in response to YOUR orders - are attacking an undefended sovereign state that has done you no harm. You are attacking my Isle and the innocent creatures that live there!

"I am an American citizen, and as a former federal employee of our great nation, I swore an allegiance to the Constitution as did you. I swore to protect the Constitution of the United States from all enemies, *foreign and domestic*, sir. Mr. President, right now you are my domestic enemy. Let there be no mistake about it!

"Once again, the most powerful nation on earth is conducting a unilateral attack on a sovereign land. It is attacking without the expressed consent and authorization of the world's policing force, the United Nations. Did we not learn our lessons of the past? How dare you, Mr. President - how dare you attack an innocent Isle and its people based on poor intelligence!

"I know what you are trying to do Mr. President. You are trying to destroy the Evil One that lives on the Isle. However, you cannot do it. No one on the surface earth can do it. I am the only one who can. So why are you wasting your bombs and prized treasury attacking my Isle when the one you seek is not even there?" As soon as I say this, the president's somber look turns to one of bewilderment.

"That is correct Mr. President. He is not on the Isle. He is here on surface earth. Therefore, why are you expending your bombs attacking my Isle beneath the sea?

"Please, sir, please allow me tell you something you obviously do not know. No matter what weapon you employ, you cannot harm my Isle. The Islanders are not at risk from your puny instruments of war. The Isle is under my spell, and you have seen my powers firsthand. All the same, the very thought that my beloved birthright country is trying to destroy an ancient Isle of Paradise that means it no harm is repugnant! The peoples of my Isle have done nothing to harm you. They are innocent. So call off your attacks. Let us work this out together."

"Miss Roblins," the President's lips say in reply, "My intelligence sources say the Evil One, as you refer to him, has acquired the means to communicate to the outside world, to others outside of the Isle. His presence is a direct threat to our nation's security. As President of the United States, I am compelled to do something about it. I must act."

"Sir, I am telling you he is not on the Isle. You declare he has the means to communicate to surface earth? The heck with that, Mr. President! He is one step further than communicating from the Isle. He is on surface earth right now having face to face discussions with evil human beings. Some are your equal heads of state."

"How do you know that, Miss Roblins," the President asks. "Our intelligence says otherwise. We have nothing to indicate he is here on the surface."

I boldly say, "Because I can read minds, Mr. President. I can look into the future Mr. President. Sir, think about this. Do you honestly believe the former KGB stooge, the self-styled president of Russia, added Crimea to the map of Russia unattended? He did not. Our mutual foe was behind the scenes orchestrating it! The Russian President knows our opponent has the strength to control everyone, be it with his mind or via his awesome power. Mr. President, Crimea is just the beginning. It will not stop there. With our mutual adversary's strength behind him, Russia will attempt to annex the entire Russian-speaking areas of eastern Ukraine. It is only a matter of time.

"Cannot you see, Mr. President? Our mutual enemy is trying to pin Russia against the West once again. In my opinion, the Evil One's efforts are working, despite our tough economic sanctions. With the Evil One's support, the Russian President is acting like nothing is happening to his economy. He knows he holds all the cards because of our mutual enemy's support.

"Then there are the evil terrorists in the Middle East. The primary terrorist organization is receiving knowledge and aid directly from him Mr. President. Now those people are using our weapons against the very people our troops died trying to protect. When our mutual enemy garners enough strength, he will unleash a weapon that will make even nuclear weapons seem like pea-shooters.

"With his tremendous powers, weapons of mass destruction will seem like nothing in comparison. Once he has enough allies here on surface earth, he will be unstoppable! Think about it, sir. All the world's previous wars and bloodshed combined into one conflict that will exceed all others ten-fold. I am talking about subjugation of the human race to one unspeakably evil creature!

"Let me be totally truthful, Mr. President. Here on surface earth no one, not even I, can do a darned thing about our adversary, at least not yet. While my powers are surprisingly strong, I do not have the capability to confront him on surface earth. I can only defeat him when he is present on the Isle. As my powers increase, I shall someday have the power to confront him on surface earth if it comes to that. That is our salvation, Mr. President.

"There is another clear-cut ray of hope. Each day our enemy remains on surface earth he grows weaker. His power slowly deteriorates. The importance of this is clear. He must return to Spardom to replenish his core at least once every ten days, or he will ultimately die. Once he is back on the Isle, he must remain for an additional ten days.

"It is then, and only then, I can destroy him. Working together, we can make this come about. You do what you must up here on surface earth to confront the Russian bureaucrats through diplomatic or military efforts. You and your coalition continue to tackle the terrorists. I honestly do not care what you do, just as long as it achieves your objectives and spares innocent American lives.

"I ask that you trust me when I say I will do what I must do on the Isle to defeat our adversary. Also, Mr. President, please call off your naval vessels and aircraft. They are just wasting their time and American taxpayer's dollars while giving my Isle's inhabitants one heck of a fire-works show."

The President stares at me. I am reading his thoughts. He believes what I have been saying. He knows anyone, who has my powers, must be true to her word. Besides, if I able to go from surface earth to Spardom and back again, so can the Evil One.

The President does not know what to do to stop Russia and the terrorists from continued conquests. The American people do not want another war of that he is certain. The Iraq and Afghanistan wars tired the nation. There was such a horrible loss of life and thousands upon thousands of young men and women scarred for life. The President is somewhat indecisive, understandably so. After a few mo-ments, he decides to listen to what I have to say.

"Okay, Miss Roblins, I will listen to your plan." He picks up his phone. I sigh with relief as I read his thoughts. "This is the President. Get me the Secretary of Defense. Hello, Tom - George. I want you to call off the attack on the Isle. That's correct. Call it off and have our forces return to port. No, they are not to loiter in the area. They are to re-turn to port. Raise DEFCON to condition four as well. Cor-rect. I'll explain later. Thanks, Tom."

I say, "Thank you, Mr. President. Sir, I think it pru-dent for everyone to leave this room except Ms. Wickham. She is the only one I will entrust with what I have to say to you. You will have a credible witness to my conversation unless, of course, you're taping our conversation like an in-famous former president."

The President is a Democrat. He laughs. Then his mood quickly turns serious yet again. He hesitates for a few moments before deciding. "Agreed. For Ms. Wickham's piece of mind and well-being, I do insist one armed Marine stay behind. I think that prudent, don't you, Miss Roblins?

"I must also ask you one more thing as a fellow head of state. Give me your word you will not use any more of your magic in the Oval Office, okay?" He glances at a painting of George Washington hanging on the wall. "Otherwise, I do believe our beloved first American President will turn over in his grave. I am sure he and the Founding Fathers had no concept of what is happening right now in this office or the world for that matter."

With a smile, I nod in agreement and say, "I give you my word, Mr. President, and I will no longer use magic in the Oval Office."

Addressing his chief of staff, the President says, "Joseph, please ask Sergeant Edwards to step inside."

Just as Sergeant Edwards steps inside the Oval Office, I say aloud, "Lindsial if you please?" Lindsial suddenly turns visible. She has been standing to my right this entire time. She is wearing the light brown robe Bratle sewed for her so long ago. Her sheathed sword hangs from her right hip. Her bow and quiver of arrows hang loosely over her right shoulder. She seems to look at the President. She curtsies. Then she smiles and says, "It is a pleasure to meet you, sir."

I smile at the President and say, "Yes Mr. President, she has been here all along."

He laughs. "Well, I'll be darned, weapons and all. That explains the metal detector going haywire. I guess it's the sword and arrow tips." He glances at the Marine and says, "Stand at ease Sergeant. These two charming ladies mean us no harm."

The President has regained his composure to a degree. He orders, "With the exception of Ms. Wickham and Sergeant Edwards and Miss Roblins and her companion here, I ask all of you to leave the Oval Office. Before you go, may I caution you? Everything you've seen and heard in this office in the past twenty minutes did not occur. I am classifying it Top Secret, so protect it accordingly. That includes not discussing it with each other or with others who have equal access. It is strictly on a need to know basis. And others do not have the need to know. Thank you."

I am exhausted. It has been a long year. I must admit · it has been an exciting adventure since I opened the package Mustache Bobby gave to me on the eve of my twenty·

ninth birthday. It has been both satisfying and daring. That goes without saying.

Lindsial and I left Spardom ten days ago, and I already miss it. I particularly miss my other Group of Seven friends. I also miss Jakebe, Clover and the other ziplips, the dwarf-like tilbells. I miss E-mah, Nicolas, S-Shea and their fellow centaurs, and, of course, my darling Hannahlo. I cannot wait to return to them. Unfortunately, there are issues to attend to here on surface earth. There is also dreadful business to attend to when I return to my Isle. The latter will have to wait, at least for now.

I lean over to give Lindsial a peck on her cheek. As I do, my thought transference says, "Thanks, hon. I know you're as tired of this bureaucratic garbage as I am. As soon as business is finished here, I promise you can hit me with a snowball, just not too hard!"

I motion with my hand toward the chair beside me. I watch as the President's lips say, "By all means, Miss Roblins, please have a seat." Looking at Lindsial, he adds, "Please have a seat as well lady with many weapons." The three of us laugh.

The President of the United States stares at Lindsial and me for the longest time. As he sizes us up, he shakes his head now and then. He also smiles. I am happy to notice his smile is genuine and non-political.

I stretch my legs before me. I ask in a whisper, "Mr. President, about that coffee - that is if you have hazelnut cream..."

The End

We have added a special bonus - chapter one of book two of the *Eva Roblins and the Enchanted Gate* series: *Conquest of the Hidden Valley*, "No Fair Throwing Snowballs when you're invisible."

CHAPTER ONE OF BOOK TWO

CONQUEST
OF THE HIDDEN VALLEY

No Fair Throwing Snowballs when you're Invisible

It has taken us nearly two hours to travel from the White House to the neighborhood of my apartment in Washington, DC suburbia. We're still a good ten to fifteen minutes away from home. There's hardly any traffic on the road. But there is plenty of snow, perhaps five to six inches. More snow is falling by the minute. Thankfully, the plows are out in full force. During this entire period, Lindsial has been chatting away without a break in her stride. Now I know how my parents must have felt when I was a child. I talked incessantly. I bet I drove my parent's nuts when we took lengthy trips in the car!

I cannot help but laugh at the irony of it all. I am deaf, have been since I was fifteen. I cannot hear what Lindsial is saying as she chatters away. Fortunately, I am telepathic. I can sense in my mind everything that escapes her mouth or her thoughts. For this reason, being deaf is no biggie for me, not like it was a year ago before I left surface earth. If Lindsial's nonstop chattering were to bother me too much, I could always block her thoughts. But I do not want to do that. Lindsial is my best friend. Besides, I had to block her thoughts once before. Both of us have regretted it ever since.

She and I were on the ancient Isle of Spardom. It is the Isle where I rule as princess. Well, I guess you can say I rule the Isle. I was on the Isle about nine months. I didn't accomplish too much. I battled on three separate occasions and ticked off a lot of things that hate me and want me dead. I did befriend some amazing, nice creatures while on Spardom. The more I think about it, I guess it was a somewhat fruitful stay, after all. The only reason I'm back on surface earth is due to my country attacking my Isle. They didn't damage it, but their actions made me angry, as you can well imagine!

The Isle of Spardom sank below the ocean's surface nearly three centuries ago. The ruling monarch at the time, Queen April, made it so. I am her lineage descendant, the heir to the Isle's crown. A set of Isle laws, called Chronicles, told of a Prophesy narrating how I would become the Princess of Spardom on my twenty-ninth birthday. I'm now twenty-nine years of age, and I'll never grow a day older - more of that later.

An invisible bubble of magical energy protects the Isle from enormous pressure. Thanks to the bubble, living creatures abound on the Isle. The air is breathable. The Isle has a sun, moon, and stars. There are majestic mountains, a huge lake, forests and much more. It's an unbelievably beautiful paradise full of wondrous creatures, except for the things that hate me.

Lindsial and I were under attack, along with others in our group and faerie elves we befriended. The faerie elves are called *ziplips*. With my fire-producing *credo aduro* spell, I easily handled the vicious, elf mutants called *morgalps* that were attacking us. Lindsial and the others were doing a super job battling the beasts as well. The beasts had us outnumbered over twenty to one, yet we hung in there.

Morgalps are ugly creatures. Their lower bodies resemble that of wolves. Their upper bodies and heads are similar to elves. They have quick intellect like elves. Morgalps have long rubbery appendages in place of arms. The appendages are quite strong. They can reach out and grab you from more than twenty feet away. I know firsthand how frightening their grip can be. Ten to fifteen morgalps held me in their tentacles toward the end of the battle. I could not escape, so I died on the battlefield after a *storngful* scorpion slashed at my breasts. Amazingly, life was restored to me by a great unicorn named E-mah, and here I am. I'll provide more details recounting what happened a bit later in this story.

Storngfuls are huge scorpions, perhaps as large as lions on surface earth. Like many scorpions on surface earth, these creatures have poisonous venom in their stingers. It was when the storngfuls arrived that I had blocked my thoughts, both incoming and outgoing. I did not want to risk their reading my mind. I also did not want for others' thoughts to invade my mind. Let me tell you, too many thoughts coming into your mind at once can be mightily distracting! We were in the middle of the battle of our lives. I needed to concentrate. So I blocked everything, coming and going.

With the exception of Lindsial, I had turned the others in our *Group of Seven* invisible with my *invisibilis* spell. I wanted them to escape. But I goofed - big time. I planned on Lindsial, who can turn others invisible, to hold my hand. That way the two of us would disappear. I cannot work my invisibilis spell on myself. Unfortunately, because I blocked Lindsial from my thoughts, she had no clue of my intentions. She was invisible, busily fighting morgalps on the periphery of the battlefield. There I was, defenseless, all alone, and held by morgalp tentacles as a storngful lashed at me with its stinger.

Now you can see why I do not want to block Lindsial from my thoughts and vice versa. Perhaps I will need to do so again someday in a crisis. I hope not. Then again, I do block my thoughts from her from time to time so I can tease her. I'm about to do so in a few minutes.

As we gradually proceed down the road, following a slow-moving snow plow, Lindsial is still talking - nonstop. I'm reading her thoughts. She conveys via telepathy, "And I still cannot believe you did that to the Vice President, Eva! I mean, turning the others invisible - especially General Powers - was understandable. But, turning the Vice President invisible, that took some guts!"

I respond via telepathy, "Well, the President didn't seem to be listening, Lindsial. I cast spells to turn the lights on and off. I made his picture frames crash on their faces. I even made his pen scribble notes. Then I lifted him and his chair off of the floor! He just didn't get it. I had to do something dramatic to get his attention."

Lindsial laughs. "I fully understand. The coolest part was when you made General Powers float to stand beside you. Then you repeated what he said in his mind nine months ago, calling you a redheaded idiot and all. Did you see the look on his face?"

"Yes, I did. The sexist moron deserved everything that he got. To be honest with you, Lindsial, I do feel badly that I turned the others invisible. Just the same, like my Papa always said, *sometimes ya gotta do what ya gotta do because ya gotta do it*. I'm just relieved the President and I came to terms. I'm glad he halted the bombing, torpedoing, and the depth-charging of our beloved Isle."

"So, do you think he is going to allow you to follow through with your plan?" Lindsial conveys. "Do you trust him?"

"I don't think he has any other choice than to let me proceed," I convey. "Besides, he has his hands full with the problem in the Middle East. Then there are the continued tensions in Eastern Europe. China is rattling its saber in the Pacific. North Korea is still a pain in the butt. I think he and I are strong partners when it comes to what needs to be done to defeat the Evil One. Whether I trust him or not, that remains to be seen."

"Interesting…" Lindsial conveys. "I find it interesting that the wizard Zarof, I mean the Evil One knows how to come and go as he pleases. He must have super magical powers to pull off that one. The Isle's bubble is supposedly impenetrable. Maybe his powers are as strong as yours, Eva? What do you think?"

"Something tells me his powers are strong. Then again, something tells me he lacks some of the powers that I possess. For instance, I do not think he was able to read my mind during the last battle. Plus, according to E-mah, he must return every ten days to Spardom or he will perish. Then he must remain on the Isle for an additional ten days before returning here. On the other hand, I can come and go as I please; at least that is what E-mah said. I hope she's right. We will be on surface earth exactly ten days tonight. If I'm going to go, I'm going to go today."

I suddenly make a gurgling noise, cough, sputter, and groan. Then I purposely allow my Volkswagen Beetle to veer a bit in the slushy snow. I laugh as Lindsial tightly grips her seatbelt. I'm messing with her, but she doesn't see the humor in my actions. In fact, she doesn't see anything at all. Lindsial is blind.

Despite her blindness, Lindsial can visualize movements, changes in mass, density, and discern image outlines in her mind. She has a special gift called *echolocation*. Lindsial emits sounds that are beyond human and elf hearing. She listens to the echoes of the sounds that return from various objects. That way she can identify the objects. Her gift of echolocation is as fine-tuned as that of a flying bat. It is as accurate as biological sonar. I watched her echolocation firsthand on Spardom. She hit morgalps with her arrows, and she sliced a huge spider's stinger with her sword. Her echolocation is amazing - almost as amazing as her weaponry skills! Lindsial is a courageous warrior. When she's invisible, she's practically invincible.

Her thoughts seem to yell, "Stop that, Eva! You're not a bit funny. For crying out loud, you've already died once. I cannot allow you to die again. My heart was breaking. I cried uncontrollably the entire time you were in a coma. I love you too much to go through that again. So stop fooling around, okay?"

"Okay," I say aloud. "I'm sorry. Hey, I see the neighborhood gas station. We're almost home!"

Lindsial seems to peer out the window. Her thoughts convey, "A gas station, huh? It appears like nothing in my mind but a big something or other. I'll never get used to all these large objects you call buildings." She pauses, and then she conveys, "Okay. So let me get this straight. We get home. We eat lunch. We dress in snow stuff. Then you and I play in the snow, right?"

I'm still not finished teasing Lindsial. I am twenty-nine years old. Lindsial looks like she's twelve-years-old. She is reborn, so, despite her youthful looks, she might be as old as three centuries. All the same, I cannot help but think of her as my child or younger sister. I say aloud, "Naw, I'm pretty tired, honey. I don't feel like playing in the snow. Some of the snow should be here tomorrow unless it melts. We can play then if there's any snow left. I need to take a nap."

"No way are you going to take a nap!" Lindsial's mind conveys. "You promised Eva, you promised! I have never experienced snow in my entire life until this morning. And we were in such a rush to get to the White House we could not even play in it. All I could do was feel its coldness with my hands and listen to it crunch beneath my feet. We're going to throw snowballs and make a snowman. You promised. To heck with your nap! You can nap later. You're not so old, Eva that you need a nap. You're only twenty-nine years old. I have you beat big time! Take a nap - pooh!"

I cannot help but laugh. I say aloud, "Oh, but you felt snowflakes on your face when we were on Spardom, the night we departed. Then I saw you trying to catch them with your tongue as they fell from the sky. Weren't you playing with snow then? Certainly you couldn't see the snowflakes, but you could feel them. You were playing with them with your tongue. I saw you."

"That wasn't the same," Lindsial says via thought transference. "We were all keyed-up since you were leaving Spardom. Although I more or less figured you were taking me with you, I wasn't certain. As a result, I was worried. Besides, catching a few snowflakes with my tongue doesn't count like playing in the snow. You promised, Eva, you promised! You said you would show me how to roll a snow-ball. You said I could throw it at you. You said that your-self in the Oval Office."

She pauses, "And oh, what's this? You're blocking your thoughts aren't you? Hah! That's why you're talking aloud. You're just messing with my head, aren't you? You are too mean to me Eva! If you weren't driving this ghastly thing you call a car, I would beat you up!" She laughs. "But I'll let you off the hook this time. I don't want us to crash!" She laughs again.

I chuckle loudly. I unblock my outgoing thoughts and convey, "Yes, dear. I'm just messing with you. After we eat, we can play outside. Cindy left some smaller-sized snow pants and boots that should fit you. I'd give you mine, but the boots I'm wearing are the only ones I have. Yup, we're going to eat and then it is building a snowman time. And don't forget, you promised not to hit me too hard with snowballs, correct?"

Lindsial sticks her tongue out at me. She conveys, "Af-ter what you just did to me, I'm going to hit you as hard as I can. I'll be invisible too, so you won't know what direction the snowballs are coming."

She and I both laugh. I have this feeling I'm in for a world of hurt when it comes to a snowball fight with Lind-sial. She may be blind, but her echolocation is dead right accurate. No problem, I can still beat her at arm wrestling - barely.

As we pull into my driveway, I roll down the window and yell my thanks to the driver of the snowplow. The snow is deep. We would not have made it from the White House to my apartment without the aid of the snowplow.

We would have had to stay the night in a hotel. Thankfully, the President arranged for the District of Columbia Mayor to have a snowplow precede us all the way to here. The forty-five mile trip took nearly three hours, but it was well worth it. I dread the thought that we would have had to stay in a hotel. Lindsial would have driven me nuts if we didn't play outside in the snow. Then again, she would have made me play in it outside the hotel, like it or not.

Now that we're in my apartment, I cannot help but think of my human friend, Cindy. She was here yesterday, tidying up a bit. She also prepared today's dinner. It's in the refrigerator. All I have to do is microwave it. Since my apartment was unlived in for nine months, Cindy took it upon herself to check on it once a week. She also paid my rent each month. I owe her nine months rent.

I continued to receive my salary while I was on Spardom, so paying her one lump sum of back rent is no biggie. I have tons of money in the bank. It won't do me much good on Spardom. There are no Wal-Mart's, Seven-Eleven's, or grocery stores on the Isle. In fact, there are no buildings at all. At least I don't think there are. But it's nice to know I have a nest egg here on surface earth. To be honest with you, Cindy's checking on my apartment was no small feat. She lives in Maryland. I live past Tyson's Corner in Virginia.

Cindy is - or I should say she was my supervisor at the Central Intelligence Agency - CIA. I resigned my position at the Agency this very morning. Cindy was also my surrogate mother, for one whole year. After I had turned eighteen, she continued to look after me, just like a mother would. My mother died when I was seven years old. My Papa died when I was seventeen. Cindy has been my friend for going on twelve years. I love her very much.

She would be here with us now. However, she wanted to get home after our meeting with the President earlier today. She has a teenage daughter who is off from school because of the snowstorm. Like Lindsial and me, Cindy and her daughter, Faith, are going to play in the snow. The

DC area seldom gets snow. When it does, it's usually a whopper of a storm. Everything closes and folks hibernate for a day or two. It's supposed to get in the mid-forties to-morrow, so most of the snow will be gone by tomorrow night. I expect Cindy will visit then. At least I hope so.

After eating a hearty meal of roast beef, mashed pota-toes, and gravy, and snow peas, along with corned bread, Lindsial and I are ready to go play outside. Lindsial dons the boots and snow pants. As she dresses, I cannot help but laugh. She is too cute in her snow clothes! I help her put on a scarf. Then I help her put on earmuffs. Lastly, I help her put on her mittens. It is funny how one can take certain things for granted. I've been experiencing snow all my life. Lindsial is experiencing it for the first time. She is clueless when it comes to cold weather attire.

It's about twenty-five degrees outside. Not too terribly cold, but cold enough to see your breath. Lindsial is amazed when I tell her she should be able to detect water vapor from her breath when she exhales. I take lots of pic-tures of her as she puffs her cheeks and blows. She cannot see her breath, but I can. It warms my heart as I watch her having so much fun. Afterward, we build a snowman. It's not too tall, maybe three feet, with two button eyes and a pickle for a nose. Its grinning lips are thin slices of red pepper. I take my scarf and tie it around its neck, or rather in between its head and torso. I top it off with a New York Yankees baseball cap.

Lindsial touches the snowman from everywhere on its head to its wide round body. She is visualizing in her mind what the snowman looks like as it stands before her. I can-not help but shed a few tears. I've been deaf since I was fif-teen. Lindsial has been blind since birth. I wish I could trade places with her if only for a day or two. Before I be-came telepathic, being deaf sucked. Being blind must be awful.

Lindsial and I take turns posing alongside the snow-man as we take pictures for posterity. Because she doesn't know how to use a camera properly and cannot see where to point, I'm missing from many of the photos. She doesn't know, but I grin when I look at some of the pictures she has taken. Some pictures are of trees, the sky, the ground, and parked cars. Luckily, more than a few turned out all right. I plan on developing the finest pictures. I will take them with us when we return to Spardom in a few days. I bet the others will be excited to see them!

I'm hiding behind a tree as Lindsial throws snowballs at me. She has a darned good aim, especially when considering she is using echolocation! I get smacked in the side of my head now and then when I peek from behind the tree. Most of the time, she hits me square in my chest. I also hit her. I smack her in her side, her back, and her front as she scampers from tree to tree. I never could throw snowballs this well before I left for Spardom. I guess my throwing of a relatively heavy spear on the Isle has improved my aim. My beloved elf mermaid, Ariel·e taught me well!

I caution Lindsial to not turn invisible. The neighbors are watching. We do not want them to see an elf disappear. All of sudden, I am hit in my side. Then I'm hit almost simultaneously in my front. I convey via telepathy, "I don't want you turning invisible. It's too risky out here in the open. A human may see you."

Lindsial conveys, "Oh, don't be such a spoilsport. Just because I'm hitting you now and then doesn't mean I'm cheating. I'm not invisible, Eva. I promised you I wouldn't turn invisible, so I won't."

Just as my mind reads her thoughts, two snowballs fly through the air from two directions to hit me on my sides. Then I watch as Lindsial scampers from behind her tree to another tree. She tosses a snowball as she runs. What in the world is going on here? Is some magic at play? I saw Lindsial virtually at the same time two snowballs flew at me from two new directions.

I shout aloud, "Lindsial, please come here at once!" Thinking I may have injured myself or worse, Lindsial hurries to me. I read her lips. As a deaf elf, I'm proficient at doing so. She says aloud, "What's wrong, Eva? Are you okay? Are you hurt?" Both of us have blocked our minds from incoming thoughts. We have blocked our outgoing thoughts as well. It is a force of habit, a defense mechanism of sorts. Evil things on Spardom taught us to be ever on our guard when it comes to our telepathic powers.

I whisper, "Lindsial, something weird is happening here. I saw you over there." I point to the tree where she was hiding a moment ago. Although she is blind, she follows my gaze as I point · remarkable! "And even though you were over there, I was hit by two snowballs that came from two directions." I point to my left and right. "Something isn't proper here, Lindsial."

"Goodness," Lindsial says. "Maybe something evil followed us from Spardom. I hope not!" She stands motionless. She clenches her fists. She has spotted something with her mind; I'm sure of it. I watch her lips say, "Eva, something's out there. I can visualize it in my mind, with echolocation. It's to your right, about fifteen feet away, next to a tree. Can you see it?"

I look. I cannot see anything but falling snow, trees, cars parked alongside the road and houses. "No, I don't see anything unusual. Does it have a shape or something? What does it appear to be in your mind?"

I watch Lindsial's lips as she whispers, "I think it's a person, a tiny person, maybe three and one-half feet tall at best. Wait a minute." She frowns as she seems to concentrate intently. "Eva, I think it's invisible. Hold on. Something much taller, perhaps a bit taller than you is now standing by its side."

I stare where Lindsial is facing. I still do not see a thing. I unblock my mind, just for the heck of it. As I do, I detect what appear to be words of a child. I think they're coming from the direction where Lindsial told me to look! The thoughts say, "Do you think we should tell them now?"

Thoughts from someone or something that is also unknown answers, "Yes, I guess we should." I suspect the originator of these thoughts is older, perhaps a teenager. "But before we do, let's throw some more snowballs. We're having too much fun! Besides, they can't see us. I'm sure they don't mind if we play a bit longer."

Just as the thoughts go silent, I stare in bewilderment. Two things have scooped up snow from the ground! I stare as two something's form snowballs in midair! I instinctively duck as a snowball flies in my direction. Lindsial ducks as well. With her echolocation, she is much quicker than me. The snowball misses her. The one thrown at me hits me square in the forehead.

I yell, "Stop it, whoever you are - no fair throwing snowballs when you're invisible! Besides, the humans will know something magical is happening. Show yourselves, now!" Just as I say this, Lindsial starts laughing. She has unblocked her mind.

Lindsial conveys, "Eva, well, I'll be darned. I think we are about to meet Estefany and Jade. How do you like that? I can detect their presence even though they're invisible. One's much shorter than the other - that must be Jade. The taller one is undoubtedly Estefany. Hannahlo had described them to me before we left the Isle."

"Estefany and Jade," I stammer. "E-mah says they were to accompany us on the next phase of our journey. She said they were on a secret spying mission. I doubt these two are Estefany and Jade."

Suddenly, youthful thoughts once again enter my mind. "Aw shucks. They know we're here, and they know who we are. We might as well show ourselves."

With that, two elves appear. One is rather small. She is about eight years old. The other is taller than me, perhaps five-foot-seven inches, give or take an inch. She is about sixteen years of age. The younger elf has coal-black, shoulder length hair, and beautiful eyes of jade. Of course, she must be Jade! The other elf has olive skin with shoulder-length black hair. She is lovely as well. She must be Estefany! Both elves are grinning from ear to ear.

Lindsial walks over to the two elves. She reaches out to touch their faces, their necks, and their hair. She conveys, "It's a pleasure to meet you, Estefany and Jade. I am Lindsial." She glances in my general direction and says, "As you probably know, this is Princess Eva."

Both elves smile and curtsy. Their minds say in unison, "It's a pleasure to meet you Princess Eva and elfin Lindsial."

I am flabbergasted. I convey via thought transference, "Hello you two. It's a pleasure to meet you at last. But what in the world are you doing here? I thought you were to accompany us on the next phase of our journey. E-mah said you were on a special mission, spying on something or other."

I watch as Estefany's lips say, "Oh, we were spying here on surface earth. We were watching the Evil One, Zarof, as he scurried here and there making mischief. We've been on surface earth for over a month. We are instructed to accompany you when you return to Spardom. About the next phase of your journey, E-mah said that was your meeting with the President. We had checked out the White House before you arrived this morning. We wanted to ensure it was safe for you to enter."

Wow! I imagine how the Secret Service would react if they knew there were two invisible elves snooping around inside the White House. It was bad enough that Lindsial turned up in the Oval Office with her bow and arrows and sword. When the President escorted us through the hallway, the Secret Service bubbas went berserk when they saw Lindsial with her weapons. The President had to tell them repeatedly to holster their weapons.

"How did you get here?" Lindsial's mind conveys.

"Oh, our lady, Lindsial," Estefany conveys, "E-mah knows similar spells as those of Princess Eva. We traveled unhindered from Spardom to surface earth. The only problem is we have no way to return. E-mah's magic works one-way only. We're supposed to return with you two." She looks at me, smiles, and then she says, "That is if you do not mind, Princess Eva."

I'm now standing close to the two elves. I give both of them a loving hug, and then I kiss them on the top of their heads. I convey, "Of course, it would be an honor to have you accompany us to Spardom. I still have business to attend to here on surface earth. We depart in a few days. In the meantime, we can get to know each other better."

Jade, who's cuter than a button, conveys via telepathy, "Can we go inside your house, too, Princess Eva? I've never been inside a real house before. I bet it's pretty and comfy." She stares at me with her gorgeous, sparkling, jade-colored eyes. "Please, Princess Eva, pretty, pretty please?" She curtsies. I melt inside. How could I refuse that look? She is the most darling eight-year-old elf I've ever seen!

"Of course you can," I convey. "In fact, I have a fancy comforter you might like. It's from a famous Walt Disney movie. I have the movie as well, plus many more children's movies. I like watching them with subtitles. Would you like to see the movie?"

"Oh yes," Jade conveys as she jumps up and down. "I would love to watch a movie. I've heard about them, but I never watched them. We're going to have a great time! Can I have some surface earth popcorn, too? Maybe something you call soda? And if we have time, can you take me roller skating, Princess Eva? I bet that would be loads of fun!"

Jade takes hold of my hand and starts to drag me through the snow in the direction of my apartment. Meanwhile, Lindsial and Estefany are chatting away as we stroll through the park.

Then unexpectedly a snowball is flying through the air. It hits me square on my chest. I yell aloud, "Oh no, not again!"

Lindsial laughs. Her thoughts convey, "Oh it's you. I'd recognize your shape anywhere. Show yourself, Clover! And stop throwing snowballs at Princess Eva." She gleefully claps her mittens together and adds, "Eva, Ziplip Clover is here - this is too cool!"

Clover - what in the world is Clover doing here? I thought she was on Spardom in the Land of the Unseen undergoing battle training like the rest of the ziplips. How did she get here? Why is she here? Goodness, these elves are full of surprises!

Clover turns visible. She is standing about fifteen feet from me. She has the silliest grin on her face. If you recall from the last story in the *Enchanted Gate* series, *Return of the Princess*, Clover is the only four-winged ziplip on Spardom. Like the other ziplips, she can turn invisible and fly. She is also an expert archer. Every ziplip on Spardom wears a different colored cap. Clover wears a bright green cap. Her skin color is emerald green, which almost matches her unblinking green eyes. She stands around four feet tall. Thankfully, she is wearing a heavy coat. Humans who may be watching will not see her wings.

I convey, "Clover, it's wonderful to see you. But what in the world are you doing here? How did you get from Spardom to surface earth?"

Clover curtsies, and then she conveys, "It is a pleasure to see you again, Princess Eva. I am at your service." She smiles a playful grin. "I hope you are not angry, Princess Eva." She looks at Lindsial, "Or you either, elfin Lindsial." Looking at me she adds, "You see, Princess Eva, I overheard you telling E-mah and Hannahlo about the wonderful things here on surface earth. I couldn't resist. I had to see them for myself. I'm sorry."

She smiles, curtsies again, and says, "Please don't be angry, please? When you, Lindsial and the others of the Group of Seven were outside the Land of the Unseen, I was there. I was invisible. You asked elfin Lindsial via telepathy if she would take your hand when you asked her to. I figured you were going to return to surface earth. So..." She hesitates a bit, and then looking at Lindsial she conveys, "So, I held Lindsial's other hand." She manages a meek smile and adds, "So here I am! Please don't be angry with me, Princess Eva - you either elfin Lindsial, please."

I am flabbergasted. Lindsial is laughing. Estefany and Jade are laughing as well. Lindsial conveys, "So that what was in my other hand - your hand! I thought I felt something, but I couldn't tell what it was. It was you, Clover! Pretty darned cool I'll say. You are one ingenious ziplip!"

She laughs again.

I know I should be a bit angry at Clover, especially since I'm the Princess of Spardom and all. However, I am certain Clover's actions are quite innocent. She's just different; that's all. And yes, she's feisty and bold, and daring, spontaneous, gorgeously cute, devoted, and...

I say aloud, "Well, I'm glad you're here safe and sound, Clover. I hope you understand you could have been hurt or worse. It's not easy to transport from beneath the sea at one thousand fathoms to surface earth. I hope you know that."

With a bashful smile and an accompanying curtsy, Clover says, "Yes, milady, I know. I am sorry. Please do not be angry with me. I just wanted to see surface earth. I knew of no other way to get here. It's pretty exciting, to say the least." She curtsies once more.

"Okay then," I say aloud. "Let's head to my apartment. We have plenty of food, lots of room, and loads of stories to tell." I look at Estefany and Jade and say, "I'm curious what you two have discovered on surface earth." Then waving my index finger at Clover I say with a grin, "And you, young elfin four-winged Clover. I want you to tell me what you have been up to for the past ten days. Hopefully, you didn't allow anyone to see your wings."

Clover nods, and conveys, "No milady Eva. I've been in your house the entire time, invisible." She adds with a timid smile, "Except when I was with you and Lindsial in the President's Oval Office. Wasn't it gorgeous, Princess Eva? It was incredible, wasn't it?"

What?

www.evaroblins.com

CARROT TOP

I am a proud redhead, a bona fide rarity
Freckles on my back · some you'll never see

I'm called too late for supper, thing on a pup,
For red grows on my head like tomato catsup

I am pure uniqueness · my face rubicund,
Pleased by my birthright · a redhead fine spun

A carrot top am I, for certain this is me,
Amazed by copycats dyeing manes pointlessly

When the day is done, when tresses are gone
I'll still be a pure redhead · second to none

I'M SORRY

I'm sorry I'm not pretty just like you
I'm sorry I'm quite odd to look at too
I'm sorry you mock me ever so much
I'm sorry you fear all that I touch

I'm sorry I have such peculiar ways
I'm sorry you dread my living days
I'm sorry if it should happen to you
And I question · what will you do?

Will you call my name, someday when
Outcast you too shall need a friend;
Or will you dread each new waking day
Wishing like me you could fade away?